Praise for
*Eleanor Oliphant Is Completely Fine*

Winner of the Costa First Novel Award and
the British Book Awards Book of the Year

Shortlisted for the Desmond Elliott Prize

Longlisted for the Women's Prize for Fiction

"Deadpan, heartbreaking, and humorous all at once."
—NPR.org

"A charmer . . . satisfyingly quirky."
—*The New York Times*

"Move over, Ove (in Fredrik Backman's *A Man Called Ove*)—
there's a new curmudgeon to love. . . . A remarkable debut."
—*Booklist* (starred review)

"Heart-wrenching yet humorous; dark yet full of life—the
debut novel from this Glasgow-based author is nothing short
of extraordinary." —*Hello! Canada*

"The book occupies that sweet spot between literary and com-
mercial fiction: a highly readable but beautifully written story
that's as perceptive and wise as it is funny and endearing."
—*The Guardian*

"Sweet and satisfying . . . will speak to introverts who have
ever felt a little weird about their place in the world."
—*Bustle*

"The kind of book you'll want to devour in a single sitting."
—*Vox*

"Endearing, [a] whip-smart read . . . Perfectly paced, odd, shocking, and hilarious . . . A fascinating story about loneliness, hope, tragedy, and humanity. Honeyman's delivery is wickedly good, and Eleanor won't leave you anytime soon."
—Associated Press

"Hilarious, deadpan, and irresistible."  —*Kirkus Reviews*

"[A] captivating debut . . . A must-read for those who love characters with quirks."  —*BookPage*

"The book is wonderfully, quirkily funny. You both ache for Eleanor . . . and laugh with her."  —*Seattle Times*

"An absolute joy, laugh-out-loud funny but deeply moving."
—*Express UK*

"Eleanor Oliphant is more than Completely Fine. She is Unforgettable, Brilliant, Funny and Life-Affirming."
—*The Daily Mail*

"Honeyman's wonderful debut novel hits the summer read sweet spot: an intelligent, complex, funny, heartbreaking book that you'll want to read in a single sitting."
—*The Irish Times*

"If you thought Fredrik Backman's Ove was a charming curmudgeon, you'll instantly fall for Eleanor."  —HelloGiggles

"I loved this beautiful, funny, heartbreaking book."
—Kristin Hannah, *New York Times* bestselling author of *The Great Alone*

"Eleanor Oliphant is a truly original literary creation: funny, touching, and unpredictable. Her journey out of dark shadows is expertly woven and absolutely gripping."
—Jojo Moyes, *New York Times* bestselling author of *The Giver of Stars*

"Like a contemporary Jane Eyre . . . Honeyman's debut will have you rooting for Eleanor with every turning page. I loved this story."    —Paula McLain, *New York Times* bestselling author of *The Paris Wife* and *Love and Ruin*

"So powerful—I completely loved *Eleanor Oliphant Is Completely Fine*."

—Fiona Barton, *New York Times* bestselling author of *The Suspect*, *The Child*, and *The Widow*

"A compulsive, irresistible narrative that arcs toward compassion and light."

—Mona Awad, award-winning author of *Bunny* and *13 Ways of Looking at a Fat Girl*

"Funny, moving, original, thought-provoking . . . I'm a fully paid up member of the Eleanor Oliphant fan club, and I can't wait to see what Gail writes next."

—Clare Mackintosh, *New York Times* bestselling author of *After the End*

"In an extraordinarily difficult year socially and politically, I cannot help picking a book that gave me immense joy. From page one, I had no idea where it was going, but I immediately loved Eleanor precisely for how difficult she was, how deliciously awkward in so many situations that made me laugh out loud at her rejection of social mores. Nothing prepared for the slow warming of her heart, and the way it blew her world wide open."

—Attica Locke, award-winning author of *Pleasantville* and *Bluebird, Bluebird*

"*Eleanor Oliphant Is Completely Fine* made me laugh, made me cry, and the entire time I beamed with joy at the beauty of this story. I fell in love with Eleanor and never wanted the book to end."    —Krysten Ritter, actress, producer, and author of *Bonfire*

# ELEANOR OLIPHANT IS COMPLETELY FINE

Gail Honeyman is a graduate of the universities of Glasgow and Oxford. *Eleanor Oliphant Is Completely Fine* is a #1 *New York Times* bestseller and has won awards around the globe, including the Costa First Novel Award, the British Book Awards Book of the Year, the BAMB Readers' Choice Award, and the Author's Club Best First Novel. It was shortlisted for the Desmond Elliot Prize and was longlisted for the Women's Prize for Fiction. This is Honeyman's debut novel and she lives in Glasgow, Scotland.

# Eleanor Oliphant

is completely fine

~

Gail Honeyman

PENGUIN

an imprint of Penguin Canada, a division of
Penguin Random House Canada Limited

Published in this edition, 2021

1 2 3 4 5 6 7 8 9 10

LIBRARY AND ARCHIVES CANADA CATALOGUING IN PUBLICATION

Title: Eleanor Oliphant is completely fine / Gail Honeyman.
Names: Honeyman, Gail, author.
Description: Originally published: Toronto : Viking, 2017.
Identifiers: Canadiana 20200365177 | ISBN 9780735242098 (softcover)
Classification: LCC PR6108.O5 E44 2021 | DDC 823/.92—dc23

Cover design by Jaya Miceli
Cover art: Soleila420 / Getty Images
Interior design by Amy Hill

Printed and bound in the United States of America

www.penguinrandomhouse.ca

Penguin
Random House
Canada

*For my family*

"Loneliness is hallmarked by an intense desire to bring the experience to a close; something which cannot be achieved by sheer willpower, or by simply getting out more, but only by developing intimate connections. This is far easier said than done, especially for people whose loneliness arises from a state of loss or exile or prejudice, who have reason to fear or mistrust as well as long for the society of others. . . .

"The lonelier a person gets, the less adept they become at navigating social currents. Loneliness grows around them, like mould or fur, a prophylactic that inhibits contact, no matter how badly contact is desired. Loneliness is accretive, extending and perpetuating itself. Once it becomes impacted, it is by no means easy to dislodge."

—Olivia Laing in *The Lonely City: Adventures in the Art of Being Alone*

# Eleanor
# Oliphant

## is completely fine

# Good Days

# 1

When people ask me what I do—taxi drivers, dental hygienists—I tell them I work in an office. In almost nine years, no one's ever asked what kind of office, or what sort of job I do there. I can't decide whether that's because I fit perfectly with their idea of what an office worker looks like, or whether people hear the phrase *work in an office* and automatically fill in the blanks themselves—lady doing photocopying, man tapping at a keyboard. I'm not complaining. I'm delighted that I don't have to get into the fascinating intricacies of accounts receivable with them. When I first started working here, whenever anyone asked, I told them that I worked for a graphic design company, but then they assumed I was a creative type. It became a bit boring to see their faces blank over when I explained that it was back office stuff, that I didn't get to use the fine-tipped pens and the fancy software.

I'm nearly thirty years old now and I've been working here since I was twenty-one. Bob, the owner, took me on not long after the office opened. I suppose he felt sorry for me. I had a degree in Classics and no work experience to speak of, and I turned up for the interview with a black eye, a couple of missing teeth and a broken arm. Maybe he sensed, back then, that I would never aspire to anything more than a poorly paid office job, that I would be content to stay with the company and save him the bother of ever having to recruit a replacement. Perhaps he could also tell that I'd never need to take time off to go on honeymoon, or request maternity leave. I don't know.

~

It's definitely a two-tier system in the office; the creatives are the film stars, the rest of us merely supporting artists. You can tell by looking at us which category we fall into. To be fair, part of that is salary-related. The back office staff gets paid a pittance, and so we can't afford much in the way of sharp haircuts and nerdy glasses. Clothes, music, gadgets—although the designers are desperate to be seen as freethinkers with unique ideas, they all adhere to a strict uniform. Graphic design is of no interest to me. I'm a finance clerk. I could be issuing invoices for anything, really: armaments, Rohypnol, coconuts.

From Monday to Friday, I come in at 8:30. I take an hour for lunch. I used to bring in my own sandwiches, but the food at home always went off before I could use it up, so now I get something from the high street. I always finish with a trip to Marks & Spencer on a Friday, which rounds off the week nicely. I sit in the staff room with my sandwich and I read the newspaper from cover to cover, and then I do the crosswords. I take the *Daily Telegraph*, not because I like it particularly, but because it has the best cryptic cross-word. I don't talk to anyone—by the time I've bought my Meal Deal, read the paper and finished both cross-words, the hour is almost up. I go back to my desk and work till 5:30. The bus home takes half an hour.

I make supper and eat it while I listen to the *Archers*. I usually have pasta with pesto and salad—one pan and one plate. My childhood was full of culinary contradiction, and I've dined on both hand-dived scallops and boil-in-the-bag cod over the years. After much reflection on the political and sociological aspects of the table, I have realized that I am completely uninterested in food. My preference is for fodder that is cheap, quick and simple to procure and prepare, whilst providing the requisite nutrients to enable a person to stay alive.

After I've washed up, I read a book, or sometimes I watch television if there's a program the *Telegraph* has recommended that day. I usually (well, always) talk to Mummy on a Wednesday evening for fifteen minutes or so. I go to bed around ten, read for half an hour and then put the light out. I don't have trouble sleeping, as a rule.

On Fridays, I don't get the bus straight after work but instead I go to the Tesco Metro around the corner from the office and buy a margherita pizza, some Chianti and two big bottles of Glen's vodka. When I get home, I eat the pizza and drink the wine. I have some vodka afterward. I don't need much on a Friday, just a few big swigs. I usually wake up on the sofa around 3 a.m., and I stumble off to bed. I drink the rest of the vodka over the weekend, spread it throughout both days so that I'm neither drunk nor sober. Monday takes a long time to come around.

My phone doesn't ring often—it makes me jump when it does—and it's usually people asking if I've been mis-sold Payment Protection Insurance. I whisper *I know where you live* to them, and hang up the phone very, very gently. No one's been in my flat this year apart from service professionals; I've not voluntarily invited another human being across the threshold, except to read the meter. You'd think that would be impossible, wouldn't you? It's true, though. I do exist, don't I? It often feels as if I'm not here, that I'm a figment of my own imagination. There are days when I feel so lightly connected to the earth that the threads that tether me to the planet are gossamer thin, spun sugar. A strong gust of wind could dislodge me completely, and I'd lift off and blow away, like one of those seeds in a dandelion clock.

The threads tighten slightly from Monday to Friday. People phone the office to discuss credit lines, send me e-mails about contracts and estimates. The employees I share an office with—Janey, Loretta, Bernadette and Billy—would notice if I didn't turn up. After a few days (I've often wondered how many) they would worry that I hadn't phoned in sick—so unlike me—and they'd dig out my address from the personnel files. I suppose they'd call the police in the end, wouldn't they? Would the officers break down the front door? Find me, covering their faces, gagging at the smell? That would give them something to talk about in the office. They hate me, but they don't actually wish me dead. I don't think so, anyway.

〜

I went to the doctor yesterday. It feels like eons ago. I got the young doctor this time, the pale chap with the red hair, which I was pleased about. The younger they are, the more recent their training, and that can only be a good thing. I hate it when I get old Dr. Wilson; she's about sixty, and I can't imagine she knows much about the latest drugs and medical breakthroughs. She can barely work the computer.

The doctor was doing that thing where they talk to you but don't look at you, reading my notes on the screen, hitting the return key with increasing ferocity as he scrolled down.

"What can I do for you this time, Miss Oliphant?"

"It's back pain, Doctor," I told him. "I've been in agony." He still didn't look at me.

"How long have you been experiencing this?" he said.

"A couple of weeks," I told him.

He nodded.

"I think I know what's causing it," I said, "but I wanted to get your opinion."

He stopped reading, finally looked across at me.

"What is it that you think is causing your back pain, Miss Oliphant?"

"I think it's my breasts, Doctor," I told him.

"Your breasts?"

"Yes," I said. "You see, I've weighed them, and they're almost half a stone—combined weight, that is, not each!" I laughed. He stared at me, not laughing. "That's a lot of weight to carry around, isn't it?" I asked him. "I mean, if I were to strap half a stone of additional flesh to your chest and force you to walk around all day like that, your back would hurt too, wouldn't it?"

He stared at me, then cleared his throat.

"How . . . how did you . . . ?"

"Kitchen scales," I said, nodding. "I just sort of . . . placed one on top. I didn't weigh them both, I made the assumption that they'd be roughly the same weight. Not entirely scientific I know, but—"

"I'll write you a prescription for some more pain-killers, Miss Oliphant," he said, talking over me and typing.

"Good-bye then, Doctor," I said. "Thank you so very much for your time." My tone went completely over his head. He was still, apparently, engrossed in his notes. That's the only downside to the younger ones; they have a terrible bedside manner.

≈

That was yesterday morning, in a different life. Today, *after*, the bus was making good progress as I headed for the office. It was raining, and everyone else looked miserable, huddled into their overcoats, sour morning breath steaming up the windows. Life sparkled toward me through the drops of rain on the glass, shimmered fragrantly above the fug of wet clothes and damp feet.

I have always taken great pride in managing my life alone. I'm a sole survivor—I'm Eleanor Oliphant. I don't need anyone else—there's no big hole in my life, no missing part of my own particular puzzle. I am a self-contained entity. That's what I've always told myself, at any rate. But last night, I'd found the love of my life. When I saw him walk onstage, I just *knew*. He was wearing a very stylish hat, but that wasn't what drew me in. No—I'm not that shallow. He was wearing a three-piece suit, *with the bottom button of his waistcoat unfastened*. A true gentleman leaves the bottom button unfastened, Mummy always said—it was one of the signs to look out for, signifying as it did a sophisticate, an elegant man of the appropriate class and social standing. His handsome face, his voice . . . here, at long last, was a man who could be described with some degree of certainty as "husband material."

Mummy was going to be thrilled.

# 2

At the office, there was that palpable sense of Friday joy, everyone colluding with the lie that somehow the weekend would be amazing and that, next week, work would be different, better. They never learn. For me, though, things *had* changed. I had not slept well, but despite that, I was feeling good, better, best. People say that when you come across "the one," you just know. Everything about this was true, even the fact that fate had thrown him into my path on a Thursday night, and so now the weekend stretched ahead invitingly, full of time and promise.

One of the designers was finishing up today—as usual, we'd be marking the occasion with cheap wine and expensive beer, crisps dumped in cereal bowls. With any luck, it would start early, so I could show my face and still leave on time. I simply *had* to get to the shops before they closed. I pushed open the door, the chill of the air-con making me shudder, even though I was wearing my jerkin. Billy was holding court. He had his back to me, and the others were too engrossed to notice me slip in.

"She's mental," he said.

"Well, we know she's mental," Janey said, "that

was never in doubt. The question is, what did she do this time?"

Billy snorted. "You know she won those tickets and asked me to go to that stupid gig with her?"

Janey smiled. "Bob's annual raffle of crap client freebies. First prize, two free tickets. Second prize, four free tickets . . ."

Billy sighed. "Exactly. Total embarrassment of a Thursday night out—a charity gig in a pub, starring the marketing team of our biggest client, plus various cringeworthy party pieces from all their friends and family? And, to make it worse, with *her*?"

Everyone laughed. I couldn't disagree with his assessment; it was hardly a Gatsby-esque night of glamour and excess.

"There was one band in the first half—Johnnie something and the Pilgrim Pioneers—who weren't actually that bad," he said. "They mostly played their own stuff, some covers too, classic oldies."

"I know him—Johnnie Lomond!" Bernadette said. "He was in the same year as my big brother. Came to our house for a party one night when Mum and Dad were in Tenerife, him and some of my brother's other mates from Sixth Year. Ended up blocking the bathroom sink, if I remember right . . ."

I turned away, not wishing to hear about his youthful indiscretions.

"Anyway," said Billy—he did not like being interrupted, I'd noticed—"she absolutely *hated* that band. She just sat there frozen; didn't move, didn't clap, anything. Soon as they finished, she said she needed to go home. So she didn't even make it to the interval, and I had to sit there on my own for the rest of the gig, like, literally, Billy No-Mates."

"That's a shame, Billy; I know you were wanting to take her for a drink afterward, maybe go dancing," Loretta said, nudging him.

"You're so funny, Loretta. No, she was off like a shot. She'd have been tucked up in bed with a cup of cocoa and a copy of *Reader's Digest* before the band had even finished their set."

"Oh," said Janey, "I don't see her as a *Reader's Digest* reader, somehow. It'd be something much weirder, much more random. *Angling Times*? *What Caravan?*"

"*Horse and Hound*," said Billy firmly, "and she's got a subscription." They all sniggered.

I laughed myself at that one, actually.

~

I hadn't been expecting it to happen last night, not at all. It hit me all the harder because of that. I'm someone who likes to plan things properly, prepare in advance and be organized. This came out of nowhere; it felt like a slap in the face, a punch to the gut, a burning.

I'd asked Billy to come to the concert with me, mainly because he was the youngest person in the office; for that reason, I assumed he'd enjoy the music. I heard the others teasing him about it when they thought I was out at lunch. I knew nothing about the concert, hadn't heard of any of the bands. I was going out of a sense of duty; I'd won the tickets in the charity raffle, and I knew people would ask about it in the office.

I had been drinking sour white wine, warm and tainted by the plastic glasses the pub made us drink from. What savages they must think us! Billy had insisted on buying it, to thank me for inviting him. There was no question of it being a date. The very notion was ridiculous.

The lights went down. Billy hadn't wanted to watch the other acts, but I was adamant. You never know if you'll be bearing witness as a new star emerges, never know who's going to walk onto the stage and set it alight. And then *he* did. I stared at him. He was light and heat. He blazed. Everything he came into contact with would be changed. I sat forward on my seat, edged closer. At last. I'd found him.

≈

Now that fate had unfurled my future, I simply *had* to find out more about him; the singer, the answer. Before I tackled the horror that was the month-end accounts, I thought I'd have a quick look at a few sites—Argos, John Lewis—to see how much a computer would cost. I suppose I could have come into the office during the weekend and used one, but there was a high risk that someone else would be around and ask what I was doing. It's not like I'd be breaking any rules, but it's no one else's business, and I wouldn't want to have to explain to Bob how I'd been working weekends and yet still hadn't managed to make a dent in the huge pile of invoices waiting to be processed. Plus, I could do other things at home at the same time, like cook a trial menu for our first dinner together. Mummy told me, years ago, that men go absolutely crazy for sausage rolls. The way to a man's heart, she said, is a homemade sausage roll, hot, flaky pastry, good quality meat. I haven't cooked anything except pasta for years. I've never made a sausage roll. I don't suppose it's terribly difficult, though. It's only pastry and mechanically recovered meat.

I switched on the machine and entered my password, but the whole screen froze. I turned the computer off and on again, and this time it didn't even get as far as the password prompt. Annoying. I went to see Loretta, the office manager. She has overinflated ideas of her own administrative abilities, and in her spare time makes hideous jewelry, which she then sells to idiots. I told her my computer wasn't working, and that I hadn't been able to get hold of Danny in IT.

"Danny left, Eleanor," she said, not looking up from her screen. "There's a new guy now. Raymond Gibbons? He started last month?" She said this as though I should have known. Still not looking up, she wrote his full name and telephone extension on a Post-it note and handed it to me.

"Thank you so much, you've been extremely helpful as usual, Loretta," I said. It went over her head, of course.

I phoned the number but got his voice mail: "Hi, Raymond here, but also *not* here. Like Schrödinger's cat. Leave a message after the beep. Cheers."

I shook my head in disgust, and spoke slowly and clearly into the machine.

"Good morning, Mr. Gibbons. My name is Miss Oliphant and I am the finance clerk. My computer has stopped working and I would be most grateful if you could see your way to repairing it today. Should you require any further details, you may reach me on extension five-three-five. Thank you most kindly."

I hoped that my clear, concise message might serve as an exemplar for him. I waited for ten minutes, tidying my desk, but he did not return my call. After two hours of paper filing and in the absence of any communication from Mr. Gibbons, I decided to take a very early lunch break. It had crossed my mind that I ought to ready myself physically for a potential meeting with the musician by making a few improvements. Should I make myself over from the inside out, or work from the outside in? I compiled a list in my head of all of the appearance-related work which would need to be undertaken: hair (head and body), nails (toe and finger), eyebrows, cellulite, teeth, scars . . . all of these things needed to be updated, enhanced, improved. Eventually, I decided to start from the outside and work my way in—that's what often happens in nature, after all. The shedding of skin, rebirth. Animals, birds and insects can provide such useful insights. If I'm ever unsure as to the correct course of action, I'll think, "What would a ferret do?" or, "How would a salamander respond to this situation?" Invariably, I find the right answer.

I walked past Julie's Beauty Basket every day on my way to work. As luck would have it, they had a cancelation. It would take around twenty minutes, Kayla would be my therapist, and it would cost forty-five pounds. Forty-five! Still, I reminded myself as Kayla led me toward a room downstairs, he was worth it. Kayla, like the other employees, was wearing a white outfit resembling surgical scrubs and white clogs. I approved of this pseudo-medical apparel. We went into an uncomfortably small room, barely large enough to accommodate the bed, chair and side table.

"Now then," she said, "what you need to do is pop off your . . ." she paused and looked at my lower half ". . . erm, trousers, and your underwear, then pop up onto the couch. You can be naked from the waist down or, if you prefer, you can pop these on." She placed a small packet on the bed. "Cover yourself with the towel and I'll pop back in to see you in a couple of minutes. OK?"

I nodded. I hadn't anticipated quite so much popping.

Once the door had closed behind her, I removed my shoes and stepped out of my trousers. Should I keep my socks on? I thought, on balance, that I probably should. I pulled down my underpants and wondered what to do with them. It didn't seem right to drape them over the chair, in full view, as I'd done with my trousers, so I folded them up carefully and put them into my shopper. Feeling rather exposed, I picked up the little packet that she'd left on the bed and opened it. I shook out the contents and held them up: a very small pair of black underpants, in a style which I recognized as "Tanga" in Marks & Spencer's nomenclature, and made from the same papery fabric as tea bags. I stepped into them and pulled them up. They were far too small, and my flesh bulged out from the front, sides and back.

The bed was very high and I found a plastic step underneath that I used to help me ascend. I lay down; it was lined with towels and topped with the same scratchy blue paper that you find on the doctor's couch. Another black towel was folded at my feet, and I pulled it up to my waist to cover myself. The black towels worried me. What sort of dirty staining was the color choice designed to hide? I stared at the ceiling and counted the spotlights, then looked from side to side. Despite the dim lighting, I could see scuff marks on the pale walls. Kayla knocked and entered, all breezy cheerfulness.

"Now then," she said, "what are we doing today?"

"As I said, a bikini wax, please."

She laughed. "Yes, sorry, I meant what kind of wax would you like?"

I thought about this. "Just the usual kind . . . the candle kind?" I said.

"What shape?" she said tersely, then noticed my expression. "So," she said patiently, counting them off on her fingers, "you've got your French, your Brazilian or your Hollywood."

I pondered. I ran the words through my mind again, over and over, the same technique I used for solving crossword anagrams, waiting for the letters to settle into a pattern. French, Brazilian, Hollywood . . . French, Brazilian, Hollywood . . .

"Hollywood," I said, finally. "Holly would, and so would Eleanor."

She ignored my wordplay, and lifted up the towel. "Oh . . ." she said. "Okaaaay . . ." She went over to the table and opened a drawer, took something out. "It's going to be an extra two pounds for the clipper guard," she said sternly, pulling on a pair of disposable gloves.

The clippers buzzbuzzbuzzed and I stared at the ceiling. This didn't hurt at all! When she'd finished, she used a big, fat brush to sweep the shaved hair onto the floor. I felt panic start to rise within me. I hadn't looked at the floor when I came in. What if she'd done this with the other clients—were their pubic hairs now adhering to the soles of my polka-dot socks? I started to feel slightly sick at the thought.

"That's better," she said. "Now, I'll be as quick as I can. Don't use perfumed lotions in the area for at least twelve hours after this, OK?" She stirred the pot of wax that was heating on the side table.

"Oh, don't worry, I'm not much of a one for unguents, Kayla," I said. She goggled at me. I'd have thought that staff in the beauty business would have better-developed people skills. She was almost as bad as my colleagues back at the office.

She pushed the paper pants to one side and asked me to pull the skin taut. Then she painted a stripe of warm wax onto my pubis with a wooden spatula, and pressed a strip of fabric onto it. Taking hold of the end, she ripped it off in one rapid flourish of clean, bright pain.

"*Morituri te salutant*," I whispered, tears pricking my eyes. This is what I say in such situations, and it always cheers me up to no end. I started to sit up, but she gently pushed me back down.

"Oh, there's a good bit more to go, I'm afraid," she said, sounding quite cheerful.

Pain is easy; pain is something with which I am familiar. I went into the little white room inside my head, the one that's the color of clouds. It smells of clean cotton and baby rabbits. The air inside the room is the palest sugar almond pink, and the loveliest music plays. Today, it was "Top of the World" by the Carpenters. That beautiful voice . . . she sounds so blissful, so full of love. Lovely, lucky Karen Carpenter.

Kayla continued to dip and rip. She asked me to bend my knees out to the sides and place my heels together. Like frog's legs, I said, but she ignored me, intent on her work. She ripped out the hair from right underneath. I hadn't even considered that such a thing would be possible. When she'd finished, she asked me to lie normally again and then pulled down the paper pants. She smeared hot wax onto the remaining hair and ripped it all off triumphantly.

"There," she said, removing the gloves and wiping her brow with the back of her hand, "now doesn't that look *so* much better!"

She passed me a hand mirror so I could look at myself. "But I'm completely bare!" I said, horrified.

"That's right, a Hollywood," she said. "That's what you asked for."

I felt my fists clench tight, and shook my head in disbelief. I had come here to start to become a normal woman, and instead she'd made me look like a child.

"Kayla," I said, unable to believe the situation I now found myself in, "the man in whom I am interested is a normal adult man. He will enjoy sexual relations with a normal adult woman. Are you trying to imply that he's some sort of pedophile? How *dare* you!"

She stared at me, horrified. I had had enough of this.

"Please, leave me to get dressed now," I said, turning my face to the wall.

She left and I climbed down from the couch. I pulled my trousers on, consoled by the thought that the hair would surely grow back before our first intimate encounter. I didn't tip Kayla on the way out.

~

When I returned to the office, my computer still wasn't working. I sat down gingerly and called Raymond in IT again, but it went straight to his preposterous message. I decided to go upstairs and find him; from his voice mail greeting, he sounded like the kind of person who would ignore a ringing telephone and sit around doing nothing. Just as I pushed my chair back, a man approached my desk. He was barely taller than me, and was wearing green training shoes, ill-fitting denim trousers and a T-shirt showing a cartoon dog lying on top of its kennel. It was stretched taut against a burgeoning belly. He had pale, sandy hair, cut short in an attempt to hide the fact that it was thinning and receding, and patchy blond stubble. All of his visible skin, both face and body, was very pink. A word sprang to mind: porcine.

"Erm, Oliphant?" he said.

"Yes—Eleanor Oliphant—I am she," I said.

He lurched toward my desk. "I'm Raymond, IT," he said. I offered him my hand to shake, which eventually he did, rather tentatively. Yet more evidence of the lamentable decline in modern manners. I moved away and allowed him to sit at my desk.

"What seems to be the problem?" he asked, staring at my screen. I told him. "Okey dokey," he said, typing noisily. I picked up my *Telegraph* and told him I'd be in the staff room; there was little point in my standing around while he mended the computer.

The crossword setter today was "Elgar," whose clues are always elegant and fair. I was tapping my teeth with the pen, pondering twelve down, when Raymond loped into the room, interrupting my train of thought. He looked over my shoulder.

"Crosswords, eh?" he said. "Never seen the point of them. Give me a good computer game any day. *Call of Duty*—"

I ignored his inane wittering. "Did you fix it?" I asked him.

"Yep," he said, sounding pleased. "You had quite a nasty virus. I've cleaned up your hard drive and reset the firewall. You should run a full system scan once a week, ideally." He must have noticed my uncomprehending expression. "Come on, I'll show you." We walked along the corridor. The floor squeaked beneath his hideous training shoes. He coughed.

"So . . . you, eh, have you worked here long, Eleanor?" he said.

"Yes," I replied, increasing my pace.

He managed to keep up with me, but was slightly out of breath.

"Right," he said. He cleared his throat. "I started here a few weeks ago. I was at Sandersons before. In town. Do you know them?"

"No," I said.

We reached my desk and I sat down. He hovered, too close. He smelled of cooking and, faintly, of cigarettes. Unpleasant. He told me what to do and I followed his instructions, committing them to memory. By the time he had finished, I had reached the limit of my interest in technological matters for the day.

"Thank you for your assistance, Raymond," I said, pointedly. Raymond saluted, and heaved himself to his feet. A man with a less military bearing was hard to imagine.

"No bother, Eleanor. See you around!"

I very much doubt it, I thought, opening up the spreadsheet which listed this month's overdue accounts. He loped off with a strange bouncy walk, springing too hard on the balls of his feet. A lot of unattractive men seem to walk in such a manner, I've noticed. I'm sure training shoes don't help.

The other night, the singer had worn beautiful leather brogues. He was tall, elegant and graceful. It was hard to believe that the singer and Raymond were members of the same species. I shifted uncomfortably in my chair. There was throbbing pain and the beginnings of an itch *downstairs*. Perhaps I should have put my underpants back on.

≈

The leaving do started around half past four, and I made sure to clap extravagantly at the end of Bob's speech and say, "Hear, hear, bravo!" loudly, so that everyone noticed me; I left at 4:59 p.m. and walked to the shopping mall as fast as the chafing occasioned by my newly hairless epidermis allowed. I got there by quarter past, thank God. *Bird in the hand* is what I was thinking, given the importance of the task, so I simply headed straight into the first big department store I saw and took the lift to the Electrical Department.

A young man with a gray shirt and a shiny tie was staring at the banks of giant TV screens. I approached, and informed him that I wished to purchase a computer. He looked scared.

"*Desktop laptop tablet*," he intoned. I had no idea what he was talking about.

"I haven't bought a computer before, Liam," I explained, reading his name badge. "I'm a very inexperienced technology consumer."

He pulled at the collar of his shirt, as though trying to free his enormous Adam's apple from its constraints. He had the look of a gazelle or an impala, one of those boring beige animals with large, round eyes on the sides of its face. The kind of animal that always gets eaten by a leopard in the end.

This was a rocky start.

"What will you be using it for?" he asked, not making eye contact.

"That's absolutely none of your business," I said, most offended.

He looked like he might cry, and I felt bad. He was only young. I touched his arm, even though I hate touching.

"I'm afraid I'm a bit anxious because it is absolutely imperative that I am able to go online this weekend," I explained. His nervous expression remained in place.

"Liam," I said slowly, "I simply need to purchase some sort of computer equipment that I can use in the comfort of my own home in order to conduct some Internet-based research. I may in time send electronic messages from it. That is all. Do you have something suitable in stock?"

The boy stared heavenward and thought deeply. "A laptop and mobile Internet access?" he said. Why was he asking me, for goodness' sake? I nodded and handed over my debit card.

When I got home, slightly giddy at how much money I'd spent, I realized that there was nothing to eat. Friday was margherita pizza day, of course, but my routine was, for the first time ever, somewhat out of kilter. I recalled that I had a flyer in the tea towel drawer, something that was put through my letter box a while ago. I found it easily and smoothed it out. There were money-off coupons along the bottom, which had expired. I guessed the prices would have gone up, but assumed that the phone number had stayed the same, and they presumably still sold pizzas. Even these old prices were ridiculous, though, and I actually laughed out loud at them. In Tesco Metro, the pizzas cost a quarter of that price.

I decided that I'd go for it. Yes, it was extravagant and indulgent, but why not? Life should be about trying new things, exploring boundaries, I reminded myself. The man on the other end of the line told me that the pizza would arrive in fifteen minutes. I brushed my hair, took off my slippers and put my work shoes back on. I wondered how they managed with the black pepper. Would the man bring a pepper mill with him? Surely he wouldn't grind it over the pizza while he stood on the doorstep? I put the kettle on in case he wanted a cup of tea. They had told me on the phone how much it would cost and I took out the money, put it in an envelope and wrote *Pizza Pronto* on the front. I didn't bother with the address. I wondered whether it was the done thing to tip, and wished I had someone to ask. Mummy wouldn't be able to advise. She doesn't get to decide what she eats.

The flaw with the pizza plan was the wine. They didn't deliver it, the man on the phone said, and actually sounded quite amused that I'd asked. Strange— what could be more normal than pizza and wine? I couldn't see how I was going to acquire something to drink in time to have with the pizza. I really needed something to drink. I worried over it as I waited for the delivery.

In the end, the pizza experience was extremely disappointing. The man simply thrust a big box into my hand and took the envelope, which he then rudely ripped open right in front of me. I heard him mutter *fuck's sake* under his breath as he counted the coins. I had been collecting fifty-pence pieces in a little ceramic dish, and this had seemed the perfect opportunity to use them up. I'd popped an extra one in for him, but received no thanks for it. Rude.

The pizza was excessively greasy and the dough was flabby and tasteless. I decided immediately that I would never eat delivered pizza again, and definitely not with the musician. If we ever found ourselves in need of pizza and too far from a Tesco Metro, one of two things would happen. One: we would take a black cab into town and dine at a lovely Italian restaurant. Two: he would make pizza for us both, from scratch. He'd mix the dough, stretching and kneading it with those long, tapered fingers, stroking it until it did what he wanted. He'd stand at the cooker, simmering tomatoes with fresh herbs, reducing them to a rich sauce, slick and slippery with a sheen of olive oil.

He'd be wearing his oldest, most comfortable jeans, a pair that sat snugly on his slim hips, bare feet tapping as he sang softly to himself in his delicious voice and stirred. When he'd assembled the pizza, topping it with artichokes and fennel shavings, he'd put it in the oven and come and find me, take me by the hand and lead me into the kitchen. He'd have set the table, a dish of gardenias in the center, tea lights flickering through colored glass. He'd slowly ease the cork from a bottle of Barolo with a long, satisfying pop and place it on the table, then pull out my chair for me. Before I could sit, he'd take me in his arms and kiss me, his hands around my waist, pulling me so close that I could feel the pulse of blood in him, smell the sweet spiciness of his skin and the warm sugar of his breath.

~

I'd finished eating my poor-quality pizza and was jumping up and down on the box, trying to crush it small enough to fit into the bin, when I remembered the brandy. Mummy always said that brandy is good for shocks and I'd bought some, several years ago, just in case. I'd put it in the bathroom cabinet, with all the other emergency items. I went to check and there it was, behind the rolled-up bandages and the wrist supports—a bottle of Rémy Martin, full and unopened. I unscrewed the cap and took a drink. It wasn't as nice as vodka, but it wasn't bad.

I was very apprehensive about the laptop, never having set up a new computer before, but it was actually pretty easy. The mobile Internet thing was straightforward too. I took the brandy and the laptop to the kitchen table, typed his name into Google and hit return, then put my hands over my eyes. Seconds later I peeped through my fingers. There were hundreds of results! It seemed that this was going to be quite easy, so I decided to ration the pages; after all, I had the entire weekend, so there was no point in rushing.

The first link took me to his own web page, which was entirely taken up with photographs of him and his band. I moved closer to the screen until my nose was almost touching it. I had neither imagined him, nor overestimated the extent of his beauty. The next link took me to his Twitter page. I allowed myself the pleasure of reading the three latest messages, two of which were wry and witty, the third utterly charming. In it, he was professing his professional admiration for another musician. Gracious of him.

Next, his Instagram page. He had posted almost fifty photos. I clicked on one at random, a head shot in close-up, candid and relaxed. He had a Roman nose, perfectly straight, classically proportioned. His ears were also perfect, exactly the right size, the whorls of skin and cartilage flawlessly symmetrical. His eyes were light brown. They were light brown in the way that a rose is red, or that the sky is blue. They defined what it meant to be light brown.

There were rows and rows of photographs on the page and my brain forced my finger to press the button and return to the search engine. I scanned the rest of the sites that Google had found. There were video clips of performances on YouTube. There were articles and reviews. This was only the first page of the search results. I would read every piece of information that I could find about him, get to know him properly—after all, I'm very good at research, and at problem solving. I don't mean to boast; I'm merely stating the facts. Finding out more about him was the right thing to do, the sensible approach, if it turned out that he was going to be the love of my life. I picked up the brandy, a new notebook and a fine-tipped pen that I'd borrowed from the office, and went over to the sofa, ready to make a start on my plan of action. The brandy was both warming and soothing, and I kept sipping.

When I awoke, it was just after 3 a.m., and the pen and notebook were lying on the floor. Slowly, I recalled getting sidetracked, starting to daydream as the brandy slipped down. The backs of my hands were tattooed with black ink, his name written there over and over, inscribed inside love hearts, so that barely an inch of skin remained unsullied. A mouthful of brandy remained in the bottle. I downed it and went to bed.

# 3

Why him? Why now? On Monday morning, waiting at the bus stop, I tried to work it out. It was a tricky one. Who can understand the workings of fate, after all? Far greater minds than mine had tried, and failed, to arrive at a conclusion. There he was, a gift from the gods—handsome, elegant and talented. I was fine, perfectly fine on my own, but I needed to keep Mummy happy, keep her calm so she would leave me in peace. A boyfriend—a husband?—might just do the trick. It wasn't that *I* needed anyone. I was, as I previously stated, perfectly fine.

Having perused at length the available photographic evidence over the course of the weekend, I had concluded that there was something particularly mesmerizing about his eyes. My own are a similar shade, although they're nowhere near as beautiful, of course, containing no such shimmering copper depths. Looking at all those photographs, I was reminded of someone. It was only a half memory, like a face under ice or blurred by smoke, indistinct. Eyes just like mine, eyes set in a little face, wide and vulnerable, full of tears.

Ridiculous, Eleanor. It was disappointing that I had allowed myself, even for a moment, to indulge in sentimentality. Plenty of people in the world had light brown eyes like mine, after all—that was a scientific fact. It was statistically inevitable that some of them would have made eye contact with me during the course of a routine social interaction.

Something else was troubling me, though. All the studies show that people tend to take a partner who is roughly as attractive as they are; like attracts like, that is the norm.

I was under no illusions. In terms of looks, he was a ten and I am . . . I don't know what I am. Not a ten, certainly. Of course, I hoped he would see beyond superficialities, look a bit deeper, but that said, I knew that his profession would require him to have a partner who was at least presentable. The music business, show business, is all about image, and he couldn't be seen with a woman whose appearance would be perceived by simpletons as inappropriate. I was well aware of that. I'd have to try my best to look the part.

He'd posted some new photos online, two head shots, close profiles, right and left. He was perfect in both, and they were identical—objectively, literally, he did not have a bad side. Of course, a defining characteristic of beauty is symmetry, that's another thing all the studies agree on. I wondered what gene pool had created such handsome progeny. Did he have brothers or sisters, perhaps? If we ever got together, I might even be able to meet them. I didn't know much about parents in general, or siblings in particular, having had quite an . . . unconventional upbringing myself.

I feel sorry for beautiful people. Beauty, from the moment you possess it, is already slipping away, ephemeral. That must be difficult. Always having to prove that there's more to you, wanting people to see beneath the surface, to be loved for yourself, and not your stunning body, sparkling eyes or thick, lustrous hair.

In most professions, getting older means getting better at your job, earning respect because of your seniority and experience. If your job depends on your looks, the opposite is true—how depressing. Suffering other people's unkindness must be difficult too; all those bitter, less attractive people, jealous and resentful of your beauty. That's incredibly unfair of them. After all, beautiful people didn't ask to be born that way. It's as unfair to dislike someone because they're attractive as it is to dislike someone because of a deformity.

It doesn't bother me at all when people react to my face, to the ridged, white contours of scar tissue that slither across my right cheek, starting at my temple and running all the way down to my chin. I am stared at, whispered about; I turn heads. It was reassuring to think that he would understand, being something of a head-turner himself, albeit for very different reasons.

～

I eschewed the *Telegraph* today in favor of alternative reading matter. I had spent an obscene amount of money on a small selection of women's magazines, flimsy and lurid ones, thick, glossy ones, all of them promising a range of wonders, simple but life-enhancing changes. I had never purchased such items before, although I had, of course, leafed through a few in hospital waiting rooms and other institutional settings. I noted that, disappointingly, none of them had a cryptic crossword; indeed, one contained a "soap-star word search" that would insult the intelligence of a seven-year-old. I could have bought three bottles of wine or a liter of premium-brand vodka for the price of that little pile. Nevertheless, after careful consideration, I'd worked out that they were the most reliable and accessible source of the information that I needed.

These magazines could tell me which clothes and shoes to wear, how to have my hair styled in order to fit in. They could show me the right kind of makeup to buy and how to apply it. This way, I would disappear into everywoman acceptability. I would not be stared at. The goal, ultimately, was successful camouflage as a human woman.

Mummy has always told me that I am ugly, freakish, *vile*. She's done so from my earliest years, even before I acquired my scars. So I felt very happy about making these changes. Excited. I was a blank canvas.

At home that evening, I looked into the mirror above the washbasin while I washed my damaged hands. There I was: Eleanor Oliphant. Long, straight, light brown hair that runs all the way down to my waist, pale skin, my face a scarred palimpsest of fire. A nose that's too small and eyes that are too big. Ears: unexceptional. Around average height, approximately

average weight. I *aspire* to average . . . I've been the
focus of far too much attention in my time. Pass me
over, move along please, nothing to see here.

I don't often look in the mirror, as a rule. This has
absolutely nothing to do with my scars. It is because
of the unsettling gene mix that looks back at me. I see
far too much of Mummy's face there. I cannot distinguish any of my father's features, because I have never
met him and, to the best of my knowledge, no photographic records exist. Mummy almost never mentioned him, and on the rare occasions when he came
up, she referred to him only as "the gametes donor."
Once I'd looked up this term in her *New Shorter
Oxford English Dictionary* (from the Greek γαμέτης,
"husband"—did this juvenile etymological adventuring spark my love of classics?), I spent several years
wondering about this strange set of circumstances.
Even at that tender age, I understood that assisted
conception was the antithesis of careless, spontaneous
or unplanned parenthood, that it was the most delib-
erate of decisions, undertaken only by women who
were serious and dedicated in their quest to be mothers. I simply could not believe, given the evidence and
my own experience, that Mummy had ever been such
a woman, could ever have wished for a child so
intensely. As it transpired, I was right.

Finally, I summoned the courage to inquire directly as to the circumstances of my creation, and to
seek any available information about the mythical
donor of spermatozoan, my father. As any child

would in such circumstances—possibly even more so, in *my* particular circumstances—I had been harboring a small but intense fantasy about the character and appearance of my absent parent. She laughed and laughed.

"Donor? Did I really say that? It was simply a *metaphor*, darling," she said.

Another word I'd have to look up.

"I was actually trying to spare your feelings. It was more of a . . . compulsory donation, shall we say. I had no choice in the matter. Do you understand what I'm telling you?"

I said that I did, but I was fibbing.

"Where does he live, Mummy?" I asked, feeling brave. "What does he look like, what does he do?"

"I can't remember what he looked like," she said, her tone dismissive, bored. "He smelled like high game and liquefied Roquefort, if that's any help." I must have looked puzzled. She leaned forward, showed me her teeth. "That's rotting flesh and stinking, moldy cheese to you, darling." She paused, regained her equanimity.

"I don't know if he's alive or dead, Eleanor," she said. "If he's alive, he's probably very rich by dubious, unethical means. If he's dead—and I sincerely hope that he is—then I imagine he's languishing in the outer ring of the seventh circle of hell, immersed in a river of boiling blood and fire, taunted by centaurs."

I realized at that point that it probably wasn't worth asking if she had kept any photos.

# 4

It was Wednesday evening. Mummy time. However much I might wish it were otherwise, she always managed to get through to me in the end. I sighed and turned off the radio, knowing I would have to wait until Sunday's omnibus now to find out whether Eddie Grundy's cider had fermented successfully. I felt a flash of desperate optimism. What if I didn't have to talk to her? What if I could talk to someone else, anyone else?

"Hello?" I said.

"Oh, hiya, hen, it's just me. Some weather the day, eh?"

It was hardly surprising that my mother had become institutionalized—that, one assumed, was a given, considering the nature of her crime—but she had gone far, far further than necessary by occasionally adopting the accent and argot of the places where she has been detained. I assumed this helped her ingratiate herself with her fellow residents, or, perhaps, with the staff. It may simply have been to amuse herself. She's very good at accents, but then she's a woman with a broad range of gifts. I was poised, *en garde*, for this conversation, as one always had to be with her. She was a formidable adversary. Perhaps it was foolhardy, but I made the first move.

"It's only been a week, I know, but it feels like an age since we last spoke, Mummy. I've been so busy with work, and—"

She cut across me, nice as pie on this occasion, switching her accent to match mine. That voice; I remembered it from childhood, heard it still in my nightmares.

"I know what you mean, darling," she said. She spoke quickly. "Look, I can't talk for long. Tell me about your week. What have you been doing?"

I told her that I had attended a concert, mentioned the leaving do at work. I told her absolutely nothing else. As soon as I heard her voice, I felt that familiar, creeping dread. I'd been so looking forward to sharing my news, dropping it at her feet like a dog retrieving a game bird peppered with shot. Now I couldn't shake the thought that she would pick it up and, with brutal calm, simply tear it to shreds.

"Oh a concert, that sounds marvelous—I've always been fond of music. We're treated to the occasional performance here, you know; a few of the residents will have a singsong in the recreation room if the mood takes them. It really is . . . quite something."

She paused, and then I heard her snarl at someone.

"Will ah fuck, Jodi—ahm talkin tae ma lassie here, and ahm no gonnae *curtail* ma conversation for a wee skank like you." There was a pause. "No. Now *fuck off.*" She cleared her throat.

"Sorry about that, darling. She's what's known as a 'junkie'—she and her similarly addicted friends were caught purloining perfume from Boots. Midnight Heat by Beyoncé, would you believe." She lowered her voice again. "We're not exactly talking criminal masterminds in here, darling—I think Professor Moriarty can rest easy for now."

She laughed, a cocktail party tinkle—the light, bright sound of a Noel Coward character enjoying an amusing exchange of bon mots on a wisteria-clad terrace. I tried to move the conversation forward.

"So . . . how are you, Mummy?"

"Fabulous darling, just fabulous. I've been 'crafting'—some nice, well-meaning ladies have been teaching me how to embroider cushions. Sweet of them to volunteer their time, no?" I thought of Mummy in possession of a long, sharp needle, and an icy current ran up and down my spine.

"But enough of me," she said, the jagged edge in her voice hardening. "I want to hear about *you*. What are your plans for the weekend? Are you going out dancing, perhaps? Has an admirer asked you on a date?"

Such venom. I tried to ignore it.

"I'm doing some research, Mummy, for a project." Her breathing quickened.

"Is that right? What kind of research? Research into a *thing*, or research into a *person*?"

I couldn't help myself. I told her.

"A person, Mummy," I said.

She whispered so softly that I could hardly hear her.

"Ah, so the game's afoot, is it? Do tell . . ." she said. "I'm all ears, darling."

"There's really nothing to tell yet, Mummy," I said, looking at my watch. "I simply came across someone . . . nice . . . and I want to find out a bit more about . . . that someone." I needed to polish and perfect things before I plucked up the courage to share my shiny new jewel with her, set it before her for her approval. In the meantime, let me get away, let this end, *please*.

"How marvelous! I shall look forward to regular updates on this project of yours, Eleanor," she said brightly. "You know how much I'd love for you to find someone *special*. Someone *appropriate*. All these talks we've had, over the years: I've always had the impression that you're missing out, not having someone significant in your life. It's good that you've started looking for . . . your other half. A partner in crime, as it were." She laughed quietly.

"I'm not lonely, Mummy," I said, protesting. "I'm fine on my own. I've always been fine on my own."

"Well now, you haven't *always* been on your own, have you?" she said, her voice sly, quiet. I felt sweat cling to the back of my neck, dampening my hair. "Still, tell yourself whatever you need to get you through the night, darling," she said, laughing. She has a knack for amusing herself, although no one else laughs much in her company. "You can always talk to me, you know.

About anything. Or anyone." She sighed. "I do so love
to hear from you, darling . . . You wouldn't understand, of course, but the bond between a mother and
child, it's . . . how best to describe it . . . *unbreakable.*
The two of us are linked forever, you see—same blood
in my veins that's running through yours. You grew
inside me, your *teeth* and your *tongue* and your *cervix*
are all made from my cells, my genes. Who knows
what little surprises I left growing inside there for you,
which codes I set running? Breast cancer? Alzheimer's?
You'll just have to wait and see. You were fermenting
inside me for all those months, nice and cozy, Eleanor.
However hard you try to walk away from that fact,
you can't, darling, you simply can't. It isn't possible to
destroy a bond that strong."

"That may or may not be true, Mummy," I said
quietly. Such audacity. I don't know where I found the
courage. The blood was pounding through my body
and my hands quivered.

She responded as though I had not spoken.

"Right, so we'll keep in touch, yes? You carry on
with your little project, and I'll speak to you at the
same time next week? That's settled, then. Must
dash—cheerio!"

It was only when the air went dead that I noticed
I'd been crying.

# 5

Friday at last. When I arrived at the office, my colleagues were already clustered around the kettle, talking about soap operas. They ignored me; I have long since ceased to initiate any conversation with them. I hung my navy jerkin on the back of my chair and switched on my computer. I had not slept well again the previous evening, being somewhat unsettled by my conversation with Mummy. I decided to make a refreshing cup of tea before I got started. I have my own mug and spoon, which I keep in my desk drawer for hygiene reasons. My colleagues think this strange, or at least I assume so from their reactions, and yet they are happy to drink from filthy vessels, washed carelessly by unknown hands. I cannot even countenance the notion of inserting a teaspoon, licked and sucked by a stranger barely an hour beforehand, into a hot beverage. Filthy.

I stood at the sink while I waited for the kettle to boil, trying not to listen to their conversation. I gave my little teapot another hot rinse, just to be sure, and drifted into pleasurable thoughts, thoughts of him. I wondered what he was doing at this very moment—writing a song, perhaps? Or would he still be asleep?

I wondered what his handsome face would look like in repose.

The kettle clicked off and I warmed the teapot, then spooned in some first-flush Darjeeling, my mind still focused on the putative beauty of my slumbering troubadour. Childish laughter from my colleagues began to intrude upon my thoughts, but I assumed this was to do with my choice of beverage. Knowing no better, they are content to drop a bag of poorest-quality blended tea into a mug, scald it with boiling water and then dilute any remaining flavor by adding fridge-cold milk. Once again, for some reason, it is I who am considered strange. But if you're going to drink a cup of tea, why not take every care to maximize the pleasure?

The giggling continued, and Janey started to hum. There was no attempt at concealment now; they were laughing loud and hard. She stopped humming and started singing. I recognized neither the melody nor the lyrics. She stopped, unable to go on because she was laughing so much, still performing a strange backward walk.

"Morning, Wacko Jacko," Billy called out to me. "What's with the white glove?"

So that was the source of their amusement. Unbelievable.

"It's for my eczema," I said, talking slowly and patiently, the way you explain things to a child. "I had a very bad flare-up on Wednesday evening and the skin on my right hand is extremely inflamed. I'm wearing this cotton glove to prevent infection." The laughter died away, leaving a long pause. They looked at each other silently, rather like ruminant animals in a field.

I didn't often interact with my colleagues in this informal, chatty way, which gave me cause to stop and consider whether I ought to make the most of the opportunity. Bernadette's fraternal connection to the object of my affections—surely it would be the work of moments to glean some additional, useful information about him from her? I didn't think I was up to a protracted interaction—she had a very loud, grating voice and a laugh like a howler monkey—but it was surely worth a few moments of my time. I stirred my tea in a clockwise direction while I prepared my opening gambit.

"Did you enjoy the rest of the concert the other night, Billy?" I said. He looked surprised at my question, and there was a pause before he answered.

"Aye, it was OK," he said. Articulate as ever. This was going to be hard work.

"Were the other singers of a similar standard to . . ." I paused and pretended to wrack my brains ". . . to Johnnie Lomond?"

"They were all right, I guess," he said, shrugging. Such insight, such clear, descriptive prose. Bernadette piped up, as I knew she would, unable to resist an opportunity to draw attention to herself by any means available.

"I know him, Johnnie Lomond," she told me proudly. "He used to be pals with my brother, at school."

"Really?" I said, not, for once, having to feign interest. "Which school was that?"

The way she said the name of the establishment implied that I ought to be aware of it. I tried to look impressed.

"Are they still friends?" I asked, stirring my tea again.

"Not really," she said. "He came to Paul's wedding, but I think they drifted apart after that. You know what it's like—when you're married with kids, you sort of lose touch with your single pals, don't you? You don't have that much in common anymore . . ."

I had neither knowledge nor experience of the situation she'd described, but I nodded as though I did, while all the while the same phrase was scrolling across my brain: he is single, he is single, he is single.

I took my tea back to my desk. Their laughter seemed to have turned into low whispering now. It never ceases to amaze me, the things they find interesting, amusing or unusual. I can only assume they've led very sheltered lives.

~

Janey the secretary had got engaged to her latest Neanderthal, and there was a presentation for her that afternoon. I'd contributed seventy-eight pence to the collection. I only had coppers in my purse or else a five-pound note, and I certainly wasn't going to put such an extravagant sum into the communal envelope to buy something unnecessary for someone I barely knew. I must have contributed hundreds of pounds over the years to all the leaving presents, baby gifts and special birthdays, and what had I ever received in return? My own birthdays pass unremarked.

Whoever had chosen the engagement gift had selected wineglasses and a matching carafe. Such accoutrements are unnecessary when you drink vodka—I simply use my favorite mug. I purchased it in a charity shop some years ago, and it has a photograph of a moon-faced man on one side. He is wearing a brown leather blouson. Along the top, in strange yellow font, it says *Top Gear*. I don't profess to understand this mug. It holds the perfect amount of vodka, however, thereby obviating the need for frequent refills.

Janey was planning a short engagement, she'd simpered, and so, of course, the inevitable collection for the wedding present would soon follow. Of all the compulsory financial contributions, that is the one that irks me most. Two people wander around John Lewis picking out lovely items for themselves, and then they make other people pay for them. It's bare-faced effrontery. They choose things like plates, bowls and cutlery—I mean, what are they doing at the moment: shoveling food from packets into their mouths with their bare hands? I simply fail to see how the act of legally formalizing a human relationship necessitates friends, family and coworkers upgrading the contents of their kitchen for them.

I've never actually been to a wedding ceremony. I was invited to Loretta's evening reception a couple of years ago, along with everyone else from the office. It was in a horrible hotel near the airport, and we organized a minibus to get there; I had to contribute to the cost of that, in addition to my bus fare into town and back. Guests were obliged to buy their own drinks all evening, which shocked me. Entertaining is not my area of expertise, I'll admit that, but surely, if you are a host, you are responsible for ensuring that your guests are provided with a libation? That's a basic principle of hospitality, in all societies and cultures, and has been since recorded time. In the event, I drank tap water—I rarely imbibe alcohol in public. I only really enjoy it when I'm alone, at home. They did at least serve tea and coffee later in the evening, free of charge; this was accompanied by poor-quality savory pastries and, bizarrely, slices of Christmas cake. For hours and hours, there was a disco, and terrible people danced in a terrible way to terrible music. I sat on my own and no one asked me to dance and I was absolutely fine with that.

The other guests did seem to be enjoying themselves, or at least I assume that to have been the case. They were shuffling on the dance floor, red-faced and drunk. Their shoes looked uncomfortable, and they were shouting the words of the songs into each other's faces. I'll never go to such an event again. It simply wasn't worth it, just for a cup of tea and a slice of cake. The evening wasn't completely wasted, however, because I managed to slip almost a dozen sausage rolls into my shopper, wrapped in serviettes, for later. Unfortunately, they weren't very tasty—nowhere near as good as the always reliable Greggs.

≈

When the grim engagement presentation was over, I zipped up my jerkin and turned off my computer, excited at the thought of switching on my personal laptop at home as soon as I could. There might be some useful information online about his school days, given the nugget of new information I'd inveigled from Bernadette earlier. How wonderful if there was a class photograph! I'd love to see how he looked in his youth, whether he'd always been beautiful, or whether he'd blossomed into a glorious butterfly at a relatively late stage. My money was on him being stunning from birth. There might be a list of prizes he'd won! Music, obviously, English, probably: he wrote such wonderful lyrics, after all. Either way, he definitely struck me as a prizewinner.

I try to plan my exits from the office so that I don't need to talk to anyone else on the way out. There are always so many questions. *What are you up to tonight? Plans for the weekend? Booked a holiday yet?* I've no idea why other people are always so interested in my schedule. I'd timed it all perfectly, and was maneuvering my shopper over the threshold when I realized that someone had pulled the door back and was holding it open for me. I turned around.

"All right, Eleanor?" the man said, smiling patiently as I unraveled the string on my mittens from my sleeve. Even though they were not required in the current temperate atmosphere, I keep them in situ, ready to don as the eventual change in season requires.

"Yes," I said, and then, remembering my manners, I muttered, "Thank you, Raymond."

"No bother," he said.

Annoyingly, we began walking down the path at the same time.

"Where are you headed?" he asked. I nodded vaguely in the direction of the hill.

"Me too," he said.

I bent down and pretended to refasten the Velcro on my shoe. I took as long as I could, hoping that he would take the hint. When eventually I stood up again, he was still there, arms dangling by his sides. I noticed that he was wearing a duffle coat. A duffle coat! Surely they were the preserve of children and small bears? We started to walk downhill together and he took out a packet of cigarettes, offered me one. I reared back from the packet.

"How disgusting," I said. Undeterred, he lit up.

"Sorry," he mumbled. "Filthy habit, I know."

"It is," I said. "You'll die years earlier than you would have otherwise, probably from cancer or heart disease. You won't see the effects on your heart or your lungs for a while, but you'll notice it in your mouth—gum disease, loss of teeth—and you've already got the smoker's characteristically dull, prematurely lined skin. The chemical constitution of cigarettes includes cyanide and ammonia, you know. Do you really want to willingly ingest such toxic substances?"

"You seem to know an awful lot about fags for a nonsmoker," he said, blowing a noxious cloud of carcinogens from between his thin lips.

"I did briefly consider taking up smoking," I admitted, "but I thoroughly research all activities before commencement, and smoking did not in the end seem to me to be a viable or sensible pastime. It's financially rebarbative too," I said.

"Aye," he nodded, "it does cost a fortune, right enough." There was a pause. "Which way are you going, Eleanor?" he asked.

I considered the best response to this question. I was heading home for an exciting rendezvous. This highly unusual occasion—an appointment with a visitor to my home—meant that I needed to curtail this tedious, unplanned interaction posthaste. I therefore ought to pick any route but the one Raymond would be taking. But which one? We were about to pass the chiropody clinic and inspiration struck.

"I have an appointment over there," I said, pointing to the chiropodist's opposite. He looked at me. "Bunions," I improvised. I saw him looking at my shoes.

"I'm sorry to hear that, Eleanor," he said. "My mother's the same; she's got terrible trouble with her feet."

We waited at the pedestrian crossing, and he was silent at last. I watched an old man stagger down the opposite side of the road. He was small and square, and had caught my eye because of his tomato-red sweater, which burst out from beneath his standard-issue pensioner grays and muted pastels. Almost in slow motion, the old man began to weave and wobble erratically, swaying wildly from side to side, his bulging carrier bags creating a sort of human pendulum.

"Drunk in the daytime," I said quietly, more to myself than to Raymond. Raymond opened his mouth to reply when the old man finally toppled, fell backward hard and lay still. His shopping exploded around him, and I noticed he'd bought Tunnock's Caramel Logs and a jumbo pack of sausages.

"Shit," said Raymond, stabbing at the button on the crossing control.

"Leave him," I said. "He's drunk. He'll be fine."

Raymond stared at me.

"He's a wee old man, Eleanor. He smacked his head on that pavement pretty hard," he said.

Then I felt bad. Even alcoholics deserve help, I suppose, although they should get drunk at home, like I do, so that they don't cause anyone else any trouble. But then, not everyone is as sensible and considerate as me.

Finally, the green man flashed and Raymond jogged

across the road, having flung his cigarette into the gutter. No need to be a litter lout, I thought, walking at a more measured pace behind him. When I reached the other side, Raymond was already kneeling beside the old man, feeling for a pulse in his neck. He was talking loudly and slowly, silly nonsense like *Hiya, old-timer, how you doing?* and *Can you hear me, mister?* The old man didn't respond. I leaned over him and sniffed deeply.

"He's not actually drunk," I said. "You'd smell it, if he were drunk enough to fall over and pass out." Raymond started loosening the man's clothing.

"Call an ambulance, Eleanor," he said quietly.

"I don't possess a mobile telephone," I explained, "although I'm open to persuasion with regard to their efficacy." Raymond rummaged in his duffle coat pocket and tossed me his.

"Hurry up," he said, "the old guy's out cold."

I started to dial 999, and then a memory punched me full in the face. I couldn't do it again, I realized, I simply couldn't live and listen to a voice saying *Which service do you require, caller?* then to approaching sirens. I touched my scars, and then threw the phone back at Raymond.

"You do it," I said. "I'll sit with him." Raymond swore under his breath and stood up.

"Keep talking, and don't move him," he said. I took off my jerkin and placed it over the man's torso.

"Hello," I said, "I'm Eleanor Oliphant." Keep talking to him, Raymond had said, so I did.

"What a lovely sweater!" I said. "You don't see that color often on a woolen garment. Would you describe it as vermillion? Or carmine, perhaps? I rather like it. I wouldn't attempt such a shade myself, of course. But, against the odds, I think you just about carry it off. White hair and red clothing—like Father Christmas. Was the sweater a gift? It looks like a gift, all soft and expensive. It's far too nice a thing to buy for yourself. But perhaps you *do* buy nice things for yourself—some people do, I know. Some people think nothing of treating themselves to the best of everything. Mind you, looking at the rest of your clothes, and the contents of your shopping bag, it seems highly unlikely that you're that sort of person."

I braced myself and took three deep breaths, then slowly put out my hand and placed it over his. I held it gently for as long as I could bear.

"Mr. Gibbons is calling an ambulance," I said, "so don't worry, you won't be lying here in the middle of the street for long. There's no need to be anxious; medical care is completely free of charge in this country, and the standard is generally considered to be among the best in the world. You're a fortunate man. I mean, you probably wouldn't want to fall and bump your head in, say, the new state of South Sudan, given its current political and economic situation. But here in Glasgow . . . well, you've struck it lucky, if you'll pardon the pun."

Raymond hung up and scuttled over.

"How's he doing, Eleanor?" he said. "Has he come round yet?"

"No," I said, "but I've been talking to him, like you asked."

Raymond took the man's other hand.

"Poor old soul," he said.

I nodded. Surprisingly, I felt an emotion that I recognized as anxiety or concern in relation to this elderly stranger. I sat back, and my buttocks bumped against something large and curvaceous. When I turned around to check, it was a huge plastic bottle of Irn-Bru. I stood up and stretched my spine out, and then started to collect the spilled shopping and put it into the carrier bags. One of them was torn, so I went into my shopper and took out my favorite Bag for Life, the Tesco one with lions on it. I packed all the comestibles and placed the bags by the old man's feet. Raymond smiled at me.

We heard the sirens and Raymond handed me my jerkin. The ambulance pulled up alongside us and two men got out. They were in the middle of a conversation and I was surprised at how proletarian they sounded. I thought they'd be more like doctors.

"All right," said the older one, "what do we have here, then? The old boy's taken a tumble, has he?"

Raymond filled him in and I watched the other one; he was bent over the old man, taking his pulse, shining a little torch into his eyes and tapping him gently to try to elicit a response. He turned to his colleague.

"We need to get moving," he said.

They fetched a stretcher and were fast and surprisingly gentle as they lifted the old man and strapped him on. The younger man wrapped a red fleece blanket around him.

"Same color as his jumper," I said, but they both ignored me.

"You coming with him?" the older man asked. "Only room for one in the back, mind."

Raymond and I looked at one another. I glanced at my watch. The visitor was due *chez Oliphant* in half an hour.

"I'll go, Eleanor," he said. "You don't want to miss your chiropody appointment."

I nodded, and Raymond climbed in beside the old man and the paramedic, who was busy connecting drips and monitors. I picked up the shopping bags and lifted them high enough to pass across to Raymond.

"Look," said the paramedic, sounding slightly tetchy, "this isn't the Asda van. We don't deliver shopping."

Raymond was on the phone, and I heard him talking, apparently to his mother, telling her that he'd be late, before he quickly hung up.

"Eleanor," he said, "why don't you give me a call in a bit, and maybe you could bring his stuff over to him?" I considered this, nodded, watched as he rummaged in his coat pocket and took out a Biro. He grabbed my hand. I gasped and stepped to the side, shocked, placing my hand firmly behind my back.

"I need to give you my phone number," he said patiently.

I took out my little notebook from my shopper, which he returned with a page covered in blue scribble, his name barely legible there, and a series of numbers scrawled below it in an awkward, childish hand.

"Give it an hour or so," he said. "Your bunions will be dealt with by then, won't they?"

# 6

I had barely had time to get home and divest myself of my outer garments when the doorbell rang, ten minutes earlier than I'd been expecting. Probably trying to catch me out. When I opened it, slowly, keeping the chain on, it wasn't the person I'd been expecting. Whoever it was, she wasn't smiling.

"Eleanor Oliphant? June Mullen, Social Work," she said, stepping forward, her progress blocked by the door.

"I was expecting Heather," I said, peering around.

"Heather's off sick, I'm afraid; we've no idea when she'll be back. I've taken over her cases."

I asked to see some form of official identification— I mean, you can't be too careful. She gave a tiny sigh, and began to look in her bag. She was tall, carefully dressed in a black trouser suit and white shirt. As she bent her head, I noticed the white stripe of scalp at the parting in her shiny, dark bob. Eventually, she looked up and thrust out a security pass, with a huge council logo and a tiny photo. I scrutinized it carefully, looked from the photograph to her face and back again several times. It wasn't a flattering shot, but I didn't hold that against her. I'm not particularly photogenic myself. In real life, she was about my age, with smooth, unlined skin and a slash of red lipstick.

"You don't look like a social worker," I said. She stared at me but said nothing. Not again! In every walk of life, I encounter people with underdeveloped social skills with alarming frequency. Why is it that client-facing jobs hold such allure for misanthropes? It's a conundrum. I made a mental note to return to the topic later, unhooked the chain and invited her in. I showed her into the lounge, listening to her high heels clicking across the floor. She asked if she could have a quick tour; I'd been expecting that, of course. Heather used to do that too; I assume that it's part of the job, checking to make sure that I'm not storing my own urine in demijohns or kidnapping magpies and sewing them into pillowcases. She complimented me unenthusiastically on the interiors as we went into the kitchen.

I tried to see my home through the eyes of a visitor. I'm aware that I am very fortunate to live here, social housing in this area being virtually nonexistent these days. I couldn't possibly afford to live in this postcode otherwise, certainly not on the pittance that Bob pays me. Social Services arranged for me to move here after I had to leave my last foster placement, the summer immediately before I started university. I'd just turned seventeen. Back then, a vulnerable young person who'd grown up in care would be allocated a council flat close to her place of study without it being too much of a problem. Imagine that.

It took me a while to get around to decorating, I remember, and I finally painted the place in the summer after I graduated. I bought emulsion and brushes after cashing a check I received in the post from the University Registry, along with my degree parchment; it turned out that I'd won a small prize, set up in the name of some long-dead classicist, for the best finals performance in a paper on Virgil's *Georgics*. I graduated *in absentia* of course; it seemed pointless to process onto the stage with no one there to applaud me. The flat hadn't been touched since then.

I suppose, trying to be objective, that it was looking rather tired. Mummy always said that an obsession with home interiors was tediously bourgeois and, worse still, that any kind of "do-it-yourself" activities were very much the preserve of the hoi polloi. It's quite frightening to think about the ideas that I may have absorbed from Mummy.

The furniture was provided by a charity that helps vulnerable young people and ex-offenders when they move into a new home: donated, mismatched things for which I was most grateful at the time, and continue to be. It was all perfectly functional, so I'd never seen the need to replace any of it. I didn't clean the place very often, I supposed, which might contribute to what I could see might be perceived as a general air of neglect. I didn't see the point; I was the only person who ever ate here, washed here, went to sleep and woke up here.

This June Mullen was the first visitor I'd had since November last year. They come around every six months or so, the Social Work visits. She's my first visitor this calendar year. The meter reader hasn't been yet, although I must say I prefer it when they leave a card and I can phone in my reading. I do love call centers; it's always so interesting to hear all the different accents and try to find out a bit about the person you're talking to. The best part is when they ask, at the end, *Is there anything else I can help you with today, Eleanor?* and I can then reply, *No, no thank you, you've completely and comprehensively resolved my problems.* It's always nice to hear my first name spoken aloud by a human voice too.

Apart from Social Work and the utility companies, sometimes a representative from one church or another will call round to ask if I've welcomed Jesus into my life. They don't tend to enjoy debating the concept of proselytizing, I've found, which is disappointing. Last year, a man came to deliver a Betterware catalog, which turned out to be a most enjoyable read. I still regret not purchasing the spidercatcher, which really was a very ingenious device.

June Mullen declined my offer of a cup of tea as we returned to the living room, and after sitting down on the sofa, she pulled my file from her briefcase. It was several inches thick, held together precariously by a rubber band. Some unknown hand had written OLIPHANT, ELEANOR, in marker pen on the top right-hand corner and dated it July 1987, the year of my birth. The buff folder, tattered and stained, looked like a historical artifact.

"Heather's handwriting is atrocious," she muttered, running a manicured fingernail down the page at the top of the pile of papers. She spoke quietly, to herself rather than to me. "Biannual visits . . . continuity of community integration . . . early identification of any additional support needs . . ."

She continued to read, and then I saw her face change and she glanced at me, her expression a mixture of horror, alarm and pity. She must have got to the section about Mummy. I stared her out. She took a deep breath, looked down at the papers and then exhaled slowly as she looked up at me again.

"I had no idea," she said, her voice echoing her expression. "Do you . . . you must miss her terribly?"

"Mummy?" I said. "Hardly."

"No, I meant . . ." she trailed off, looking awkward, sad, embarrassed. Ah, I knew them well—these were the holy trinity of Oliphant expressions. I shrugged, having no idea whatsoever what she was talking about.

Silence sat between us, shivering with misery. After what felt like days had passed, June Mullen closed the file on her lap and gave me an overly bright smile.

"So, Eleanor, how have you been getting on, generally, since Heather's last visit, I mean?"

"Well, I haven't become aware of any additional support needs, and I'm fully integrated into the community, June," I said.

She smiled weakly. "Work going OK? I see you're

a . . ." she consulted the file again ". . . you work in an office?"

"Work is fine," I said. "Everything's fine."

"What about home?" she said, looking round the room, her eyes lingering on my big green pouf, which is shaped like a giant frog and was part of the charity furniture donation I'd received when I first moved in. I'd grown very fond of his bulbous eyes and giant pink tongue over the years. One night, a vodka night, I'd drawn a big housefly, *Musca domestica*, on his tongue with a pilfered Sharpie. I'm not artistically gifted in any way, but it was, in my humble opinion, a fair rendering of the subject matter. I felt that this act had helped me to take ownership of the donated item, and created something new from something secondhand. Also, he had looked hungry. June Mullen seemed unable to take her eyes off it.

"Everything's fine here, June," I reiterated. "Bills all paid, cordial relations with the neighbors. I'm perfectly comfortable."

She flicked through the file again, and then inhaled. I knew what she was about to say, recognizing full well the change in tone—fear, hesitancy—that always preceded the subject matter.

"You're still of the view that you don't want to know anything else about the incident, or about your mother, I understand?" No smiling this time.

"That's right," I said. "There's no need—I speak to her once a week, on a Wednesday evening, regular as clockwork."

"Really? After all this time, that's still happening? Interesting . . . Are you keen to . . . maintain this contact?"

"Why wouldn't I be?" I said, incredulous. Where on earth does the Social Work Department find these people?

She deliberately allowed the silence to linger, and, although I recognized the technique, I could not stop myself from filling it, eventually.

"I think Mummy would like it if I tried to find out more about . . . the incident . . . but I've no intention of doing so."

"No," she said, nodding. "Well, how much you want to know about what happened is entirely up to you, isn't it? The courts were very clear, back then, that anything like that was to be entirely at your discretion?"

"That's correct," I said, "that's exactly what they said."

She looked closely at me, as so many people had done before, scrutinizing my face for any traces of Mummy, enjoying some strange thrill at being *this close* to a blood relative of the woman the newspapers still occasionally referred to, all these years later, as *the pretty face of evil*. I watched her eyes run over my scars. Her mouth hung slightly open, and it became apparent that the suit and the bob were an inadequate disguise for this particular slack-jawed yokel.

"I could probably dig out a photograph, if you'd like one," I said.

She blinked twice and blushed, then busied herself by grappling with the bulging file, trying to sort all the loose papers into a tidy pile. I noticed a single sheet flutter down and land under the coffee table. She hadn't seen it make its escape, and I pondered whether or not to tell her. It was about me, after all, so wasn't it technically mine? I'd return it at the next visit, of course— I'm not a thief. I imagined Mummy's voice, whispering, telling me I was quite right, that social workers were busybodies, do-gooders, nosy parkers. June Mullen snapped the elastic band around the file, and the moment to mention the sheet of paper had passed.

"I . . . is there anything else you'd like to discuss with me today?" she asked.

"No thank you," I said, smiling as broadly as I could. She looked rather disconcerted, perhaps even slightly frightened. I was disappointed. I'd been aiming for pleasant and friendly.

"Well then, that seems to be that for the time being, Eleanor; I'll leave you in peace," she said. She continued talking as she packed away the file in her briefcase, adopting a breezy, casual tone. "Any plans for the weekend?"

"I'm visiting someone in hospital," I said.

"Oh, that's nice. Visits always cheer a patient up, don't they?"

"Do they?" I said. "I wouldn't know. I've never visited anyone in hospital before."

"But you've spent a lot of time in hospital yourself, of course," she said.

I stared at her. The imbalance in the extent of our knowledge of each other was manifestly unfair. Social workers should present their new clients with a fact sheet about themselves to try to redress this, I think. After all, she'd had unrestricted access to that big brown folder, the bumper book of Eleanor, two decades' worth of information about the intimate minutiae of my life. All I knew about her was her name and her employer.

"If you know about that, then you'll be aware that the circumstances were such that the police and my legal representatives were the only visitors permitted," I said.

She gawped at me. I was reminded of those clowns' heads in fairgrounds, the ones where you try to throw a Ping-Pong ball into their gaping mouths in order to win a goldfish. I opened the door for her, watching her eyes swivel repeatedly toward the giant customized frog.

"I'll see you in six months then, Eleanor," she said reluctantly. "Best of luck."

I closed the door with excessive gentleness behind her.

≈

She hadn't remarked upon Polly, I thought, which was odd. Ridiculously, I felt almost slighted on Polly's behalf. She'd been sitting in the corner throughout our meeting, and was clearly the most eye-catching thing in the room. My beautiful Polly, prosaically described as a parrot plant, sometimes referred to as a Congo cockatoo plant, but always known to me, in her full Latinate glory, as *Impatiens niamniamensis*. I say it out loud, often: *niamniamensis*. It's like kissing, the "m's forcing your lips together, rolling over the consonants, your tongue poking into n's and over the s's." Polly's ancestors came all the way from Africa, originally. Well, we all did. She's the only constant from my childhood, the only living thing that survived. She was a birthday present, but I can't remember who gave her to me, which is strange. I was not, after all, a girl who was overwhelmed with gifts.

She came with me from my childhood bedroom, survived the foster placements and children's homes and, like me, she's still here. I've looked after her, tended to her, picked her up and repotted her when she was dropped or thrown. She likes light, and she's thirsty. Apart from that, she requires minimal care and attention, and largely looks after herself. I talk to her sometimes, I'm not ashamed to admit it. When the silence and the aloneness press down and around me, crushing me, carving through me like ice, I *need* to speak aloud sometimes, if only for proof of life.

A philosophical question: if a tree falls in a forest and no one is around to hear it, does it make a sound? And if a woman who's wholly alone occasionally talks to a potted plant, is she certifiable? I'm confident that it is perfectly normal to talk to oneself occasionally. It's not as though I'm expecting a reply. I'm fully aware that Polly is a houseplant.

I watered her, then got on with some other household chores, thinking ahead to the moment when I could open my laptop and check whether a certain handsome singer had posted any new information. Facebook, Twitter, Instagram. Windows into a world of marvels. While I was loading the washing machine, my telephone rang. A visitor *and* a phone call! A red-letter day indeed. It was Raymond.

"I rang Bob's mobile and explained the situation to him, and he dug out your number from the personnel files for me," he said.

I mean, really. Was all of me on show in buff folders, splayed wide for anyone to flick open and do with as they wished?

"What a gross abuse of my privacy, not to mention an offense against the Data Protection Act," I said. "I'll be speaking to Bob about that next week."

There was silence on the other end of the line.

"Well?" I said.

"Oh, right. Yeah. Sorry. It's just, you said you would call and you didn't, and, well, I'm at the hospital now. I wondered, you know . . . if you wanted to bring the old guy's stuff in? We're at the Western Infirmary. Oh, and his name's Sami-Tom."

"What?" I said. "No, that can't be right, Raymond. He's a small, fat, elderly man from Glasgow. There is absolutely no possibility of him being christened *Sami-Tom*." I was beginning to develop some serious concerns about Raymond's mental capacities.

"No, no, Eleanor—it's Sammy as in . . . short for Samuel. Thom as in T-h-o-m."

"Oh," I said. There was another long pause.

"So . . . like I said, Sammy's in the Western. Visiting starts at seven, if you want to come in?"

"I said I would, and I'm a woman of my word, Raymond. It's a bit late now; tomorrow, early evening, would suit me best, if that's acceptable to you?"

"Sure," he said. Another pause. "Do you want to know how he's doing?"

"Yes, naturally," I said. The man was an extremely poor conversationalist, and was making this whole exchange terribly hard work.

"It's not good. He's stable, but it's serious. Just to prepare you. He hasn't regained consciousness yet."

"In that case, I can't imagine he'll have much use for his Irn-Bru and lorne sausage tomorrow, will he?" I asked. I heard Raymond take a breath.

"Look, Eleanor, it's entirely up to you whether you visit or not. He's in no rush for his stuff, and I guess you should throw out anything that won't keep. Like you say, the poor old soul isn't going to be making a fry-up anytime soon."

"Well, quite. In fact, I imagine that fry-ups are exactly what got him into this situation in the first place," I said.

"I've got to go now, Eleanor," he said, and put the phone down rather abruptly. How rude!

I was on the horns of a dilemma; there seemed little point in traveling to hospital to see a comatose stranger and drop off some fizzy pop at his bedside. On the other hand, it would be interesting to experience being a hospital visitor, and there was always an outside chance that he might wake up when I was there. He had rather seemed to enjoy my monologue while we were waiting for the ambulance; well, insofar as I could tell, given that he was unconscious.

As I was pondering, I picked up the fallen page from the file and turned it over. It was slightly yellowed around the edges, and smelled institutional: metallic, like filing cabinets, and grubby, touched by the unwashed skin of multiple, anonymous hands. Banknotes have a similar odor, I've noticed.

## DEPARTMENT OF SOCIAL WORK

NOTE OF CASE MEETING
March 15, 1999, 10 a.m.
Case Meeting: OLIPHANT, ELEANOR
(07/12/1987)

Present: Robert Brocklehurst (Deputy Head, Children and Families, Social Work Department); Rebecca Scatcherd (Senior Case Worker, Social Work Department); Mr. and Mrs. Reed (foster carers).

The meeting took place at the home of Mr. and Mrs. Reed, whose children, including Eleanor Oliphant, were at school at the time. Mr. and Mrs. Reed had requested the meeting, which was outside the regular scheduled sessions, in order to discuss their growing concerns about Eleanor.

Mrs. Reed reported that Eleanor's behavior had deteriorated since it was last raised at a case meeting some four months earlier. Mr. Brocklehurst requested examples, and Mr. and Mrs. Reed cited the following:

- Eleanor's relationship with their other children had almost completely broken down, particularly with John (14), the eldest;
- Eleanor was insolent and rude to Mrs. Reed on a daily basis. When Mrs. Reed attempted to discipline her, for example, by sending her upstairs to the spare room to reflect on her behavior, she had become hysterical and, on one occasion, physically violent;
- Eleanor had, on occasion, pretended to faint in an attempt to avoid being disciplined, or else in response to being disciplined;
- Eleanor was terrified of the dark and kept the family awake with hysterical crying.

She had been provided with a night-light
and reacted with violent sobbing and
tremors to any suggestion that she should
give it up, being too old for it now;

- Eleanor often refused to eat the food
which was provided for her; mealtimes
had become a source of conflict at the
family table;

- Eleanor refused point-blank to assist with
simple household chores, such as lighting
the fire or clearing out the ashes.

Mr. and Mrs. Reed reported that they were
extremely concerned about the effects of
Eleanor's behavior on their other three children (John, 14, Eliza, 9 and Georgie, 7) and,
in light of these concerns and also those
raised previously during scheduled case meetings, they wished to discuss the best way forward for Eleanor.

Mr. and Mrs. Reed again requested more
information about Eleanor's past history,
and Mr. Brocklehurst explained that this
would not be possible, and indeed was not
permitted.

Miss Scatcherd had sought a school report
from Eleanor's head teacher in advance of the
meeting, and it was noted that Eleanor was
performing well, achieving excellent grades
in all subjects. The head teacher commented

that Eleanor was an exceptionally bright and articulate child, with an impressive vocabulary. Her class teachers had reported that she was quiet and well behaved during lessons, but did not participate in discussions, although she was an active listener. Several members of the staff had noticed that Eleanor was very withdrawn and isolated during break times, and did not appear to socialize with her peers.

After lengthy discussion, and in light of the concerns raised and reemphasized by Mr. and Mrs. Reed about the impact of Eleanor's behavior on their other children, it was agreed that the most appropriate course of action would be to remove Eleanor from the family home.

Mr. and Mrs. Reed were content with this outcome, and Mr. Brocklehurst informed them that the department would be in touch in due course regarding next steps.

File note: on November 12, 1999 a Children's Panel Review of Compulsory Supervision Order concerning Eleanor Oliphant took place, at which Mr. Brocklehurst and Miss Scatcherd were present (minutes attached).

The Children's Panel concluded that, on account of Eleanor's challenging behavior in this and previous placements, foster care in

a family environment was not appropriate
at the current time. It was therefore agreed
that Eleanor should be placed in a residential
care home for the time being, and that the
decision of the panel would be reviewed in
twelve months.

(Action: R. Scatcherd to investigate avail-
ability of places in local facilities and notify
Mr. and Mrs. Reed of expected date of
removal.)

*R. Scatcherd, 11/12/99*

Liars. Liars, liars, liars.

# 7

The bus was quiet and I had a seat to myself, the old man's shopping sitting in two Bags for Life beside me. I'd thrown out the sausages and the orange cheese, but I kept the milk for myself, reasoning that it wasn't stealing as he wouldn't be able to use it anyway. I had some qualms about throwing out the other perishable items. I do understand that some people think waste is wrong, and, after careful reflection, I tend to agree. But I'd been brought up to think very differently; Mummy always said that only peasants and grubby little worker ants worried about such trivial things.

Mummy said that we were empresses, sultanas and maharanis in our own home, and that it was our duty to live a life of sybaritic pleasure and indulgence. Every meal should be an epicurean feast for the senses, she said, and one should go hungry rather than sully one's palate with anything less than exquisite morsels. She told me how she'd eaten chili-fried tofu in the night markets of Kowloon, and that the best sushi outside of Japan could be found in São Paulo. The most delicious meal of her life, she said, had been chargrilled octopus, which she'd eaten at sunset in an unassuming harbor front taverna one late summer evening on Naxos. She'd watched a fisherman land it that morning, and then sipped ouzo all afternoon while the kitchen staff battered it again and again against the harbor wall to tenderize its pale, suckered flesh. I must ask her what the food is like where she is now. I suspect that Lapsang souchong and *langues de chat* biscuits are in short supply.

I remember being invited to a classmate's house after school. Just me. The occasion was "tea." This was confusing in itself; I had, not unreasonably, been expecting afternoon tea, whereas her mother had prepared a sort of early kitchen supper for us. I can still picture it—orange and beige—three luminous fish fingers, a puddle of baked beans and a pale pile of oven chips. I had never seen, let alone tried any of these items, and had to ask what they were. Danielle Mearns told everyone in the class the next day and they all laughed and called me Beanz Meanz Weird (shortened to Beanzy, which stuck for a while). No matter, school was a short-lived experience for me. There was an incident with an over-inquisitive teacher who suggested a trip to the school nurse, after which Mummy decided that said teacher was a *barely literate, monolingual dullard whose only worthwhile qualification was a certificate in first aid*. I was homeschooled after that.

At Danielle's house, her mother gave us each a Munch Bunch yogurt for pudding, and I snuck the empty pot into my school bag so that I could study it afterward. Apparently, it was merchandise pertaining to a children's television program about animated pieces of fruit. And they said I was weird! It was a source of disgust to the other children at school that I couldn't talk about TV programs. We didn't have a television; Mummy called it the cathode carcinogen, cancer for the intellect, and so we would read or listen to records, sometimes playing backgammon or mah-jongg if she was in a good mood.

Taken aback by my lack of familiarity with frozen convenience food, Danielle Mearns' mother asked me what it was that I usually had for tea on a Wednesday night.

"There's no routine," I said.

"But what kind of things do you eat, generally?" she asked, genuinely puzzled.

I listed some of them. Asparagus velouté with a poached duck egg and hazelnut oil. Bouillabaisse with homemade rouille. Honey-glazed *poussin* with celeriac fondants. Fresh truffles when in season, shaved over cèpes and buttered linguine. She stared at me.

"That all sounds quite . . . fancy," she said.

"Oh no, sometimes it's just something really simple," I said, "like sourdough toast with Manchego cheese and quince paste."

"Right," she said, exchanging a glance with little Danielle, who was gawping at me, revealing a mouthful of partially masticated beans. Neither spoke, and Mrs. Mearns placed a glass bottle of thick red liquid on the table, which Danielle then proceeded to shake violently and slather all over the orange and beige food.

Of course, after I was taken into care, I rapidly became acquainted with a new culinary family; Aunt Bessie, Captain Birdseye and Uncle Ben all featured regularly, and now I can distinguish HP Sauce from Daddies by smell alone, like a sauce sommelier. It was one of the innumerable ways in which my old life and my new life differed. Before and after the fire. One day I was breakfasting on watermelon, feta and pomegranate seeds, the next I was eating toasted Mother's Pride smeared with margarine. That's the story Mummy told me, at any rate.

~

The bus stopped right outside the hospital. There was a shop on the ground floor selling an eclectic assortment of goods. I was aware that it was very much the done thing to take a gift when visiting a patient, but what to purchase? I didn't know Sammy from Adam. Comestibles seemed pointless, since the purpose of my visit was to bring him his own food, items that he'd only very recently selected for himself. Given that he was in a coma, reading material seemed somewhat irrelevant. There wasn't much else that might be suitable, however. The shop carried a small range of toiletries, but it seemed inappropriate for me, a stranger of the opposite sex, to present him with items pertaining to his bodily functions and, anyway, a tube of toothpaste or a packet of disposable razors did not strike me as very charming gifts.

I tried to remember the nicest gift I'd ever received. Apart from Polly the plant, I couldn't think of anything. Alarmingly, Declan came into my mind. My first and only boyfriend, I'd very nearly succeeded in erasing him from my memory altogether, so it was rather distressing to be reminded of him. I recalled an incident when, on seeing the single birthday card I'd received one year (from a journalist who'd somehow managed to track me down, with a note inside reminding me that she'd pay a substantial sum for an interview, anytime, anywhere), he claimed that I deliberately hadn't told him the date of my birthday. For my twenty-first birthday gift, he therefore punched me in the kidneys, kicked me as I lay on the floor until I passed out and then gave me a black eye when I came round, for "withholding information." The only other birthday I could recall was my eleventh. I received a sterling silver bracelet from the foster family I was living with at the time, with a teddy bear charm attached. I was very grateful to receive a present, but I didn't ever wear it. I'm not really a teddy bear sort of person.

I wondered what sort of gift the handsome singer might give me, for an anniversary, say, or for Christmas. No, wait—for Valentine's Day, the most special, romantic day of the year. He'd write a song for me, something beautiful, and then play it for me on his guitar while I sipped perfectly chilled champagne. No, not on his guitar, that was too obvious. He'd surprise me by learning the . . . bassoon. Yes, he'd play the melody on the bassoon for me.

Back to more prosaic matters. For want of anything more suitable, I bought some newspapers and magazines for Sammy, thinking that I could at least read them aloud to him. They stocked a passable selection. From his appearance and the contents of his shopping bag, I divined that Sammy was more *Daily Star* than *Daily Telegraph*. I bought a few tabloids, and decided to take him a magazine too. That was more difficult. There were so many. *Condé Nast Traveler, Yachts* and *Yachting, Now!*—how would I know which one to choose? I had no idea what interested him. I thought carefully and rationally in order to deduce the answer. The only thing I knew for sure about him was that he was an adult male; anything else would be pure speculation. I went with the law of averages, stood on tiptoe and reached up for a copy of *Playboy*. Job done.

It was too hot inside the hospital and the floors squeaked. There was a hand-gel dispenser outside the ward, and a big yellow sign above it read *Do Not Drink*. Did people actually drink sanitizing hand gel? I supposed they must—hence the sign. Part of me, a very small sliver, briefly considered dipping my head to taste a drop, purely because I'd been ordered not to. No, Eleanor, I told myself. Curb your rebellious tendencies. Stick to tea, coffee and vodka.

I was apprehensive about using it on my hands, for fear that it might inflame my eczema, but I did so nonetheless. Good hygiene is so important—heaven forfend that I would end up becoming a vector of infection. The ward was large, with two long rows of beds, one down each wall. All the inhabitants were interchangeable: hairless, toothless old men who were either dozing or staring blankly ahead, chins slumped forward. I spotted Sammy, right at the end on the left-hand side, but only because he was fat. The rest of them were bones draped with pleated gray skin. I sat down on the vinyl wipe-clean chair next to his bed. There was no sign of Raymond.

Sammy's eyes were closed but he obviously wasn't comatose. He would be on a special ward if that were the case, hooked up to machinery, wouldn't he? I wondered why Raymond had lied about it. I could tell from the regular way that Sammy's chest rose and fell that he was sleeping. I decided not to read to him, not wishing to wake him, and so I put the reading material on top of the cabinet next to his bed. I opened the compartment at the front, thinking it best to deposit the Bags for Life inside. The cabinet was empty apart from a wallet and a set of keys. I wondered if I should look in Sammy's wallet to see if it contained any clues about him, and I was about to reach forward for it when I heard someone clear their throat behind me, a phlegm-filled sound that indicated a smoker.

"Eleanor. You came," said Raymond, pulling up a chair on the opposite side of the bed. I stared at him.

"Why did you lie, Raymond? Sammy's not in a coma. He's merely asleep. That's not the same thing at all."

Raymond laughed.

"Ah, but it's great news, Eleanor. He woke up a couple of hours ago. Apparently, he's got a severe concussion and a broken hip. They reset it yesterday—he's very tired from the anesthetic, but they say he's going to be fine." I nodded, and stood up abruptly. "We should leave him in peace then," I said.

I was keen to be out of the ward, to be frank. It was too hot, and too familiar—the waffle blankets, the chemical and human smells, the hard surfaces of the metal bed frame and the plastic chairs. My hands were stinging slightly from the gel, which had seeped into the cracks in my skin. We walked together to the lift, and rode down in silence. The doors opened at the ground floor and I felt my legs speed up of their own accord toward the front door.

It was one of those beautiful midsummer evenings—eight o'clock and still full of heat and soft light. It wouldn't get dark till almost eleven. Raymond took off his jacket, revealing another ridiculous T-shirt. This one was yellow and had two white cartoon cockerels on the front. *Los Pollos Hermanos*, it said. Nonsensical. He looked at his watch.

"I'm going to pick up a carryout and head round to my mate Andy's. A few of us usually hang out there on Saturday nights, fire up the PlayStation, have a smoke and a few beers."

"Sounds utterly delightful," I said.

"What about you?" he asked.

I was going home, of course, to watch a television program or read a book. What else would I be doing?

"I shall return to my flat," I said. "I think there might be a documentary about komodo dragons on BBC4 later this evening."

He looked at his watch again, and then up at the boundless blue sky. There was a moment of silence and then a blackbird began showing off nearby, his song so spectacular that it bordered on vulgar. We both listened, and when I smiled at Raymond, he smiled back.

"Look, it's far too nice a night to be sitting inside on your own. Fancy grabbing a quick pint somewhere? I'll need to head off in an hour or so before the offy shuts, but . . ."

This required careful consideration. I had not been in a public house for many years, and Raymond could hardly be described as engaging company. I quickly concluded, however, that it would be useful for two reasons. Firstly, it would be good practice, as, if things went well, Johnnie Lomond would probably want to take me to a public house during one of our dates, and so I really ought to familiarize myself in advance with the general environs and required behaviors in such establishments. Secondly, Raymond was an IT expert—allegedly—and I needed some advice. Such advice might be expensive to obtain via official channels, but I could ask him tonight, for free. All things considered, it seemed expeditious to accede to Raymond's request. He was staring into the middle distance, and I noticed that he had lit a cigarette and smoked almost half of it while I had been pondering.

"Yes, Raymond. I will go to the pub with you for one drink," I said, nodding.

"Magic," he said.

~~

We ended up in a bar five minutes from the hospital, on a busy road. One of the tables outside was unoccupied. The metal surface was covered in circular stains and its legs looked unstable, but Raymond seemed delighted.

"Seats outside!" he said, happily throwing himself down and hanging his jacket over the back of his chair. "Right then, I'll go to the bar," he said. "What are you after, Eleanor?"

I felt a fluttering of concern in my stomach. Firstly, sitting out here, I wouldn't get to see the inside of the public house and observe what went on there. Secondly, I didn't know what to order. What did normal people drink in public houses? I decided to take control of the situation.

"Raymond, I will go to the bar. I insist. What would you like me to order for you?" He tried to argue but I stood my ground and eventually he agreed, although he seemed annoyed. I simply could not fathom why he was making such a fuss about it.

"Right, well, I suppose I'll have a pint of Guinness then. But I wish you'd let me get it, Eleanor."

I put both hands on the table and leaned forward so that my face was very close to his.

"Raymond, I will purchase the drinks. It's important to me, for reasons that I don't wish to articulate to you."

He shrugged, then nodded, and I walked off toward the door.

~

It seemed very dark inside after the sunlight, and noisy too—there was music of an unfamiliar genre pulsing loudly from large speakers. The place wasn't busy, and I was the only customer at the bar. A young man and a young woman were serving; that is to say, they were deep in conversation with each other, and every so often she would giggle like a simpleton and flick her dyed yellow hair, or he would punch her arm playfully and laugh in an overly loud, false manner. Human mating rituals are unbelievably tedious to observe. At least in the animal kingdom you are occasionally treated to a flash of bright feathers or a display of spectacular violence. Hair flicking and play fights don't quite cut the mustard.

I was bored and I knocked hard, three times, on the wooden bar, as though it were a front door. They both looked up. I asked for a pint of Guinness, which the boy began to pour from a tap. "Anything else?" he said. I was still stumped. I reasoned that part of his job would be to help customers in such situations.

"What would you recommend?" I asked him. He looked up from watching the black liquid trickle into the glass.

"Eh?"

"I said, what would you recommend for me? I don't drink in public houses, as a rule."

He looked to his left and right, as if expecting someone else to be standing there. There was a long pause.

"Erm," he said. "Well . . . Magners is very popular. With ice? Nice summer drink."

"Right," I said, "thank you. In that case, I'll have a Magners drink, please, on your recommendation." He opened a brown bottle and put it on the bar. He put some ice in a tall glass and placed it next to the bottle.

"What's that?" I said.

"The Magners."

"And what's the empty glass for?"

"It's for the Magners," he said.

"Am *I* expected to pour the drink from the bottle into the glass?" I said, puzzled. "Isn't it *your* job to do that?" He stared at me and then slowly poured the brown liquid over the ice and put it down quite hard; indeed, he practically slammed the bottle onto the counter.

"Eight pound seventy," he said, in a most unfriendly manner. I handed over a five-pound note and four pound coins, then took my change and carefully put it in my purse.

"Would you by any chance have a tray?" I asked. He tossed down a filthy, sticky tray and watched as I placed the drinks on it before turning his back on me. There is such a paucity of good manners on display in the so-called service sector!

≈

Raymond thanked me for the drink and took a big gulp. The Magners was quite pleasant, and I revised my opinion of the young barman. Yes, his customer service skills were poor, but he did at least know how to make appropriate beverage recommendations. Unprompted, Raymond started to tell me about his mother, how he was going to visit her tomorrow, something he did every Sunday. She was a widow and not terribly well. She had a lot of cats, and he helped her care for them. On and on and on he droned. I interrupted him.

"Raymond," I said. "Can I ask you something?"

He sipped his pint. "Sure."

"If I were to purchase a 'smart phone,' which type would you advise? I have been looking into the relative merits of iPhones as compared with Android devices, and I'd appreciate an insider's perspective on the cost-benefit ratio, as it were."

He looked somewhat surprised at my question, which was odd, given that he worked in IT and therefore must be asked technological questions quite frequently.

"Right, well . . ." He shook his head in a slightly canine way, as though he were clearing thoughts from it ". . . that depends on a lot of factors." He expounded on these factors at some length—without reaching any kind of useful conclusion—and then looked at his watch.

"Shit! I better run—I need to pick up some beers before I head over to Andy's, and it's nearly ten." He drained his pint, stood up and put on his jacket, even though it wasn't in the least bit cold.

"You going to be OK getting home, Eleanor?" he said.

"Oh yes," I said, "I'll walk—it's such a beautiful evening, and it's still light."

"Right then, I'll see you on Monday," he said. "Enjoy the rest of your weekend." He turned to leave.

"Raymond, wait!" I said. He turned back toward me, smiling.

"What is it, Eleanor?"

"The Guinness, Raymond. It was three pounds fifty." He stared at me. "It's OK," I said, "there's no rush. You can give it to me on Monday, if that's easier."

He counted out four pound coins and put them on the table. "Keep the change," he said, and walked off. Extravagant! I put the money in my purse, and finished my Magners. Emboldened by the apples, I decided to take a detour on the way home. Yes. Why not? It was time for a spot of reconnaissance.

# 8

There is no such thing as hell, of course, but if there was, then the sound track to the screaming, the pitch-fork action and the infernal wailing of damned souls would be a looped medley of "show tunes" drawn from the annals of musical theater. The complete oeuvre of Lloyd Webber and Rice would be performed, without breaks, on a stage inside the fiery pit, and an audience of sinners would be forced to watch—and listen—for eternity. The very worst among them, the child molesters and the murderous dictators, would have to perform them.

Save for the exquisite oeuvre of a certain Mr. Lomond, I have yet to find a genre of music I enjoy; it's basically audible physics, waves and energized particles, and, like most sane people, I have no interest in physics. It therefore struck me as bizarre that I was humming a tune from *Oliver!* I mentally added the exclamation mark, which, for the first time ever, was appropriate. *Who will buy this wonderful evening?* Who indeed?

One of the foster carers kept a video library of musicals that we worked our way through *en famille* at weekends, and so, although I fervently wish that I wasn't, I'm very familiar with the work of Lionel Bart, Rodgers and Hammerstein et al. Knowing I was *here on the street where he lived* was giving me a funny feeling, fluttery and edgy, verging on euphoric. I could almost understand why that frock-coated buffoon from *My Fair Lady* had felt the need to bellow about it outside Audrey Hepburn's window.

Finding out where the musician lived had been easy. He had posted a picture of a lovely sunset on Twitter:

> @johnnieLrocks
> The view from my window:
> how lucky am I?
> #summerinthecity #blessed

It showed rooftops, trees and sky, but there was also a pub in the corner of the photograph, right at the end of the street, its name clearly visible. I found it in seconds, thanks to Google.

The street, like most in this part of the city, was made up of tenements. They all had a secure main front door with named buzzers on the outside wall, one for each flat inside the building. This was the right street. Which side should I start with? Even numbers, I decided. He was an even sort of man, not an odd one. I had a puzzle to solve. I hummed as I worked, and couldn't remember the last time I'd felt like this—light, sparkly, quick. I suspected that it might be what happiness felt like.

It was fascinating to see all the different names on the buzzers, and the manner in which they were displayed. Some were scribbled in Biro on a sticker and placed carelessly over the button. Others had typed their names in bold uppercase, printed it out and affixed it with three layers of Sellotape. A few had left their buzzer blank, or failed to replace their name when the elements had made the ink run, rendering it illegible. I really hoped he wasn't one of those, but I kept a list of their locations in my notebook, just in case. If I had eliminated all the legible names without coming across his, I'd have to go back and work my way through the list of blank ones.

Ah, but how could I have doubted him? Halfway down the street, the most even of even numbers, there he was: *Mr. J. Lomond Esq.* I stood before the buzzer, examining the letters. They were written neatly but artistically in classic black ink on thick white paper. It was so him.

It seemed unlikely that he, a popular, handsome man with the world at his feet, would be at home on a Saturday night, so, just to see how it felt, I gently touched his buzzer with the tip of my index finger. There was a crackle, and then a man's voice spoke. I was somewhat taken aback, to say the least.

"Hello?" he said again.

A deep voice, well spoken, measured. Honey and smoke, velvet and silver. I quickly scanned the list and selected another resident's name at random.

"Pizza delivery for . . . McFadden?" I said. I heard him sigh.

"They're on the top floor," he said, and hung up. The door buzzed and clicked open. Without stopping to think too much about it, I went inside.

The musician was upstairs on the first floor, in the flat on the right-hand side. There was a discreet brass nameplate above the bell. I stood and listened. I could hear nothing from inside, just the hum of the stair light and faint sounds from the street below. On the floor above, a television was blaring. I took out my notebook and tore off a blank page. I placed it over the nameplate and took out my pencil, then began a brass rubbing. Within moments, I had a stunning facsimile of the plate, which I placed carefully into my bag, between the pages of the notebook. The exterior doors were open and his interior door, a typical Victorian design of mahogany and opaque etched glass, was tantalizingly close.

I stood as near as I dared. I could hear nothing from within, and there was no visible movement. I could almost make out the shape of a bookcase, and a painting. A cultured man. How much we had in common!

I stiffened. There: soft fingers on vibrating steel, and a chord shimmered into the air, nebulous and milky, like light from an old, old star. A voice: warm and low and gentle, a voice to cast spells, charm snakes, shape the course of dreams. I could do nothing but turn toward it and lean closer. I pressed myself against the glass. He was writing a song, working it all out—words, music, *feelings*. What a rare privilege, to be permitted to eavesdrop on the very moment of creation! He sang of nature, my handsome Orpheus. His voice. His voice!

I tipped my head back and closed my eyes. I pictured a sky. It was blue black, soft and dense as fur. Across and over the expanse of night, into the velvet depths of it, light was scattered, enough for a thousand darknesses. Patterns revealed themselves; the eye, exquisitely dazzled, sought out snail-shell whorls and shattered pearls, gods and beasts and planets. As we stood still, yet we rotated, and, whilst turning, moved in a larger circle, round and round the sun, and oh, the dizzying momentum of it . . .

The music stopped and there was a sudden, blurry movement. I stepped back, and quickly started to walk upstairs, my heart hammering. Nothing. I stood on the upper landing and waited for a few minutes. Nothing.

I tiptoed down and placed myself outside his door again. The music had started up once more, but I did not wish to disturb him. I was only there to see where he lived, after all . . . there was no harm in looking. Mission accomplished.

It was sheer spendthrift madness, but once on the street, I hailed a passing black cab to take me home. The evening had lingered slowly, but now it was definitely night, and I did not care to be abroad. The dark is where bad things happen. I estimated that the taxi was likely to cost in the region of six pounds, but I had no choice. I put on my seat belt and closed the glass panel that separated me from the driver. I had no desire to hear his views on association football, the city council or any other topic. I had only one thing on my mind. Or, more accurately, one person.

~

I realized after an hour or two that I wasn't going to be able to sleep after my earlier adventuring. I put on the light and looked down at my nightdress. I have two, to allow for alternate washing. They are identical, both of them ankle-length with a high neckline, made of cozy brushed cotton. They're lemon-colored (the shade reminds me of explosively fizzy boiled sweets, not a feature of my early childhood but a comforting image nonetheless). When I was young, for a treat, Mummy would pop a pimento-stuffed olive into my mouth, or, occasionally, an oily anchovy from a coffin-shaped yellow-and-red tin. She always stressed to me that sophisticated palates erred toward savory flavors, that cheap, sugary treats were the ruin of the poor (and their teeth). Mummy always had very sharp, very white teeth.

The only acceptable sweet treats, she said, were proper Belgian truffles (Neuhaus, *nom de dieu*; only tourists bought those nasty chocolate seashells) or plump Medjool dates from the souks of Tunis, both of which were rather difficult to source in our local Spar. There was a time, shortly before . . . the incident . . .

when she shopped only at Fortnum's, and I recall that in that same period she was in regular correspondence with Fauchon over perceived imperfections in their *confiture de cerises*. I remember the pretty red stamps on the letters from Paris: *Liberté, Egalité, Fraternité*. Not exactly a credo of Mummy's.

I folded my pillow in half to support me as I sat up. Sleep still felt far away, and I was in need of soothing. I reached down into the gap between the mattress and the wall and sought my old faithful, its edges rounded and softened with years of handling. *Jane Eyre*. I could open up the novel at any page and immediately know where I was in the story, could almost visualize the next sentence before I reached it. It was an old Penguin Classic, Ms. Brontë's portrait gracing the cover. The bookplate inside read: *Saint Eustace Parish Church Sunday School, Presented to Eleanor Oliphant for Perfect Attendance, 1998*. I had a very ecumenical upbringing, all told, having been fostered by Presbyterians, Anglicans, Catholics, Methodists and Quakers, plus a few individuals who wouldn't recognize God if he pointed his electric Michelangelo finger at them. I submitted to all attempts at spiritual education with equally bad grace. Sunday school, or its equivalent, did at least get me out of whatever house I was living in, and sometimes there were sandwiches, or, more rarely, tolerable companions.

I opened the book at random, in the manner of a lucky dip. It fell open at a pivotal scene, the one where Jane meets Mr. Rochester for the first time, startling his horse in the woods and causing him to fall. Pilot is there too, the handsome, soulful-eyed hound. If the book has one failing, it's that there is insufficient mention of Pilot. You can't have too much dog in a book.

Jane Eyre. A strange child, difficult to love. A lonely only child. She's left to deal with so much pain at such a young age—the aftermath of death, the absence of love. It's Mr. Rochester who gets burned in the end. I know how *that* feels. All of it.

Everything seems worse in the darkest hours of the night; I was surprised to hear that the birds were still singing, although they sounded angry. The poor creatures must hardly sleep in summer, when the light glimmers on and on. In the half dark, in the full dark, I remember, I remember. Awake in the shadows, two little rabbit heartbeats, breath like a knife. I remember, I remember . . . I closed my eyes. Eyelids are really just flesh curtains. Your eyes are always "on," always *looking*; when you close them, you're watching the thin, veined skin of your inner eyelid rather than staring out at the world. It's not a comforting thought. In fact, if I thought about it for long enough, I'd probably want to pluck out my own eyes, to stop looking, to stop *seeing* all the time. The things I've seen cannot be unseen. The things I've done cannot be undone.

Think about something nice, one of my foster parents would say when I couldn't sleep, or on nights when I woke up sweating, sobbing, screaming. Trite advice, but occasionally effective. So I thought about Pilot the dog.

—

I suppose I must have slept—it seems impossible that I wouldn't have dropped off for at least a moment or two—but it didn't feel like it. Sundays are dead days. I try to sleep as long as possible to pass the time (an old prison trick, apparently—thank you for the tip, Mummy) but on summer mornings, it can be difficult. When the phone rang just after ten, I'd been up for hours. I'd cleaned the bathroom and washed the kitchen floor, taken out the recycling and arranged all the tins in the cupboard so that the labels were facing forward in zetabetical order. I'd polished both pairs of shoes. I'd read the newspaper and completed all the crosswords and puzzles.

I cleared my throat before I spoke, realizing that I hadn't uttered a word for almost twelve hours, back when I told the taxi driver where to drop me off. That's actually quite good, for me—usually, I don't speak from the point at which I state my destination to the bus driver on Friday night, right through until I greet his colleague on Monday morning.

"Eleanor?" It was Raymond, of course.

"Yes, this is she," I said, quite curtly. For goodness' sake, who did he expect? He coughed extravagantly: filthy smoker.

"Erm, right. I just wanted to let you know that I'm going in to see Sammy again today—wondered if you wanted to come with me?"

"Why?" I said.

He paused for quite a while—strange. It was hardly a difficult question.

"Well . . . I phoned the hospital and he's much better—he's awake—and he's been moved into the general medical ward. I thought . . . I suppose I thought it'd be nice if he met us, in case he had any questions about what happened to him."

I wasn't thinking very quickly and had no time to consider the ramifications. Before I quite knew what had happened, we had arranged to meet at the hospital that afternoon. I hung up and looked at the clock on the living room wall, above the fireplace (it's one I got in the Red Cross shop: electric blue circular frame, Power Rangers; adds a kind of rakish joie de vivre to the living room, I've always thought). I had several hours until the rendezvous.

I decided to take my time getting ready, and looked cautiously at myself in the mirror while the shower warmed up. Could I ever become a musician's muse? I wondered. What was a muse, anyway? I was familiar with the classical allusion, of course, but, in modern-day, practical terms, a muse seemed simply to be an attractive woman whom the artist wanted to sleep with.

I thought about all those paintings: voluptuous maidens reclining in curvaceous splendor, waiflike ballerinas with huge limpid eyes, drowned beauties in clinging white gowns surrounded by floating blossoms. I was neither curvaceous nor waiflike. I was normal-sized and normal-faced (on one side, anyway).

Did men ever look in the mirror, I wondered, and find themselves wanting in deeply fundamental ways? When they opened a newspaper or watched a film, were they presented with nothing but exceptionally handsome young men, and did this make them feel intimidated, inferior, because they were not as young, not as handsome? Did they then read newspaper articles ridiculing those same handsome men if they gained weight or wore something unflattering?

These were, of course, rhetorical questions.

I looked at myself again. I was healthy and my body was strong. I had a brain that worked fine, and a voice, albeit an unmelodious one; smoke inhalation all those years ago had damaged my vocal cords irreparably. I had hair, ears, eyes and a mouth. I was a human woman, no more and no less.

Even the circus freak side of my face—my damaged half—was better than the alternative, which would have meant death by fire. I didn't burn to ashes. I emerged from the flames like a little phoenix. I ran my fingers over the scar tissue, caressing the contours. I didn't burn, Mummy, I thought. I walked through the fire and I lived.

There are scars on my heart, just as thick, as disfiguring as those on my face. I know they're there. I hope some undamaged tissue remains, a patch through which love can come in and flow out. I hope.

# 9

Raymond was waiting outside the front door of the hospital. I saw him bend down to light the cigarette of a woman in a wheelchair—she'd brought her drip out with her, on wheels, so that she could destroy her health at the same time as taxpayers' money was being used to try and restore it. Raymond chatted to her as she smoked, puffing away himself. He leaned forward and said something and the woman laughed, a harridan's cackle that ended in a prolonged bout of coughing. I approached with caution, fearing the noxious cloud might envelop me to deleterious effect. He spotted me coming, stubbed out his cigarette then ambled toward me. He was wearing a pair of denim trousers which were slung unpleasantly low around his buttocks; when his back was turned I saw an unwelcome inch of underpant—a ghastly imperial purple—and white skin covered in freckles, reminding me of a giraffe's hide.

"Hiya, Eleanor," he said, rubbing his hands on the front of his thighs as though to clean them. "How're you doing today?"

Horrifically, he leaned forward as though to embrace me. I stepped back, but not before I'd had a chance to smell the cigarette smoke and another odor, something unpleasantly chemical and pungent. I suspected it was an inexpensive brand of gentleman's cologne.

"Good afternoon, Raymond," I said. "Shall we go inside?"

We took the lift to Ward 7. Raymond recounted the events of the previous evening to me at tedious length; he and his friends had apparently "pulled a late one," whatever that meant, completing a mission on *Grand Theft Auto* and then playing poker. I wasn't sure why he was telling me this. I certainly hadn't asked. He finally finished speaking and then inquired about my evening.

"I conducted some research," I said, not wishing to sully the experience by recounting it to Raymond.

"Look!" I said. "Ward 7!" Like a child or a small pet, he was easily distracted, and we took turns to use the alcohol hand rub before we went in. Safety first, although my poor ravaged skin had barely recovered from the previous dermatological onslaught.

Sammy was in the last bed nearest to the window, reading the *Sunday Post*. He glared at us over the top of his spectacles as we approached; his demeanor was not friendly. Raymond cleared his throat.

"Hi there, Mr. Thom," he said. "I'm Raymond, and this is Eleanor." I nodded at the old man. Raymond kept talking. "We, eh, we found you when you had your funny turn, and I went with you in the ambulance to hospital. We wanted to come by today and say hello, see how you were doing . . ."

I leaned forward and extended my hand. Sammy stared at it.

"Eh?" he said. "*Who* did you say you were?" He looked quite perturbed, and not a little aggressive. Raymond started to explain again, but Sammy held up his hand, palm facing forward, to silence him. Given that he was wearing candy-striped pajamas and his white hair was as fluffy and spiky as a baby pigeon's, he nevertheless cut a surprisingly assertive figure.

"Now hold on, wait a minute," he said, and leaned toward his bedside cabinet, grabbing something from the shelf. I took an involuntary step back—who knew what he might be about to pull out of there? He inserted something into his ear and fiddled about for a moment, a high-pitched squeal emitting from that side of his head. It stopped, and he smiled.

"Right then," he said, "that's better. *Now* the dog can see the rabbit, eh? So, what's the story with you pair—church, is it? Or are you trying to rent me a telly again? I don't want one, son—I've already told your pals. There's no way I'm paying good money just to lie here and watch all *that* shite! Fatties doing ballroom dancing, grown men baking cakes, for the love of God!"

Raymond cleared his throat again and repeated his introduction, while I leaned forward and shook

Sammy's hand. His expression changed instantly and he beamed at us both.

"Oh, so it was *you* pair, was it? I kept asking the nurses who it was that had saved my life—'Who brought me in?' I said. 'How did I get here?'—but they couldn't tell me. Have a seat, come on, sit down next to me and tell me all about yourselves. I can't thank you enough for what you did, I really can't." He nodded, and then his face became very serious. "All you hear these days is that everything's going to hell in a hand-cart, how everybody's a pedophile or a crook, and it's not true. You forget that the world is full of ordinary decent people like yourselves, Good Samaritans who'll stop and help a soul in need. Just wait till the family meet you! They'll be over the moon, so they will."

He leaned back on his pillows, tired out from the effort of talking. Raymond fetched me a plastic seat, then another for himself.

"How are you feeling, then, Mr. Thom?" Raymond asked him. "Did you have a good night?"

"Call me Sammy, son—there's no need to stand on ceremony. I'm doing fine, thanks; I'll be right as rain in no time. You and your wife here saved my life, though, no two ways about it."

I felt Raymond shift in his chair, and I leaned forward.

"Mr. Thom," I said.

He raised his eyebrows, then waggled them at me in quite a disconcerting way. "Sammy," I said, correcting myself, and he nodded at me.

"I'm afraid I have to clarify a couple of factual inaccuracies," I said. "Firstly, we did not save your life. Credit for that must go to the Ambulance Service, whose staff, although somewhat brusque, did what was necessary to stabilize your condition whilst they brought you here. The medical team at the hospital, including the anesthetist and the orthopedic surgeon who operated on your hip, alongside the many other health-care professionals who have carried out your postoperative care—it is they who saved you, if anyone did. Raymond and I merely summoned assistance and kept you company until such time as the National Health Service took responsibility."

"Aye, God bless the NHS, right enough," said Raymond, interrupting rudely. I gave him one of my sternest looks.

"Furthermore," I continued, "I should clarify *posthaste* that Raymond and myself are merely coworkers. We are most certainly *not* married to one another." I stared hard at Sammy, making sure that he was in no doubt. Sammy looked at Raymond. Raymond looked at Sammy. There was a silence which, to me, seemed slightly awkward. Raymond sat forward in his chair.

"So, eh, where do you live then, Sammy? What were you up to the other day when you had your accident?" he asked.

Sammy smiled at him.

"I'm local, son—born and bred," he said. "I always get my bits and pieces from the shops on a Friday. I'd been feeling a bit funny that morning, right enough, but I thought it was just my angina. Never expected to find myself in here!"

He took a toffee from a large bag on his lap, then offered them to us. Raymond took one; I declined. The thought of malleable confectionery, warmed to body temperature on Sammy's groin (albeit encased in flannel pajamas and a blanket) was repellent.

Both Sammy and Raymond were audible masticators. While they chomped, I looked at my hands, noticing that they looked raw, almost burned, but glad of the fact that the alcohol rub had removed the germs and bacteria which lurked everywhere in the hospital. And, presumably, on me.

"What about you two—did you have far to come today?" Sammy asked. "Separately, I mean," he added quickly, looking at me.

"I live on the South Side," Raymond said, "and Eleanor's . . . you're in the West End, aren't you?" I nodded, not wishing to disclose my place of residence any more precisely. Sammy asked about work, and I let Raymond tell him, being content to observe. Sammy looked rather vulnerable, as people are wont to do when they are wearing pajamas in public, but he was younger than I'd originally thought—not more than seventy, I'd guess—with remarkably dark blue eyes.

"I don't know anything about graphic design," Sammy said. "It sounds very fancy. I was a postman all my days. I got out at the right time, though; I can live on my pension, so long as I'm careful. It's all changed now—I'm glad I'm not there anymore. All the messing about they've done with it. In my day, it was a proper public service . . ."

Raymond was nodding. "That's right," he said. "Remember when you used to get your post before you left the house in the morning, and there was a lunchtime delivery too? It comes in the middle of the afternoon now, if it comes at all . . ."

I have to admit, I was finding the post office chat somewhat tedious.

"How long are you likely to be in here, Sammy?" I said. "I only ask because the chances of contracting a postoperative infection are significantly increased for longer-stay patients—gastroenteritis, *Staphylococcus aureus*, *Clostridium difficile*—"

Raymond interrupted me again. "Aye," he said, "and I bet the food's rank as well, eh, Sammy?"

Sammy laughed. "You're not wrong there, son," he said. "You want to see what they served up for lunch today. Supposed to be Irish stew . . . looked more like Pedigree Chum. Smelled like it too."

Raymond smiled. "Can we get you anything, Sammy? We could nip to the shop downstairs, or else pop back later in the week, bring stuff in, if you need it?"

Raymond looked at me for confirmation and I nodded. I had no reason to dismiss the suggestion. It was actually quite a pleasant feeling, thinking that I might be able to help an elderly person who was suffering due to inadequate nutrition. I started to think about what to bring him, types of food that could be transported without mishap. I wondered if Sammy might enjoy some cold pasta and pesto; I could make a double portion for supper one evening and bring the leftovers to him the next day in a Tupperware tub. I did not own any Tupperware, having had no need of it until this point. I could go to a department store to purchase some. That seemed to be the sort of thing that a woman of my age and social circumstances might do. Exciting!

"Ach, son, that's awful kind of you," Sammy said, deflating my sense of purpose somewhat, "but there's really no need. The family are in here every day, twice a day." He said this last part with evident pride. "I can't even finish half the stuff they bring. There's just so much of it! I end up having to give most of it away," he said, indicating the other men on the ward with an imperious wave of his hand.

"What constitutes your family?" I asked, slightly surprised by this revelation. "I had assumed you were single and childless, like us."

Raymond shifted uncomfortably in his seat.

"I'm a widower, Eleanor," Sammy said. "Jean died five years ago—cancer. Took her quick, in the end." He paused and sat up straighter. "I've two sons and a daughter. Keith's my eldest, married with two wee ones. They're cheeky monkeys, those boys," he said, his eyes crinkling. "Gary's my other son; Gary and Michelle—they're not married, but they live together. That seems to be the way of it these days. And Laura, my youngest . . . well, God knows about Laura. Divorced twice by the age of thirty-five, can you believe it? She's got her own wee business, a nice house and a car . . . she just can't seem to find a good man. Or when she does find one, she can't hang on to him."

I found this interesting. "I'd counsel your daughter not to worry," I said, with confidence. "In my recent experience, the perfect man appears when you're least expecting it. Fate throws him into your path, and then providence ensures that you will end up together." Raymond made a strange sound, something between a cough and a sneeze.

Sammy smiled kindly at me. "Is that right? Well, you can tell her yourself, hen," he said. "They'll all be here soon."

A nurse walked past as he said this and had clearly overheard. She was grossly overweight and was wearing rather attractive white plastic clogs teamed with striking black-and-yellow-striped socks—her feet looked like big fat wasps. I made a mental note to ask her where she'd purchased them before we left.

"There's a maximum of three visitors to a bed," she said, "and we're strictly enforcing that rule today, I'm afraid." She didn't look afraid. Raymond stood up.

"We'll go, and let your family visit, Sammy," he said. I stood up too; it seemed appropriate.

"No rush, no rush now," Sammy said.

"Shall we return later in the week?" I asked. "Is there a magazine or a periodical you'd like us to bring?"

"Eleanor, it's like I said—you two saved my life, we're family now. Come and visit anytime you like. I'd love to see you, hen," Sammy said. His eyes were damp, like periwinkles in seawater. I held out my hand again and instead of shaking it, he clasped both of mine in his. Normally I would be horrified, but he surprised me. His hands were large and warm, like an animal's paws, and mine felt small and fragile inside them. His fingernails were quite long and gnarly, and there were curly gray hairs on the backs of his hands, running all the way up and under his pajama sleeves.

"Eleanor, listen," he said, staring me in the eye and gripping my hands tightly, "thanks again, lass. Thanks for taking care of me and bringing in my shopping." I found that I didn't want to remove my hands from the warmth and strength of his. Raymond coughed, his lungs no doubt reacting to the absence of carcinogens over the last half hour or so.

I swallowed hard, suddenly finding it difficult to speak. "I'll return later in the week, then, with comestibles," I said eventually. "I promise." Sammy nodded.

"Cheers then, big man," Raymond said, placing a meaty hand on Sammy's shoulder. "See you soon, eh?"

Sammy waved to us as we made our way out of the ward, and was still waving and smiling as we turned the corner and headed toward the lift.

Neither of us spoke until we got outside.

"What a lovely guy, eh?" Raymond said, somewhat redundantly.

I nodded, trying to hold on to the feeling of my hands in his, cozy and safe, and the look of kindness and warmth in his eyes. I found, to my extreme consternation, that nascent tears were forming in my eyes, and I turned away to rub them before they could spill over. Annoyingly, Raymond, usually the least observant of men, had noticed.

"What are you doing for the rest of the day, Eleanor?" Raymond asked gently. I looked at my watch. It was almost four.

"I suppose I'll return home, perhaps read for a while," I said. "There's a radio program on later where people write in to request excerpts of items they've enjoyed during the week. That can often be reasonably entertaining."

I was also thinking that I might buy some more vodka, just a half bottle, to top up what remained. I yearned for that brief, sharp feeling I get when I drink it—a sad, burning feeling—and then, blissfully, no feelings at all. I had also seen the date on Sammy's newspaper and remembered that today was, in fact, my birthday. Annoyingly, I'd forgotten to ask the nurse where she had purchased her wasp socks—those could have been my present to myself. I decided that I might buy some freesias instead. I have always loved their delicate scent and the softness of their colors—they have a kind of subdued luminosity which is much more beautiful than a garish sunflower or a clichéd red rose.

Raymond was looking at me. "I'm going to my mum's now," he said.

I nodded, blew my nose and zipped up my jerkin in preparation for the journey home.

"Listen—d'you fancy coming with me?" Raymond said, just as I was turning toward the gate.

Under no circumstances, was my immediate thought.

"I go over most Sundays," he went on. "She doesn't get out much—I'm sure she'd love to see a new face."

"Even one like mine?" I said. I couldn't imagine that anyone would take any particular pleasure in looking at my face, either for the first or for the thousand and first time. Raymond ignored me and began to rummage in his pockets.

I thought about his suggestion while he lit up another cigarette. I could still purchase vodka and birthday flowers on the way home, after all, and it might be interesting to see the inside of another person's home. I tried to think of the last time I had done so. I had stood in the hallway of my downstairs neighbors' flat a couple of years ago, when I was delivering a parcel I'd taken in for them. The place had smelled strongly of onions, and there was an ugly standard lamp in the corner. A few years before that, one of the receptionists had hosted a party at her flat and invited all the women from work. It was a beautiful flat, a traditional tenement with stained glass and mahogany and elaborate cornices. The "party," however, had merely been a pretext, a ruse of sorts to provide her with the opportunity to attempt to sell us sex toys. It was a most unedifying spectacle: seventeen drunken women comparing the efficacy of a range of alarmingly large vibrators. I left after ten minutes, having downed a tepid glass of Pinot Grigio and parried an outrageously impertinent question from a cousin of the host about my private life.

I'm familiar with the concept of bacchanalia and Dionysian revels, of course, but it strikes me as utterly bizarre that women should want to spend an evening together drinking and purchasing such items, and, indeed, that this should pass as "entertainment." Sexual union between lovers should be a sacred, private thing. It should not be a topic for discussion with strangers over a display of edible underwear. When the musician and I spent our first night together, the joining of our bodies would mirror the joining of our minds, our souls. His otherness, the flash of dark hair in his armpit, the buttons of bone at his clavicle. The blood scent in the crook of his elbow. The warm softness of his lips, as he takes me in his arms and . . .

"Erm, Eleanor? Hello? I was just saying . . . we'll need to go now to catch the bus, if you're coming to Mum's?"

I dragged myself back to the unwelcome present and the squat figure of Raymond, with his grubby hooded sweatshirt and dirty training shoes. Perhaps Raymond's mother would prove intelligent and charming company. I doubted it, based on the evidence of her progeny, but one never knew.

"Yes, Raymond. I will accompany you to your mother's house," I said.

# 10

Of course Raymond didn't have a car. I would guess he was in his midthirties, but there was something adolescent, not fully formed, about him. It was partly the way he dressed, of course. I had yet to see him in normal, leather footwear; he wore training shoes at all times, and seemed to own a wide range of colors and styles. I have often noticed that people who routinely wear sportswear are the least likely sort to participate in athletic activity.

Sport is a mystery to me. In primary school, sports day was the one day of the year when the less academically gifted students could triumph, winning prizes for jumping fastest in a sack, or running from Point A to Point B more quickly than their classmates. How they loved to wear those badges on their blazers the next day! As if a silver in the egg-and-spoon race was some sort of compensation for not understanding how to use an apostrophe.

At secondary school, PE was simply unfathomable. We had to wear special clothes and then run endlessly around a field, occasionally being told to hold a metal tube and pass it to someone else. If we weren't running, we were jumping, into a sandpit or over a small bar on legs. There was a special way of doing this; you couldn't simply run and jump, you had to do some strange sort of hop and skip first. I asked why, but none of the PE teachers (most of whom, as far as I could ascertain, would struggle to tell you the time) could furnish me with an answer. All of these seemed strange activities to impose on young people with no interest in them, and indeed I'm certain that they merely served to alienate the majority of us from physical activity for life. Fortunately, I am naturally lithe and elegant of limb, and I enjoy walking, so I have always kept myself in a reasonable state of physical fitness. Mummy has a particular loathing for the overweight ("Greedy, lazy beast," she'd hiss, if one waddled past us in the street) and I may perhaps have internalized this view to some extent.

Raymond wasn't overweight, but he was doughy and a bit paunchy. None of his muscles were visible, and I suspect he only ever used the ones in his forearms with any degree of regularity. His sartorial choices did not flatter his unprepossessing physique: slouchy denims, baggy T-shirts with childish slogans and images. He dressed like a boy rather than a man. His toilette was sloppy too, and he was usually unshaven—it was not a beard as such, but patchy stubble, which merely served to make him look unkempt. His hair, a mousy, dirty blond, was cut short and had been given minimal attention—at most, perhaps a rub with a grubby towel after washing. The overall impression was of a man who, whilst not exactly a vagrant, had certainly slept rough in a flophouse or on a stranger's floor the previous evening.

"Here's our bus, Eleanor," Raymond said, nudging me rudely. I had my travel pass ready but, typically, Raymond did not possess one, preferring to pay well over the odds for want of a few moment's advance planning. He did not, it transpired, even have the correct change, and so I had to lend him a pound. I would be sure to recoup it at work tomorrow.

The journey to his mother's house took about twenty minutes, during which I explained the benefits of a travel pass to him, including where one could purchase such an item and how many journeys one needed to take in order to break even or, indeed, to effectively travel for free. He did not seem particularly interested, and didn't even thank me when I'd finished. He is a spectacularly unsophisticated conversationalist.

We walked through a small estate of square white homes; there were four different house designs interspersed in a predictable pattern. Each had a newish car in the driveway, and evidence of children—small bicycles with stabilizers, a basketball hoop fixed to the garage wall—but there was neither sight nor sound of any. The streets were all named after poets—Wordsworth Lane, Shelley Close, Keats Rise—no doubt chosen by the building company's Marketing Department. They were all poets that the kind of person who'd aspire to such a home would recognize, poets who wrote about urns and flowers and wandering clouds. Based on past experience, I'd be more likely to end up living in Dante Lane or Poe Crescent.

I was very familiar with such environs, having lived in several virtually identical houses in virtually identical streets during foster placements. There would be no pensioners here, no friends sharing a house and no one living alone, save for the occasional transitory divorcé. Newish cars lined up in driveways, two per house, ideally. Families came and went, and the whole place felt temporary, somehow, like theatrical scenery that had been hastily assembled and could be shifted at any time. I shuddered, chasing away the memories.

Raymond's mother lived in a neat terrace behind the newer houses, a row of tiny pebble-dashed semis. It was social housing; the streets here were named after obscure local politicians. Those who had purchased their homes had fitted UPVC double-glazed front doors, or added little porches. Raymond's family homestead was unmodified.

~

Raymond ignored the front door and walked around the side of the house. The back garden had a shed with net curtains in the window, and a square of green lawn marked by clothes poles. Washing flapped on the line, pegged out with military precision, a row of plain white sheets and towels and then a line of alarming elasticated undergarments. There was a vegetable patch, with tropically lush rhubarb and neat rows of carrots, leeks and cabbages. I admired the symmetry and precision with which they had been laid out.

Raymond pushed open the back door without knocking, shouting hello as he walked into the little kitchen. It smelled deliciously of soup, salty and warm, probably emanating from the large pot that sat on the hob. The floor and all the surfaces were immaculately clean and tidy, and I felt certain that, were I to open a drawer or cupboard, everything inside would be pristine and neatly arranged. The décor was plain and functional, but with occasional flashes of kitsch—there was a large calendar with a lurid photograph of two kittens in a basket, and a cloth tube to store plastic bags and designed to resemble an old-fashioned doll hung on a door handle. A single cup, glass and plate were stacked on the drainer.

We walked into a tiny hall, and I followed Raymond into the living room which, again, was spotless, and reeked of furniture polish. A vase of chrysanthemums sat on the window ledge, and an uncurated jumble of framed photographs and ornaments was protected by the smoked-glass doors of an outmoded dresser like holy relics. An old woman in an armchair reached forward for a remote to mute an enormous television. It was showing that program where people take old things to be valued and then, if it turns out they are worth something, pretend they like them too much to sell them. Three cats lounged on the sofa; two glared at us, the third merely opened one eye and then went back to sleep, not deigning us worthy of a response.

"Raymond, son! Come in, come in," the old woman said, pointing to the sofa and leaning forward in her chair to shoo the creatures off.

"I've brought a friend from work, Mum, hope that's OK?" he said, walking forward and kissing her on the cheek. I stepped forward and held out my hand.

"Eleanor Oliphant, pleased to meet you," I said. She took my hand, then clasped it in both of hers, much as Sammy had done.

"Lovely to see you, hen," she said. "I'm always pleased to meet Raymond's friends. Sit down, won't you? You'll be needing a cup of tea, I'm sure. What do you take in it?" She made to stand, and I noticed the wheeled walking frame by the side of the chair.

"Stay where you are, Mum, I'll get it," Raymond said. "Shall I make us all a nice cuppa?"

"That'd be lovely, son," she said. "There's some biscuits too—Wagon Wheels—your favorites."

Raymond went off to the kitchen and I sat on the sofa to the right of his mother.

"He's a good boy, my Raymond," she said proudly. I was unsure how best to respond, and opted for a short nod. "So you work together," she said. "Do you fix computers too? My goodness, girls can do just about anything these days, can't they?"

She was as neat and tidy as her house, her blouse fastened at the neck with a pearl brooch. She wore wine-colored velvet slippers with a sheepskin trim, which looked cozy. She was in her seventies, I'd guess, and I noticed, when I shook her hand, that her knuckles were swollen to the size of gooseberries.

"I work in accounts, Mrs. Gibbons," I said. I told her a bit about my job, and she appeared to be fascinated, nodding along and occasionally saying "Is that right?" and "My my, isn't that interesting." When I ended my monologue, having exhausted the already limited conversational opportunities afforded by accounts receivable, she smiled.

"Are you local, Eleanor?" she asked gently. Usually I abhor being questioned in this manner, but it was clear that her interest was genuine and without malice, so I told her where I lived, being deliberately vague as to the precise location. One should never disclose one's exact place of residence to strangers.

"You don't have the accent, though?" she said, framing it as another question.

"I spent my early childhood down south," I said, "but I moved to Scotland when I was ten."

"Ah," she said, "that explains it." She seemed happy with this. I've noticed that most Scottish people don't inquire beyond "down south," and I can only assume that this description encapsulates some sort of generic Englandshire for them, boat races and bowler hats, as though Liverpool and Cornwall were the same sorts of places, inhabited by the same sorts of people. Conversely, they are always adamant that every part of their own country is unique and special. I'm not sure why.

Raymond returned with the tea things and a packet of Wagon Wheels on a garish plastic tray.

"Raymond!" his mother said. "You might have put the milk into a jug, for heaven's sake! We've got a guest!"

"It's only Eleanor, Mum," he said, then looked at me. "You don't mind, do you?"

"Not at all," I said. "I always use the carton at home too. It's merely a vessel from which to convey the liquid into the cup; in fact, it's probably more hygienic than using an uncovered jug, I would have thought."

I reached forward for a Wagon Wheel. Raymond was already chewing on his. The pair of them chatted about inconsequential matters and I settled into the sofa. Neither of them had particularly strident voices, and I listened to the carriage clock on the mantelpiece tick loudly. It was warm, just on the right side of oppressively hot. One of the cats, lying on its side in front of the fire, stretched out to its full length with a shudder, and then went back to sleep. There was a photograph next to the clock, the colors muted with age. A man, obviously Raymond's father, grinned broadly at the camera, holding up a champagne flute in a toast.

"That's Raymond's dad," his mother said, noticing. She smiled. "That was taken the day Raymond got his exam results." She looked at him with obvious pride. "Our Raymond was the first one in the family to go to university," she said. "His dad was pleased as punch. I only wish he could have been there for your graduation. What a day that was, eh, Raymond son?" Raymond smiled, nodded.

"He had a heart attack not long after I started uni," he explained to me.

"Never got to enjoy his retirement," his mother said. "It often happens that way." They both sat quietly for a moment.

"What did he do for a living?" I asked. I wasn't interested, but I felt it was appropriate.

"Gas engineer," Raymond said.

His mother nodded. "He worked hard all his days," she said, "and we never wanted for anything, did we, Raymond? We had a holiday every year, and a nice wee car. At least he got to see our Denise married, anyway—that's something."

I must have looked puzzled.

"My sister," Raymond explained.

"Och, for goodness' sake, Raymond. Too busy talking about football and computers, no doubt, and I don't suppose she wants to hear about that sort of thing anyway. Boys, eh, Eleanor?" She shook her head at me, smiling.

This was puzzling. How on earth could you forget that you had a sister? He hadn't forgotten, I supposed—he'd simply taken his sibling for granted: an unchanging, unremarkable fact of life, not even worthy of mention. It was impossible for me to imagine such a scenario, alone as I was. Only Mummy and I inhabit the Oliphant world.

His mother was still talking. "Denise was eleven when Raymond came along—a wee surprise and a blessing, so he was."

She looked at him with so much love that I had to turn away. At least I know what love looks like, I told myself. That's something. No one had ever looked at me like that, but I'd be able to recognize it if they ever did.

"Here, son, get the album out. I'll show Eleanor those photos of that first holiday in Alicante, the summer before you started school. He got stuck in a revolving door at the airport," she said, sotto voce, leaning toward me confidentially.

I laughed out loud at the look of utter horror on Raymond's face.

"Mum, Eleanor doesn't want to be bored to death looking at our old photos," he said, blushing in a way that I supposed some people might consider charming. I thought for a moment about insisting that I'd love to see them, but he looked so miserable that I couldn't do it. Conveniently, my stomach gave a loud rumble. I'd only had the Wagon Wheel since my lunchtime repast of spaghetti hoops on toast. She coughed politely.

"You'll stay for your tea, won't you, Eleanor? It's nothing fancy, but you're very welcome."

I looked at my watch. It was only five thirty—an odd time to eat, but I was hungry, and it would still allow me time to go to Tesco on the way home.

"I'd be delighted, Mrs. Gibbons," I said.

We sat around the small table in the kitchen. The soup was delicious; she said she'd used a pork knuckle to make stock, and then shredded the meat through the soup, which was also full of vegetables from the garden. There was bread and butter and cheese, and afterward we had a cup of tea and a cream cake. All the while, Mrs. Gibbons regaled us with tales of her neighbors' various eccentricities and illnesses, along with updates on the activities of their extended family, which seemed to be of as little relevance to Raymond as they were to me, judging by his expression. He teased his mother frequently and affectionately, and she responded with mock annoyance, gently slapping him on the arm or chiding him for his rudeness. I was warm and full and comfortable in a way I couldn't remember feeling before.

Raymond's mother heaved herself to her feet and reached for her walking frame. She had crippling arthritis in her knees and hips, Raymond told me, while she hobbled upstairs to the bathroom. The house wasn't really suitable for someone with limited mobility, but she refused to move, he said, because she'd lived all her adult life there and it was the place where she'd brought up her family.

"Now then," she said, returning from upstairs, "I'll wash these few dishes and then we can settle down and watch a bit of telly." Raymond got straight to his feet.

"Sit down, Mum, let me do it—it won't take a minute. Eleanor will help me, won't you, Eleanor?"

I stood up and began gathering up the plates. Mrs. Gibbons protested vehemently, but eventually sat back down in her chair, slow and awkward, and I heard a tiny sigh of pain.

Raymond washed and I dried. This was his suggestion—somehow, he'd noticed my red, sore hands, although he didn't make a hullaballoo about it. He'd merely nudged me away from the sink and thrust a tea towel—a rather jaunty one with a Scottie dog sporting a tartan bow tie—into my damaged fingers.

The tea towel was soft and fibrous, as though it had been washed many times over, and had been ironed carefully into a neatly pressed square. I cast an eye over the plates before stacking them on the table for Raymond to put away. The crockery was old but good quality, painted with blowsy roses and edged in faded gilt. Mrs. Gibbons saw me looking at it. There was certainly nothing wrong with her powers of observation.

"That was my wedding china, Eleanor," she said. "Imagine—still going strong almost fifty years later!"

"You, or the china?" Raymond said, and she tutted and shook her head, smiling. There was a comfortable silence as we worked on our respective tasks.

"Tell me, are you courting at the moment, Eleanor?" she asked.

How tedious.

"Not presently," I said, "but I have my eye on someone. It's only a matter of time." There was a crash from the sink as Raymond dropped the ladle onto the draining board with a clatter.

"Raymond!" his mum said. "Butterfingers!"

I'd been keeping track of the musician online, of course, but he'd been rather quiet, virtually speaking. A couple of Instagram snaps of some meals he'd had, a few tweets, uninteresting Facebook updates about other people's music. I didn't mind. It was merely a matter of biding my time. If I knew one thing about romance, it was that the perfect moment for us to meet and fall in love would arrive when I least expected it, and in the most charming set of circumstances. That said, if it didn't happen soon, I'd need to take matters into my own hands.

"And what about your family?" she said. "Do they live close by? Any brothers or sisters?"

"No, unfortunately," I said. "I would have loved to have had siblings to grow up with." I thought about this. "It's actually one of the greatest sources of sadness in my life," I heard myself say. I had never uttered such a sentence before, and, indeed, hadn't even fully formed the thought until this very moment. I surprised myself. *And whose fault is that, then?* A voice, whispering in my ear, cold and sharp. Angry. Mummy. I closed my eyes, trying to be rid of her.

Mrs. Gibbons seemed to sense my discomfort. "Oh, but I'm sure that must mean you've got a lovely close relationship with your mum and dad, then? I bet you mean the world to them, being the only one."

I looked at my shoes. Why had I selected them? I couldn't remember. They had Velcro fastenings for ease of use and they were black, which went with everything. They were flat for comfort, and built up around the ankle for support. They were, I realized, hideous.

"Don't be so nosy, Mum," Raymond said, drying his hands on the tea towel. "You're like the Gestapo!"

I thought she'd be angry, but it was worse than that; she was apologetic.

"Oh, Eleanor, I'm sorry, love, I didn't mean to upset you. Please, hen, don't cry. I'm so sorry."

I was crying. Sobbing! I hadn't cried so extravagantly for years. I tried to remember the last time; it was after Declan and I split up. Even then, those weren't emotional tears—I was crying with pain because he'd broken my arm and two ribs when I'd finally asked him to move out. This simply wasn't on, sobbing in the kitchen of a colleague's mother. Whatever would Mummy say? I pulled myself together.

"Please don't apologize, Mrs. Gibbons," I said, my voice croaking and then splitting like a teenage boy's as I tried to calm my breath, wiping my eyes on the tea towel. She was literally wringing her hands and looked on the verge of tears herself. Raymond had his arm around her shoulder.

"Don't upset yourself, Mum. You didn't mean anything by it, she knows that—don't you, Eleanor?"

"Yes, of course!" I said and, on impulse, leaned across and shook her hand. "Your question was both reasonable and appropriate. My response, however, was not. I'm at a loss to explain it. Please accept my apologies if I've made you feel uncomfortable."

She looked relieved. "Thank God for that, hen," she said. "I wasn't expecting tears in my kitchen today!"

"Aye, it's usually your cooking that makes me cry, Ma," Raymond said, and she laughed quietly. I cleared my throat.

"Your question took me unawares, Mrs. Gibbons," I said. "I never knew my father, and I know nothing about him, not even his name. Mummy is currently . . . let's just say she's hors de combat." I received blank looks from both of them—I was clearly not among Francophones. "I don't ever see her, she's . . . inaccessible," I explained. "We communicate once a week, but . . ."

"Of course—that would make anyone sad, love, of course it would," she said, nodding sympathetically. "Everyone needs their mum now and again, doesn't matter how old they are."

"On the contrary," I said, "if anything, weekly contact is too much for me. Mummy and I—we're . . . well, it's complicated . . ."

Mrs. Gibbons nodded sympathetically, wanting me to continue. I, on the other hand, knew that it was time to stop. An ice-cream van went past in the street, the chimes playing "Yankee Doodle," pitched a few painful hertz below the correct notes. I recalled the words, feathers in caps and macaroni, from some deep and completely useless vault of memories.

Raymond clapped his hands together in fake bonhomie.

"Right then, time's marching on. Mum, go and sit down—your program's about to start. Eleanor, could you maybe give me a hand and bring in the washing?"

I was glad to help, glad to be moving away from Mummy-related conversation. There were various chores Mrs. Gibbons needed assistance with—Raymond had elected to change the cats' litter trays and empty the bins, so I'd certainly drawn the long straw with the laundry.

Outside, the early evening sun was weak and pale. There was a row of gardens to the right and the left, stretching off in both directions. I placed the laundry basket on the ground and took the peg bag (on which, in looping cursive, someone had helpfully stitched "Pegs') and hung it on the line. The washing was dry and smelled of summer. I heard the syncopated thud of a football being kicked against a wall, and girls chanting as a skipping rope skimmed the ground. The distant chimes of the ice-cream van were now almost inaudible. Someone's back door slammed, and a man's voice shouted a furious reprimand at—one hoped—a dog. There was birdsong, a descant over the sounds of a television drifting through an open window. Everything felt safe, everything felt *normal*. How different Raymond's life had been from mine—a proper family, a mother and a father and a sister, nestled among other proper families. How different it was still; every Sunday, here, this.

Back indoors, I helped Raymond swap the sheets on his mother's bed for the clean ones I'd brought in from the line. Her bedroom was very pink and smelled of talcum powder. It was clean and nondescript—not like a hotel room, more like a bed and breakfast, I imagined. Save for a fat paperback and a packet of extra strong mints on the bedside table, there was nothing personal in the room, no clue to the owner's personality. It struck me that, in the nicest possible way, she didn't really have a personality; she was a mother, a kind, loving woman, about whom no one would ever say, "She was crazy, that Betty!" or, "You'll never guess what Betty's done now!" or, "After reviewing psychiatric reports, Betty was refused bail on grounds that she posed an extreme risk to the general public." She was, quite simply, a nice lady who'd raised a family and now lived quietly with her cats and grew vegetables. This was both nothing and everything.

"Does your sister help out with your mother, Raymond?" I asked. He was grappling with the duvet and I took it from him. There is a knack to such things. Raymond is a man without the knack. He put on the pillowcases (flowers, ruffles) instead.

"Nah," he said, concentrating. "She's got two kids, and they're a bit of a handful. Mark works offshore, so she's a single parent for weeks at a time, really. It's not easy. It'll be better when the kids are at school, she says."

"Ah," I said. "Do you—do you enjoy being an uncle, then?" Uncle Raymond: a somewhat unlikely role model, I felt. He shrugged.

"Yeah, they're good fun. There's not much to it, to be honest; I just slip them some cash at Christmas and birthdays, take them to the park a couple of times a month. Job done."

I would never be an aunt, of course. Probably just as well.

"You had a lucky escape with Mum and the photo albums this time, Eleanor," Raymond said. "She'll bore the pants off you next time about the grandkids, just you wait and see."

He was making a lot of assumptions there, I thought, but I let it pass. I looked at my watch, surprised to see it was after eight.

"I must be off, Raymond," I said.

"If you want to hang on for another hour or so, I'll be done here and we can get the bus together?" he said. I declined, naturally.

I went downstairs and thanked Mrs. Gibbons for "tea." She, in turn, thanked me profusely for coming and for helping with the chores.

"Eleanor, it's been lovely, so it has," she said. "I haven't been beyond the garden for months now—these knees of mine—so it's a pleasure to see a new face, and such a friendly one at that. You've been a great help around the house too—thanks, hen, thanks very much."

I smiled at her. Twice in one day, to be the recipient of thanks and warm regard! I would never have suspected that small deeds could elicit such genuine, generous responses. I felt a little glow inside—not a blaze, more like a small, steady candle.

"Come back anytime, Eleanor—I'm always in. You don't have to come with"—she jabbed a finger Raymond-ward—"*him*, just come yourself, if you like. You know where I am now. Don't be a stranger."

On impulse, I leaned forward and brushed my cheek (not the scarred one, the normal one) close to hers. It wasn't a kiss or an embrace, but it was as close as I was able to come.

"Cheerio!" she said. "Safe home, now!"

Raymond walked me to the end of the road to show me where the bus stop was located. I'd probably have a bit of a wait, it being Sunday, he said. I shrugged; I was used to waiting, and life has taught me to be a very patient person.

"See you tomorrow, then, Eleanor," he said.

I took out my travel pass and showed it to him. "Unlimited travel!" I said. He nodded, gave a small smile. Miraculously, the bus arrived. I raised my hand and climbed on board. I stared straight ahead as the bus pulled away to avoid any awkwardness with waving.

It had been quite a day. I felt drained, but something had crystallized in my mind. These new people,

new adventures . . . this contact. I found it overwhelming, but, to my surprise, not at all unpleasant. I'd
coped surprisingly well, I thought. I'd met new people, introduced myself to them, and we'd spent prob-
lem-free social time together. If there was one thing
I could take from today's experiences, it was this: I
was nearly ready to declare my intentions to the musician. The time for our momentous first encounter was
drawing ever closer.

# 11

I didn't see Raymond on Monday, or on Tuesday. I didn't think about him, although my mind did return to Sammy and to Mrs. Gibbons on occasion. I could, of course, visit either or both of them without Raymond being there. Indeed, both had stressed that to me on Sunday. But would it be better if he were by my side? I suspected that it would, not least because he could always fill a silence with banal, inane comments and questions should the need arise. In the meantime, I'd gone to the mobile telephone emporium with the least garish fascia in the closest location to the office and, on the highly suspect advice of a bored salesperson, had eventually purchased a reasonably priced handset and "package" which allowed me to make calls, access the Internet and also do various other things, most of which were of no interest to me. He'd mentioned apps and games; I asked about crosswords, but was very disappointed with his response. I was familiarizing myself with the manual for the new device, rather than completing the VAT details on Mr. Leonard's invoice, when, very much against my will, I became aware of the conversation going on around me, due to its excessive volume. It was, of all things, on the topic of our annual Christmas lunch.

"Yeah, but they have entertainment laid on there! And lots of other big groups go, so we can meet new people, have a laugh," Bernadette was saying.

Entertainment! I wondered if that would involve a band, and, if so, might it be *his* band? A very early Christmas miracle? Was this fate interceding once again? Before I could ask for details, Billy jumped in.

"You just want to cop off with some drunk guy from Allied Carpets under the mistletoe," Billy said. "There's no way I'm paying sixty quid a head for a dry roast turkey dinner and a cheesy afternoon disco. Not just so's you can scout for talent!"

Bernadette cackled and slapped him on the arm.

"No," she said, "it's not that. I just think it might be more fun if there's a bigger crowd there, that's all . . ."

Janey looked slyly at the others, thinking that I hadn't seen her. I saw her eyes flick up to my scars, as they often did.

"Let's ask Harry Potter over there," she said, not quite sotto voce, and then turned to address me.

"Eleanor! Hey, Eleanor! You're a bit of a girl about town, aren't you? What do you reckon: where should we go for the office Christmas lunch this year?"

I looked pointedly at the office wall calendar, which, this month, displayed a photograph of a green articulated lorry.

"It's the middle of summer," I said. "I can't say I've really given it any thought."

"Yeah," she said, "but we've got to get something booked up now, otherwise all the good places get taken and you get left with, like, Wetherspoons or a rubbish Italian."

"It's a matter of supreme indifference to me," I said. "I shan't be going anyway." I rubbed at the cracked skin between my fingers—it was healing, but the process was painfully slow.

"Oh, that's right," she said, "you never go, do you? I'd forgotten about that. You don't do the Secret Santa either. Eleanor the Grinch, that's what we ought to call you." They all laughed.

"I don't understand that cultural reference," I said. "However, to clarify, I'm an atheist, and I'm not consumer oriented, so the midwinter shopping festival otherwise known as Christmas is of little interest to me."

I went back to my work, hoping it would inspire them to do the same. They are like small children, easily distracted, and content to spend what feels like hours discussing trivialities and gossiping about people they don't know.

"Sounds like *somebody* had a bad experience in Santa's grotto back in the day," said Billy, and then, thankfully, the phone rang. I smiled sadly. He couldn't even begin to imagine the sort of bad experiences I'd had, *back in the day*.

It was an internal call: Raymond, asking if I wanted to go and visit Sammy again with him tonight. A Wednesday. I'd miss my weekly chat with Mummy. I'd never missed one, not in all these years. But then, what could she actually do about it, after all? There couldn't be much harm in skipping it, just this once, and Sammy was in need of nutritious food. I said yes.

≈

Our rendezvous was scheduled for five thirty. I'd insisted that we meet outside the post office, fearing the reaction of my coworkers were we to be observed leaving work together. It was a mild, pleasant evening, so we decided to walk to hospital, which would take only twenty minutes. Raymond was certainly in need of the exercise.

"How was your day, Eleanor?" he said, smoking as we walked. I changed sides, trying to position myself downwind of the noxious toxins.

"Fine, thank you. I had a cheese-and-pickle sandwich for lunch, with ready-salted crisps and a mango smoothie." He blew smoke out of the side of his mouth and laughed.

"Anything else happen? Or just the sandwich?"

I thought about this. "There was a protracted discussion about Christmas lunch venues," I said. "Apparently it's been narrowed down to TGI Fridays, because 'it's a laugh' "—here, I tried out a little finger-waggling gesture indicating quotation marks, which I'd seen Janey doing once and had stored away for future reference; I think I carried it off with aplomb—"or else the Bombay Bistro Christmas Buffet."

"Nothing says Christmas like a lamb biryani, eh?" Raymond said.

He stubbed out his cigarette, discarding it on the pavement. We arrived at the hospital and I waited while Raymond, typically disorganized, went into the shop on the ground floor. There really is no excuse for being unprepared. I had already gone to Marks & Spencer before meeting him, and had purchased some choice items there, including a tub of pumpkin seeds. I suspected Sammy was in dire need of zinc. Raymond came out swinging a carrier bag. In the lift, he opened it and showed me what he'd bought.

"Haribo, the *Evening Times*, big tub of sour cream and chive Pringles. What more could a man ask for, eh?" he said, looking quite proud of himself. I did not dignify this with a response.

We paused at the ward entrance; Sammy's bed was surrounded by visitors. He saw us and beckoned us over. I looked around, but the stern nurse with the stripy socks was nowhere to be seen. Sammy was reclining regally on a mound of pillows, addressing the assembled throng.

"Eleanor, Raymond—great to see you! Come and meet the family! This is Keith—the kiddies are at home with their mum—and this is Gary and Michelle, and this"—he indicated a blond woman who was texting with impressive focus on her mobile telephone— "is my daughter Laura."

I was aware of everyone smiling and nodding, and then they were shaking our hands, slapping Raymond's back. It was quite overwhelming. I'd put on my white cotton gloves, rather than use the hand gel—I reasoned

that I could run them through a boil wash as soon as
I got home. This occasioned a certain hesitancy in the
handshakes, which was strange—surely a cotton bar-
rier between our respective skin surfaces could only
be a good thing?

"Thanks so much for taking care of my dad, guys,"
the older brother, Keith, said, wiping his hands on the
front of his trousers. "It means a lot, to know he wasn't
on his own when it happened, that he had people
looking out for him."

"Hey, now," said Sammy, nudging him with his
elbow, "I'm not some doddery old invalid, you know.
I can look after myself." They smiled at one another.

"Course you can, Dad. I'm just saying, it's nice to
have a friendly face around sometimes, eh?"

Sammy shrugged, not conceding the point but
graciously allowing it to pass.

"I've got some good news for you two," Sammy
said to us, leaning back contentedly into his pillows
while Raymond and I deposited our carrier bags like
myrrh and frankincense at the foot of his bed. "I'm
getting out on Saturday!"

Raymond high-fived him, after some initial awkwardness whereby Sammy had no idea why a podgy
hand had been thrust in his face.

"He's coming to stay at mine for a couple of weeks,
just till he gets confident with the walking frame,"
his daughter Laura said, finally looking up from her
phone. "We're having a wee party to celebrate! You're

both invited, of course," she added, somewhat less than enthusiastically.

She was staring at me. I didn't mind. In fact, I actually prefer that to surreptitious, sneaky glances—from her, I got a full and frank appraisal, filled with fascination, but with no trace of fear or disgust. I brushed my hair off my face, so that she could get a better view.

"This Saturday?" I said.

"Now, Eleanor, don't you dare say you're busy," Sammy said. "No excuses. I want you both there. End of."

"Who are we to argue?" Raymond said, smiling. I thought about it. A party. The last party I'd been to—apart from that appalling wedding reception—was on Judy Jackson's thirteenth birthday. It had involved ice-skating and milkshakes, and hadn't ended well. Surely no one was likely to vomit or lose a finger at an elderly invalid's welcome home celebration?

"I shall attend," I said, inclining my head.

"Here's my card," Laura said, passing one each to Raymond and to me. It was black and glossy, embossed with gold leaf, and said *Laura Marston-Smith, Esthetic Technician, Hair Stylist, Image Consultant*, with her contact details set out below.

"Seven o'clock on Saturday, yeah? Don't bring anything, just yourselves."

I tucked the card carefully into my purse. Raymond had thrust his into his back pocket. He couldn't take his eyes off Laura, I noticed, apparently hypnotized rather in the manner of a mongoose before a snake. She was clearly aware of this. I suspected she was used to it, looking the way she did. Blond hair and large breasts are so clichéd, so obvious. Men like Raymond, pedestrian dullards, would always be distracted by women who looked like her, having neither the wit nor the sophistication to see beyond mammaries and peroxide.

Raymond tore his eyes away from Laura's décolletage and looked at the wall clock, then, pointedly, at me.

"We shall depart," I said, "and meet again on Saturday." Once again, there was an overwhelming onslaught of salutations and handshakes. Sammy, meanwhile, was rummaging in the bags we'd brought. He held up a packet of organic curly kale.

"What the hell is this?" he said, incredulous. *Zinc*, I whispered to myself. Raymond hustled me out of the ward rather brusquely, I felt, and before I'd even had a chance to mention that the squid salad would need to be eaten promptly. The ambient temperature in the hospital ward was very warm.

# 12

The next day, whilst waiting for the kettle to boil, my eye was drawn to a leaflet which had been discarded on top of the office recycling bag, alongside a pile of holiday brochures and well-thumbed gossip magazines. It was for a department store in town—not one I had ever frequented—and set out an introductory offer, featuring a frankly spectacular one-third reduction in the price of a "Deluxe Pamper Manicure." I tried and failed to imagine what a deluxe pamper manicure might involve. How might one introduce luxury and pampering into the process of shaping and painting a nail? It was, literally, beyond my imagining. I felt a thrill of excitement. There was only one way to find out. With my animal grooming regime in mind, I would turn my attention to my talons.

I had somewhat neglected my self-improvement plans of late, distracted by Sammy's unfortunate accident and the events which had resulted from it. But it was time to refocus on my goal: the musician. I indulged in the sin of pride for a moment. My nails grow exceedingly fast, and they are strong and shiny. I attribute this to a diet high in the requisite vitamins, minerals and fatty acids, which are obtained from my well-planned luncheon regime. My nails are a tribute to the culinary excellence of the British high street. Not being a vain person, I merely cut them with clippers when they grow too long to allow for comfortable data input, and file down the resulting sharp corners so that they do not snag on fabric or scrape my skin unpleasantly when I am bathing. So far, so perfectly adequate. My nails are always clean—clean nails, like clean shoes, are fundamental to self-respect. Whilst I am neither stylish nor fashionable, I am always clean; that way, at least, I can hold my head up when I take my place, however unexalted, in the world.

≈

I headed into town during my lunch break, eating my sandwich on the way in order to save time. On reflection, I wished that I had selected a less obtrusive filling; egg and cress was perhaps not the most judicious choice for a busy, warm train carriage, and both the sandwich and I were attracting disapproving looks from our fellow travelers. I abhor eating in public at the best of times, so the eight-minute journey was not a pleasant experience for anyone concerned.

I found the nail concession at the rear of the Beauty Hall, a vast chandelier-lit barn of mirrors, scents and noise. I felt like a trapped animal—a steer or a rabid dog—and imagined the chaos I'd cause if, careering wildly, I was corralled in there against my will. I clutched the leaflet tight in my fist, balled up inside my jerkin pocket.

"Nails Etcetera"—to what extras did the Latin term refer? I wondered—appeared to consist of two bored children in white tunics, a breakfast bar with four stools and a rack of polishes in every hue from clear to tar. I approached with caution.

"WelcometoNailsEtcetraHowCanIHelpYou-Today," said the smaller girl-child. It took me a moment to translate.

"Good afternoon," I said slowly, and in an exaggeratedly modulated voice, to give her a clue as to how one ought to speak in order to communicate effectively. She and her companion were both staring, their expressions a combination of alarm and . . . well, alarm, mainly. I smiled in what I hoped was a reassuring manner. They were so young, after all—perhaps this was some sort of work experience and they were awaiting the return of their teacher.

"I'd like a Deluxe Pamper Manicure, please," I said, as clearly as I could. There was a long, still pause where nothing happened. The shorter one was first to wake from her trance.

"Take a seat!" she said, indicating the nearest stool. Her companion remained transfixed. The shorter one (Casey, according to her name badge) bustled about distractedly and then perched opposite, having first set down a kidney bowl slopping with hot, soapy water. She swiveled the rack of polishes toward me.

"What color would you like?" she said. My eye was drawn to a bright green hue, the same shade as a poisonous Amazonian frog, the tiny, delightfully deadly ones. I handed it to her. She nodded. She wasn't actually chewing gum, but her demeanor was very much that of a gum chewer.

She took my hands and placed the tips of all ten fingers into the warm water. I kept a watchful eye to ensure that no other flesh made contact with the unknown detergent substances, for fear of inflaming my eczema. I sat there for several minutes, feeling rather foolish, while she rummaged in a nearby drawer and returned with a variety of stainless steel tools, carefully laid out on a tray. Her catatonic companion had finally sprung to life and was chatting enthusiastically to a coworker at a different concession; I couldn't discern the topic, but it seemed to prompt some eye-rolling and shrugging.

Casey deemed the moment apposite to remove my hands from the water, and she then laid them on a folded flannel. She carefully patted each fingertip dry. I wondered why she hadn't simply asked me to remove my hands, using her voice, and passed me the towel, so I could dry them using my hands, since I was enjoying, at current point of reporting, full use and motor function in all limbs and extremities. Perhaps that was what pampering meant, though—literally, not having to lift a finger.

Casey set to work with the tools, pushing back my cuticles and trimming them where required. I essayed some chitchat, aware that this was the done thing in the circumstances.

"Have you worked here long?" I asked.

"Two years," she said, to my astonishment—she appeared to be around fourteen years of age and, to the best of my knowledge, child labor was still outlawed in this country.

"And did you always want to be a . . ." I grappled for the word ". . . manicurist?"

"Nail technician," she corrected me. She was intent on her task and did not look at me while she talked, which I approved of enormously. There is categorically no need for eye contact when the person concerned is wielding sharp implements.

"I wanted either to work with animals or to be a nail technician," she continued. She had moved on to a hand massage now. More deluxe pampering, presumably, although I found it rather pointless and ineffectual, and was concerned for potential allergic reactions. Her hands were tiny, almost as small as mine (which are, unfortunately, abnormally small, like a dinosaur's). I would have preferred a man's hands: larger, stronger, firmer. Hairier.

"So yeah," she said, "I couldn't decide between animals or nails, so I asked my mum, and she said I should go for nail technician." She picked up an emery board and began to shape my nails. It was an awkward process, one that would have definitely been easier to do oneself.

"Is your mother an economist or a qualified careers adviser?" I said. Casey stared at me. "Because, if not, then I'm not sure that her advice was necessarily informed by the latest data on earnings projections and labor market demand," I said, quite concerned for her future prospects.

"She's a travel agent," Casey said firmly, as if that settled the matter. I let it drop—it was no concern of mine, after all, and she seemed happy enough at her work. The thought did strike me, as she painted on various coats of various varnishes, that she could have perhaps combined the two professions by becoming a dog groomer. However, I elected to keep my counsel on the matter. Sometimes, when you tried to help with suggestions, it could lead to misunderstandings, not all of them entirely pleasant.

She placed my hands into a small machine which was, I assumed, a hair dryer for nails, and a few minutes later the deluxe pampering was done. All in all, the experience had been rather underwhelming.

She advised me of the price—it was, frankly, extortionate. "I have a leaflet!" I said. She nodded, not even asking to check it, and deducted the requisite one-third, stating the revised amount, which still left me reeling. I reached for my shopper. She said "Stop!" in a very alarming fashion. I did.

"You'll smudge them," she said. She leaned forward. "I'll get your purse out for you, if you like?"

I was concerned that this might be some elaborate ruse to part me from even more of my hard-earned cash, so I watched her like the proverbial hawk as she reached inside my bag. Too late, I remembered the unfinished remains of the egg sandwich which lay within—she gagged ostentatiously as she removed my purse. A slight overreaction, I felt—yes, the odor which escaped was somewhat sulfurous, but still, no need for pantomime. I kept my eyes fixed on her fingers (unpainted, I noticed) as she extracted the required notes and replaced the purse in the shopper very carefully.

I stood up, ready to take my leave. Her erstwhile companion had returned, and cast a glance at my hands, their tips gleaming green. "Nice," she said, her tone and body language implying strongly that she had little interest in the topic. Casey became slightly more animated. "Would you like a loyalty card?" she said. "Have five manicures and the sixth one's free!"

"No thank you," I said. "I shan't be having a manicure again. I can do the same thing myself at home, better, for nothing." Their mouths fell open slightly, but with that I was off, making my way back out into the world, dodging the squirters and the sample-pushers on my way past the perfume counters. I longed to be outside in natural light and fresh air again. The gilded confines of the Beauty Hall were not my preferred habitat; like the chicken that had laid the eggs for my sandwich, I was more of a free-range creature.

≈

I got home after work and opened my wardrobe. What to wear to a party? I had two pairs of black trousers and five white blouses—well, they were white originally—which I wore to work. I had a comfortable pair of slacks, two T-shirts and two jumpers, which I wore at weekends. That left my special occasion outfit. I'd bought it for Loretta's wedding reception years ago, and had worn it on a handful of occasions since, including a special visit to the National Museum of Scotland. The exhibition of newly discovered Roman trove had been tremendous; the journey to Edinburgh, far less so.

The train interior had been more like a bus than the Orient Express, replete with hard-wearing fabrics in stain-concealing colors and gray plastic fittings. The worst thing, apart from the other travelers—my goodness, the hoi polloi do get about these days, and they eat and drink in public with very few inhibitions—was the incessant noise from the loudspeakers. It seemed there was an announcement every five minutes from the mythical conductor, imparting sagacious gems such as *large items should be placed in the overhead luggage racks*, or that *passengers should report any unattended items to the train crew as soon as possible*. I wondered at whom these pearls of wisdom were aimed; some passing extraterrestrial, perhaps, or a yak herder from Ulan Bator who had trekked across the steppes, sailed the North Sea and found himself on the Glasgow–Edinburgh service with literally no prior experience of mechanized transport to call upon?

The special occasion outfit was, I realized, somewhat outmoded now. Lemon was not a color that suited me particularly well—fine for nightgowns, worn in the privacy of my bedroom, but hardly suitable for a sophisticated gathering. I'd go to the shops tomorrow and purchase something new; I'd be able to wear it again when I was out at a restaurant or at the theater with my true love, so the money would not be wasted. Feeling happy with this decision, I made my usual *pasta con pesto* and listened to the *Archers*. There was a convoluted story line involving a very unconvincing Glaswegian milkman, and I did not particularly enjoy the episode. I'd washed up and settled down with a book about pineapples. It was surprisingly interesting. I like to read as widely as possible for many reasons, not least in order to broaden my vocabulary to assist with crossword solving. Then the silence was very rudely interrupted.

"Hello?" I said, somewhat tentatively.

"Oh, so it's 'Hello,' is it? 'Hello'—that's all you've got to say to me? And where the hell were you last night, lady? Hmm?" She was playing to the gallery again.

"Mummy," I said. "How are you?" I tried my best to steady myself.

"Never mind how I am. Where were you?"

"I'm sorry, Mummy," I said, trying to keep my voice even. "I was . . . I was with a friend, visiting another friend in hospital, actually."

"Oh, Eleanor," she said, her voice oozingly oleaginous, "you don't *have* friends, darling. Now come on, tell me where you *really* were, and I want the truth this time. Were you doing something naughty? Tell Mummy, there's a good girl."

"Honestly, Mummy, I was out with Raymond"—there was a snort—"visiting this nice old man in hospital. He fell in the street and we helped him and—"

"SHUT YOUR LYING LITTLE CAKE HOLE!" I flinched, dropped the book, picked it up again.

"You know what happens to liars, don't you, Eleanor? You remember?" Her voice was back to sickly sweet. "I don't mind how bad the truth is, but I won't tolerate lies, Eleanor. You of all people should know that, even after all this time."

"Mummy, I'm sorry if you don't believe me, but it's true. Raymond and I went to hospital to visit a man we'd helped when he had an accident. It's true, I swear it!"

"Really?" she drawled. "Well, that's just delightful, isn't it? You can't be bothered to talk to your own mother, and yet you spend your Wednesday evenings visiting some geriatric, accident-prone stranger? Charming."

"Please, Mummy, let's not fight. How are you? Have you had a good day?"

"I don't want to talk about *me*, Eleanor. I already know all about *me*. I want to talk about *you*. How is your project coming along? Any news for Mummy?"

I might have known she'd remember. How much should I tell her? Everything, I supposed.

"I went to his house, Mummy," I said. I heard the click of a lighter and then a long exhaled breath. I could almost smell the smoke from her Sobranie.

"Oooh," she said. "Interesting." She took in another lungful and expelled it with a sigh. "Who's this 'he'"?

"He's a musician, Mummy." I didn't want to tell her his name quite yet—there is a power in naming things, and I wasn't quite ready to cede it to her yet, to hear those precious syllables rolled in her mouth, for her to spit them out again. "And he's handsome and clever and, well, I think he's the perfect man for me, really. I knew it as soon as I saw him."

"That all sounds rather marvelous, darling. And you went to his house, did you? Tell me, what did you find there?"

I sniffed. "The thing is, Mummy . . . I didn't actually . . . go inside." This wasn't going to be easy. She liked doing bad things, and I didn't. It was as simple as that. I spoke quickly, hoping to head off the inevitable criticism. "I just wanted to have a quick look, make sure he lived somewhere app . . . appropriate," I said, stumbling over the words in my haste to get them out.

She sighed. "And how are you supposed to know whether it's nice if you didn't go inside? You always were overcautious and lily-livered, darling," she said, sounding bored.

I looked at my hands. The chipped green nails looked so garish in this light.

"What you have to do, Eleanor," she said, "is grasp the nettle. Do you know what I mean by that?"

"I think so," I whispered.

"I'm simply telling you that you mustn't keep pussyfooting around, Eleanor." She sighed. "Life is all about taking decisive action, darling. Whatever you want to do, do it—whatever you want to take, grab it. Whatever you want to bring to an end, END IT. And live with the consequences."

She started to talk quietly, speaking so softly that I could hardly hear her. This, I knew from experience, did not bode well.

"This man . . ." she murmured. "This man sounds as if he has some potential, but, like most people, he'll be weak. That means that you have to be strong, Eleanor. Strength conquers weakness—that's a simple fact of life, isn't it?"

"I suppose so," I said sullenly, pulling a face. Childish, I know, but Mummy does tend to bring out the worst in me. The musician was very handsome and very talented. I knew, as soon as I set eyes on him, that we were destined to be together. Fate would see to that. I didn't need to take any more . . . decisive action, apart from ensuring that our paths crossed again— once we met properly, the rest was, surely, already written in the stars. I suspected that Mummy wasn't going to be pleased with this approach, but I was more than accustomed to that. I heard her breathe in, then out, and felt the soft menace through the ether.

"Don't you go getting sidetracked, now, Eleanor— don't go ignoring Mummy, will you? Oh, you think you're so smart now, don't you, with your *job* and your *new friends*. But you're not smart, Eleanor. You're someone who lets people down. Someone who can't be trusted. Someone who failed. Oh yes, I know exactly what you are. And I know how you'll end up. Listen, the past isn't over. The past is a living thing. Those lovely scars of yours—they're from the past, aren't they? And yet they still live on your plain little face. Do they still hurt?"

I shook my head, but said nothing.

"Oh, they do—I know they do. Remember how you got them, Eleanor. Was it worth it? For *her*? Oh, there's room on your other cheek for a bit more hurt, isn't there? Turn the other cheek for Mummy, Eleanor, there's a good girl."

And then there was only silence.

# 13

On the bus to work on Friday, I felt strangely calm. I hadn't drunk vodka after the chat with Mummy, but only because I didn't have any, and I didn't want to go out alone in the dark to buy some. Always alone, always dark. So, instead, I had made a cup of tea and read my book, distracted occasionally by my flashing green fingernails as I turned the pages. I'd had enough of tropical fruit for the time being, and needed something more conducive to matters of the heart. *Sense and Sensibility*. It's another one of my favorites: top five, certainly. I love the story of Elinor and Marianne. It all ends happily, which is highly unrealistic, but, I must admit, narratively satisfying, and I understand why Ms. Austen adhered to the convention. Interestingly, despite my wide-ranging literary tastes, I haven't come across many heroines called Eleanor, in any of the variant spellings. Perhaps that's why the name was chosen for me.

After a few, familiar chapters, I went to bed and did not sleep at all. A night without repose, however, seemed to have no ill effects, surprisingly, and I felt bright and alert as the bus made its way through the morning traffic. Perhaps I was one of those people, like the late Baroness Thatcher, who simply did not require sleep? I picked up a copy of the free newspaper that is always discarded on bus seats, and began to flick through it. An orange woman I'd never heard of had got married for the eighth time. A captive panda had apparently "reabsorbed" its own fetus, thereby ending its pregnancy—I looked out of the window for a moment as I tried and failed to understand the reproductive system of the panda—and, on page ten, evidence had been uncovered of the systematic and widespread abuse of underage boys and girls in a series of care homes. The news stories were reported in that order.

I shook my head, and was about to discard the newspaper when a small advertisement caught my eye. The Cuttings, it said, with a logo of a bullet train hurtling along a track. I noticed it because the answer to twelve across in yesterday's crossword had been *Shinkansen*. Such small coincidences can pepper a life with interest. I looked at the content, which appeared to be an announcement of forthcoming events at said venue. Sandwiched between two artistes I'd never heard of was a listing for Friday. Tonight.

There was the name of a band—obviously, I'd never heard of them—and there, in smaller font, was the musician! I dropped the paper, picked it up again. No one had noticed. I ripped out the advert, folded it carefully and placed it in the inside pocket of my shopper. This was it, the opportunity I'd been waiting for. Written in the stars, delivered to me by fate. This bus, this morning . . . and tonight.

I looked up the venue when I got to the office. It seemed that he would be playing at 8 p.m. I needed to shop for a party—and now a gig—outfit after work, which did not leave much time. Judging by the website, The Cuttings seemed to be the sort of place where one would feel most comfortable when fashionably attired. How, then, would I manage to be there for eight, dressed and ready? Ready to meet him? Was it too soon? Should I wait until another time, prepare properly? I'd read somewhere that one only gets a single chance to make a first impression—I'd dismissed the trite phrase at the time, but perhaps there was some truth in it. If the musician and I were going to be a couple, our first encounter needed to be a memorable one.

I nodded to myself, having made up my mind. I'd go to the shops straight after work, buy a new outfit and wear it to the concert. Oh, Eleanor, it couldn't be that easy, could it? I knew from experience that life was never this straightforward, so I tried to anticipate any potential problems and how best I might address them. What would I do with the clothes I was currently wearing? The answer came to me easily: my shopper was big enough to hold them. What about dinner? I am not a woman who functions well on an empty stomach, and it would be embarrassing to faint at his feet for any reason other than an excess of emotion. Well, couldn't I purchase some food from a café after work, and still manage to arrive at The Cuttings for 7:45 p.m.? Yes, I could. That would allow me plenty of time to select a seat near the front for the best possible view. My view of him, and his view of me, of course. All of the problems solved.

I couldn't resist a quick look online to see if he was as excited as I was about tonight. Ah, thank you, Twitter:

> @johnnieLrocks
> Soundcheck: done. Haircut:
> done. Get your fat backsides
> down to Cuttings tonight,
> mofos.
> #nextbigthing
> #handsomebastard

A man of few words. I had to google "mofo" and must confess to being slightly alarmed by the result. Still, what did I know of the wild ways of rock stars? They used an unfamiliar argot that he'd teach me in due course, no doubt. Could the lessons start tonight? It was hard to believe that, in a matter of a few hours, I'd be in his presence. Ah, the thrill of anticipation!

I had a missive for him in my shopper which I hadn't sent yet. Another sign that fate was smiling on me today. Earlier in the week, I'd copied out a verse for him, one I'd always loved, using a Bic Biro. What a cost-effective miracle of engineering this instrument is! I'd selected the card with care: it was blank, and the front displayed an etching of a most endearing hare—long ears, powerful legs and a surprisingly assertive face. It was gazing upward at the moon and stars, its expression impossible to fathom.

Greeting cards are preposterously expensive, given that they are fabricated from a small piece of printed cardboard. You get an envelope with it, I suppose, but still. You would have to work for almost half an hour in a minimum-wage occupation in order to earn enough to purchase a nice greeting card and a second-class stamp. This was a revelation; I'd never actually sent a card to anyone before. Now that I would be seeing him tonight, however, I had no need to attach a postage stamp. I could present my humble gift in person.

Emily Dickinson's beautiful poem is called "Wild Nights—Wild Nights!" and combines two elements of which I am inordinately fond: punctuation, and the theme of finding, at long last, a soul mate.

Lovely. I read the poem over again, licked the glue of the envelope with care—it was deliciously bitter—and then wrote his name on the front in my best handwriting. I hesitated as I put it back in my shopper. Was tonight really the best night for poetry? My reluctance was strange; the card was bought and paid for, after all. I wondered, however, whether I might be better off waiting to see what happened at the gig before taking things to an epistolary level. There was no need to be reckless.

≈

Five o'clock took forever to arrive. I traveled on the underground into town for speed, and went into the closest department store to the station, the same one where I'd purchased my laptop. It was 5:20 p.m., and the store would close in less than an hour. Womenswear was on the first floor (when did Ladieswear become Womenswear? I wondered) and I took the escalator, being unable to find the stairs. The shop floor was vast, and I decided to request assistance. The first woman I saw was matronly, and did not seem well placed to dispense fashion advice. The second was in her late teens or early twenties, and therefore too callow to advise me. The third, in the manner of Goldilocks, was just right—around my age, well groomed, sensible-looking. I approached with caution.

"Excuse me, I wonder if I could possibly ask for your assistance?" I said.

She stopped folding sweaters and turned to me, smiling insincerely.

"I'm attending a concert at a fashionable venue, and I wondered if you might assist me with the selection of an appropriate ensemble?"

Her smile broadened and looked more genuine.

"Well, we do offer a personal shopper service," she said. "I could make you an appointment, if you like?"

"Oh no," I said, "it's for this evening. I really do need something right now, I'm afraid." She looked me up and down.

"Where is it that you're going?"

"The Cuttings," I said proudly. She stuck out her bottom lip, nodded once, slowly.

"What are you, a twelve?" I nodded, impressed that she had been able to size me up so accurately by sight alone. She checked her watch.

"Follow me," she said. It seemed that there were a variety of stores within the store, and she took me to the least prepossessing outlet. "OK, off the top of my head," she said, "these . . ." a pair of ridiculously slender black denim trousers ". . . with this . . ." a black top, similar to a T-shirt but in faux silk, with a keyhole of fabric missing from the back.

"Really?" I said. "I was thinking more along the lines of a nice dress, or a skirt and blouse." She looked me up and down again.

"Trust me," she said.

The changing room was small and smelled of unwashed feet and air freshener. The jeans looked too small but, miraculously, they stretched around me and I was able to fasten them. The top was loose, with a high neck. I felt appropriately covered up, if nothing else, although I couldn't see the cutout section at the back. I looked exactly like everyone else. I supposed that was the point. I kept the outfit on, pulled off the tags and placed them on the floor, then folded up my work clothes and put them into my shopper. I picked up the tags for the woman to process on her cash register.

She was hovering outside when I emerged. "What do you think?" she said. "Looks good, doesn't it?"

"I'll take them," I said, handing her the bar codes.

I had forgotten about the security devices clipped onto the clothes, however, and we had quite a struggle to remove them. I had to come behind the desk, in the end, and kneel backward beside her so she could detach them using the magnetic machine fixed to the counter. We ended up laughing about it, actually. I don't think I've ever laughed in a shop before. After I'd paid, trying not to think about how much money I'd spent, she came out from behind the desk again.

"D'you mind if I say something? It's just . . . shoes."

I looked down. I was wearing my work shoes, the flat, black, comfortable pair with the Velcro fastenings.

"What's your name?" she said. I was bemused. Why was my name relevant to a footwear purchase? She was waiting, expecting an answer.

"It's Eleanor," I admitted with great reluctance, having considered giving a false name or nom de plume. I certainly wasn't going to tell her my surname.

"The thing is, Eleanor, you need an ankle boot with skinny jeans, really," she said, as seriously as though she were a hospital consultant giving medical advice. "D'you want to come over to Footwear and take a look?" I hesitated. "I'm not on commission or anything," she said quietly, "I just . . . I just think it'll really finish off the outfit if you've got the right shoes."

"Accessories maketh the woman, eh?" I said. She didn't smile.

She showed me boots that made me laugh out loud, so ridiculous were they in both heel height and narrowness of fit. Finally, we agreed on a pair that were sufficiently stylish but in which I could also walk without risk of spinal injury, thereby meeting both of our requirements. Sixty-five pounds! Good grief, I thought, as I handed over my card again. Some people have to live on that for a week.

I shoved my black shoes into my shopper. I saw her eyeing that too, then looking over at the handbag section. "Oh, I'm afraid not," I said, "I've exhausted my funds for the time being."

"Ah, well," she said, "just stash it in the cloakroom and you'll be fine." I had no idea what she meant, but time's winged chariot was hurrying near.

"Thank you very much indeed for your assistance, Claire," I said, leaning forward to read her name badge. "It's been invaluable."

"You're welcome, Eleanor," she said. "One last thing: the store closes in ten minutes, but if you're quick, you can nip down and get a wee makeover before you head out—Beauty's on the ground floor beside the exit. Go to Bobbi Brown, tell them Claire sent you."

With that she was off, the till already spewing out its reckoning of the day's takings, bolstered in part by my own not inconsiderable contribution.

I asked to speak to Bobbi, and the woman at the makeup counter giggled.

"We've got a right one here," she said, to no one in particular.

There were so many mirrors, I wondered if that might encourage a person to talk to themselves.

"Sit yourself up there, my love," she said, pointing to a ridiculously high stool. I managed to clamber aboard, but it was not a dignified procedure, and I was somewhat hindered by my new boots. I sat on my hands, to hide them—the red, broken skin seemed to burn under the harsh overhead lighting, which showed up every flaw, every damaged inch.

She pushed my hair out of my face. "Right then," she said, looking me over, too close. "D'you know, that won't even be a problem. Bobbi's got some marvelous concealers that can match any skin tone. I can't get rid of it, but I can certainly minimize it."

I wondered if she always talked about herself in the third person.

"Are you talking about my face?" I said.

"No, silly, your scar. Your face is lovely. You've got very clear skin, you know. Now, just watch this." She had a tool belt around her waist in the manner of a joiner or plumber, and her tongue poked out of the corner of her mouth as she worked.

"We've only got ten minutes till the store closes," she said, "so I'll focus on camouflage and eyes. D'you like a smoky eye?"

"I don't like anything to do with smoking," I said, and, bizarrely, she laughed again. Strange woman.

"You'll see . . ." she said, pushing my head back, asking me to look up, look down, turn to the side . . . there was so much touching, with so many different implements, and she was so close that I could smell her minty gum, not quite masking the coffee she'd drunk earlier. A bell rang, and she swore. The intercom announced that the store was now closed.

"Time's up, I'm afraid," she said, stepping back to admire her handiwork. She passed me a hand mirror. I didn't really recognize myself. The scar was barely noticeable, and my eyes were heavily rimmed and ringed with charcoal, reminding me of a program I'd watched recently about lemurs. My lips were painted the color of Earl Haig poppies.

"Well," she said, "what do you think?"

"I look like a small Madagascan primate, or perhaps a North American raccoon," I said. "It's charming!"

She laughed so much she had to cross her legs, and she shooed me down from the chair and toward the door.

"I'm supposed to try and sell you the products and brushes," she said. "If you want any, come back tomorrow and ask for Irene!"

I nodded, waved good-bye. Whoever Irene was, there was literally more chance of me purchasing weapons-grade plutonium from her.

# 14

The musician must have been experiencing a maelstrom of emotions at this moment. A shy, modest, self-effacing man, a man who is forced to perform because of his talent, to share it with the world, not because he wants to, but because he simply has to. He sings in the way that a bird sings; his music is a sweet, natural thing that comes like rain, like sunlight, something that, perfectly, just *is*. I thought about this as I ate my impromptu dinner. I was in a fast-food restaurant for the first time in my adult life, an enormous and garish place just around the corner from the music venue. It was mystifyingly, inexplicably busy. I wondered why humans would willingly queue at a counter to request processed food, then carry it to a table which was not even set, and then eat it from the paper? Afterward, despite having paid for it, *the customers themselves* are responsible for clearing away the detritus. Very strange.

After some contemplation, I had opted for a square of indeterminate white fish, which was coated in bread crumbs and deep fried and then inserted between an overly sweet bread bun, accompanied, bizarrely, by a processed cheese slice, a limp lettuce

leaf and some salty, tangy white slime which bordered on obscenity. Despite Mummy's best efforts, I
am no epicure; however, surely it is a culinary truth
universally acknowledged that fish and cheese do
not go together? Someone really ought to tell Mr.
McDonald. There was nothing to tempt me from
the choice of desserts, so I opted instead for a coffee,
which was bitter and lukewarm. Naturally, I had
been about to pour it all over myself but, just in time,
had read the warning printed on the paper cup, alert-
ing me to the fact that hot liquids can cause injury. A
lucky escape, Eleanor! I said to myself, laughing quietly. I began to suspect that Mr. McDonald was a
very foolish man indeed, although, judging from the
undiminished queue, a wealthy one.

I checked my watch, then picked up my shopper
and put on my jerkin. I left the remains of my dinner
where it was—what, after all, is the point of eating
out if you have to clear up yourself? You might as well
have stayed at home.

It was time.

~

The flaw in my plan, the hamartia, was this: there
were no tickets available. The man at the box office
actually laughed at me.

"It's been sold out for a couple of days now, love,"
he said. I explained, patiently and slowly, that I only
wanted to watch the first half, the opening act, and
suggested that they'd surely be able to admit one

additional person, but it was impossible, apparently—
fire regulations. For the second time in days, I felt
tears come. The man laughed again.

"Don't cry, love," he said. "Honestly, they're not
even that good." He leaned over confidentially. "I
helped the singer bring his gear in from his car this
afternoon. Bit of an arsehole, to be honest with you.
You shouldn't let a wee bit of success go to your head,
that's all I'm saying. Nice to be nice, eh?"

I nodded, wondering which singer he was talking
about, and moved to the bar area to gather my thoughts.
I wouldn't gain entry without a ticket, that much was
clear. And there were no tickets available. I ordered a
Magners drink, remembering from last time that I'd
be required to pour it myself. The barman was well
over six feet tall and had created strange, enormous
holes in his earlobes by inserting little black plastic
circles in order to push back the skin. For some reason, I was reminded of my shower curtain.

This comforting thought of home gave me the
courage to examine his tattoos, which snaked across
his neck and down both arms. The colors were very
beautiful, and the images were dense and complex.
How marvelous to be able to read someone's skin, to
explore the story of his life across his chest, his arms,
the softness at the back of his neck. The barman had
roses and a treble clef, a cross, a woman's face . . . so
much detail, so little unadorned flesh. He saw me
looking, smiled.

"Got any yourself?"

I shook my head, smiled back and hurried off to a table with my drink. His words resonated in my head. Why didn't I have any tattoos? I had never given it a moment's thought, and I'd never consciously decided either to have or not have one. The more I thought about it, the more I was drawn to the idea. Perhaps I could have one on my face, something complex and intricate which incorporated my scar, making it a feature? Or, better still, I could have one done somewhere secret. I liked that idea. The inside of my thigh, the back of my knee, the sole of my foot, perhaps.

I finished the Magners and the barman came over to remove my glass.

"Same again?" he asked.

"No thank you," I said. "Can I ask you something?" I stopped picking off the remains of the nail polish. "Two things, actually. One: does it hurt, and two, how much does a tattoo cost?" He nodded, as if he'd been expecting my questions.

"Hurts like fuck, I'm not gonna lie," he said. "In terms of cost, it depends on what you're having done—there's a big difference between *Mum* on your bicep and a massive tiger across your back, you know?"

I nodded; this made perfect sense.

"Lot of cowboys around, though," he said, warming to his theme. "You want to go to Barry, in Thornton Street, if you're getting one. Barry's sound."

"Thank you very much," I said. I hadn't expected this outcome from the evening, but then life has a way of surprising you sometimes.

Outside, I realized there was no point in waiting around. The musician would doubtless be going on to a glamorous after-party, somewhere that glittered and pulsed, to celebrate. As of tonight, I was only familiar with two venues, McDonald's and the unpleasant bar I'd visited with Raymond, and it was hardly likely to be held in either of those.

Come on, Eleanor, I told myself. Tonight was simply not meant to be. The card would remain undelivered in my shopper for the time being. I assuaged my disappointment with the consoling thought that, when it did finally happen, the encounter would be perfect, and not some short notice, ad hoc meeting in a music club. Also, I'd have broken in my new boots by then, and so would be able to walk normally. I was already tired of the glances my semi-hobbled gait had been attracting.

@johnnieLrocks
Wondering if my stuff is a wee
bit too challenging for some
people yeah? Dont go to gigs
if you can't handle new
sounds. #misunderstood
#truth

@johnnieLrocks
Happens to all the greats
when they first start out, tho
#Dylan #Springsteen
#amgigging

# 15

I took a taxi home in the end. It was only once I got indoors that I remembered I had no vodka. I simply went to bed. I awoke early the next day and decided to walk to the local shop to buy provisions, having disrupted my usual routine because of the failed attempt to meet the singer yesterday. I picked up some milk, a packet of bread rolls and a tin of spaghetti hoops. I had intended to buy Alphabetti Spaghetti, but, on impulse, chose hoops instead. It's good to keep an open mind, although I'm well aware that hoops and letters all taste the same. I'm not stupid.

The owner was a charming Bangladeshi man with an interesting birthmark. After all these years, we were of course on cordial terms, which was pleasant. I placed the goods on the counter and scanned the shelves behind him while he rang up the items on the till. He smiled and announced the total.

"Thank you," I said, and pointed to the shelves behind him. "May I also please have two of the liter bottles of Glen's vodka?"

His eyebrows shot to the top of his head momentarily, and then his face became impassive.

"I'm afraid I can't sell alcohol to you, Miss Oliphant," he said, looking not a little embarrassed. I smiled.

"Mr. Dewan, I'm both extremely flattered and somewhat concerned as to the state of your eyesight," I said. "I have, in fact, only just entered my thirty-first year." I felt a little bubble of pleasure shimmer inside me. Bobbi Brown had said that I had nice skin (the live sections, at any rate), and now Mr. Dewan had mistaken me for a teenager!

"It's ten past nine in the morning," he said, quite curtly—a small queue had built up behind me.

"I'm well aware of the time," I said. "Might I be so bold as to suggest that what your customers choose to have for breakfast is none of your concern?"

He spoke so quietly that I had to lean in to hear him.

"It's illegal to sell alcohol before 10 a.m., Miss Oliphant. I could lose my license."

"Really?" I said, fascinated. "I had absolutely no idea! I'm afraid my knowledge of licensing law is patchy at best." He stared at me.

"That'll be 5.49 pounds," he repeated, took my ten-pound note, and rendered my change, all the while keeping his eyes firmly on his shoes. I sensed a change in our hitherto cordial relationship but was at a loss to understand why. He didn't even say good-bye.

~

Annoyingly, it meant that I would have to go out again later to get my vodka. Why couldn't you just purchase it in the same way that you bought, say, milk—to wit, at any shop at any time that it was open? Ridiculous. I suppose it's to ensure that alcoholics are protected from themselves for at least a few hours each day; although, rationally, that makes no sense. If I were chemically and psychologically addicted to alcohol, I'd ensure I had a ready supply to hand at all times, buying in bulk and stockpiling. It was an illogical law; really, what was the difference between buying vodka at ten past nine in the morning and at ten past ten?

Vodka is, for me, merely a household necessity, like a loaf of bread or a packet of tea. The very best thing about it is that it helps me to sleep. Sometimes, when night comes, I lie there in the darkness and I can't prevent myself remembering: fear, and pressure, but mostly fear. On nights like those, Mummy's voice hisses inside my head, and another voice, a smaller, timid one, nestles in close to my ear, so close that I can feel her hot, panicky breath moving across the tiny hairs that transmit the sound, so close she barely needs to whisper. That small voice; it breaks apart, pleading: *Eleanor, please help me, Eleanor* . . . over and over and over again. On those nights I need the vodka, or else I'd break apart too.

≈

I decided to carry on walking toward the big supermarket, which was around twenty minutes away. It would be a more efficient use of my time, allowing me to purchase everything at once, rather than going home and having to go out again. My shopper was feeling rather heavy, and so I put it down and unfolded the collapsible frame that was stored in one of the inside compartments. I built it up, fitted the bag, *et voilà*! A shopper on wheels. It made a rather inharmonious trundling sound, but this was more than compensated for by the efficacy with which it transported heavier items.

The supermarket in question carried a wide range of quality goods—not just food and drink, but toasters, sweaters, Frisbees and novels. It wasn't a Tesco Metro, it was a Tesco Extra. It was, in short, one of my favorite places in the world.

# 16

Tesco! Bright lights, clear labeling, 3 FOR 2 and BOGOF and ANY 3 FOR £5. I took a trolley, because I enjoy pushing them. I stuck my shopper in the child's seat, and it was quite tricky to peer round it, but that only made the exercise more fun. I didn't go straight to the vodka; instead, I perused each aisle in turn, starting upstairs in the electrical goods section and then, downstairs, taking my time over tampons and tomato feed and Ainsley Harriot's Spice Sensation couscous.

I gravitated toward the in-store bakery and stopped dead by the well-fired morning rolls, barely able to believe my eyes. The musician! How blessed I am to live in a compact city, where lives can intersect so readily. Ah, but who's to say it was accidental, I thought. As previously noted, the machinations of fate are often beyond human ken, and perhaps greater forces were at work here, throwing us into one another's path in the unlikeliest of circumstances. Buffeted by fate, I felt like a Thomas Hardy heroine this morning (although I silently and passionately entreated fate not to create any future encounters for us in the vicinity of exploding sheep).

Keeping my eyes on the musician, I ducked behind my protruding child-seated shopper in the trolley, then slowly rolled toward him. I stood as close as I dared. He looked tired and pale, but was still handsome, albeit in a rugged, very casually groomed way. He tossed a loaf of sliced white into his basket and glided off toward the meat counter. Once again, I found myself at a disadvantage. I was not physically ready to introduce myself, being somewhat less than soigné at this hour on a weekend, and not wearing my new clothes or boots. Nor had I prepared an opening conversational gambit. I did not even have the greeting card in my bag to pass to him. Lesson: I must be prepared at all times.

I decided it would be wise to stop following him, despite my overwhelming curiosity as to what he would purchase next, as I feared my meta-trolley might be somewhat conspicuous. Instead, I went straight to Wines and Spirits and bought three big bottles of premium-brand vodka. I had only intended to purchase two bottles of Glen's, but the promotional offer on Smirnoff was remarkable. Oh, Mr. Tesco, I simply cannot resist your marvelous bargains.

As luck would have it, the musician was waiting at the checkouts when I arrived. There was one person behind him, so I took refuge in the same queue with this convenient buffer between us. What a well-chosen selection of shopping! Eggs, bacon, orange juice ("with bits"—bits of what? I wondered) and Nurofen tablets. I had to stop myself from leaning forward and explaining that he was wasting his money—this branded nonsteroidal anti-inflammatory drug was in fact simply ibuprofen 200 mg, the generic version of which was readily available for sale at perhaps one-quarter of the price. But that couldn't be my opening. I'd need something more alluring, more memorable, for our first exchange.

He took out a beautifully battered leather wallet and paid with a credit card, although I noted that the total sum was less than eight pounds. I expect, rather like a member of the royal family, that he is simply too important to carry cash. During his exchange with the cashier—a middle-aged woman who, rather bizarrely, seemed completely oblivious to the manifest charms of the handsome man standing before her—I noticed another missed opportunity. This time, I couldn't resist. I took out my brand-new phone, accessed my pristine Twitter account and waited till he had paid and had left the building. I typed quickly and pressed send.

@eloliph
A Tesco Club Card is a thing of
beauty and a joy forever. You
should DEFINITELY sign up for
one. A Concerned Friend xx

@johnnieLrocks
Tesco: stop pushing Big
Brother spy-slash-loyalty card
on here. It like living in a
police state, yo #hungover
#leavemealone
#fightthepower

# 17

Of course, I already knew that we lived not far from one another, but it had not occurred to me that our lives might intersect in any unplanned way. Sometimes this place feels more like a village than a city, really. So we shared a love of Tesco. Unsurprising. I wondered where else our existences overlapped. Perhaps we frequented the same post office, for example, or had our prescriptions dispensed by the same pharmacist? I reflected again on the importance of being ready, at any time, for an encounter, of looking my best and having something appropriate to say. I was going to need more than one outfit.

Sammy's homecoming party tonight was at seven, and Raymond had offered to meet me beforehand near Laura's house. At first, I thought that he was being surprisingly and uncharacteristically thoughtful, but then I realized that he simply didn't want to arrive alone. Some people, weak people, fear solitude. What they fail to understand is that there's something very liberating about it; once you realize that you don't need anyone, you can take care of yourself. That's the thing: it's *best* just to take care of yourself. You can't protect other people, however hard you try. You try, and you fail, and your world collapses around you, burns down to ashes.

That said, I did sometimes wonder what it would be like to have someone—a cousin, say, or a sibling—to call on in times of need, or even just to spend unplanned time with. Someone who knows you, cares about you, who wants the best for you. A houseplant, however attractive and robust, doesn't quite cut the mustard, unfortunately. Pointless even to speculate, though. I had no one, and it was futile to wish it were otherwise. After all, it was no more than I deserved. And, really, I was fine, fine, fine. Was I not here, after all, out in the world, and going to a party? Dressed in my finery and awaiting an acquaintance? Look out, Saturday night, here comes Eleanor Oliphant! I allowed myself a little smile.

In the end, my mood soured somewhat, as I had to wait twenty-five minutes for Raymond. I find lateness exceptionally rude; it's so disrespectful, implying unambiguously that you consider yourself and your own time to be so much more valuable than the other person's. Raymond eventually clambered out of a minicab at quarter past seven, just when I was on the verge of leaving.

"Hiya, Eleanor!" he said, full of good cheer. He was clutching a clinking carrier bag and a bunch of cheap carnations. Laura had specifically told us not to bring anything. Why had he ignored her polite request?

"Raymond, the invitation was for 7 p.m.," I said. "We arranged to meet here at 6:50 p.m., and we are now inexcusably late on account of your tardiness. It's very disrespectful to our hostess!" I could not bear to look at him. Inexplicably, he laughed.

"Chill, Eleanor," he said.

I mean, really. Chill!

"No one ever goes to a party on time. It's ruder to do that than to be fifteen minutes late, believe me." He looked me up and down. "You look nice," he said. "Different . . ."

I did not appreciate this crass attempt to change the subject. "Shall we go?" I said, quite curtly. He ambled along beside me, smoking as usual.

"Eleanor," he said, "honestly, don't stress about it. When people say seven o'clock, they mean, like, seven thirty, earliest. We'll probably be the first people there!"

I was thrown by this.

"But why?" I said. "Why on earth would you state one time whilst meaning something completely different, and how are people supposed to know?"

Raymond extinguished his cigarette and dropped it into the gutter. He put his head on one side, considering.

"I don't know how you know, now I come to think of it," he said. "You just do." He thought some more. "It's like, you know when you invite people over, and you say come at eight, it's always a nightmare if some . . . if a person actually arrives at eight, because you're not ready, you haven't had time to tidy up, take the rubbish out or whatever? It feels quite . . . passive aggressive, almost, if someone actually arrives on time or—oh God—early?"

"I have absolutely no idea what you're talking about," I said. "If I were to invite people to attend at eight, then I'd be ready for them at eight. It's sloppy time management otherwise."

Raymond shrugged. He had made no effort whatsoever to dress smartly for the party, sporting his usual uniform of training shoes (green ones) and a T-shirt. This one said *Carcetti for Mayor*. Unfathomable. He was wearing a denim jacket, paler than his denim trousers. I hadn't considered that a suit could be fashioned from denim, but there it was.

Laura's house was at the end of a neat cul-de-sac of small, modern houses. There were several cars in the driveway. We approached the front door and I noticed that she had red geraniums in window boxes. I find geraniums somewhat unsettling; that rich, sticky scent when you brush against them, a brackish, vegetable smell that's the opposite of floral.

Raymond rang the doorbell—the chime played the opening chords to Beethoven's Third Symphony. A very small boy, his face smeared with, one hoped, chocolate, answered and stared at us. I stared back at him. Raymond stepped forward.

"All right, mate?" he said. "We're here to see your granddad."

The boy continued staring at us, somewhat unenthusiastically. "I'm wearing new shoes," he stated, apropos of nothing. At that moment, Laura appeared behind him in the hallway.

"Auntie Laura," he said, not turning round, and sounding distinctly unimpressed, "it's more people for the party."

"I see that, Tyler," she said. "Why don't you go and find your brother, see if you can blow up some more balloons for us?" He nodded and ran off, his little feet thumping on the stairs.

"Come in," she said, smiling at Raymond. "Dad'll be pleased to see you." She didn't smile at me, which is the normal state of affairs in most encounters I have with other people.

We entered, Raymond wiping his feet elaborately on the doormat. I copied him. It was truly an unforeseen day when I would look to Raymond for social guidance.

He handed over the flowers and the clinking bag, and Laura looked pleased. I realized that, despite her entreaty at the hospital, I ought to have brought something to hand over too. I was going to explain that she had told us not to, and I had simply done her the courtesy of respecting her wishes, but before I could speak, Raymond blurted out, "These are from Eleanor and me."

She peered into the carrier bag—I fervently hoped it wasn't Haribo and Pringles again—and thanked us both. I nodded in acknowledgment.

She showed us into the living room, where Sammy and his family were seated. Banal pop music was playing softly, and a low table was covered with little bowls of beige snacks. Laura was wearing a dress, wrapped around her like black bandages, and teetered in heels with a two-inch platform. Her blond hair was—I grappled for the correct terms—both tall and fat, and tumbled well past her shoulders in glossy waves. Even Bobbi Brown might have thought the amount of makeup she was wearing de trop. Raymond's mouth hung slightly open, just wide enough to post a letter through, and he seemed somewhat dazed. Laura appeared entirely indifferent to his response.

"Raymond! Eleanor!" Sammy shouted, waving from deep within an enormous velvet armchair. "Laura, get them both a drink, would you? We're on the Prosecco," he said, confidentially.

"No more for you, Dad," his elder son said. "Not with those painkillers."

"Och, come on, son—you only live once!" Sammy said brightly. "After all, there's worse ways to go, eh, Eleanor?"

I nodded. He was, of course, absolutely right. I should know.

Laura appeared with two flutes of urine-colored fizzy liquid—much to my surprise, I drank mine down in three gulps. It was dry and biscuity, and extremely delicious. I wondered if it was expensive, and whether it might in due course come to replace vodka as my beverage of choice. Laura noticed, and topped up my glass.

"You're like me—I only drink bubbles," she said approvingly.

I looked around.

"You have a very beautiful home," I said.

She nodded.

"It's taken me a couple of years to get everything the way I like it, but I'm happy with it now," she said.

I was struck by how coordinated everything was, how clean and gleaming. There were textures everywhere—feathers and flock, velvet, silk—and jewel colors.

"It's like an aerie where a beautiful bird would nest," I said. "A quetzal, or an imperial eagle."

She appeared to be struggling for an appropriate response, strangely. Surely a simple "thank you" would have sufficed?

After a silence, not too uncomfortable because of the fizzy bubble drink, she asked me about work, and I explained what I did, and how I knew Raymond. We looked over at him—he was perched on the arm of Sammy's chair, laughing at something one of her brothers had said.

"You could do worse, you know," she said, with a sly smile. "I mean, if you tidied him up a bit, decent haircut . . ."

It took me a moment to grasp what she meant.

"Oh no," I said, "you completely misunderstand. I already have someone. He's handsome and sophisticated and talented—a cultured, educated man." Laura smiled.

"Aren't you the lucky one! How did you two meet, then?"

"Well, we haven't, as yet," I explained, "but it's only a matter of time."

She threw her head back and laughed, a deep throaty sound that seemed wrong coming from such a slight, feminine woman.

"You're hilarious, Eleanor," she said. "You'll have to come round for drinks some time. And if you ever decide to cut your hair, bear me in mind, yeah? I'll give you mates' rates."

I thought about this. I had been slacking somewhat with my makeover list, after the frankly disconcerting wax experience at the salon and the unremarkable changes that had been wrought on my nails. I supposed I ought to press on with it. Normally, I wasn't at all interested in my hair and I hadn't had it cut since I was thirteen years old. It ran down to my waist, straight and light brown—just hair, nothing more, nothing less. I barely noticed it, in truth. I knew, though, that for the singer to fall in love with me, I'd need to make much more of an effort.

"This is, in fact, serendipitous timing, Laura," I said, drinking more of the delicious bubbles—my glass seemed miraculously to have refilled itself. "I had been planning something of a reinvention. Might next week be suitable for you to effect a change of hairstyle?"

She picked up her phone from a console table and tapped away.

"How's Tuesday at three?" she said.

We were allocated twenty-five days of annual leave, and I had used three—a recovery day after painful root canal work, one of my biannual daytime Social Work visits, and an extra day I'd added onto a bank holiday weekend in order to allow me to finish a particularly lengthy but thrilling volume on the history of ancient Rome without interruption.

"Tuesday would be splendid," I said.

She shimmered off toward the kitchen, and reappeared with a tray of malodorous, warm snacks which she passed around the room. The space had filled up with people, and the overall volume level was very loud. I stood for several minutes examining the bibelots and objets which she had artfully placed around the room. More from boredom than necessity, I went to use the bathroom, a tiny cloakroom under the stairs which was also shiny and warm, gleaming white and scented, improbably, with figs—the smell, I eventually realized, emanating from a lit candle in a glass jar on the shelf below the mirror. Candles in a bathroom! I suspected that Laura was something of a sybarite.

I walked into the room at the end of the hall, which was, as I had correctly guessed, the kitchen. This room was also full of people and noise, but I could make out black marble work tops, gloss cream cabinets and lots of chrome. Her home was so . . . shiny. She was shiny too, her skin, her hair, her shoes, her teeth. I hadn't even realized before; I am matte, dull and scuffed.

Feeling the need to escape the noise and heat for a moment, I opened the back door and stepped out onto a patio. The garden was small and contained little in the way of botanical life, being mostly paved with concrete slabs or covered in slippery decking. Dusk was falling, but the sky felt small here, and I felt penned in by a high fence which ran on all three sides. I breathed in, deeply, hoping for cool night air. Instead, my nasal passages were assaulted by tar, nicotine and other poisons.

"Nice night, eh?" said Raymond, loitering unnoticed in the shadows and, just for a change, puffing on a cigarette. I nodded.

"I came out for some fresh air," he said, without a hint of irony. "I shouldn't drink fizz, it knocks me for six." I realized that I was somewhat discombobulated myself.

"I think I'm ready to go home now," I said, a little unsteady on my feet. It was, however, a lovely feeling.

"Come and sit down for a minute," Raymond said, steering me toward a pair of wooden armchairs. I was glad to do so, as my new boots rendered my balance somewhat precarious at the best of times. Raymond lit another cigarette—he seemed to be becoming a chain smoker.

"They're a nice family, aren't they?" he said.

"Laura is going to cut my hair," I blurted out. I've no idea why.

"Is she now?" He smiled.

"You like her," I stated, nodding sagely. I was a woman of the world, after all.

He laughed.

"She's gorgeous, Eleanor, but she's really not my type." His cigarette end glowed red in the semi-darkness.

"What *is* your type?" I asked, finding to my surprise that I was actually interested.

"I don't know. Someone less . . . high maintenance, I guess. Someone . . . wait a minute."

I was more than content to sit still while he walked off, returning minutes later with a bottle of wine and two garishly decorated paper cups sporting cartoon rodents on skateboards.

"Rastamouse," I read aloud, slowly. "What on earth is this?"

"Give it here," Raymond said, and poured us both a . . . cup. We tapped our vessels together. There was no clink.

"I thought I'd found the perfect person for me," he said, staring at the back of the garden. "Didn't work out, though."

"Why not?" I said, although I could, in fact, think of many reasons why someone might not want to be with Raymond.

"Thing is, I'm still not entirely sure. I wish I *did* know—it would make things easier . . ."

I nodded—it seemed like the appropriate thing to do.

"Helen said it wasn't me, it was her." He laughed, not an amused laugh, though. "I can't believe she came out with that old chestnut. After three years . . . you'd think she'd have known before then that it wasn't working for her. I don't know what changed. *I* didn't change . . . I don't think I did, anyway . . ."

"People can be . . . unfathomable," I said, stumbling slightly over the word. "I often find that I don't understand why they do and say things."

He nodded.

"We had a lovely wee flat, went on some great holidays. I was . . . I was actually thinking about asking her to marry me. Christ . . ." He stared at the paving stones and I tried and failed to picture Raymond in a morning suit, top hat and cravat, let alone a kilt.

"It's fine," he said, after a while. "It's quite a laugh, sharing with the guys, and I've got this new job. Things are OK. It's just . . . I dunno. She said I was too nice. What exactly am I meant to do with that? I mean . . . become more of a bastard? Should I have hit her, or cheated on her?"

I realized he wasn't really talking to me; it was like in a play, when a character just talks out loud for no apparent reason. I knew the answer to his question, however.

"No, Raymond," I said. "You would never have done either of those things." I finished my cup of wine and poured some more. "I lived with a man called

Declan for a couple of years. He used to punch me in the kidneys, slap me—he fractured twelve bones, all in all. He stayed out some nights and then came home and told me about the women he'd been with. It was my fault, all my fault. But still, I know he shouldn't have done that. I know it now, anyway."

Raymond stared at me. "Jesus, Eleanor. When was this?"

"Several years ago," I said. "While I was still at university. He saw me in the Botanic Gardens one day, just came up and started talking to me. I know it sounds ridiculous, looking back. By the end of the week, he'd moved in."

"Was he a student too?" Raymond said.

"No, he said reading books was a waste of time, boring. He didn't work either; couldn't find a job that suited him, he said. It's not easy to find a job that suits you, I suppose, is it?"

Raymond was looking at me with a strange expression on his face.

"Declan wanted to help me learn how to be a better person," I said. Raymond lit yet another cigarette.

"How did it end?" he said, not looking at me, blowing smoke up into the air in a long stream, like a very unterrifying dragon.

"Well," I told him, "he broke my arm again, and when I went to hospital, they somehow guessed that it hadn't happened the way I'd said. He'd told me to tell them that I'd had a fall, but they didn't believe me." I took another large sip. "Anyway, a nice nurse came and spoke to me, and explained that people who truly love you don't hurt you, and that it wasn't right to stay with someone who did. The way she explained it, it all made sense. I should have been able to work it out for myself, really. I asked him to leave when I got home and, when he wouldn't, I called the police, like she'd suggested. And that was that. Oh, and I changed the locks."

He said nothing, and stared with intense concentration at his shoes. Without looking at me, he put out his hand and touched my arm, patted it very tentatively, as one would a horse or a dog (if one were frightened of horses or dogs). He shook his head gently, for a long time, but seemed unable to articulate a response. No matter; I didn't require one. The whole thing was ancient history now. I was happy being alone. Eleanor Oliphant, sole survivor—that's me.

"I'm going to go home now, Raymond," I said, standing up quickly. "I'm going to get a taxi."

"Good idea," he said, finishing his drink. He took out his phone. "But you're not going to wander the streets on your own and try to hail one, not at this time of night. I'll call you one—look, I've got an app!" He showed me his phone, beaming.

"What am I supposed to be looking at?" I said, peering at the screen. He ignored me and checked the message. "It'll be here in five minutes," he said.

He waited with me in the hall until the cab arrived, then walked me to the vehicle and held the door open for me. I saw him peering in at the driver, a middle-aged woman who looked tired and bored, as I climbed into the backseat.

"Are you coming too?" I said, wondering why he was hesitating on the curb. He checked his watch, ruffled his hair and looked from the house to the taxi and back again.

"Nah," he said. "I think I'll hang around here for a bit. See what happens."

I turned to watch him as the car moved off. He staggered slightly as he walked up the path, and I saw Laura framed in the doorway, two glasses in her hands, one of them offered out to him.

# 18

Raymond sent me an electronic mail message at work the next week—it was very odd, seeing his name in my in-box. As I'd expected, he was semiliterate.

> Hi E, hope all good with u. Got a wee favor to
> ask. Sammy's son Keith has invited me to his
> 40th this Saturday (ended up staying late at
> that party BTW, it was a rite laugh). Fancy
> being my plus one? It's at the golf club, there's
> a buffet? No worries if not—let me no. R

A buffet. In a golf club. The Lord giveth and the Lord taketh away. And two parties in a month! More parties than I had been to in two decades. I hit reply:

> Dear Raymond,
> I should be delighted to accompany you to the
> birthday celebration.
>                         Kind regards,
>                                 Eleanor Oliphant (Ms.)

Moments later, I received a response: ☺

Twenty-first-century communication. I fear for our nation's standards of literacy.

I had arranged to have the afternoon off that day for my appointment at the hairdressers, but ate my lunch in the staff room first as usual, with the *Telegraph* crossword, a tuna and sweet corn bloomer, salt and vinegar crisps and orange juice, with bits. I must thank the musician, in due course, for introducing me to the pleasure of bits. After this delicious repast, and with a small grin of triumph at the thought of my colleagues having to remain behind at their desks for the rest of the afternoon, I took a bus into town.

Heliotrope was in a smart street in the city center, on the ground floor of a Victorian sandstone building. It was certainly not the sort of place I'd usually frequent—loud music, aggressively fashionable staff and far too many mirrors. I imagined this might be where the musician went for a haircut, and that made me feel slightly better about it. Perhaps one day we'd be sitting side by side in those black leather chairs, holding hands under the hair dryers.

I waited for the receptionist to finish her phone call, and stepped away from the huge vase of white and pink lilies on the counter. Their smell snagged in the back of my throat, like fur or feathers. I gagged; it wasn't something meant for humans.

I'd forgotten how noisy hairdressers' salons were, the constant hum of dryers and inane chat, and positioned myself in the window seat, having donned a black nylon kimono which, I was alarmed to see, was already sprinkled with short hair clippings snipped from a previous client. I quickly brushed them off.

Laura arrived, looking just as glamorous as before, and led me toward a seat in front of a terrifying row of mirrors.

"Did you have a good time on Saturday?" she said, fussing around with a stool until she was seated behind me at the same height. She didn't look at me directly, but into the mirror, where she addressed my reflection; I found myself doing the same. It was strangely relaxing.

"I did," I said. "It was a splendid evening."

"Dad's doing my nut in already, staying in the spare room," she said, smiling, "and I've got another two weeks of it. I don't know how I'll cope." I nodded.

"Parents can certainly be challenging, in my experience," I said. We exchanged a sympathetic glance.

"Now then, what are we doing for you today?" she said, unfastening the rubber band at the bottom of my braid and fanning it out. I stared at my reflection. My hair was mousy brown, parted in the center, straight and not particularly thick. Human hair, doing what human hair does: growing on my head.

"Something different," I said. "What would you suggest?"

"How brave are you prepared to be, Eleanor?" Laura asked. This was the correct question. I am brave. I am brave, courageous, Eleanor Oliphant.

"Do whatever you want," I said. She looked delighted.

"Color too?"

I considered this.

"Would it be a normal human hair color? I don't think I'd like pink or blue or anything like that."

"I'll give you a shoulder-length, lightly layered choppy bob, with caramel and honey pieces woven through and a long sweeping fringe," she said. "How does that sound?"

"It sounds like an incomprehensible pile of gibberish," I said. She laughed at my reflection, and then stopped, perhaps because I wasn't laughing.

"Trust me, Eleanor," she said earnestly. "It'll be beautiful."

"Beautiful is not a word normally associated with my appearance," I said, highly skeptical. She patted my arm.

"Just you wait," she said gently. "MILEY!" she screeched, almost causing me to fall from my chair. "Come and help me mix up some color!"

A short, chubby girl with bad skin and beautiful eyes came trotting up. Laura gave a prescription involving percentages and codes which might as well have been for gunpowder.

"Tea? Coffee? Magazine?" Laura said. I could scarcely believe it when I found myself, five minutes later, sipping a cappuccino and perusing the latest edition of *OK!* magazine. Look at me, I thought.

"Ready?" Laura asked. Her hand, warm and soft, brushed against the back of my neck as she took the hank and heft of my hair and twisted it into a rope behind me. The slow noise of the scissors slicing through it was like the sound of embers shifting in a fire: tinkly, dangerous. It was over in a moment. Laura held the hair aloft, a triumphant Delilah.

"I'll cut it properly after the color's done," she said. "We just need a level playing field at this stage." Because I was sitting motionless, it didn't feel any different. She dropped the hair on the floor where it lay like a dead animal. A skinny boy, who looked like he'd rather be doing almost anything else, was sweeping up very, very slowly, and nudged my hair creature into his dustpan with a long-handled brush. I watched his progress round the salon in the mirror. What happened to all the hair afterward? The thought of a day's or a week's worth bundled into a bin bag, the smell of it and the soft, marshmallowy pillowing of it inside, made me feel slightly queasy.

Laura approached wheeling a trolley, then proceeded to daub various thick pastes onto selected strands of my hair, alternating between bowls. After each section of gunk was applied, she folded the painted hair into squares of tinfoil. It was a fascinating procedure. After thirty minutes, she left me sitting with a foil head and a red face, then returned pushing a hot lamp on a stand, which she placed behind me.

"Twenty minutes and you'll be done," she said.

She brought me more magazines, but the pleasure had waned—I had quickly tired of celebrity gossip, and it seemed that the salon didn't take *Which?* or *BBC History*, much to my disappointment. A thought kept nudging me, and I ignored it. Me, brushing someone else's hair? Yes. Someone smaller than me, sitting on a chair while I stood behind and combed out the tangles, trying my best to be gentle. She hated the snags and tugs. Thoughts of this type—vague, mysterious, unsettling—were precisely the sort that vodka was good for obliterating, but unfortunately I'd only been offered a choice of tea or coffee. I wondered why hair salons didn't provide anything stronger. A change of style can be stressful, after all, and it's hard to relax in such a noisy, bright environment. It would probably encourage customers to give bigger tips too. Tipsy equals tips, I thought, and laughed silently.

When the buzzer sounded on the heat lamp, the color-mixing girl came over and led me to the "backwash," which was, by any other name, a sink. I allowed the tinfoil to be unwrapped from my hair. She ran warm water through it, and then shampooed it clean. Her fingers were firm and deft, and I marveled at the generosity of those humans who performed intimate services for others. I hadn't had anyone else wash my hair since as far back as I could remember. I suppose Mummy must have washed it for me when I was an infant, but it was hard to imagine her performing any tender ministrations of this type.

After the shampoo was rinsed away, the girl performed a "shiatsu head massage." I have never known such bliss. She kneaded my scalp with firm tenderness and precision, and I felt the hairs stand up on my forearms, then a bolt of electricity run down my spine. It ended about nine hours before I would have liked it to.

"You had a lot of tension in your scalp," she said sagaciously, while she rinsed out the conditioning cream. I had no idea how to respond, and opted for a smile, which serves me well on most occasions (not if it's something to do with death or illness, though— I know that now).

Back in the same chair, my shorter, colored hair combed out, Laura returned with her sharp scissors.

"You can't see the color properly when it's wet," she said. "Just you wait!"

In the end, the cutting only took ten minutes or so. I admired her dexterity and the confidence with which she undertook the task. The drying took much longer, with considerable and elaborate hairbrush action. I read my magazine, electing, at her prompting, not to look up until the styling was finished. The dryer was switched off, chemicals were sprayed, lengths and angles were examined and a few additional snips undertaken here and there. I heard Laura's laugh of delight.

"Look, Eleanor!" she said.

I raised my head from *Marie Claire*'s in-depth report into female genital mutilation. My reflection showed a much younger woman, a confident woman with glossy hair that brushed her shoulders and a fringe that swept across her face and sat just over her scarred cheek. Me? I turned to the right and then to the left. I looked in the hand mirror Laura was holding behind my head so that I could see the back, smooth and sleek. I swallowed hard.

"You've made me shiny, Laura," I said. I tried to stop it, but a little tear ran down the side of my nose. I wiped it away with the back of my hand before it could dampen the ends of my new hair. "Thank you for making me shiny."

# 19

Bob had called me in for a meeting. He stared at me when I went into his office. I wondered why.

"Your hair!" he said, eventually, as though guessing the answer to a question. I hadn't found it easy to style this morning, but I thought I'd made a fair attempt. I put my hands to my head.

"What's wrong with it?" I said.

"Nothing's wrong with it. It looks . . . it looks nice," he said, smiling and nodding. There was a moment's awkwardness. Neither of us was used to Bob commenting on my appearance.

"I had it cut," I said, "obviously."

He nodded.

"Sit down, Eleanor." I looked around. To say Bob's office was untidy was rather to understate the degree of chaos in which it was always to be found. I lifted a pile of brochures from the chair which faced his desk and placed them on the floor. He leaned forward. Bob has aged very badly during the time that I've known him; his hair has almost all fallen out and he has put on quite a lot of weight. He looks rather like a dissolute baby.

"You've worked here for a long time, Eleanor," he said. I nodded; that was factually correct. "Did you know that Loretta is going off on leave for the fore-seeable?" I shook my head. I am not interested in the petty tittle-tattle of quotidian office life. Unless it's gossip about a certain singer, of course.

"I can't say I'm surprised," I said. "I always doubted her grasp of the basic principles of value-added tax," I shrugged, "so perhaps it's for the best."

"Her husband's got testicular cancer, Eleanor," he said. "She wants to look after him."

I thought about this for a moment.

"That must be very difficult for them both," I said. "But, if detected early enough, the survival and recov-ery rates for cancer of the testes are good. If you're male and you are unfortunate enough to get any sort of cancer, that's probably the best type to have."

He fiddled with one of his fancy black pens. "So," he said. "I'm going to be needing a new office manager, for the next few months at least." I nodded. "Would you be interested, Eleanor? It'd mean a bit more money, a bit more responsibility. I think you're ready for it, though."

I considered this.

"How much more money?" I asked. He wrote a sum on a Post-it note, tore it from the pad and passed it across to me. I gasped. "In addition to my current salary?"

I had visions of taking taxis to work rather than getting the bus, of upgrading to Tesco Finest every-thing, and of drinking the kind of vodka that comes in chunky opaque bottles.

"No, Eleanor," he said. "That amount would be your new salary."

"Ah," I said.

If that were the case, then I would need to consider the risk/reward ratio carefully. Would the increase in salary compensate adequately for the increased amount of tedious administration work I'd be required to undertake, the augmented levels of responsibility for the successful functioning of the office and, worse still, for the significantly increased degree of interaction that I'd need to undertake with my colleagues?

"May I take a few days to consider it, Bob?" I said.

He nodded. "Of course, Eleanor. I expected you to say that."

I looked at my hands.

"You're a good worker, Eleanor," he said. "How long has it been now—eight years?"

"Nine," I said.

"Nine years, and you've never had a day off sick, never used all your annual leave. That's dedication, you know. It's not easy to find these days."

"It's not dedication," I said. "I simply have a very robust constitution and no one to go on holiday with."

He looked away and I stood up, ready to leave.

He cleared his throat. "Oh, one other thing, Eleanor. Because Loretta's so busy preparing all the handover stuff . . . could I ask you to help out with something?"

"Ask away, Bob," I said.

"The office Christmas lunch—do you think you could organize it this year?" he said. "She won't have time before she finishes up, and I've already had people in my office whingeing that if we don't book somewhere now . . ."

". . . they'll end up in Wetherspoons," I said, nodding. "Yes, I'm familiar with the issues, Bob. If you wish it, I'd certainly be willing to organize the lunch. Do I have carte blanche with regard to venue, menu and theme?"

Bob nodded, already busy at his computer again.

"Sure," he said. "The company will chip in a tenner per head—after that, it's up to you guys to choose where to go and how much extra you want to pay."

"Thank you, Bob," I said. "I won't let you down."

He wasn't listening, engrossed with whatever was on his screen. My head was buzzing. Two major decisions to make. Another party to go to. And handsome, talented Johnnie Lomond, *chanteur extraordinaire* and potential life partner on the horizon. Life was very intense.

When I sat back down at my computer, I stared at the screen for some time, not actually reading the words. I felt slightly sick at the thought of all the dilemmas I faced, to the extent that, although it was almost lunchtime, I had no desire to buy and eat my Meal Deal. It might be helpful to talk to someone about it all, I realized. I remembered that from the past. Apparently, talking was good; it helped to keep anxieties in perspective. People had kept saying that. *Talk to someone, do you want to talk about it, tell me how you feel, anything you want to share with the group, Eleanor? You do not have to say anything, but it may harm your defense if you do not mention when questioned something which you later rely on in court. Miss Oliphant, can you tell us in your own words what you recall of the events that took place that evening?*

I felt a tiny trickle of sweat run down my back, and a fluttering in my chest like a trapped bird. The computer made that annoying ping which indicates the arrival of an electronic message. I clicked on it without thinking. How I despise these Pavlovian responses in myself!

> Hi E, you still on for Keith's party on
> Saturday? Meet you at the station—8ish? R

He had attached a graphic: a photograph of a famous politician's face, next to a head shot of a dog that looked exactly like him. I snorted—the resemblance was uncanny. Underneath he'd written Wednesday morning LOLs, whatever that meant.

Impulsively I typed straight back:

> Good morning, Raymond. The canine/
> ministerial graphic was most amusing. Would
> you happen to be free for lunch at 12:30 by
> any chance? Regards, Eleanor

There was no reply for almost fifteen minutes, and I began to regret my impulsive decision. I hadn't ever invited anyone to join me for lunch before. I conducted my usual online checks for any updates from the musician—there was nothing new on Facebook, Twitter or Instagram, sadly. It made me feel anxious when he went quiet. I suspected it meant he was either very sad, or, perhaps more worryingly, that he was very happy. A new girlfriend?

I felt queasy, and was thinking that perhaps I wouldn't go for the full Meal Deal today, just an anti-oxidant smoothie and a small bag of wasabi peanuts, when another message arrived.

> Soz—had to deal with a helpdesk call. Told him to switch it off and switch it back on again LOL. Yeh, lunch would be good. See you out front in 5? R.

I hit reply.

> That would be fine. Thank you.

Daringly, I didn't put my name, because I realized he'd know it was from me.

~

Raymond was late, arriving in eight rather than the promised five minutes, but I decided not to make anything of it on this one occasion. He suggested we go to a café he liked around the corner.

It wasn't the sort of place I would normally frequent, being rather bohemian and shabby-looking, with mismatched furniture and a lot of cushions and throws. What was the likelihood of them being

laundered on any sort of regular basis? I wondered.
Minimal at best. I shuddered at the thought of all
those microbes; the warmth of the café and the dense
fibers of the cushions would be a perfect breeding
ground for dust mites and perhaps even lice. I sat at
a table with ordinary wooden chairs and no soft
furnishings.

Raymond seemed to know the waiter, who greeted
him by name when he brought the menus. The staff
seemed to be the same sort of person as him: unkempt,
scruffy, badly dressed, both the men and the women.

"The falafel's usually good," he said, "or the
soup—" pointing to the Specials board.

"Cream of cauliflower and cumin," I said, reading aloud. "Oh no. No, I really don't think so."

I was still in gastric turmoil after my meeting with
Bob, and so I simply ordered a frothy coffee and a
cheese scone. Whatever Raymond was eating smelled
disgusting, like gently reheated vomit. He ate noisily
with his mouth partially open, so that I had to look
away. It made it easier to broach the subject of Bob's
offer and the task he had entrusted me with.

"May I ask you something, Raymond?" I said. He
slurped his cola and nodded. I looked away again.
The man who had served us was lounging at the
counter, nodding his head in time with the music. It
was a cacophonous din, with too many guitars and
not enough melody. It was, I thought, the sound of
madness, the kind of music that lunatics hear in their

heads just before they slice the heads off foxes and throw them into their neighbor's back garden.

"I've been offered a promotion, to the position of office manager," I said. "Do you think I should accept?"

He stopped chomping and took another slurp of his drink.

"That's brilliant, Eleanor," he said, smiling. "What's stopping you?"

I had a nibble of my scone—it was unexpectedly delicious, much nicer than the ones you get in Tesco. I never thought I'd find myself thinking that about anything.

"Well," I said, "on the plus side, I would get paid more money. Not a huge amount more, but still . . . enough to allow me to upgrade on certain items. On the other hand, it would entail more work and more responsibility. And the office is largely staffed by shirkers and idiots, Raymond. Managing them and their workloads would be quite a challenge, I can assure you."

He snorted with laughter, then coughed—it appeared that his cola had gone down the wrong way.

"I see your point," he said. "What it boils down to is, is the extra money worth the extra hassle?"

"Quite," I said, "you've summarized my dilemma very neatly."

He paused, chomped some more.

"What's your game plan, Eleanor?" he asked.

I had no idea what he meant, which must have been evident from my facial expression.

"What I mean is, do you plan to stay in office administration long term? If you do, it could be good—a new title and salary. When you come to take the next step, you'll be in a much better position."

"What do you mean, 'next step'?" I said. The man was incapable of speaking in plain English.

"When you apply for another job, with another company, I mean," he explained, waving his fork around. I shrank back, fearful that some microspots of spittle might reach me.

"Well, you don't want to work at By Design forever, do you?" he said. "You're, what, twenty-six, twenty-seven?"

"I recently turned thirty Raymond," I said, surprisingly pleased.

"Really?" he said. "Well, you're not planning to spend the rest of your life doing Bob's books, are you?"

I shrugged; I genuinely hadn't given it a moment's thought.

"I suppose so," I said. "What else would I do?"

"Eleanor!" he said, shocked for some reason. "You're bright, you're conscientious, you're . . . very well organized," he said. "There are lots of other jobs you could do."

"Really?" I said, dubious.

"Sure!" he said, nodding vigorously. "I mean, you're numerate, right? You're well spoken. Do you know any other languages?"

I nodded. "I have a very good grasp of Latin, actually," I said.

He pursed his whiskery little mouth. "Hmm," he said, gesturing to the waiter, who came over and cleared our table. He returned with two coffees and an unrequested saucer of chocolate truffles.

"Enjoy, guys!" he said, placing the dish with a flourish.

I shook my head, not believing that anyone would actually say such a thing.

Raymond returned to his theme.

"There are lots of places that would be looking to hire an experienced office manager, Eleanor," he said. "Not just graphic design—it could be a GP practice, or an IT company or, well . . . loads of places!" He shoved a truffle in his mouth. "Do you want to stay in Glasgow? You could move to Edinburgh, or London or . . . well, the world's your oyster really, isn't it?"

"Is it?" I said. Again, it had never crossed my mind to move cities, live somewhere else. Bath, with its fabulous Roman remains, York, London . . . it was all a bit too much.

"It occurs to me that there are many things in life that I've never considered doing, Raymond. I suppose I hadn't realized that I had any control over them. That sounds ridiculous, I know," I said.

He looked very serious, and leaned forward.

"Eleanor, it can't have been easy for you. You don't have any brothers or sisters, your dad's never been around and you said that you have quite a . . . difficult relationship with your mum?"

I nodded.

"Are you seeing anyone at the moment?" he asked.

"Yes," I said.

He looked expectant; bizarrely, he seemed to require a more detailed response than this. I sighed, shook my head. I spoke as slowly and clearly as I could.

"I'm seeing you right now, Raymond. You're sitting right in front of me."

He snorted with laughter.

"You know fine well what I mean, Eleanor." It became apparent that I didn't.

"Have you got a boyfriend?" he said, patiently.

I hesitated. "No. Well . . . there is someone. But no, I suppose the factually correct answer at this point in time is no, for the time being, at least."

"So you have a lot to deal with on your own," he said, not as a question but as a statement of fact. "You shouldn't give yourself a hard time for not having a ten-year career plan."

"Do *you* have a ten-year career plan?" I asked. It seemed unlikely.

"Nah," he said, smiling. "Does anybody? Anybody normal, I mean?"

I shrugged. "I'm not really sure I know any normal people," I said.

"None taken, Eleanor," he said, laughing.

I pondered this, then realized what he meant.

"I didn't mean any offense, Raymond," I said. "Sorry."

"Don't be daft," he said, gesturing for the bill. "So, when do you have to decide about the job? I think you should take it, for what it's worth," he said. "Nothing ventured, eh? Plus, I'm sure you'd make a great office manager."

I looked at him closely, waiting for a follow-up remark or a snide comment, but, much to my surprise, neither was forthcoming. He took out his wallet and paid the bill. I protested vehemently but he flat-out refused to allow me to contribute my share.

"You only had a coffee and a scone," he said. "You can buy me lunch when you get your first office manager's paycheck!" He smiled.

I thanked him. No one had ever bought me lunch before. It was a very pleasant feeling, to have someone incur expenditure on my behalf, voluntarily, expecting nothing in return.

The hour was up just as we got back to the office building, and so we said a brief good-bye before returning to our respective desks. This was the first day in nine years that I'd eaten lunch with a companion, and that I hadn't done the crossword. Strangely, I felt no concern about the crossword whatsoever. Perhaps I'd do it this evening instead. Perhaps I'd simply recycle the newspaper without even attempting it. As Raymond had pointed out, the world was full of infinite possibility. I opened my e-mail and typed him a message.

> Dear R, thank you very much for lunch. Kind
> regards, E

I supposed it made sense, in a way, shortening the
names. It was obvious who was addressing whom,
after all. He replied quickly:

> No worries, good luck with your decision. See
> you Saturday! R

Life felt like it was moving very fast indeed at the
moment, a whirlwind of possibilities. I hadn't even
thought about the musician this afternoon. I logged
on to my computer and started researching venues for
the Christmas lunch. This was going to be quite the
event, I decided. It would be unlike any other Christmas
lunch. It would be important to eschew cliché and
precedent. I would do something different, something
that would surprise and delight my co-workers, sub-
vert their expectations. It wouldn't be easy. One thing
I knew for certain was this: Bob's ten-pound budget
would be the basis of the event, and no one would
need to contribute further. I still resented all the
monetary payments I'd been forced to make over the
years to have a terrible time in a terrible place with
terrible people on the last Friday before the twenty-
fifth of December.

After all, how hard could it be? Raymond had
really been most encouraging over lunch. If I could
perform scansion on the *Aeneid*, if I could build a
macro in an Excel spreadsheet, if I could spend the

last nine birthdays and Christmases and New Year's Eves alone, then I'm sure I could manage to organize a delightful festive lunch for thirty people on a budget of ten pounds per capita.

# 20

Saturday morning passed in a blur of household chores. I'd started wearing rubber gloves to protect my hands, and, although unsightly, they were helping. The ugliness didn't matter—after all, there was no one to see me.

Gathering up the detritus of the previous evening, I noticed that I had failed to consume all of my vodka allocation; the best part of a half bottle of Smirnoff was extant. Mindful of my gauche faux pas at Laura's party, I put it in a Tesco carrier bag to present to Keith tonight. I pondered what else I should take for him. Flowers seemed wrong; they're a love token, after all. I looked in the fridge, and popped a packet of cheese slices into the bag. All men like cheese.

I arrived five minutes early at the train station nearest to the party venue. Mirabile dictu, Raymond was already there! He waved at me and I waved back. We set off toward the golf club. Raymond walked quickly, and I began to worry that I wouldn't be able to keep pace with him in my new boots. I noticed him glance at me, and then he slowed his steps to match mine. I realized that such small gestures—the way his mother had made me a cup of tea after our meal without asking, remembering that I didn't take sugar, the way Laura had placed two little biscuits on the saucer when she brought me coffee in the salon—such things could mean so much. I wondered how it would feel to perform such simple deeds for other people. I couldn't remember. I *had* done such things in the past, tried to be kind, tried to take care, I knew that I had, but that was *before*. I tried, and I had failed, and all was lost to me afterward. I had no one to blame but myself.

It was quiet out in the suburbs; the views were open, with no tenements or high-rise blocks to obscure the distant hills. The light was soft and gentle—summer was drifting ever onward and the evening seemed delicate, fragile. We walked in silence, the kind that you didn't feel the need to fill.

I was almost sad when we arrived at the squat, white clubhouse. It was halfway to dark by then, with both a moon and a sun sitting high in a sky that was sugar almond pink and shot with gold. The birds were singing valiantly against the coming night, swooping over the greens in long, drunken loops. The air was grassy, with a hint of flowers and earth, and the warm, sweet outbreath of the day sighed gently into our hair and over our skin. I felt like asking Raymond whether we should keep walking, walk over the rolling greens, keep walking till the birds fell silent in their bowers and we could see only by starlight. It almost felt like he might suggest it himself.

The front door to the clubhouse burst open and three children came running out, laughing at the tops of their voices, one wielding a plastic sword.

"Here we are, then," said Raymond, softly.

≈

It was an odd venue for a social gathering. The corridors were lined with notice boards, all pinned with impenetrable messages about Ladders and Tee Times. A wooden panel at the end of the entrance hall bore a long list of men's names in golden letters, starting in 1924 and ending, this year, somewhat improbably, with a Dr. Terry Berry. The décor was a discomfiting mix of institutional (a look with which I'm very familiar) and outdated family home—nasty patterned curtains, hard-wearing floors, dusty dried flower arrangements.

When we walked into the function suite, we were met with a wall of sound; a mobile discotheque had been set up and the floor was already packed with dancers, ages ranging from five to eighty, all illuminated randomly by some unimpressive colored lights. The dancers seemed to be pretending to ride a horse in time to the music. I looked up at Raymond, very much out of my depth.

"Christ," he said, "I need a drink."

I followed him gratefully to the bar. The prices were gratifyingly low, and I drank my Magners quite fast, comfortable in the knowledge that I'd brought enough money for several more, although Raymond had, despite my protests, purchased this one. We found a table as far away from the source of the noise as possible.

"Family dos," Raymond said, shaking his head. "It's bad enough when it's your own family; when it's someone else's . . ."

I looked around. I had no prior experience of such events, and the main thing that struck me was disparity; age range, social class and the sartorial choices made by the guests.

"You can choose your friends . . ." Raymond said, toasting me with his pint glass.

"But you can't choose your family!" I replied, delighted to be in a position to complete the well-known phrase. It was only a quick crossword clue, not a cryptic one, but still.

"This is exactly like my dad's fiftieth, Mum's sixtieth, my sister's wedding," Raymond said. "A shite DJ, overexcited kids high on sugar, people who haven't seen each other for years catching up and pretending they like each other. Bet you anything there'll be a buffet with vol-au-vents, and a fight in the car park at closing time."

I was intrigued.

"But surely it must be fun?" I said. "Catching up with family? All those people, pleased to see you, interested in your life?" He looked at me carefully.

"D'you know what, Eleanor? It is. I'm just being a grumpy bastard—sorry." He finished his pint. "Same again?" he said. I nodded, and then remembered.

"No, no, it's my turn," I said. "Will you have the same again?"

He smiled.

"That'd be great. Thanks, Eleanor."

I picked up my shopper and made my way to the bar. I caught Sammy's eye en route—he was sitting in an armchair surrounded by friends and family members, as usual. I went over.

"Eleanor, love!" he said. "How are you? Great party, eh?"

I nodded.

"I can't believe my wee boy's forty. It seems like yesterday he was off to school for his first day. You should see the photo—he's got no front teeth, the wee scamp! And look at him now."

He pointed across the room to where Keith was standing with his wife, their arms round one another's waists, laughing at something an older man was saying.

"That's all you ever want for your kids: for them to be happy. I just wish my Jean was here to see it . . ."

I pondered this. Was that what people wanted for their children, for them to be happy? It certainly sounded plausible. I asked Sammy if I could purchase a drink for him, although he did, to my inexpert eye, already seem somewhat intoxicated.

"You're fine, hen," he said, "I've already got these waiting for me!"

The table was covered with short glasses of amber liquid. I said I'd see him again later and went to the bar.

There was quite a queue, but I was enjoying the atmosphere. Blessed relief—the DJ was taking a break, and I could see him over in the corner, swigging from a can and talking morosely into his mobile telephone. There was a background hum of noise, male and female voices and a lot of laughter. The children seemed to have multiplied, and had gravitated toward one another in order to form a merry band of mischief makers. It was clear that the adults were all occupied with the party, so they could run and whoop and chase each other with unsupervised abandon. I smiled at them, envied them slightly.

All of the people in the room seemed to take so much for granted: that they would be invited to social events, that they would have friends and family to talk to, that they would fall in love, be loved in return, perhaps create a family of their own. How would I celebrate my own fortieth birthday? I wondered. I hoped I would have people in my life to mark the occasion with me when the time came. Perhaps the musician, the light of my new life? One thing was certain, however: I would not, under any circumstances, be celebrating in a golf club.

When I returned to our table, it was empty. I put Raymond's pint down and sipped my Magners. I supposed he'd found someone more interesting to talk to. I sat and watched the dancing—the DJ was back behind the decks, and had selected a cacophonous racket from a silver box of records, something about a man after midnight. I allowed my mind to wander. I've found this to be a very effective way of passing the time; you take a situation or a person and start to imagine nice things that might happen. You can make anything happen, anything at all, inside a daydream.

I felt a hand on my shoulder and jumped.

"Sorry," Raymond said. "I nipped to the Gents, got talking to someone on the way back."

I felt the heat where his hand had been; it was only a moment, but it left a warm imprint, almost as though it might be visible. A human hand was exactly the right weight, exactly the right temperature for touching another person, I realized. I'd shaken hands a fair bit over the years—more so recently—but I hadn't been touched in a lifetime.

Of course, Declan and I had had regular sexual intercourse, whenever he wanted to, but he never really *touched* me. He made me touch him, told me how and when and where, and I did so. I had no choice in the matter, but I remembered feeling like another person at those times, like it wasn't my hand, like it wasn't my body. It was simply a case of waiting for it to be over. I was thirty years old, I realized, and I had never walked hand in hand with anyone. No one had ever rubbed my tired shoulders, or stroked my face. I imagined a man putting his arms around me and holding me close when I was sad or tired or upset; the warmth of it, the weight of it.

"Eleanor?" Raymond said.

"Sorry, I was miles away," I said, sipping my Magners.

"Seems to be going well," he said, gesturing around the room. I nodded.

"I was chatting with Sammy's other son, Gary, and his girlfriend," he said. "They're a good laugh."

I looked around again. What would it be like in future, going to events like this on the arm of the musician? He'd make sure I was comfortable, dance with me if I wanted to (unlikely), make friends with the other guests. And then, at the end of the evening, we'd slip away together, home, to nest like turtledoves.

"We seem to be the only people here who aren't part of a couple," I told him, having observed the other guests.

He screwed up his face. "Aye—listen, thanks for coming with me. It's shite going to stuff like this on your own, isn't it?"

"Is it?" I said, interested. "I don't have a control situation to compare it with."

He looked at me. "You've always been on your own, then?" he said. "You mentioned that guy last week, the one that . . ." I saw him reach for words, "the one that you were with when you were at uni?"

"As you know, I was with Declan for a couple of years," I said. "And you also know how that turned out." More Magners. "You get used to being on your own," I said. "Actually, it really is much better than being punched in the face or raped."

Raymond choked on his pint, and took a moment
to recover himself. He spoke very gently.

"You do realize, Eleanor, that those are not your
only options, don't you? Not all men are like Declan,
you know."

"I *do* know!" I said, brightly. "I've met one!"

In my mind's eye, I saw the musician bringing
me freesias, kissing the nape of my neck. Raymond
looked uncomfortable, for some reason.

"I'll just nip to the bar," he said. "You still on the
Magners?" I felt strange, stirred up. "I'll have a vodka
with cola, please," I said, knowing from experience
that vodka would be good for whatever ailed me. I
watched Raymond shuffle off. If he would only stand
up straight, and shave! He needed to buy some nice
shirts and some proper shoes, and read a book or two
instead of playing computer games. How could he
ever hope to find a nice girl otherwise?

Keith came up to the table and thanked me for
coming. I gave him his birthday present, which he
seemed to find genuinely surprising. He looked at
each item in turn with an expression that I found
hard to read, but I quickly eliminated "boredom" and
"indifference." I felt happy; it was a nice feeling, giving someone a gift, the kind of unique, thoughtful
present that he wouldn't have received from anyone
else. He put the carrier bag on a nearby table.

"Would you, eh, would you like to dance, Eleanor?"

My heart started to pump faster. Dance! Could I?

"I'm not sure I know how," I said.

Keith laughed, and pulled me to my feet.

"Come on," he said, "you'll be fine."

We'd only just reached the wooden dancing area when the music changed, and he groaned.

"I'm sorry," he said, "but there's no way. I'm going to have to sit this one out. Birthday boy privileges!"

I watched as some people left the dance floor and others flocked to take their place. The music had a lot of brass instruments and a fast beat. Michelle, Gary's girlfriend, beckoned me over and pulled me into a small group of women, around the same age, who smiled at me and looked very happy. I joined in with what seemed to be jigging on the spot. Some people moved their arms as though they were jogging, some people were pointing at nothing; it appeared that you were supposed to move your body around in any way you saw fit, as long as it was in time with the music, which was a steady eight beats, helpfully marked out by a drum. Then the beat changed abruptly and everyone started doing the same thing, making strange shapes with their arms above their head. It took me a moment or two to learn the shapes, and then I was able to copy them. Free-form jigging, communal shapes in the air; free-form jigging, communal shapes in the air. Dancing was easy!

I found myself not thinking about anything, sort of like how the vodka worked, but different, because I was with people and I was singing. YMCA! YMCA! Arms in the air, mimicking the letters—what a marvelous idea! Who knew that dancing could be so logical?

During the next free-form jigging section, I started
to wonder why the band was singing about, presumably, the Young Men's Christian Association, but
then, from my very limited exposure to popular music,
people did seem to sing about umbrellas and fire-
starting and Emily Brontë novels, so, I supposed, why
not a gender- and faith-based youth organization?

The song finished and another one began; this one
was not nearly so much fun, being entirely free-form
jigging with no communal arm patterns in between,
but nevertheless I remained on the dance floor, with
the same group of smiling women, feeling that I was
in the swing of things now. I was beginning to understand why people might find dancing enjoyable,
although I wasn't sure I could manage an entire evening of it. I felt a quick tap on my shoulder and turned
around, expecting Raymond to be there, a smile ready
as I thought how he'd like to hear about the arm-shape
dance, but it wasn't him.

It was a man in his mid- to late thirties, whom
I'd never met before. He smiled and raised his eyebrows, like a question, and then simply started free-
form jigging in front of me. I turned back to the group
of smiling women, but the circle had reformed without me. The man, red-faced, short, with the pasty
look of someone who has never eaten an apple, continued to jig enthusiastically, if somewhat unrhythmi-
cally. At a loss as to how to respond, I resumed my
dancing. He leaned forward and said something,

which, naturally, was rendered inaudible by the volume of the music.

"I beg your pardon?" I shouted.

"I said," he shouted, much louder than before, "how do you know Keith?"

What a bizarre question to ask a stranger.

"I assisted his father when he had an accident," I said. I had to repeat this twice before the man understood—perhaps he had some sort of hearing impairment. When it had finally penetrated, he looked intrigued. He lunged forward toward me with what I could only describe as a leer.

"Are you a nurse?" he said.

"No," I said, "I'm a finance administration assistant." He seemed to be at a bit of a loss for words after that, and I looked ceiling-ward as we jigged in order to discourage further conversation; it was quite challenging to dance and speak at the same time.

When the song ended, I'd had enough for the time being, and felt in fairly urgent need of refreshment.

"Can I get you a drink?" the man yelled, over the top of the next song. I wondered whether the DJ had ever considered introducing a five-minute break between records, to allow people to go to the bar or the lavatory in peace. Perhaps I should suggest that to him later.

"No thank you," I said. "I don't want to accept a drink from you, because then I would be obliged to purchase one for you in return, and I'm afraid I'm simply not interested in spending two drinks' worth of time with you."

"Eh?" he said, cupping his hand around his ear. Clearly he had tinnitus or some other hearing impairment. I communicated via mime, simply shaking my head and waving my index finger, while mouthing NO. I turned around and went in search of the lavatory before he attempted any further conversation.

It was difficult to find, located down a corridor, and I could only see signs for a Powder Room. This, it eventually transpired, meant Lavatories. Why don't people just call things what they are? It's confusing. There was a queue, which I joined, standing behind a very inebriated woman who was dressed inappropriately for her age. I do feel that tube tops are best suited to the under twenty-fives, if, indeed, they are suited to anyone.

A sheer, sparkly jacket was doing an inadequate job of covering up her enormous, crepey bosom. Her makeup, which would have been subtle had it been intended for a stage performance in the Royal Albert Hall, had started to run. For some reason, I could imagine this woman sobbing on the stairs at the end of the night. I surprised myself with the insight, but there was something rather febrile about her demeanor which led one to this conclusion.

"How much of your life do you think you've wasted queuing for the bogs?" she asked, conversationally. "They never have enough of them, do they?"

I didn't speak, as I was trying to calculate the approximate queuing time, but she didn't seem to mind that I hadn't responded.

"It's all right for the men, isn't it?" she went on, in an angry tone. "There's never a queue for the Gents. Sometimes I feel like just going in there, squatting over the urinal. Ha!" she said. "Imagine their faces!" She laughed, a long, smoky laugh that turned into a protracted cough.

"Oh, but I think it would be terribly unhygienic in the Gentlemen's toilets," I said. "They don't seem to mind so much about cleanliness and that sort of thing."

"No," she said, her voice full of bitterness, "they just come in, piss everywhere and then waltz off, leaving someone else to clean up after them." She gazed unsteadily off into the distance, clearly with a specific individual in mind.

"I feel quite sorry for them, actually," I said. She glared at me, and I hurried to clarify my statement. "I mean, imagine having to micturate in a row, alongside other men, strangers, acquaintances, friends even? It must be dreadful. Just think how odd it would be if we had to display our genitals to one another when we finally reached the front of this queue!"

She belched, very gently, and stared with uninhibited frankness at my scars. I turned my head away.

"You're a bit mental, aren't you?" she said, not in the least aggressively, but slurring her words somewhat. It was hardly the first time I'd heard this.

"Yes," I said, "yes, I suppose I am." She nodded, like I had confirmed a long-held suspicion. We didn't talk after that.

When I returned to the function suite, the mood had changed—the pace of the music was slower. I went to the bar and bought myself a Magners and a vodka and cola, and, after a moment's thought, a pint of beer for Raymond. It was quite tricky to carry it all back to our little table, but I managed without spilling a drop. I was glad to sit down, after all the jigging and queuing, and finished my vodka in two gulps—dancing was thirsty work. Raymond's denim coat was still slung over the back of his chair, but there was no sign of him. I thought he had perhaps gone outside to smoke. I had a lot to tell him, about the dancing, about the queue lady, and I was looking forward to doing so.

The music changed again, and was now even slower. Lots of people left the floor, and those who remained drifted together. It was a strange sight, like something from the natural world; monkeys, perhaps, or birds. The women all put their arms around the men's necks, and the men put their arms around the women's waists. They swayed from side to side, shuffling their feet awkwardly, either looking into one another's faces, or else resting their heads on each other's shoulders.

It was some sort of mating ritual, clearly. But then, might it not be quite pleasurable, to sway in time to slow music, pressed close against someone rather wonderful? I looked at them all again, the various sizes and shapes and permutations of them. And there, in the middle, was Raymond, dancing with Laura. He was speaking into her ear, close enough to be able to smell her perfume. She was laughing.

The drink I'd bought him was going to go to waste. I picked it up and drank it down, the whole pint, acrid and bitter tasting. I stood up and put on my jerkin. I'd visit the Powder Room one more time, and then I would get the train back into town. The party, it seemed, was over.

# 21

Monday, Monday. Things didn't feel right; I hadn't been able to relax yesterday, hadn't been able to settle to anything. I just felt on edge, somehow. If my mood was a crossword clue, the answer would be "discombobulated." I tried to think why, but was unable to arrive at a plausible conclusion. I'd ended up taking the bus into town in the afternoon (free of charge—thank you, travel pass) and gone back to see Bobbi Brown. Once again, Ms. Brown herself had failed to report for duty—I feared her work ethic was somewhat lacking—and a different lady had made me up, almost the same as last time. On this occasion, I'd purchased the multiple products and tools required to re-create the same face at home.

The total cost exceeded my monthly council tax bill by some margin, but I was in such a strange mood that this did not deter me. I kept the painted face on all day, and had reapplied it this morning, in an almost exact facsimile. The lady had shown me what to do, including the careful blending of concealer over my scars. The smoky eye was a bit uneven today but that, she had said, was the beauty of a smoky eye—it didn't need to be precise.

I'd forgotten I'd done it, until I got to the office and Billy whistled, a wolf whistle, in fact, which made the others turn and look.

"New hair, bit of lippy," he said, nudging me with his elbow. I shrank back. "Somebody's hoping to get herself a bit of action, if I'm not mistaken?"

The women gathered round. I was wearing my new outfit too. "You look lovely, Eleanor!" "Black really suits you." "I love those boots, where did you get them?" I examined their faces, looking out for sly glances, waiting for a punch line. None was forthcoming.

"Where did you get your hair done, by the way?" Janey said. "It's a very flattering cut."

"Heliotrope, in town," I said. "Laura did it. She's a friend of mine," I said proudly. Janey looked impressed. "I might try them out," she said. "My hairdresser is moving up north, so I'm looking for someone new. Does your friend do wedding hair, d'you know?"

I rummaged in my shopper. "Here's her card," I said, "why not give her a call?"

Janey beamed at me. Could this be right? I smiled back quickly—if in doubt, smile, remember—and made for my desk.

Was this how it worked, then, successful social integration? Was it really that simple? Wear some lipstick, go to the hairdressers and alternate the clothes you wear? Someone ought to write a book, or at least an explanatory pamphlet, and pass this information on. I had had more attention from them today (nonmalevolent, positive attention, that is) than I'd had in the last few years. I smiled to myself, pleased that I'd unlocked part of the puzzle. An electronic message arrived.

> You ran off on Saturday without saying cheerio—everything OK? R.

I hit reply.

> Fine, thank you. I had simply had enough of the dancing and other people. E.

He replied instantly.

> Lunch? Usual place, 12:30? R.

Much to my surprise, I realized that I actually liked the idea of having lunch with Raymond, and was genuinely pleased to be asked. We had a Usual Place! I steeled myself as best I could, and, with teeth gritted, using only one finger I typed:

> C U there E.

I sat back, feeling a bit queasy. Illiterate communication was quicker, that was true, but not by much. I'd saved myself the trouble of typing four whole characters. Still, it was part of my new credo, trying new things. I'd tried it, and I very definitely did not like it. LOL could go and take a running jump. I wasn't made for illiteracy; it simply didn't come naturally. Although it's good to try new things and to keep an open mind, it's also extremely important to stay true to who you really are. I read that in a magazine at the hairdressers.

Raymond was already there when I arrived, chatting to a different yet almost identical young man with a beard from the one who'd served us last time. I ordered a frothy coffee and a cheese scone again, which made Raymond smile.

"You're a creature of habit, Eleanor, aren't you?" I shrugged.

"You look nice, by the way," he said. "I like your . . ." He gestured indistinctly at my face. I nodded.

"People seem to like me better with makeup on, for some reason," I said. He raised his eyebrows and shrugged, apparently as stumped as I was.

The bearded man brought our food and Raymond began shoveling it into his face.

"Did you have a good time on Saturday, then?" he asked. I wished it had been between mouthfuls, but it was, in fact, horrifically, *during* one.

"Yes, thank you," I said. "It was the first time I've tried dancing, and I quite enjoyed it." He kept forking the food into his mouth. The process, and the noise, seemed almost industrial in its relentlessness.

"Did *you* enjoy yourself?" I asked.

"Mmm," he said. "It was fun, wasn't it?" He wasn't using a knife, but held a fork in his right hand like a child or an American. He smiled.

I considered asking whether he and Laura had danced again that evening, whether he'd escorted her home, but decided against it. It was none of my

business, after all, and intrusive questions are very
ill-mannered.

"Eh, so . . . did you decide about the promotion?
Are you going to take it?"

I had, of course, been pondering this in spare
moments throughout the preceding days. I had looked
for signs, clues—none were forthcoming, however,
except that, last Friday, twelve across had read: *in
favor of (upward) movement (9)*. I had taken this as
an encouraging omen.

"I'm going to say yes," I said.

He smiled, put down his fork and held up his
hand. I realized I was meant to place mine against his
in what I now recognized as a "high five."

"Nice one," he said, resuming his lunch. "Con-
gratulations."

I felt a flash of happiness, like a match being struck.
I couldn't recall ever having been congratulated on
anything before. It was very pleasant indeed.

"How's your mother, Raymond?" I asked him,
having enjoyed the moment and the last of the scone.
He talked about her for a while, told me she'd been
asking after me. I felt slightly concerned about this, a
default anxiety pertaining to maternal inquisitive-
ness, but he put my mind at rest.

"She really liked you—said to tell you to pop over
anytime," he said. "She's lonely."

I nodded. I had recognized that. He excused himself and plodded off to the bathroom, and I gazed
around the café while I awaited his return. Two

women around my age were seated at the table next to me, each with a brightly dressed baby. Both infants were in car seats; one was asleep, the other stared dreamily at a beam of sunlight as it danced on the wall. The coffee machine hissed into life behind us, and I watched alarm ripple in waves across his face. In slow motion, his sweet pink mouth puckered into a kiss and then opened wide to release a wail at quite momentous volume. His mother glanced down and, reassured that he was fine despite the noise, continued her conversation. The crying got louder. It made evolutionary sense, I supposed, that a baby's cries of distress would be tuned to precisely the right pitch and volume to make them impossible for an adult human to ignore.

He was winding himself up now, fists balled furiously, his face getting redder by the minute. I closed my eyes, tried and failed to ignore the noise. *Please stop crying, please stop crying. I don't know why you are crying. What do I need to do to make you stop? I don't know what to do. Are you hurt? Are you ill? Hungry. I don't know what to do. Please don't cry. There isn't anything to eat. Mummy will be back soon. Where's Mummy?* My hand was shaking as I picked up my coffee cup, and I breathed as slowly as I could, staring at the tabletop.

The crying ceased. I looked up and saw the baby, lying quietly in his mother's arms now as she covered his face with kisses. I breathed out. My heart soared for him.

≈

When Raymond returned, I paid for lunch, since he had paid last time; I was really starting to get the hang of the concept of a payment schedule. He insisted on leaving the tip, however. Five pounds! All the man had done was carry our food from the kitchen to the table, a job for which he was already being recompensed by the café owner. Raymond was reckless and profligate— no wonder he couldn't afford proper shoes or an iron.

We walked back slowly to the office, and Raymond told me in detail about some computer server issue that I did not understand (and didn't particularly care to) that he would have to deal with that afternoon. In the lobby, he turned toward the stairs, where his office was located.

"See you soon, yeah?" he said. "Take care."

He actually sounded like he meant both; that he would indeed see me soon, and that he wished me to take care of myself. I felt a warmth inside, a cozy, glowy feeling like hot tea on a cold morning.

"Take care yourself, Raymond," I said, and I meant it.

≈

That evening, I had planned to relax with a cup of Bovril and listen to a very interesting radio program about South American politics, after completing my usual checks on what Johnnie Lomond was up to.

He'd sent a desultory tweet about a character in a television program and posted a photograph on Facebook of a new pair of boots he wanted. A slow news day, then. Hearing from Mummy on a Monday was an unexpected, unwelcome surprise.

"Eleanor, darling. Not our usual time to talk, I know, but I was thinking about you. Just wanted to say hello, see how you were getting on, you know the sort of thing."

I was silent, shocked by the unscheduled intrusion into my evening.

"Well?" she said. "I'm waiting, darling . . ."

I cleared my throat.

"I, er . . . I'm fine, Mummy. You were—*thinking* about me?" This was a first.

"Mmm. Two things really: first of all, do you want me to see if I can give you a hand with your project? I can't do much from where I am, obviously, but I might be able to, I don't know, pull some strings? Might there perhaps be some way I could engineer a little visit, come and help you? I mean, I know it sounds impossible, but one never knows . . . mountains can always be moved and so on—"

"No, Mummy, oh no, no, no . . ." I said, gabbling. I heard her take in a breath, and forced my words into order. "What I mean, Mummy"—I heard the hiss as she released the air trapped in her lungs—"is that it's very kind of you to offer, but I think I'm going to decline."

"Might one ask why?" she said, sounding some-what put out.

"It's just . . . I really do think I've got everything under control here," I said. "I think it'd be better if you . . . stayed put, as it were. I'm not sure there's anything more you can do at this point."

"Well, darling . . . if you're sure. But I'm very effi-cient, you know? And, to be frank, you're a bit of a bumbling idiot at times."

I sighed, as quietly as I could.

"And furthermore," she went on, "I'm getting rather impatient now. Things need to move forward with this man, you know? A bit more action, Eleanor—that's what's needed, darling." She was starting to sound calmer now.

"Yes, Mummy. Yes, you're absolutely right of course." It was true that, since the time when I'd first seen the musician, my interest and therefore my prog-ress had been subsumed by more pressing matters over the last few weeks. There were so many other things to be getting on with—Raymond, the new job, Sammy and his family . . . But she was right.

"I'll try to move things along a bit faster," I said. That had placated her, I hoped, and she started to say her good-byes.

"Oh wait, Mummy—hang on a second. You said there were two things—what was the second thing you were thinking about?"

"Oh yes," she said, and I heard her dismissive sideways hiss of cigarette smoke. "It was just that I wanted to tell you that you're a pointless waste of human tissue. That was all. Bye then, darling!" she said, bright as a knife.

Silence.

@johnnieLrocks
Newsflash! Am leaving Pilgrim
Pioneers. No hard feelings
TOTALLY respect those guys
#soloartist #astarisborn (1/2)

@johnnieLrocks
I'm going solo in a different,
stronger musical direction.
More soon. Peace out
#iconoclast (2/2)

# 22

Mummy got in touch again on Wednesday as usual, the interval between our conversations all too brief.

"What ho!" she said. "Me again! Anything new to share with Mummy?"

In the absence of any other salient news since Monday, I told her about Keith's birthday party.

"Quite the social butterfly these days, aren't you, Eleanor?" she said, her voice unpleasantly sweet.

I said nothing; it's usually the safest course of action.

"What did you wear? I bet you looked ridiculous. For the love of God, please tell me you didn't attempt to dance, daughter mine." She somehow intuited the answer from my tense silence.

"Oh dear," she said. "Dancing's for the beautiful people, Eleanor. The thought of you, lumbering about like a walrus . . ." She laughed long and hard. "Oh, thank you, thanks very much, darling. That's made my night, it really has." She laughed again. "Eleanor, dancing!"

"How are you, Mummy?" I said quietly.

"Fine, darling, just fine. It's chili night tonight, always a treat. We're going to watch a film later.

The wonder of Wednesdays!" Her tone was breezy, cheerful—it had a borderline manic quality that I recognized.

"I got promoted, Mummy," I said, unable to keep a little flash of pride from my voice. She snorted.

"Promoted! How *incredibly* impressive, darling. What does that mean—an extra five pounds a month?"

I said nothing.

"Still," she said, her voice dripping with patronizing sweetness, "*good for you*, darling. I mean it, really, *well done*." I looked at the floor, felt tears come.

She spoke to someone else, a semi-snarl; "Naw, ah fucking didnae! Ah said *Sex and the City 2*! Aye, I did! I thought we were taking a vote. Eh? Again? Oh, for fuck's . . ." She spoke directly to me again.

"My fellow residents have elected to watch *The Shawshank Redemption* yet again, if you can believe it; it's only been, oooh, twenty consecutive Wednesdays now . . .

"Listen—don't go getting sidetracked from your project with all this *new job* and *birthday party* nonsense. There's a task in hand, and you need to remain focused on it. Faint heart never won fair chap, you know. Imagine if you were to provide me with a handsome, appropriate son-in-law, Eleanor. That would be *normal*, darling, wouldn't it? We'd be a *normal* family then."

She laughed, and I did too—the concept was just too bizarre to contemplate.

"I was cursed with daughters," she said sadly, "and yet I always wanted a son. A son-in-law will do at a push—so long as he's suitable. You know: polite, thoughtful, considerate, well behaved. He is all of those things, isn't he, this *project* of yours, Eleanor? A well-dressed man? Well spoken? You know I've always tried to impress upon you how appropriate it is to talk properly and look the part."

"He seems very nice, Mummy," I said. "Very suitable. Handsome and talented and successful. Glamorous!" I said, warming to my theme. Obviously, I knew next to nothing about him, so I was embellishing the scant information I'd gleaned about Johnnie Lomond from my research. It was quite fun.

Her tone was dismissive, with an undercurrent of menace. The default tone.

"Oh God, I'm bored now. I'm bored of this conversation, and I'm bored of waiting for you to complete this project. Off you trot, Eleanor. For heaven's sake, please don't trouble yourself by being proactive and pushing forward with it. Oh no, heaven forfend. Please—continue to do nothing. Go and sit in your empty little flat and watch television on your own, just like you do Every. Single. Night."

I heard her shout, "I'm coming! Dinnae start without me!" The click of a lighter, an intake of breath.

"Must dash, Eleanor. Toodle-oo!"

Dead air.

I sat down and watched television alone, like I do Every. Single. Night.

I suppose one of the reasons we're all able to continue to exist for our allotted span in this green and blue vale of tears is that there is always, however remote it might seem, the possibility of change. I never thought, in my strangest imaginings, that I would find my job anything other than eight hours of drudgery. It was a source of astonishment to me that, on many days of the week now, I'd check my watch and see that hours had gone by without my noticing. The office manager role involved numerous new tasks that I had to learn and perfect. None of them was beyond the wit of man, obviously, but some were reasonably complex, and I was surprised at how enthusiastically my brain responded to the new challenges placed before it. My colleagues had appeared somewhat underwhelmed upon hearing the news that I would be managing them, but, thus far at least, there had been no sign of mutiny or insubordination. I kept myself to myself, as always, and allowed them to get on with their jobs (or what passed for doing their jobs, insofar as they never actually did very much, and tended to make a mess of the few tasks they actually attempted). For the time being, at least, the status quo prevailed, and they were, so far, no more ineffectual than they'd been prior to my installation.

The new role meant interacting with Bob more frequently, and I discovered that he was actually quite an amusing interlocutor. He shared a lot of details about the day-to-day running of the business with me, and was delightfully indiscreet about clients. Clients, I soon learned, could be very demanding; I still had limited direct contact with them, which suited me just fine.

From what I could gather, they would routinely be completely unable to articulate their requirements, at which point, in desperation, the designers would create some artwork for them based on the few vague hints they had managed to elicit. After many hours of work, involving a full team of staff, the work would be submitted to the client for approval. At that point, the client would say, "No. That's exactly what I *don't* want."

There would be several tortuous iterations of this process before the client finally declared his or herself satisfied with the end results. Inevitably, Bob said, the artwork that was signed off on at the end of the process was virtually identical to the first piece of work submitted, which the client had immediately dismissed as unsuitable. It was no wonder, I thought, that he kept the staff room well stocked with beer, wine and chocolate, and that the art team availed themselves of it quite so frequently.

I'd started planning the Christmas lunch too. I had only vague ideas at the moment, but, like our clients, I was very clear as to what I *didn't* want. No chain restaurants or hotels, no turkey, no Santa; nowhere that said "corporate entertainment" or "office party" on their website. It would take time to track down the

perfect venue and plan the perfect event, but I had
months yet.

Raymond and I continued to meet for lunch, roughly
once per week. It was always on a different day, which
annoyed me, but he was a man who was extremely
resistant to routine (something that shouldn't have surprised me). One day, he e-mailed me less than twenty-
four hours after we'd met, to invite me for lunch again
the very next day. I could almost believe that someone
might enjoy, or at least tolerate, my company over the
duration of a brief luncheon, but it stretched credibil-
ity to think that it could happen twice in one week.

> Dear R, I'd be delighted to meet you for lunch
> again, but am somewhat perplexed due to the
> proximity to our previous meeting. Is
> everything in order? Regards, E

He replied thus:

> Got something I need to tell you. See you at
> 1230 R

We were so habituated to our lunchtime meetings
that he did not even need to specify the venue.

When I arrived, he wasn't there, so I perused a
newspaper that was lying on the chair next to me.
Strangely, I'd come to like this shabby place; the staff,
whilst off-putting in appearance, were uniformly
pleasant and friendly, and now more than one of
them was able to say "The usual, is it?" to me, and
then bring my coffee and cheese scone without my

having to request it. It's very vain and superficial of me, I know, but it made me feel like someone in an American situation comedy, being a "regular," having a "usual." The next step would have been effortlessly witty badinage, but unfortunately we were still some way away from that. One of the staff—Mikey—came over with a glass of water.

"Do you want yours now, or are you waiting for Raymond?" he said.

I told him I was expecting Raymond imminently, and Mikey began wiping down the table next to me.

"How's tricks, anyway?" he asked.

"I'm fine," I said. "It feels like we're getting toward the last days of summer." This was something I had been thinking as I walked to the café, feeling gentle rays on my face, seeing a few red and gold leaves among the green. Mikey nodded.

"I'm finishing up here at the end of the month," he said.

"Oh!" I said. "That's a pity." Mikey was kind and gentle, and always brought truffles with the coffees, without being asked or seeking additional payment.

"Have you found a new position somewhere else?" I said.

"No," he said, perching on a chair beside me. "Hazel's really poorly again." Hazel, I knew, was his girlfriend, and they lived nearby with their bichon frise and their baby, Lois.

"I'm very sorry to hear that, Mikey," I said. He nodded.

"They thought they'd got rid of it all the last time, but it's come back, spread to the lymph nodes and the liver. I just wanted to, you know . . ."

"You wanted to spend the time she has left with Hazel and Lois, rather than serving cheese scones to strange women," I said, and, gratifyingly, he laughed.

"That's about the size of it," he said. I braced myself, then put my hand on his arm. I was going to say something, but then I couldn't think what was the right thing to say, so I just kept silent, and looked at him, hoping he'd intuit what I meant—that I was desperately sorry, that I admired him for caring so much about Hazel and Lois and looking after them, that I understood, perhaps more than most, about loss, about how difficult things must be, and would continue to be. However much you loved someone, it wasn't always enough. Love alone couldn't keep them safe . . .

"Thanks, Eleanor," he said gently. He thanked me!

Raymond arrived and threw himself into his seat.

"All right, mate?" he asked Mikey. "How's Hazel doing?"

"Not bad, Raymond, not bad. I'll get you a menu." After he'd left, I leaned forward. "You knew already about Hazel?" I said. He nodded.

"It's shite, isn't it? She's not even thirty, and wee Lois isn't two yet."

He shook his head. Neither of us spoke—there really wasn't anything else to say. Once we had ordered, Raymond cleared his throat.

"I've got something to tell you, Eleanor. It's more bad news—sorry."

I sat back in my chair, and looked up at the ceiling, readying myself.

"Go on," I said. There's very little in life that I couldn't imagine, or brace myself for. Nothing could be worse than what I've already experienced—that sounds like hyperbole, but it's a literal statement of fact. I suppose it's actually a source of strength, in a strange way.

"It's Sammy," he said.

I hadn't been expecting that.

"He passed away at the weekend, Eleanor. A massive coronary. It was quick, at least." I nodded. It was both a surprise and not a surprise.

"What happened?" I said. Raymond started eating, telling me the details between—and during—mouthfuls. I'm not sure what it would take to put that man off his food. The Ebola virus, perhaps.

"He was at Laura's," he said, "just watching the telly. No warning, nothing."

"Was she there at the time?" I asked. Please God, let her have been spared that. Trying to live on afterward, trying to manage the guilt and the pain and the horror of it all . . . I would not wish that on another human being. I would happily assume her burden if I could. I'd barely notice it, I'm sure, on top of my own.

"She was upstairs, getting ready to go out," he said. "Got a hell of a shock when she came down and found him on the sofa like that."

So it wasn't her fault. She couldn't have saved him, even if she'd tried. It was fine—well, as fine as death could be. I considered the facts further.

"He was alone at the time death occurred, then," I said, intrigued. "Do the police suspect foul play?"

He choked on his halloumi burger and I had to pass him a glass of water.

"For fuck's sake, Eleanor!" he said.

"I'm sorry," I said, "it was just something that popped into my mind."

"Aye, well, sometimes best not to say the first thing that pops into your mind out loud, eh?" he said quietly, not looking at me.

I felt terrible. I felt terrible for Sammy and for his family, I felt terrible for upsetting Raymond without meaning to, I felt terrible for the waiter and his girlfriend and their poor little baby. All this death, all this suffering, happening to nice people, good people who'd done nothing to deserve it, and no one able to stop it . . . Tears came, and the more I tried to fight them, the more they came. The lump in my throat was burning, burning like fire, no please, not fire . . .

Raymond had slid around to the seat beside me and put his arm around my shoulders. He spoke in a soft, low voice.

"Ah please, Eleanor, don't cry. I'm really sorry . . . I didn't mean to snap at you, I really didn't . . . please, Eleanor . . ."

The strange thing—something I'd never expected—was that it actually made you feel better when someone put their arm around you, held you close. Why? Was it some mammalian thing, this need for human contact? He was warm and solid. I could smell his deodorant, and the detergent he used to wash his clothes—over both scents there lay a faint patina of cigarettes. A Raymond smell. I leaned in closer.

Eventually, I managed to regain control of my emotions, and the embarrassing tears abated. I sniffed, and he returned to his own side of the table, rummaged in his jacket pocket and passed me a packet of tissues. I smiled at him, took one and blew my nose. I was aware that I was making a most unladylike honking sound, but what else could I do?

"Sorry," I said.

He gave me a feeble smile.

"I know," he said. "It's really hard, isn't it?"

I took a moment to process everything that he'd told me.

"How's Laura? What about Keith and Gary?"

"They're in bits, as you'd expect."

"I'm going to attend the funeral," I said, decisively.

"Me too," he said. He slurped on his cola. "He was a funny old bloke, wasn't he?"

I smiled, swallowed down the lump in my throat. "He was nice," I said. "You could tell that straightaway, even when he was unconscious on the pavement."

Raymond nodded. He reached across the table and squeezed my hand. "At least he had a few weeks with his family after the accident, eh? Good weeks—his wee party, Keith's fortieth. He got a chance to spend time with all the people he loved."

I nodded. "Can I ask you something, Raymond?" I said.

He looked at me.

"What's the etiquette for funerals? Are mourners still required to wear black, and are hats de rigueur?"

He shrugged. "No idea . . . just wear whatever you want, I guess. Sammy's not the kind of guy who'd be bothered about that sort of thing, is he?"

I pondered this. "I'll wear black," I said, "to be on the safe side. No hat, though."

"No, I'm not wearing a hat either," said Raymond, and we actually laughed. We laughed far longer than his feeble witticism merited, just because it felt good.

We didn't speak on the walk back to the office. The weak sun was in our faces, and I held mine up to it for a moment, like a cat. Raymond was scuffing through the light carpet of fallen leaves, his red training shoes flashing through all the bronze. A gray squirrel bounded in fluid semicircles across our path, and there was that almost autumnal smell in the air, apples and wool. We didn't even speak when we got inside. Raymond took both my hands in his and squeezed them, just for a second, and then released them at my sides. He went upstairs and I walked around the corner to my office.

I felt like a newly laid egg, all swishy and gloopy inside, and so fragile that the slightest pressure could break me. There was already an e-mail waiting for me by the time I sat down at my desk.

C U Friday Rx

Was a response required? I suspected it was, so I just sent this:

X

# 23

I was getting the hang of this shopping business. I had returned to the same department store and, after seeking advice from a different shop assistant, had purchased a black dress, black tights and black shoes. This was my first dress since childhood, and it felt strange to have my legs on public display. She had tried to steer me toward vertiginous heels again—why are these people so incredibly keen on crippling their female customers? I began to wonder if cobblers and chiropractors had established some fiendish cartel. On reflection, though, she was correct in stating that the fitted black dress did not really "go" with either my new boots (too informal, apparently) or my Velcro work shoes (it appeared that nothing did, much to my surprise; I had thought that they were the very definition of versatility).

We compromised with some improbably named "kitten heels," which, contrary to what one might think, had nothing to do with cats. They were heels which were easy to walk in, but which were, nonetheless, "very feminine." On what basis was this decided, and by whom? Did it matter? I made a mental note to research gender politics and gender identity at some point. There would be a book about it—there were books about everything.

On this trip, I'd even bought a handbag, judging that my shopper probably wouldn't be appropriate for a funeral. The fabric was imprinted with a very jaunty pattern, and I felt it might stand out at a graveside. The wheels could also be a bit squeaky.

The bag I finally settled on was impractical, being far too small to carry, for example, either a hardback book or a bottle of Glen's. I examined it when I got home, stroking its glossy leather outer and silky fabric lining. It had a long gold chain which you simply placed over your shoulder, leaving your hands free.

At further horrendous expense, I'd also bought a black wool coat, single-breasted, knee-length, fitted. It was warm and plain, characteristics that I found attractive. Looking at all my purchases, spread across my bed for closer examination, I assuaged my concerns about the cost by reassuring myself that the entire outfit could be worn again and again, either together or separately. I now owned what I believed was called a "capsule wardrobe," clothes which were appropriate for most social events that the musician and I might attend together. I'd look right in them, on his arm. An evening at the ballet, perhaps? The opening night of a new play? I knew he'd be opening up uncharted worlds for me. At least now I had the appropriate shoes for them.

I'd spent more in these last few weeks than I usually spent in a year. Social interaction, it appeared, was surprisingly expensive—the travel, the clothes, the drinks, the lunches, the gifts. Sometimes it evened out in the end—like with the drinks—but, I was finding out, more often than not, one incurred a net financial loss. I'd a bit of money saved up, but it only amounted to a month's wages or so, and Bob's paychecks were far from generous. I saw now that this had only been possible because I hadn't had much requirement to spend money on the social aspects of life before now.

Mummy liked to live extravagantly, but after . . . everything changed . . . I'd learned that money was something to worry about, to ration. It had to be asked for, and then counted out into my red raw hands. I never forgot—was never allowed to forget— that someone else was paying for my clothes, the food I ate, even for the heating in the room where I slept. My foster carers received an allowance for looking after me, and I was always conscious of making sure not to cause them to exceed it by *needing* things. And especially not by *wanting* things.

"Allowance" is not a generous, lavish word. I earn my own money now, of course, but I have to be careful with it. Budgeting is a skill, and a very useful one at that—after all, if I were to run out of funds, find myself indebted, there is no one, not a single soul, on whom I could call to bail me out. I'd be destitute. I have no anonymous benefactor to pay my rent, no family members or friends who could kindly lend me the money to replace a broken vacuum cleaner or pay

the gas bill until I could return the borrowed sum to
them on payday. It was important that I did not allow
myself to forget that.

Nevertheless, I couldn't attend Sammy's funeral
in inappropriate clothing. The black dress, the assistant assured me, was smart, but could also be "dressed
down." The coat could be worn all winter. My jerkin
had more than paid for itself over the years, but I
would keep it, of course, in case it was required again
in future. I hung everything up carefully. I was ready.
Bring out your dead.

≈

Friday was bright, although it was impossible to tell
if it would stay that way. I showered and put on my
new clothes. It had been many years since I'd worn
tights, preferring a handy pair of pop socks under my
slacks, but I still remembered how to roll them on. I
was very careful, as they were thin and delicate, and
could be ripped in an instant by a careless fingernail.
I felt enclosed in them, somehow, as though I was
wearing someone else's skin.

I'd made my legs black, and my hair blond. I'd
lengthened and darkened my eyelashes, dusted a flush
of pink onto my cheeks and painted my lips a shade
of dark red which was rarely found in nature. I should,
by rights, look less like a human woman than I'd ever
done, and yet it seemed that this was the most acceptable, the most appropriate appearance that I'd ever
made before the world. It was puzzling. I supposed

I could have gone further—made my skin glow with tanning agent, scented myself with a spray made from chemicals manufactured in a laboratory, distilled from plants and animal parts. I did not want to do that. I picked up my new bag and locked the door behind me.

For safety and security reasons, I had specified that I should be collected from a location on a main road near my flat rather than disclose my home address, and an unprepossessing vehicle drew up outside the building at the correct time. The driver glanced quickly in the rearview mirror as I slid into the seat behind him, next to Raymond. It took a while, as I was conscious of my dress, trying to make sure that it did not reveal more of my legs than it was designed to.

Everything took so long. Before, I'd simply bathed, run a comb through my hair and pulled on my trousers. Being feminine apparently meant taking an eternity to do anything, and involved quite a bit of advanced planning. I couldn't imagine how it would be possible to hike to the source of the Nile, or to climb up a ladder to investigate a malfunction inside a particle accelerator, wearing kitten heels and ten denier tights.

It was hard to gauge the full effect of Raymond's outfit, but it was apparent, even from this position, that he was wearing an ironed white shirt, a black tie, and black trousers. I couldn't see his feet, and issued a silent prayer that he was not shod in training shoes, even black ones.

"You look nice," he said.

I nodded, feeling slightly self-conscious in my new dress, and looked at him again. He hadn't shaved off his odd little beard, but it had been trimmed, and his hair was combed neatly. The taxi moved off, and we joined the slow morning traffic. The radio jabbered nonsense, and we didn't look at one another or speak. There was really nothing to be said.

≈

The crematorium was in the suburbs, a 1970s monstrosity of white concrete and brutal angles. The gardens were neat in a sterile, municipal way, but, surprisingly, were full of beautiful blown roses. There were lots of mature trees around the perimeter, which pleased me. I liked to think of their roots, coursing with life, snaking under this place. We drew up in an enormous car park which was already almost full, although it was only ten thirty. The place was out of the way and would be impossible to reach by public transport, which was completely illogical. There ought to be a train or a shuttle bus, I thought. It was a place we were all guaranteed to be visiting at some point.

Raymond paid the driver and we stood for a moment, taking it in.

"Ready?" he said.

I nodded. There were lots of other mourners, moving through the grounds like slow black beetles. We walked up the path, in silent agreement that we were in no hurry to leave the trees and the roses and the sunshine and go inside. A long hearse sat at the front door, and we looked at the coffin, which was covered in wreaths. A coffin was a wooden box in which Sammy's corpse would be lying. What was he wearing in there? I wondered. I hoped it was that nice red jumper; cozy, smelling of him.

We sat down on the left-hand side of the room, in a pew not too far from the front. The place was half full already, and there was a low hum of muttered conversation, a muted, insect-like buzzing that I hadn't heard in any other venue or set of circumstances.

I picked up one of the sheets that had been placed along the pews: *Samuel McMurray Thom*, it said, *1940–2017*. Inside it told us what would happen, listed the readings and hymns, and suddenly I was overwhelmed with a desire for it to be over, not to have to be there and experience it all.

Raymond and I were silent. The room was much nicer inside than the exterior had suggested, with wooden beams and a high vaulted ceiling. The entire side wall to the left of where we were seated was glass, and we could see the rolling lawns and more of those huge, primeval trees in the background. I was glad nature should make her presence felt in the room in some way, I thought; living nature, not cut flowers. The sun was quite bright now, and the trees cast short shadows, although autumn was creeping up through a shimmer of wind in the leaves. I turned around and saw that the room was full, perhaps a hundred people, maybe more. The buzzing hum threatened to drown out the dull recorded organ music.

Something shifted in the air and silence fell. Both of his sons and four other men whose faces I recognized from the party carried Sammy's coffin down the aisle and placed it gently on a sort of raised platform with a roller belt, at the end of which was a set of red velvet curtains. I tried to remember what the platform reminded me of, and it came to me: the supermarket checkout in Tesco, where you place your items and they move toward the cashier. I leaned across to tell Raymond, but he had fished a bag of peppermints from his suit pocket and offered me one before I could speak. I popped it in and sucked.

Other people had joined us on the pew, and we'd had to shuffle up like crabs to make space for them. I was therefore in very close proximity to Mr. Raymond Gibbons. I noticed that he smelled extremely pleasant today; the peppermints, of course, but also a clean soap scent and something almost woody, like cedar. I hadn't seen him smoke a cigarette yet. I suppose even Raymond would think it inappropriate to smoke a cigarette outside a crematorium.

The rest of the family entered and sat beside Sammy's boys on the front pew; Laura was on her own, looking impossibly glamorous. Dark glasses! Indoors! Astonishing. They were followed by a jolly-looking minister. A man at a keyboard tucked away in the corner flexed his fingers and started to play, and we shuffled to our feet. The words to the hymn were printed in the booklet but I found that I could remember them from childhood. The communal singing was of extremely poor quality, more like an atonal mumble, and the minister's unpleasant voice was overly loud, perhaps because he was wearing a lapel microphone. He really ought to turn it off for the hymns, I thought—there was no need to amplify his caterwauling. Raymond, to my immense surprise, had a pleasant light tenor, and he was singing properly, unlike most other people. When did people become embarrassed to sing in public? Was it because of the decline in churchgoing? And yet the television schedule was full of singing contests in which people, however untalented, were far from shy about participating. Perhaps people are only interested in giving solo performances.

Surely this was the ultimate in disrespect—to attend a man's funeral and mumble during hymns which, however dreary, had been specifically selected to commemorate his life? I began to sing more loudly. Raymond and I were making more noise than the next four pews put together, and I was glad of it. The words were incredibly sad, and, for an atheist like myself, entirely without hope or comfort, but still; it was our duty to sing them to the best of our ability, and to sing proudly, in honor of Sammy. I sat down when it was finished, happy that Raymond and I had shown him the respect he deserved. Quite a few people turned around to look at us, presumably because they had enjoyed our vocal tribute.

The minister spoke about Sammy's life; it was interesting to hear that he'd grown up near a tiny village in the North East, on a sheep farm. He'd joined the merchant navy when he left school but, soon tiring of life at sea, he'd pitched up in Glasgow with ten pounds, a new suit and no desire whatsoever to return to farming. He'd met Jean in Woolworths, looking for a needle and thread. The minister, looking pleased with himself, said that they'd stitched a happy life together after that. There was a brief religious bit—the usual balderdash—and then, like the assistant in Tesco, he made the coffin conveyer belt move, and Sammy checked out.

Bright as a button, smile plastered on, as though this were the best part of the whole terrible event, the minister announced that we would sing the final hymn. Raymond and I made a valiant effort, but it's impossible to sing when you're crying—there's a lump like a plum stone lodged in your throat, and the music can't get past it. Raymond blew his nose and passed me a packet of tissues, which I gratefully accepted.

The family, the minister told us, would be very pleased if we would join them afterward at the Hawthorn House Hotel for light refreshments. The congregation filed out, shaking hands and mumbling meaningless platitudes. I did the same. There was a collection basket for the British Heart Foundation, "in lieu of flowers," and I saw Raymond drop in a twenty-pound note. I put in three pound coins. If anything, I felt that this was overly generous. Researching new drugs and efficacious treatments for heart disease costs hundreds of millions of pounds. Three pounds or three hundred pounds—it was hardly going to swing the balance between finding and not finding a cure, after all.

I perched on a low wall behind the crematorium and turned my face to the sun. I felt utterly exhausted. After a moment, Raymond sat beside me, and I heard the click of his lighter. I didn't even have the energy to move away. He blew out a long stream of smoke.

"All right?" he said.

I nodded. "You?"

He shrugged.

"Not a big fan of funerals, to be honest," he said. He looked away. "Reminds me of my dad. It was years ago, but it's still hard, you know?"

I nodded; that made sense. Time only blunts the pain of loss. It doesn't erase it.

"I really, really, really do not want to go to the Hawthorn House Hotel for light refreshments, Raymond," I said. "I want to stop thinking about death. I just want to go home, put on normal clothes and watch television."

Raymond stubbed his cigarette out and then buried it in the flower bed behind us.

"No one *wants* to go to these things, Eleanor,"

he said gently. "You have to, though. For the family."
I must have looked sad.

"You don't need to stay long," he said, his voice
soft and patient. "Just show face; have a cup of tea,
eat a sausage roll—you know the drill."

"Well, I hope they've at least got a high meat content and friable pastry," I said, more in hope than in
expectation, and shouldering my handbag.

~

The Hawthorn House Hotel was walking distance
from the crematorium. The woman at the reception
desk smiled, and it was impossible not to notice that
she had only one front tooth; the remaining molars
were the exact same shade as Colman's English mustard. I'm not one to make judgments about other
people's personal appearance, but really; of all the
available staff, was this woman the best choice for the
front desk? She directed us to the Bramble Suite and
flashed us a gappy, sympathetic smile.

We were among the last to arrive, as most people
had driven the short journey from the crematorium
to the hotel. The crematorium was a busy place and
the parking spaces were needed, I supposed. I'm not
sure I'd like to be burned. I think I might like to be
fed to zoo animals. It would be both environmentally
friendly and a lovely treat for the larger carnivores.
Could you request that? I wondered. I made a mental
note to write to the WWF in order to find out.

I went up to Keith and told him how very sorry
I was, and then I sought out Gary to say the same
thing. Both of them looked overwhelmed, which
was understandable. It takes a long time to learn to
live with loss, assuming you ever manage it. After all
these years, I'm still something of a work in progress
in that regard. The grandchildren sat quietly in the
corner, cowed, perhaps, by the somber atmosphere.
The other person I had to pass on my condolences to
was Laura, but I couldn't spot her. She was usually
easy to find. Today, as well as the huge sunglasses,
she'd been wearing vertiginous heels, a short black
dress with a plunging neckline and her hair was piled
on top of her head in an artful birdcage creation that
added several inches to her height.

There being no sign of her, and no sign of the
promised refreshments either, I went in search of the
lavatories. I would have put money on their having a
dusty bowl of apricot-scented potpourri beside the
washbasins, and I was right. On the way back, I spotted a telltale platform heel poking out from behind a
swagged curtain. There was a window seat recess, in
which Laura was sitting in the lap of a man who, it
soon became apparent, was Raymond, although they
were embracing so closely that it took a moment
before I could see his face and be sure. He was wearing black leather shoes, I noticed. So he did at least
possess a pair.

I went back into the Bramble Suite without disturbing them; they hadn't seen me, being very much

otherwise engaged. This was an all too familiar social scenario for me: standing alone, staring into the middle distance. It was absolutely fine. It was absolutely normal. After the fire, at each new school, I'd tried so hard, but something about me just didn't fit. There was, it seemed, no Eleanor-shaped social hole for me to slot into.

I wasn't good at pretending, that was the thing. After what had happened in that burning house, given what went on there, I could see no point in being anything other than truthful with the world. I had, literally, nothing left to lose. But, by careful observation from the sidelines, I'd worked out that social success is often built on pretending just a little. Popular people sometimes have to laugh at things they don't find very funny, do things they don't particularly want to, with people whose company they don't particularly enjoy. Not me. I had decided, years ago, that if the choice was between that or flying solo, then I'd fly solo. It was safer that way. Grief is the price we pay for love, so they say. The price is far too high.

The buffet had been laid out—yes, there were sausage rolls, but also sandwiches. Staff were dispensing indistinguishable tea and coffee from bitter-smelling urns into industrial white crockery. This wouldn't do at all. I was decidedly not in the mood for hot brown liquid, oh no. I was in the mood for cool, clear vodka.

All hotels had bars, didn't they? I wasn't a great frequenter of hostelries, but I knew that bedrooms and bars were their raison d'être. I spoke to the dentally challenged lady in reception again, who directed me down another long corridor, at the end of which lay the imaginatively named Hawthorn Lounge. I stood on the threshold and looked around. The place was deserted, the fruit machines flashing purely for their own amusement. I walked in. Just me. Eleanor, alone.

A barman was watching TV and absentmindedly polishing glasses.

"*Homes Under the Hammer,*" he said, turning toward me. I remember thinking, surprised, that he was passably attractive, and then chastising myself for the thought. My prejudice was that beautiful, glamorous people would not be at work in the Hawthorn House Hotel on a Friday lunchtime. Granted, the receptionist had confirmed my initial thoughts, but really, it was shameful of me to have these preconceptions—where on earth did they come from? (A little voice whispered the answer in my head: *Mummy.*)

The barman smiled, revealing a lovely set of teeth and clear blue eyes.

"It's a load of old shite," he said, in a voice that could strip paint from walls, after giving them a good sanding down first. *See—told you!* Mummy whispered.

"Is it?" I said. "Unfortunately I'm not generally at home during the day to see it."

"Watch it here, if you like," the man said, shrugging.

"Could I?"

"Why not?" he said. "It's not like there's much else going on, is there?" He gestured around the empty bar.

I perched on a bar stool—something I have always wanted to try—and ordered a vodka and cola. He made it slowly, added ice and lemon without asking and pushed it toward me.

"Funeral, was it?" he said.

I wondered how he knew, and then I realized that I was dressed entirely in black, that my smoky eye makeup had run somewhat and that there was no other reason to be in this particular venue at this time of day. I nodded. No further exchanges were required, and we both settled back to see how Iain and Dorothy would fare with the 1970s terrace that they'd bought at auction for £95,000, intending to renovate the bathroom, install a new kitchen and "knock through" from the lounge to the dining room.

"The finishing touch," the presenter said, "was to paint the front door . . . this fetching shade of green."

"'Green Door'," the barman said, without missing a beat, and seconds later, lo and behold, that very song began to play. We both laughed, and he pushed another vodka toward me without my having to ask.

We had moved on to *Loose Women*, another program I was unfamiliar with. I was on my fourth vodka by now, and the funeral service was there in

my mind, but it didn't hurt—like noticing you had a
stone in your shoe, but while you were sitting down
rather than walking on it.

I thought that I probably ought to attempt a sausage roll at some point, or at least put a few in my bag
for later, but then I remembered that I had brought
my new, tiny bag, into which I could fit, at most, two
savory pastries. I tutted, and shook my head.

"What's up?" said the barman. We hadn't asked
each other's names; it didn't seem necessary, somehow. I slumped forward on my stool and stared, in
clichéd fashion, into my glass.

"Oh, it's nothing," I said breezily. "I suppose I
ought to have something to eat now, really."

The barman, who had become less handsome as
time had worn on, picked up my glass, filled it back up
with vodka and a dash of cola and returned it to me.

"No rush, eh?" he said. "Why not stay here and
keep me company for a while longer?"

I looked around—the bar was still deserted.

"You might need a little lie-down after this one,
eh?" he said, tapping my glass and leaning very close
to me. I could see the enlarged pores on the sides of his
nose, some of them filled with microscopic black dots.

"Perhaps," I said. "Sometimes I do need a lie-
down after vodka and cola."

He smiled wolfishly.

"Puts you in the mood, eh?"

I tried to lift my eyebrows into a question, but,
strangely, could only make one of them rise. I'd had

too much to drink because I'd had too much pain, and there was nowhere else it could go but down, drowned in the vodka. Simple, really.

"What do you mean?" I said, hearing that I was pronouncing the consonants somewhat indistinctly.

"Funerals," he said, moving closer to me, so that his face was almost pressed against mine. He smelled of onions. "It's nothing to feel bad about," he said. "All that death . . . afterward, don't you find it really makes you want to—"

"Eleanor!" I felt a hand on my shoulder and turned round on my stool, exceptionally slowly.

"Oh, hello, Raymond!" I said. "This is . . . actually, I don't know. Excuse me, what's your name, Mr. . . . ?"

The barman had moved at what must have been lightning speed to the other end of the counter, where he had resumed his glass polishing and TV watching. Raymond gave him a look that could best be described as unfriendly, and placed a twenty-pound note on the counter.

"Wait, Raymond," I said, scrabbling for my new bag, "I've got some money in here . . ."

"Come on," he said, pulling me down rather gracelessly from my stool. "We can sort it out later."

I trotted after him in my kitten heels.

"Raymond," I said, tugging at his sleeve. He looked down at me. "I'm not going to get a tattoo," I said, "I've decided."

He looked puzzled, and I realized that I'd forgotten to tell him that I'd been considering it, ever since

I'd spoken to the barman at The Cuttings. He sat me down in a window seat off the corridor—not the same one he'd been in before—and left me there. I looked around, wondering what time it was, and whether they would have burned Sammy by now, or whether they kept all the bodies back till the end of the day to get a really good blaze going. Raymond returned, a cup of tea in one hand and a plate of savory pastries in the other.

"Get this down you," he said, "and don't move till I come back."

I discovered that I was ravenous. Mourners kept wandering past, but no one noticed me in my hidey-hole. I rather liked it. The seat was comfortable and the corridor was warm, and I felt like a little dor-mouse in a cozy nest. Next thing I knew, Raymond was there again, shaking me gently but insistently.

"Wake up, Eleanor," he said. "It's half past four. Time to go."

We took a taxi to Raymond's flat. It was on the south side of the city, an area I didn't know very well and had no cause to visit, as a rule. His flatmates were out, I was relieved to learn, stumbling slightly as we entered the hallway and trying not to laugh. He steered me in a very ungallant fashion into the living room, which was dominated by a huge television. There were lots of what I assumed were game con-soles scattered around in front of it. Aside from the computer detritus, it was astonishingly tidy.

"It doesn't look like a place where boys live," I said, surprised.

He laughed. "We're not animals, Eleanor. I'm a dab hand with the Hoover, and Desi's a bit of a neat freak, as it goes."

I nodded, relieved to know as I sat down that nothing untoward would be adhering to my new dress and tights.

"Tea?" he said.

"I don't suppose you've got any vodka or Magners drink, by any chance?" I said. He raised an eyebrow.

"I'm absolutely fine now, after the sausage rolls and the catnap," I said, and I was. I felt floaty and clean, not intoxicated, just very pleasantly numbed to sharp feelings.

He laughed. "Well, I suppose I could go for a glass of red, right enough," he said.

"Red what?" I said.

"Wine, Eleanor. Merlot, I think—whatever was on special at Tesco this week."

"Ah, Tesco," I said. "In that case . . . I think I'll join you. Just the one, though," I said. I didn't want Raymond to think I was a dipsomaniac.

He came back with two glasses and a bottle with a screw cap.

"I thought wine had corks?" I said.

He ignored me. "To Sammy," he said, and we clinked glasses like people do on television. It tasted of warmth and velvet, and a little bit like burned jam.

"Take it easy now!" he said, waggling his finger in a way I recognized was supposed to be humorous. "I don't want you falling off the sofa!"

I smiled. "How was your afternoon?" I asked, after another delicious sip. He took a very big swig.

"You mean apart from rescuing you from the clutches of a pervert?" he said.

I had no idea what he was talking about.

"Och, the afternoon was fine," he said, when it became clear I didn't know how to respond. "It all went off as well as these things can. It'll be tomorrow that it really hits them. The funeral's a big distraction; you keep busy with all the arrangements, stupid decisions about scones or biscuits, hymns—"

"They were bad hymns!" I said.

"—and then the day itself, making sure you thank people, the cortege and all that stuff . . . The family said to thank you for coming, by the way," he finished, trailing off. It was he who was drinking all the wine, I noticed—he'd already refilled his glass while I'd only had two sips.

"But the days and weeks after that . . . that's when it really starts to get hard," he said.

"Is that how it was for you?" I said.

He nodded. He'd switched on the fire, one of those gas ones that's supposed to look real, and we both stared at it. There must be some piece of wiring left over in our brains, from our ancestors, something that means we can't help but stare into a fire, watch it move and dance, warding off evil spirits and dangerous animals . . . that's what fire's supposed to do, isn't it? It can do other things too, though.

"D'you want to watch a film, Eleanor? Cheer ourselves up a bit?"

I thought about this.

"A film would be perfect," I said.

He left the room and returned with another bottle of wine and a big packet of crisps. "Sharing bag" it said. I'd never tried one, for that very reason. He ripped it down the middle and spread it out on the table in front of the sofa where we were both sitting, then topped up our glasses. He went out again and came back with a duvet which I guessed he'd removed from his bed, and a cozy-looking fleece blanket, red like Sammy's sweater, which he passed to me. I kicked off my kitten heels and snuggled under the blanket while he fiddled with what seemed like ten remote control devices. The enormous TV sprung to life, and he flicked through various channels.

"How do you feel about this one?" he said, nodding toward the screen as he wrapped himself in his duvet. The highlighted selection said *Sons of the Desert*. I had no idea what it was, but I realized that I'd happily sit here in the warmth with him and watch a golf program if that was all there was.

"Fine," I said. He was about to press play when I stopped him. "Raymond," I said, "shouldn't you be with Laura?" He looked quite taken aback.

"I saw you today," I said, "and at Keith's golf club birthday party."

His face was impassive.

"She's with her family right now, that's how it should be," he said, shrugging. I sensed he did not wish to speak about it further, and so I simply nodded.

"Ready?" he asked.

The film was black and white, and it was about a fat, clever man and a thin, stupid man who'd joined the Foreign Legion. They were patently unsuited to it. At one point, Raymond laughed so much that he sprayed wine all over his duvet. I choked on a sharing crisp not long afterward and he had to pause the film and thump me on the back to dislodge it. I was very disappointed when it ended, and also to see that we had eaten all the crisps and drunk most of the wine, although Raymond had had far more than me—I couldn't drink wine as quickly as vodka or Magners drink, it seemed.

He walked unsteadily to the kitchen and returned with a big packet of peanuts.

"Fuck," he said, "bowl." He came back with a receptacle, into which he attempted to decant the peanuts. His aim was poor, and he began to pour them all over the coffee table. I started to laugh—it was just like Stan and Ollie—and then we were both laughing. He turned off the TV and put on some music, via another mysterious remote-controlled device. I didn't recognize it, but it was pleasant; soft and undemanding. He chomped on a handful of peanuts.

"Eleanor," he said, nut crumbs falling from his mouth, "can I ask you something?"

"You may certainly ask," I said. I hoped he would swallow again before he spoke.

He looked closely at me. "What happened to your face? You don't"—he leaned forward quickly, touched my arm over the blanket—"you definitely don't have to tell me if you don't want to. I'm just being a nosy bastard!"

I smiled at him, and took a gulp of wine.

"I don't mind telling you, Raymond," I said, finding, to my surprise, that it was true—I actually wanted to tell him, now that he'd asked. He wasn't asking out of prurience or bored curiosity—he was genuinely interested, I could tell. You generally can.

"It was in a fire," I said, "when I was ten. A house fire."

"Christ!" he said. "That must have been terrible." There was a long pause, and I could almost see questions crystallizing, as though letters were emanating from his brain and forming words in the air.

"Faulty wiring? Chip pan?"

"It was started deliberately," I said, declining to explain further.

"Fucking hell, Eleanor!" he said. "Arson?"

I sipped more velvety wine, said nothing.

"So what happened after that?" he said.

"Well," I told him, "I mentioned before that I never knew my father. I was taken into care after the fire. Foster placements, children's homes, back to being fostered again—I moved every eighteen months or so, I guess. I got a place at university—I was seventeen—and the council housed me in a flat. The flat I still live in."

He looked so sad that it was making *me* sad too.

"Raymond," I said, "it's really not that unusual a story. Plenty of people grow up in far, far more challenging circumstances; it's simply a fact of life."

"Doesn't make it right, though," he said.

"I always had a bed to sleep in, food to eat, clothes and shoes to wear. I was always supervised by an adult. There are millions of children in the world who can't say the same, unfortunately. I'm a very lucky person, when you think about it."

He looked like he was going to cry—it must be all the wine. It does make people overly emotional, so they say. I could feel the unasked question hovering between us like a ghost. Don't ask, don't ask, I thought, wishing as hard as I could, crossing my fingers under the blanket.

"What about your mum, Eleanor? What happened to her?" I gulped the rest of my wine down as fast as I could.

"I'd prefer not to discuss Mummy, if that's all right, Raymond."

He looked surprised, and—a familiar response, this—slightly disappointed. To his credit, he didn't pursue the topic.

"Whatever you want, Eleanor. You can talk to me anytime, you know that, don't you?"

I nodded; I found, to my surprise, that I did.

"I mean it, Eleanor," he said, the wine making him more earnest than usual. "We're pals now, right?"

"Right," I said, beaming. My first pal! Granted, he was a poorly turned out computer repairman with a range of unfortunate social habits, but still—pals! It had certainly taken me a long, long time to acquire one; I was well aware that people of my age usually had at least one or two friends. I hadn't tried to shun them, and neither had I sought them out; it had just always been so difficult to meet like-minded people. After the fire, I never managed to find anyone who could fit the spaces that had been created inside me. I can't complain; it was entirely my own fault, after all. And anyway, I'd moved around so much during my childhood that it was hard to keep in touch with people, even if I'd wanted to. So many foster placements, all those new schools. At university, I'd fallen in love with classics, happily devoting myself to my work. Missing a few nights out at the Union to get top marks and generous praise from my tutors had felt like a fair exchange. And, of course, for a few years, there had been Declan. He didn't like me to socialize without him. Or, indeed, with him.

After graduating, I'd gone straight to working at Bob's firm, and heaven knew there were no like-minded people there. Once you get used to being on your own, it becomes normal. It certainly had become so for me.

Why, now, did Raymond want to be my friend? Perhaps he was lonely too. Perhaps he felt sorry for me.

Perhaps—incredible, this, but, I supposed, possible—he actually found me likable. Who knew? I turned toward him, wanting to ask why, wanting to tell him how glad I was to have finally found a friend, but his head had fallen onto his chest and his mouth was slightly open. He sprang back to life quickly, though.

"Wasn't sleeping," he said, "just . . . resting my eyes for a minute. It's been a hell of a day."

"It has," I said, and I meant it. I slipped my kitten heels on and asked if he could call me a taxi. I was horrified to see that it was almost nine. I peered anxiously between the curtains. It was dark now. It would be safe in the taxi, though. The drivers were all checked by the police, weren't they?

Raymond walked me down to the front of the building and opened the cab door.

"Safe home, Eleanor," he said. "Have a good weekend. See you Monday, yeah?"

"See you Monday, Raymond," I said, and I waved until the taxi turned the corner and I could no longer see him.

@johnnieLrocks
Farewell Pilgrim Pioneers gig
alert! Ending on a bang not a
whimper. Details to follow.
#dontmissit #gigofthecentury
#ditchingthedeadwood

This time, it was going to be perfect. I'd seen his tweet, and then, only hours later, my eyes locked onto the small poster in the window of the independent record shop near the office. His handsome face stopped me dead in my tracks. Two weeks' time. A Tuesday night. Perfect. The hand of fate once again, moving us like chess pieces. I had the king in my sight.

Remembering my error from The Cuttings, I memorized the name of the venue and, as soon as I got home, booked two tickets via their website, the second one as backup in case I lost the first. Perhaps Raymond could use it, come with me; although, on reflection, perhaps not. I wouldn't want him cramping my style. Purchasing two tickets turned out to be unnecessary, however, as it was only after the transaction was completed that I noticed the tickets were to be collected in person on the night. No matter.

After dinner and the *Archers*, I sat down with a pencil and a notepad and made a list of all the things I'd need to do in order to prepare. The most important thing, after securing the tickets, was to conduct a reconnaissance visit to the venue, to make sure everything would go smoothly on the night and avoid any unpleasant surprises. Here, at least, I felt Raymond could be of some assistance. We could go together to a different gig, perhaps tomorrow or the following day, and this would afford me the opportunity to scope out the setting for my forthcoming encounter with destiny.

After checking that tickets were still available for a gig scheduled for tomorrow evening, I sent an electronic message:

> Dear Raymond, would you like to come to
> Rank Dan's with me tomorrow night? E

He replied straightaway.

> Who's on?

What on earth did it matter? Surely Raymond could have googled this, if it was of such importance to him? I replied:

> Agents of Insanity

Several minutes went by.

> WTF Eleanor—didn't know you were into that
> stuff? Not really my thing, TBH, but I'll come
> along with you—it's ages since I've been to a
> gig. Have you got tix?

Why, oh why, could he not type in full and proper English sentences?

> Yes. Meet you there at 7pm. E

After five minutes had passed, I received the following:

> Cool c u then

I had almost become inured to his illiterate way of communicating by the end of this exchange. It's both good and bad, how humans can learn to tolerate pretty much anything, if they have to.

The following night, Raymond arrived late, as usual. He looked ridiculous—a black sweatshirt with a hood, and a denim jacket over the top. The sweatshirt had a skull on the front.

"Thought I'd try and look the part," he said, beaming, as he stood beside me in the doorway.

I had absolutely no idea what he was talking about. We went in, and I collected the tickets I'd purchased online. The bar was poorly lit and, as implied by the name, utterly filthy. Loutish, unkempt people of both genders sat around in Stygian gloom, and the music from the stereo system was both unfeasibly loud and unspeakably terrible.

We went downstairs to the venue. It was already almost full. As I'd stood waiting for Raymond in the doorway, I'd noticed a procession of ridiculous-looking young people entering the premises—this, it transpired, was where they were going. We were surrounded by black—black clothes, black hair, spiked and shaved and sculpted. Black makeup on both men and women, applied in a way that Bobbi Brown would not have endorsed. There were a lot of spikes everywhere too—hair, jewelry, even on backpacks. Almost no one wore normal shoes. All Hallows' Eve, I thought. Raymond returned from the bar with a plastic pint of beer for himself and, without having asked, something paler for me.

"Cider?" I shouted, over the din. "But, Raymond. I don't drink cider!"

"What do you think Magners is, you daft bint?" he said, nudging me gently with his elbow.

I sipped reluctantly—it wasn't as nice as Magners, but it would do. It was too loud to converse, so I scanned the room. The stage was small and raised only a meter or so from the floor. When I came back here, assuming Johnnie Lomond would be standing front and center, he'd be able to see me easily, even if I were forced to position myself halfway back in the crowd. Cupid does, presumably, need a tiny nudge sometimes.

The audience started making a collective animal noise and surged forward. We stayed where we were—the musicians were now on-stage and had begun to play. I put my hands to my ears, unable to believe what

I was hearing. Without exaggeration, it could only be described as the cacophonous din of hell. What on earth was *wrong* with these people? The "singer" alternated between screaming and growling.

I couldn't bear it a moment longer and ran upstairs, rushing outside into the street, panting and shaking my head like a dog in an attempt to rid my ears of the sound. Raymond followed shortly afterward.

"What's wrong, Eleanor?" he said, looking concerned. "Are you OK?"

I wiped the tears from my face.

"That wasn't music, that was . . . oh, I don't know. The horror, Raymond! The horror!"

Raymond started to laugh, proper belly laughs (for which he was very well equipped), until he was actually bent over and struggling to breathe.

"Oh, Eleanor," he said, wheezing. "I *knew* you weren't a fan of grindcore! What the fuck were you thinking?" He started giggling again.

"I just wanted to see the venue, listen to a band," I said. "That such sounds could exist—it's beyond human imagining."

Raymond had recovered himself.

"Aye, well—what is it that they say?—try everything once, except incest and morris dancing. Maybe we should add death metal to the list, eh?"

I shook my head.

"I have literally no idea what you are talking about— none of those words make any sense," I said. I took several deep breaths, until I felt almost calm again.

"Let us retire to an inn or public house, Raymond—
a quiet one—and please, allow me to buy you some
beer in recompense for this wasted evening."

"Oh, it wasn't wasted, Eleanor," he said, shaking
his head. "Your face! This is one of the best nights
out I've had in ages."

He started to laugh again, and, much to my surprise, I found myself joining in. It *was* amusing that
I had so comprehensively misunderstood the genre
of music being performed. I had a lot to learn about
music, I realized, and it would be important to do so
in order to interact appropriately with the musician.

"Have you heard of Johnnie Lomond and the
Pilgrim Pioneers?" I asked him. He shook his head.
"Why?" he said. I took out my phone and navigated
to the singer's web page. Raymond scrolled down for
a few moments, reading the text, then popped in his
earphones and listened for a minute or two.

"Sounds shit," he said dismissively, handing me
back my phone. This from a man in a skull sweatshirt!

"Really?" I said.

"He's got a standard-issue beard, an expensive guitar he doesn't know how to play and a fake American
accent. Trying to make out he's from the South . . .
aye, right, South Lanarkshire," Raymond said, blowing smoke out of the corner of his mouth with a smirk.
I wasn't sufficiently well informed to be able to agree
or disagree, so I kept quiet. Either way, I needed to
know at least a few salient facts about popular music,

and, recent aberrant opinions aside, I suspected that Raymond was my best source.

"Do you know much about music, then?" I asked, as we walked toward a pub which Raymond assured me was quiet—"A proper old man's pub," he said, whatever that was.

"Eh, aye, I guess," he said.

"Wonderful," I said. "Now please: tell me everything."

# 25

It was the day of the concert. Everything was ready. I looked the part. I felt the part. I would speed up time if I could, to get to tonight more quickly. I'd found a way to help me move forward at last. A way to replace a loss with a gain.

The musician. It was luck that he'd come along at precisely the right time. It was fate that, after tonight, my Eleanor pieces would finally start to fit together.

How exquisite the anticipation—a pain, a churning pain inside me. I did not know how to assuage it—I felt, instinctively, that vodka would not work. I would simply have to bear it until we met, and that was the nature of this peculiar, blissful burden. Only a little longer to wait now, a matter of hours. Tonight, I was going to meet the man whose love would change my life.

I was ready to rise from the ashes and be reborn.

# Bad Days

# 26

I am naked, lying on the floor, looking at the underside of the table. The pale wood is unvarnished, and there is a faded stamp bearing the imprint "Made in Taiwan." Some important items are lined up on the tabletop—I can't see them, but I can sense them above me. This hideous table, blue melamine top, rickety legs, the varnish scraped off in places by decades of careless use. How many kitchens has this table been in, before it found its way to me?

I imagine a hierarchy of happiness; first purchased in the 1970s, a couple would sit here, dining on meals cooked from brand-new recipe books, eating and drinking from wedding china like proper grown-ups. They'd move to the suburbs after a couple of years; the table, too small to accommodate their growing family, passes on to a cousin newly graduated and furnishing his first flat on a budget. After a few years, he moves in with his partner and rents the place out. For a decade, tenants eat here, a whole procession of them, young people mainly, sad and happy, sometimes alone, sometimes with friends, lovers. They'd serve fast food here to fill a gap, or five stylish courses to seduce, carbohydrates before a run and chocolate pudding for broken hearts. Eventually, the cousin sells up and the house clearance people take the table away. It languishes in a warehouse, spiders spinning silk inside its unfashionable rounded corners, bluebottles laying eggs in the rough splinters. It's given to another charity. They gave it to me, unloved, unwanted, irreparably damaged. Also the table.

The things are all laid out. Painkillers (twelve packets of twenty-four tablets, prescribed and carefully hoarded); bread knife (hardly used, shark's teeth ready to bite); drain cleaner ("cuts through all blockages, even hair and grease"—also flesh and internal organs). This table, this table where I have never sat with another person and shared a bottle of wine. This kitchen, where I have never cooked for anyone but myself. Lying here on the floor, corpse-like, I can feel spiky crumbs sticking to the bare backs of my arms, my buttocks, my thighs, my heels. It is cold. I wish I *were* a corpse. Not long, not long now.

All of the empty vodka bottles are in my sight line, dropped on the floor when they were finished. I ought to feel ashamed that someone will find the place in this state, but I feel nothing. Eventually my body will be removed and industrial cleaners will be dispatched, I suppose. The flat will be re-let. I hope the new tenants will be happy here, leave some traces of love in the walls and the floors and the gaps around the windows for the next inhabitants. I have left nothing. I was never here.

I don't know how long I have been lying like this. I don't recall how I ended up on the floor of the kitchen, or why I am naked. I reach for the bottle beside me, anxious about how much remains, instantly relieved at its heaviness. This is the last one, however. When this bottle is done, I have two choices: get off this floor, get dressed and go and buy more; or kill myself. Actually, either way, I'm going to kill myself. It's simply a case of how much vodka I drink before I do it. I take another big mouthful and wait for the pain to be released.

⁓

When I wake up again, I am in the same place. Ten minutes have passed, or ten hours—I have no idea. I move into a fetal position. If I can't be a corpse, then I wish that I was a baby, curled up in some other woman's womb, pure and longed for. I move slightly, turn my face toward the floor and vomit. It is, I notice, clear and streaked yellowish green—alcohol and bile. I haven't eaten for some time.

There are so many liquids and substances inside me, and I try to list them all as I lie here. There is earwax. The yellow pus that festers inside spots. Blood, mucus, urine, feces, chyme, bile, saliva, tears. I am a butcher's shop window of organs, large and small, pink, gray, red. All of this jumbled inside bones, encased in skin, then covered with fine hair. The skin bag is flawed, speckled with moles, freckles, little broken veins. And scars, of course. I think of a pathologist examining this carcass, noting every detail, weighing each organ. Meat inspection. Fail.

It is incomprehensible to me now that I could ever have thought that anyone would love this ambulant bag of blood and bones. Beyond understanding. I think of that night—when was it, three days ago, four?—and reach for the vodka bottle. I retch again, remembering.

≈

The day had not augured well from the start. Polly the plant had died that morning. I'm fully aware of how ridiculous that sounds. That plant, though, was the only living link with my childhood, the only constant between life before and after the fire, the only thing, apart from me, that had survived. I'd thought it was indestructible, assumed it would just go on and on, leaves falling off, new ones growing to replace them. I'd neglected my duties these last few weeks, too busy with hospitals and funerals and Facebook to water her regularly. Yet another living thing that I'd failed to look after. I wasn't fit to care for anyone, anything. Too numb to cry, I dropped the plant into the bin, pot, soil and all, and saw that, throughout all these years, it had been clinging on to life only by the slenderest, frailest of roots.

Life was so very precarious. I already knew that, of course. No one knew it better than me. I know, I know how ridiculous this is, how pathetic, but on some days, the very darkest days, knowing that the plant would die if I didn't water it was the only thing that forced me up out of bed.

Still, later that day, I'd come home from work, put the rubbish out, dressed up, made myself go out to the concert. I went alone. When I met the musician, I needed it to be just me and him, no distractions, no complications. I needed to make something happen, anything. I couldn't keep passing through life, over it, under it, around it. I couldn't go on haunting the world like a wraith. And things did happen that night. The first thing was the realization that the musician simply didn't know I was there. Why on earth had I ever thought that he would? Stupidity, self-delusion, a feeble connection to reality? Take your pick.

The shame. I had stood right at the front, ridiculously trussed up in new clothes, clownish makeup, tottering on heels. When he came onstage, I was close enough to see the double knot he'd tied in his shoelaces, the strand of hair that flopped over his eyes. His hands on the guitar, fingernails carefully manicured. The lights were bright on him, and I was in darkness. But he would see me, nonetheless. If it was meant to be, and surely it was, then he would see me, the way I'd seen him, all those weeks ago. I stood still and looked up at him. The band started to play and he opened his mouth to sing. I could see his teeth, the soft pinkness of his palate. The song finished, and another began. He spoke to the crowd but he did not speak to me. I stood and waited, waited throughout another song. And another. But still he didn't see me. And gradually, as I stood there beyond the lights, the music beating off my body without getting in and the crowd unable to permeate the layer of aloneness that encased me, encases me, I began to realize the truth. I blinked, again and again, as though my eyes were trying to clear the view before them, and it crystallized.

I was a thirty-year-old woman with a juvenile crush on a man whom I didn't know, and would never know. I had convinced myself that he was the one, that he would help to make me normal, fix the things that were wrong with my life. Someone to help me deal with Mummy, block out her voice when she whispered in my ear, telling me I was bad, I was wrong, I wasn't good enough. Why had I thought that?

He wouldn't be drawn to a woman like me. He was, objectively, a very attractive man, and could therefore select from a wide range of potential partners. He would choose an equally attractive woman a few years younger than himself. Of course he would. I was standing in a basement on a Tuesday night, alone, surrounded by strangers, listening to music I didn't like, because I had a crush on a man who didn't know, and would never know, that I existed. I realized I had stopped hearing the music.

There he was onstage, pressing guitar pedals and saying something trite about touring as he tuned. Who was this stranger, and why had I chosen him, of all the men in this city, this country, the world, to be my savior? I thought about a news story I'd read the previous day, some young fans holding a tearful vigil outside a singer's house because he'd cut his hair. I'd laughed at the time, but wasn't I behaving like them, acting like a love-struck teenager who writes fan letters in purple ink and etches his name on her schoolbag?

I didn't know the man onstage before me, didn't know the first thing about him. It was all just fantasy. Could anything be more pathetic—me, a grown woman? I'd told myself a sad little fairy tale, thinking that I could fix everything, undo the past, that he and I would live happily ever after and Mummy wouldn't be angry anymore. I was Eleanor, sad little Eleanor Oliphant, with my pathetic job, my vodka and my dinners for one, and I always would be. Nothing and no one—and certainly not this singer, who was now checking his hair in his phone during a bandmate's guitar solo—could change that. There *was* no hope, things couldn't be put right. *I* couldn't be put right. The past could neither be escaped nor undone. After all these weeks of delusion, I recognized, breathless, the pure, brutal truth of it. I felt despair and nausea mingled inside me, and then that familiar black, black mood came down fast.

~

I slept again. When I woke, my head was empty, finally, of all thoughts except physical ones: *I am cold, I am shaking.* Decision time. I decided on more vodka.

When I got to my feet, slow as evolution, I saw the mess on the floor and nodded to myself—this was a good sign. Perhaps I might actually die before I needed to choose one of the methods laid out on the table. I took a tea towel from the hook—*A Present from Hadrian's Wall*, it said. It had a centurion and an SPQR sigil on it. My favorite. I used it to wipe my face and then dropped it on the kitchen floor.

I didn't bother with underwear but simply pulled on the nearest clothes from the bedroom floor—the outfit I'd been wearing on Tuesday night. I stuck my bare feet into my Velcro work shoes and found my old jerkin hanging in the hall cupboard. I didn't know where the new coat was, I realized. My bag, however, needed to be located. I recalled that I had taken the new black handbag with me that night. It only had room for my purse and keys. The keys were on the shelf in the hall where I always put them. I found the bag in the hall too, eventually, dropped in a corner next to my shopper. My purse was empty of cash—I couldn't recall how I'd got home or when I'd bought the vodka that I'd been drinking, but I assumed it must have been en route here from the city center. Luckily, the purse still contained both of my bank cards. The concert ticket was in there too. I dropped it on the floor.

I walked down to the corner shop. It was daylight, cold, the sky ashen. When I entered, the electronic bleeper sounded and, behind the counter, Mr. Dewan looked up. I saw his eyes widen, his mouth fall open slightly.

"Miss Oliphant?" he said. His voice was cautious, quiet.

"Three liters of Glen's, please," I said. My voice sounded strange—croaky and broken. I hadn't used it for some time, I supposed, and then there was all that vomiting. He placed one before me, then seemed to hesitate.

"Three, Miss Oliphant?" he said. I nodded. Slowly, he put another two bottles on the counter, all of them now lined up like skittles that I'd need to knock over, knock back.

"Anything else?" he said. I briefly considered a loaf of bread or a tin of spaghetti, but I was not in the least bit hungry. I shook my head and offered him my debit card. My hand was shaking and I tried to control it, but failed. I punched in the numbers, and the wait for the receipt to be printed was interminable.

A pile of evening newspapers sat on the counter beside the till, and I saw that it was Friday. Mr. Dewan had fixed a mirror on the wall to see into all the shop corners, and I caught sight of myself in it. I was gray white, the color of larvae, and my hair stood on end. My eyes were dark hollows, empty, dead. I noted all of this with complete indifference. Nothing could be less important than my appearance, absolutely nothing. Mr. Dewan handed me the bottles in a blue plastic bag. The smell of it, the chemical reek of polymers, made my stomach churn even harder.

"Take care of yourself, Miss Oliphant," he said, head tilted to one side, unsmiling.

"Good-bye, Mr. Dewan," I said.

It was only a ten-minute walk home but it took half an hour—the bottles in the bag, the weight in my legs. I didn't see another living creature in the streets, not even a cat or a magpie. The light was opaque,

rendering the world in gray and black, a bleak absence
of tone that weighed heavily on me. I kicked the front
door closed behind me and stepped out of my clothes,
leaving them in the hallway where they fell. I noticed
in passing that I smelled very bad—perspiration, vomit
and a sweet staleness that must be metabolized alcohol. I took the blue carrier bag into the bedroom and
pulled on my lemon nightgown. I crawled under the
covers and reached blindly for a bottle.

I drank it with the focused, single-minded deter-
mination of a murderer, but my thoughts just could
not, would not be drowned—like ugly, bloated corpses,
they continued to float to the surface in all their pale,
gas-filled ugliness. There was the horror of my own self-
delusion, of course: him, me . . . *what was I thinking?*
Worse, far worse than that, was the shame. I curled
myself into a ball, tried to make myself occupy as
small a space in the bed as possible. Despicable. I had
made a fool of myself. I was an embarrassment, like
Mummy had always told me. A sound escaped into the
pillow, an animal whine. I couldn't open my eyes. I did
not want to see even a centimeter of my own skin.

I'd thought I could solve the problem of myself so
easily, as if the things that were done all those years
ago could actually be put right. I knew that people
weren't supposed to exist as I did, work and vodka
and sleep in a constant, static cycle in which I spun
around on myself, into myself, silent and alone. Going
nowhere. On some level, I realized that this was
wrong. I'd lifted my head up just high enough to see

that, and, desperate to change, I'd clutched at a random straw, let myself get carried away, imagining some sort of . . . future.

I cringed. No, that's wrong. Cringe denotes embarrassment, fleeting shame. This was my soul curling into whiteness, an existential blank where a person had once been. Why did I start to allow myself to think I could live a normal life, a happy life, the kind other people had? Why did I think that the singer could be part of that, help bring it about? The answer stabs at me: Mummy. I wanted Mummy to love me. I'd been alone for so long. I needed someone by my side to help me manage Mummy. Why wasn't there someone, anyone, to help me manage Mummy?

I played the scene in my head again, over and over, remembering the second thing that I'd realized that night. It was later and I'd been standing further back, right in the middle of the crowd. I'd gone to get yet another drink, and the path to the front of the stage had closed up while I'd been at the bar. I'd downed the vodka—my sixth? Seventh? I don't remember. He couldn't see my face from where I was standing, I was aware of that. The band had stopped playing—someone had broken a string and was replacing it.

He leaned in to the microphone and cocked an eyebrow. I saw his lazy, handsome smile. He peered, unseeing, into the darkness.

"What are we going to do now, then? Since Davie's taking so fucking long to change that string." He turned back toward a sullen man who gave him the finger without looking up from his guitar. "Right then, here's something to keep you entertained, ladies!" he said, then turned his back, undid his belt, dropped his jeans and wiggled his pale white buttocks at us.

Some people in the crowd laughed. Some people shouted insults. The singer retorted with an obscene gesture. I realized with uncompromising clarity that the man onstage before me was, without any doubt, an arse. The band started their next song and everyone was jumping up and down and I then was at the bar, requesting a double.

≈

Later. I woke again. I kept my eyes closed. I was curious about something. What, I wondered, was the *point* of me? I contributed nothing to the world, absolutely nothing, and I took nothing from it either. When I ceased to exist, it would make no material difference to anyone.

Most people's absence from the world would be felt on a personal level by at least a handful of people. I, however, had no one.

I do not light up a room when I walk into it. No one longs to see me or to hear my voice. I do not feel sorry for myself, not in the least. These are simply statements of fact.

I have been waiting for death all my life. I do not mean that I actively wish to die, just that I do not really want to be alive. Something had shifted now, and I realized that I didn't need to wait for death. I didn't want to. I unscrewed the bottle and drank deeply.

Ah, but things come in threes, don't they say? The best was saved for last, and it came toward the end of the set. My focus was slightly filmy by that stage—the vodka—and I didn't trust my eyes. I screwed them up, strained to confirm what I thought I was looking at. Smoke, gray, hazy, deadly smoke, emanating from the side of the stage and along the front. The room started to fill with it. The man next to me coughed; a psychosomatic action, since dry ice, stage smoke, prompts no such reflex. I felt it drift over me, saw how the lights and the lasers cut through it. I closed my eyes. In that moment, I was back there, in the house, upstairs. Fire. I heard screams, and could not tell if they were mine. The bass drum beat fast with my heart, the snare drum skittered like my pulse. The room was full of smoke, and I couldn't see. Screams, my own and hers. The bass drum, the snare. The spurt of adrenaline, speeding the tempo, nauseatingly strong, too strong for my small body, for any small body. The screaming. I pushed out, out, pushed past every obstacle, stumbling, panting, until I was outside, out in the dark black night. Back to the wall, I slumped down, sprawled on the ground, the screaming in my ears, body still pounding. I vomited. I was alive. I was alone. There was no living thing in the universe that was more alone than me. Or more terrible.

~

I woke again. I had not closed the curtains and light was coming in, moonlight. The word connotes romance. I took one of my hands in the other, tried to imagine what it would feel like if it was another person's hand holding mine. There have been times when I felt that I might die of loneliness. People sometimes say they might die of boredom, that they're dying for a cup of tea, but for me, dying of loneliness is not hyperbole. When I feel like that, my head drops and my shoulders slump and I ache, I physically ache, for human contact—I truly feel that I might tumble to the ground and pass away if someone doesn't hold me, touch me. I don't mean a lover—this recent madness aside, I had long since given up on any notion that another person might love me that way—but simply as a human being. The scalp massage at the hairdressers, the flu jab I had last winter—the only time I experience touch is from people whom I am paying, and they are almost always wearing disposable gloves at the time. I'm merely stating the facts.

People don't like these facts, but I can't help that. If someone asks you how you are, you are meant to say FINE. You are not meant to say that you cried yourself to sleep last night because you hadn't spoken to another person for two consecutive days. FINE is what you say.

When I first started working for Bob, there was an older woman in the office, only a couple of months

away from retirement. She was often absent to care
for her sister, who had ovarian cancer. This older colleague would never mention the cancer, wouldn't even
say the word, and referred to the illness only in the
most oblique terms. I understand that this approach
was considered quite usual back then. These days,
loneliness is the new cancer—a shameful, embarrassing thing, brought upon yourself in some obscure
way. A fearful, incurable thing, so horrifying that you
dare not mention it; other people don't want to hear
the word spoken aloud for fear that they might too
be afflicted, or that it might tempt fate into visiting a
similar horror upon them.

I got onto all fours, shuffled forward like an old
dog and pulled the curtains closed against the moon.
I fell back onto the covers and reached again for the
bottle.

≈

I heard banging—bang bang bang—and a man shouting my name. I was dreaming a charnel house scene
of fire, blood and violence, and it took forever to make
the transition from then to now, to realize that the
banging was real and coming from my front door. I
pulled the covers over my head but it would not stop.
I desperately wanted it to end but, despairing, I could
not think of any way to make that happen other than
answering the door. My legs were shaking and I had
to hold on to the wall as I walked. As I fumbled with
the locks, I looked down at my feet—small, white,

marble. A huge bruise, purple and green, bloomed across one, right down to my toes. I was surprised—I could feel nothing, no pain, and had no recollection of how I had acquired it. It may as well have been painted on.

I finally managed to open the door, but couldn't raise my head, didn't have the strength to look up. At least the banging had stopped. That was my only objective.

"Jesus Christ!" a man's voice said.

"Eleanor Oliphant," I replied.

# 27

When I woke again, I was lying on my sofa. The texture under my hands felt rough, strange, and it took me a few moments to realize that I was covered with towels rather than blankets. I lay still, and slowly appraised my situation. I was warm. My head was pounding. My guts were filled with a stabbing pain which pulsed regularly, like blood. I opened my mouth and heard the flesh and gums peel apart, like orange segments being separated. I was wearing my yellow nightdress.

I heard churning, bumping sounds, external to the ones in my body, and eventually placed them as coming from the washer-dryer. I slowly opened one eye—it was gummed shut—and saw that the living room was unchanged, the frog pouf staring back at me. Was I alive? I hoped so, but only because if this was the location of the afterlife, I'd be lodging an appeal immediately. Beside me on the low table in front of the sofa was a large glass of vodka. I reached out, shaking violently, and managed to pick it up and lift it to my mouth without spilling too much. I had gulped down almost half of it before I realized that it was actually water. I gagged, feeling it gurgle and churn in my stomach. Another bad sign—someone or something had turned vodka into water. This was not my preferred kind of miracle.

Lying back down again, I heard other sounds, footsteps. Someone was humming, a man. Who was in my kitchen? I was amazed at how easily the sound traveled. I was always alone here, unused to hearing another person moving around in my home. I drank some more water and started to choke, which turned into a coughing fit and ended with unproductive retching. After a minute or two, someone knocked tentatively on the living room door, and a face peeped round—Raymond.

I wanted to die—this time, in addition to actually wanting to die, I meant it in the metaphorical sense too. Oh, come on now, I thought to myself, almost amused; just how desperately, on how many levels, does a person have to wish to die before it's actually allowed to happen? Please? Raymond smiled sadly at me and spoke very quietly.

"How are you feeling, Eleanor?" he said.

"What happened?" I asked him. "Why are you in my house?"

He came into the room and stood at my feet.

"Don't worry. You're going to be fine."

I closed my eyes. Neither phrase answered my questions; neither was what I wanted to hear.

"Are you hungry?" he said gently. I thought about it. My insides felt wrong, very wrong. Perhaps part of that was related to hunger? I didn't know, so I just shrugged. He looked pleased.

"I'm going to make you some soup, then," he said. I lay back with my eyes closed.

"Not lentil," I said.

⌒

He returned after a few minutes and slowly, so slowly, I eased myself into a seated position, keeping the towels wrapped around me. He'd heated some tomato soup in a mug, and placed it on the table in front of me.

"Spoon?" I said.

He did not reply, but went off to the kitchen and came back with one. I held it in my right hand, trembling violently, and tried to sip some. I shook so much that it spilled onto the towels—I realized that there was no way I would be able to get the liquid from the mug to my mouth.

"Aye, I thought you might be best just trying to drink it," he said gently, and I nodded.

He sat on the armchair and watched me as I sipped, neither of us speaking. I set the mug down when I'd finished, feeling the warmth of it inside me, the sugar and the salt in my veins. The ticking of the Power Rangers clock above the fireplace was exceptionally loud. I finished the glass of water and, without speaking, he went to refill it.

"Thank you," I said when he returned and handed it to me.

He said nothing, stood up and left the room. The washer-dryer sounds had stopped, and I heard the door click open, more footsteps. He came back in, walked toward me and held out his hand.

"Come on," he said.

I tried to stand without assistance, but couldn't. I leaned on him, and then had to have his arm around my waist to assist me across the hallway. The bedroom door was open, the bed made up with the freshly laundered sheets. He sat me down, and then lifted my legs and helped me get under the covers. The bed smelled so fresh—warm and clean and cozy, like a little bird's nest.

"Get some rest now," he said softly, closing the curtains and turning out the light. Sleep came like a sledgehammer.

~

I must have slept for half a day at least. When I finally woke, I reached for the glass that had been placed at the side of my bed and gulped the water down. I needed water inside and out, so, taking careful, tentative steps, I walked to the bathroom and stood under the shower. The smell of the soap was like a garden. I washed away all the filth, all the external stains, and emerged pink and clean and warm. I dried myself gently, so gently, afraid that my skin would tear, and then dressed in clean clothes, the softest, cleanest clothes I'd ever worn.

The kitchen floor gleamed and all the bottles had been removed, the work tops wiped down. There was a pile of folded laundry on one of the chairs. The table was bare save for a vase, the only one I owned, filled with yellow tulips. There was a note propped against it.

*Some food in the fridge. Try to drink as much*
*water as you can. Call me when you're up Rx*

He'd scrawled his phone number at the bottom. I sat down and stared at it, and then at the sunshine brightness of the flowers. No one had ever bought me flowers before. I didn't much care for tulips, but he wasn't to know that. I started to cry, huge quivering sobs, howling like an animal. It felt like I would never stop, like I couldn't stop. Eventually, from sheer physical exhaustion, I was quiet. I rested my forehead on the table.

My life, I realized, had gone wrong. Very, very wrong. I wasn't supposed to live like this. No one was supposed to live like this. The problem was that I simply didn't know how to make it right. Mummy's way was wrong, I knew that. But no one had ever shown me the right way to live a life, and although I'd tried my best over the years, I simply didn't know how to make things better. I could not solve the puzzle of me.

I made some tea and heated up the ready meal that Raymond had left in the fridge. I was, I discovered, very hungry indeed. I washed the cup and fork afterward, stacked them beside the other clean crockery he'd left to drain. I went into the living room and picked up the phone. He answered on the second ring.

"Eleanor—thank God," he said. Pause. "How're you feeling?"

"Hello, Raymond," I said.

"How are you?" he asked again, sounding strained.

"Fine, thanks," I said. This was, I knew, the correct answer.

"For fuck's sake, Eleanor. Fine. Christ!" he said. "I'll be round in an hour, OK?"

"Really, Raymond, there's no need," I said calmly. "I've had some food"—I didn't know what time it was, and didn't want to risk guessing whether it had been lunch or dinner—"and a shower, and I'm going to read for a while and then have an early night."

"I'll be round in an hour," he said again, firmly, and then hung up.

~

When I answered the door, he was holding a bottle of Irn-Bru and a bag of jelly babies. I managed a smile.

"Come in," I said.

I wondered how he had got in before, had no recollection of opening the door to him. What had I said, what kind of state had I been in? I felt my heart start to pound, jittery and anxious. Had I sworn at him? Had I been naked? Had something terrible happened between us? I felt the Irn-Bru start to slip from my grasp and it fell on the floor and rolled around. He picked it up, gripped my elbow in his other hand and guided me to the kitchen. He sat me at the table and put the kettle on. I should have been offended that he was commandeering my living space, but instead I felt relief, overwhelming relief at being taken care of.

We sat on opposite sides of the table with a cup of tea and said nothing for a while. He spoke first. "What the fuck, Eleanor?" he said.

I was shocked to hear the wobble in his voice, as though there were tears lurking there. I simply shrugged. He began to look angry.

"Eleanor, you were AWOL from work for three days, Bob was really worried about you, we all were. I got your address from him, I came round to see if you're OK, and I find you . . . I find you . . ."

". . . preparing to kill myself?" I ask.

He rubbed his hand across his face, and I saw that he was very close to crying.

"Look, I know you're a very private person, and that's fine, but we're pals, you know? You can talk to me about stuff. Don't bottle things up."

"Why not?" I asked. "How can telling someone how bad you're feeling make it better? It's not like they can fix it, can they?"

"They probably can't fix everything, Eleanor, no," he said, "but talking can help. Other people have problems too, you know. They understand what it feels like to be unhappy. A problem shared and all that . . ."

"I don't think anyone on earth would understand what it feels like to be me," I said. "That's just a fact. I don't think anyone else has lived through precisely the set of circumstances I've lived through. And survived them, at any rate," I said. It was an important clarification.

"Try me," he said. He looked at me, and I looked at him. "OK, if not me, then try someone else. A counselor, a therapist . . ."

I snorted—a most inelegant sound.

"A counselor!" I said. "'Let's sit around and talk about our feelings and that'll magically make everything better.' I don't think so, Raymond."

He smiled. "How will you know until you try, though? What have you got to lose? There's no shame, you know, no shame at all in being . . . depressed, or having a mental illness or whatever . . ." I almost choked on my tea.

"Mental illness? What are you *talking* about, Raymond?" I shook my head.

He held up both hands in a placatory movement.

"Look, I'm not a doctor. It's just . . . well . . . I don't think that someone who gives themselves alcohol poisoning while they plan their suicide is, you know, in a very good place?"

This was such a ridiculous summation of my situation that I almost laughed. Raymond wasn't usually prone to exaggeration but this was over the top, and I couldn't allow it to stand as a factually accurate description of what had happened that night.

"Raymond, I simply had a bit too much vodka after a stressful evening, that's all. It's hardly symptomatic of an *illness*."

"Where had you been that night?" he said. "What's been going on since then?"

I shrugged. "I went to a gig," I said. "It wasn't very good."

Neither of us spoke for a while.

"Eleanor," he said eventually, "this is serious. If I hadn't come over when I did, you might be dead by now, either from the booze or from choking on your own vomit. That's if you hadn't already overdosed on the pills or whatever."

I put my head on one side and pondered this.

"All right," I said. "I concede that I was feeling very unhappy. But doesn't everyone feel sad from time to time?"

"Yes, of course they do, Eleanor," he said calmly. "But when people are feeling sad they have a little cry, maybe eat too much ice cream, stay in bed all afternoon. What they *don't* do is think about drinking drain cleaner, or opening their veins with a bread knife."

Despite myself, I shuddered at the thought of those sharp, sharp teeth. I shrugged, acquiescing.

"Touché, Raymond," I said. "I can't counter your reasoning."

He reached out and put his hands on my forearms, squeezed them. He was strong.

"Will you think about going to the doctor, at least? Wouldn't do any harm, would it?"

I nodded. Again, he was being logical, and you can't argue with logic.

"Is there anyone you want me to get in contact with?" he said. "A friend, a relative? What about your mum? She'll want to know that you've been feeling like this, won't she?" He stopped speaking, because I laughed.

"Not Mummy," I said, shaking my head. "She'd probably be absolutely delighted."

Raymond looked horrified.

"Come on, Eleanor, that's a terrible thing to say," he said, visibly shocked. "No one's mother would be happy to know their child was suffering."

I shrugged, and kept my eyes focused on the floor. "You haven't met Mummy," I said.

# 28

The next few days were somewhat challenging. On several occasions, Raymond arrived unannounced, ostensibly to bring comestibles or relaying messages from Bob, but in fact to check that I hadn't committed an act of self-slaughter. If I were to compose a concise crossword clue to describe Raymond's demeanor, it would be *the opposite of inscrutable*. I could only hope that the man refrained from playing poker on all but the most casual basis, as I feared he'd be leaving the table with an empty wallet.

It was surprising that he should bother with me, especially given the unpleasant circumstances in which he'd found me after the concert. Whenever I'd been sad or upset before, the relevant people in my life would simply call my social worker and I'd be moved somewhere else. Raymond hadn't phoned anyone or asked an outside agency to intervene. He'd elected to look after me himself. I'd been pondering this, and concluded that there must be some people for whom difficult behavior wasn't a reason to end their relationship with you. If they liked you—and, I remembered, Raymond and I had agreed that we were pals now—then, it seemed, they were prepared to maintain contact, even if you were sad, or upset, or behaving in very challenging ways. This was something of a revelation.

I wondered if that's what it would be like in a family—if you had parents, or a sister, say, who would be there, no matter what. It wasn't that you could take them for granted, as such—heaven knows, nothing can be taken for granted in this life—it was simply that you would know, almost unthinkingly, that they'd be there if you needed them, no matter how bad things got. I'm not prone to envy, as a rule, but I must confess I felt a twinge when I thought about this. Envy was a minor emotion, however, in comparison to the sorrow I felt at never having a chance to experience this . . . what was it? Unconditional love, I supposed.

But there was no use in crying over spilled milk. Raymond had shown me a little of what it must be like, and I counted myself lucky to have had the opportunity. Today, he'd arrived with a box of After Eight mints and, improbably, a helium-filled balloon.

"I know it's daft," he said, smiling, "but I was passing the market in the square, and I saw a guy selling these when I was going for my bus. I thought it might cheer you up."

I saw what he was holding and I laughed, an unexpected burst of feeling, unfamiliar. He passed me the ribbon, and the balloon soared toward my low ceiling, then bobbed against it as though it was trying to escape.

"What is it supposed to be?" I said. "Is it . . . is it *cheese*?" I had never been given a helium balloon before, and certainly not one this odd-looking.

"It's SpongeBob, Eleanor," he said, speaking very slowly and clearly as though I were some sort of idiot. "SpongeBob SquarePants?"

A semi-human bath sponge with protruding front teeth! On sale as if it were something completely unremarkable! For my entire life, people have said that I'm strange, but really, when I see things like this, I realize that I'm actually relatively normal.

I made tea for us. Raymond had put his feet up on the coffee table. I was considering asking him to remove them, but then the thought came to me that he must feel at home in my house, comfortable enough to relax here and make full use of the furniture. The idea was actually rather pleasing. He slurped his tea—a much less pleasant intrusion—and asked about the GP. Earlier in the week, after Raymond had delivered a persuasive argument about the importance of obtaining an expert, objective view of my emotional state, and of the efficacy of modern treatments should any mental health issues be diagnosed, I'd finally agreed to make an appointment at the surgery.

"I'm going tomorrow," I said. "Half past eleven."

He nodded. "That's good, Eleanor," he said. "Now, promise me you'll be completely honest with the doctor, tell her exactly what you've been feeling, what you've been going through."

I thought about this. I would tell her almost everything, I'd decided, but I wasn't going to mention the little stockpile of pills (which no longer existed in any case—Raymond had, with scant concern for the environment, flushed them down the lavatory. I'd professed irritation but was secretly glad to be rid of them), and I had also decided to say nothing about the chats with Mummy or our ridiculous, abortive project. Mummy always said that information should be divulged to professional busybodies on a need-to-know basis, and these topics weren't relevant. All the doctor needed to understand was that I was very unhappy, so that she could advise me how best to go about changing that. We didn't need to start digging around in the past, talking about things that couldn't be changed.

"Promise," I said. I had my fingers crossed, though.

# 29

When the GP signed me off work, I wondered how a life of indolence would suit me. I've always had a full-time job, having started with Bob the week after I received my degree, and in all the years since then, I've never once had cause to call in sick. Fortunately, I've been blessed with an extremely robust constitution.

That first week, the week immediately after the incident with the vodka and the visit from Raymond, I slept a lot. I must have done other things, normal things too, like going out to buy milk or having a shower, but I can't recall them now.

The doctor had somehow managed to deduce that I was suffering from depression, even with only a few scant details to go on. I managed to keep all of my most important secrets to myself. She suggested that medication and talking therapy combined was the most effective form of treatment, but I insisted that I did not wish to take any tablets, at least initially. I was worried that I might start to rely on them in the same way that I'd been relying on vodka. I did, however, reluctantly agree to see a counselor as a first step, and the inaugural session had been scheduled for today. I had been assigned to a Maria Temple—no title provided. I cared nothing for her marital status, but it would have been helpful to know in advance whether or not she was in possession of any formal medical qualifications.

Her office was located on the third floor of a modern block in the city center. The lift had transported me back in time to that least *belle* of *époques*—the 1980s. Gray gray gray, sludgy pastels, dirty plastic, nasty carpets. It smelled like it hadn't been cleaned since the 1980s either. I had been reluctant to attend the counseling session from the outset, and to do so in this setting made it even less enticing, if such a thing were possible. Sadly, the environment was all too familiar, and this was, in its own way, a comfort. The institutional corridors with floral friezes and Artex ceilings down which I have walked in my life are legion.

I knocked on the door—thin plywood, gray, no nameplate—and, too quickly, as though she had been standing right behind it, Maria Temple opened it and invited me in. The room was tiny, a dining chair and two institutional armchairs (the wipe-clean, uncomfortable kind) arranged opposite a small, low table, on which was placed a box of nonbranded "man-size" tissues. I was momentarily thrown. Their noses are, with a few exceptions, more or less the same size as our own, are they not? Did they really need a vastly bigger surface area of tissue, simply because they were in possession of an XY chromosome? Why? I suspected that I really did not want to know the answer to that question.

There was no window, and a framed print on the wall (a vase of roses, made using a computer by someone who was dead inside) was more offensive to the eye than a bare wall.

"You must be Eleanor?" she said, smiling.

"It's Miss Oliphant, actually," I said, taking off my jerkin and wondering what on earth to do with it. She pointed to a row of hooks on the back of the door, where I placed it as far away as possible from the very practical waterproof which hung there already. I sat down opposite her—the chair released a tired whump of stale air from its grubby cushions. She smiled at me. Her teeth! Oh, Ms. Temple. She had done her best, but nothing could change the size of them, I supposed. They belonged in a far bigger mouth, perhaps not even a human one. I was reminded of a photograph that the *Telegraph* had featured some time ago, of a monkey which had grabbed a camera and taken its own grinning photograph (a "selfie"). The poor woman; an adjective which one would never wish to have applied to one's teeth was *simian*.

"I'm Maria Temple, Eleanor—erm, Miss Oliphant," she said, "it's a pleasure to meet you." She looked intently at me, which made me sit forward in my seat, not wanting to show how uncomfortable I was feeling.

"Have you ever had counseling before, Miss Oliphant?" she said, taking out a notebook from her handbag. It had, I noticed, several accessories attached to it, key rings and the like—a pink, fluffy monkey, a giant metallic letter M, and, most hideous of all, a tiny, sequinned red stiletto shoe. I'd come across the type before. Ms. Temple was "fun."

"Yes and no," I said. She raised a quizzical eyebrow, but I declined to elaborate further. There was a silence, in which I heard the lift clattering again, although no further sound or evidence of human occupation followed. I felt marooned.

"OK then," she said, brightly, too brightly. "I think we'll get started. Now, first of all, I want to reassure you that everything we discuss in here together is absolutely confidential. I'm a member of all the relevant professional bodies, and we adhere to a very strict code of conduct. You should always feel comfortable and safe in this space, and, please, ask me anything, at any time, especially if you're not clear about what we're doing, or why." She seemed to be waiting for some sort of response, but I had none to offer her. I shrugged.

She settled into her chair and began reading from her notebook. "You've been referred here by your GP, I see, and you've been suffering from depression."

I nodded.

"Can you tell me a bit about how you've been feeling?" she said. Her smile had assumed a slightly fixed quality.

"I've been feeling a bit sad, I suppose," I said. I stared at her shoes. They resembled golf shoes, only without spikes. They were gold. Unbelievable.

"How long have you been feeling sad, Ele—Miss Oliphant?" She tapped her enormous teeth with her pen. "Actually, would you mind if I called you Eleanor? It would just, you know, help the discussion flow a bit more freely if we were both on first-name terms, I think. Would that be OK?" She smiled.

"I prefer Miss Oliphant, but yes, I suppose so," I said graciously. Titles were better, though. I didn't know her from Adam, after all. She wasn't my friend; she was someone who was being paid to interact with me. A bit of professional distance is highly appropriate, I feel, when, for example, a stranger is examining the back of your eyeballs for tumors, or rooting around in your dentin with a hooked instrument. Or, indeed, poking around in your brain, dragging out your feelings and letting them sit there in the room, in all their shameful awfulness.

"Great," she said brightly, and I could tell that she had realized I was most decidedly *not* "fun." We wouldn't ever be going bungee jumping or to a fancy dress party together. What else is supposed to be fun? Sing-a-longs. Sponsored runs. Magicians. I've no idea; personally, I like animals and crosswords and (until very recently) vodka. What could be more fun than that? Not belly dancing classes in the community hall. Not murder mystery weekends. Hen dos. No.

"Was there something in particular that led you to seek help from your GP?" she said. "An incident, an interaction? Telling someone how you're feeling can be a very difficult thing to do, but it's great that you took such an important first step."

"A friend suggested that I see my doctor," I said, experiencing a tiny frisson of pleasure as I used the "F" word. "Raymond," I clarified. I rather liked saying his name, the rhotic trill at the start. It was a nice name, a good name, and that at least seemed fair. He deserved some luck—after all, given his meager physical blessings, he already had enough to contend with, without being lumbered with, say, Eustace or Tyson as a first name.

"Would you like to tell me about the events leading up to your decision to visit your GP? What prompted your friend to make the suggestion?" she said. "How were you feeling, then?"

"I was feeling a bit sad and things got on top of me, that's all. So my friend suggested that I should see my GP. And the GP said I had to come here, if I didn't want to take the pills."

She looked intently at me. "Could you tell me why you were feeling sad?" she said.

I released a sigh that was longer and more unintentionally histrionic than I had been expecting. I felt my throat constrict at the end of the breath, tightening with tears. Don't cry, Eleanor. DO NOT CRY IN FRONT OF THE STRANGER.

"It's quite boring," I said, trying my best to sound nonchalant. "It was just . . . a sort of love affair that went wrong. That's all. A perfectly standard situation." There was a lengthy silence. Eventually, purely to try and get this over with as quickly as possible, I spoke again. "There was a misunderstanding. I thought . . . I misinterpreted some signals. It turned out that I had very much got the wrong impression of the person concerned."

"Has this happened to you before?" she asked, quietly.

"No," I said.

There was another lengthy silence.

"Who was this person, Eleanor? Can you talk a bit more about what happened to make you . . . how did you put it . . . misunderstand the signals? What *were* the signals?"

"Well, there was a man that I took a bit of a liking to, a little crush, you might say, and I got slightly carried away, and then I realized that, actually, I'd been a bit silly. We weren't going to be together. And he—well, it turned out that he wasn't even right for me anyway. He wasn't the man I thought he was. I felt sad about that, and I felt extremely stupid for getting it all so wrong. That's all it was . . ." I heard my voice trail off.

"OK, well . . . there are a few things I'd like to unpick in all of that. How did you meet this man? What was the nature of your relationship with him?"

"Oh, I never actually met him," I said.

She stopped writing in her notebook, and there was a bit of an awkward pause. I think, in theatrical terms, it's called a beat.

"Right . . ." she said. "So how did your . . . your paths cross, then?"

"He's a musician. I saw him perform and—well, I fell for him, I suppose you'd say."

Maria Temple spoke cautiously. "Is he . . . is he famous?"

I shook my head. "He's local. He lives here. Near me, in fact. He's not famous, as such. Yet."

Maria Temple said nothing and waited for me to continue. She didn't even raise an eyebrow. Nothing. I realized that I may have given her a slightly misleading impression of my behavior.

"To be clear," I said, "I'm not some sort of . . . stalker. I merely found out where he lives, and I copied out a poem for him, which I didn't even send. And I tweeted him once, but that's all. That's not a crime. All of the information I needed was in the public domain. I didn't break any laws or anything like that."

"And you've never found yourself in this sort of situation before, Eleanor, with anyone else?" So she thought I might be some sort of obsessive, serially fixated on strangers. Charming.

"No, never," I said firmly and truthfully. "He was just . . . he caught my eye, piqued my interest, that's all. He was, you know, handsome . . ."

There was another long pause.

Finally, Maria Temple sat back in her chair and began to speak, which was a relief. It was exhausting, answering all these questions, talking about myself and worrying whether I sounded as stupid, as embarrassingly naïve as I thought I did.

"Here's a scenario. I'll run it by you and you can see what you think. Let's say, for the sake of argument, Eleanor, that you *had* developed a crush on this man. These sorts of feelings are generally a sort of emotional 'trial run' for a real relationship. They're very intense. Does that sound reasonable, plausible so far?" I stared at her.

"So," she went on, "there you were, quite enjoying your crush, *feeling the feelings*. Tell me, what happened to bring this to an end all of a sudden? What crushed the crush, as it were?"

I slumped back into my seat. She had taken me by surprise with her startlingly accurate summary of how things had been, and then asked a very interesting, pertinent question. Despite the gold shoes and the novelty key rings, I could see already that Maria Temple was no fool. This was all going to take me a while to process, but in the meantime, I tried to gather my thoughts into some sort of coherent response.

"I suppose on some level I actually felt the whole thing *was* real, and that, when we finally met, we'd fall in love and get married and so on. I felt, I don't know, somehow ready for a relationship like that. People— men—like him don't cross my path very often. It seemed only right not to let the opportunity pass by. And I felt sure that . . . certain people . . . would be pleased that I'd found him. When he and I were finally in the same room together, though, something that I'd worked hard to make happen, the whole thing just sort of . . . dissolved. Does that make any sense?"

She nodded encouragingly.

"I suppose I realized, right there in that room, that I'd been stupid, acting like a teenager rather than a thirty-year-old woman. He wasn't even special, I'd been focused on him, but really, it could have been anyone. I'd been trying to please M—"

Nodding, she interrupted me, thankfully stopping me from going too far.

"There are actually a number of issues I'd like to suggest we explore over the next few sessions," she said. "We've been talking about recent events here today, but at some point I'd like to hear a bit about your childhood—"

"Absolutely not," I said, folding my arms and staring at the carpet. *The lady does not need to know what goes on in this house.*

"I understand that it can be a very difficult thing to talk about," she said.

"I don't want to talk about any of that, Maria. Please, do *not* ask me to talk about Mummy."

Damn, damn, damn. She leaped on that, of course. Mummy's always the star turn, the big draw.

"What sort of relationship do you have with your mother, Eleanor? Are you close?"

"Mummy's in contact quite regularly. Too regularly," I said. The cat was out of the bag now.

"You two don't get on, then?" she said.

"It's . . . complicated." I noticed myself physically as well as metaphorically squirming in my seat.

"Can you tell me why?" Maria asked, bold as brass, nosy, intrusive. Shameless.

"No," I said.

There was a very long pause.

"I know that it's difficult, really difficult, to talk about painful things, but, as I said, that's the best route to helping us move forward. Let's start very slowly. Can you tell me *why* you don't feel comfortable talking about your mother?"

"I . . . she wouldn't want me to," I said. That was true. I remembered the last—and only—time I'd done it, with a teacher. It wasn't a mistake you made twice.

My left leg had begun to tremble; just a little quiver, but once it started, I couldn't get it to stop. I threw my head back and made a noise, a sort of sigh mixed with a cough, to try to distract her eye from it.

"OK," she said patiently. "If it's all right with you, to finish up, I'd like to suggest that we try something a bit different. It's called the empty-chair exercise," she said. I folded my arms and stared at her.

"Basically, I'd like you to imagine that this chair here"—she indicated the lone upright dining chair—"is your mother."

She anticipated my response.

"Now, I know this might feel silly, or embarrassing, but please, just try and go with it. No one's judging you here. This is a safe space." I twisted my hands together anxiously in my lap, mirroring the feeling in my stomach.

"Are you willing to give it a try?"

I stared at the door, willing myself out of it, willing the hands of the clock to tick round to the hour.

"Eleanor," she said gently, "I'm here to help you, and you're here to help yourself, aren't you? I think you want to be happy. In fact, I know you do. Who doesn't? We can work together in this room toward helping you achieve that. It's not going to be easy, or quick, but I really think it could be worth it. What have you got to lose, after all? You're going to be here for an hour either way. Why not give it a try?"

She had made a fair point, I supposed. I looked up and slowly unfolded my arms.

"Great!" she said. "Thank you, Eleanor. So . . . let's imagine that this chair here is your mother. What do you want to tell her, right now? If you could say anything, right here, without being interrupted? Without fear of judgment? Come on, don't worry. Anything you like . . ."

I turned to face the empty chair. My leg was still trembling. I cleared my throat. I was safe. She wasn't really here, she wasn't really listening. I thought back to that house, the cold, the damp smell, the wallpaper with the cornflowers and the brown carpet. I heard the cars passing by outside, all of them driving to nice places, safe places, while we were here, left all alone or—worse—left with her.

"Mummy . . . please," I said. I could hear my voice outside of my own head, disembodied in the room, floating. It was high and very, very quiet. I breathed in.

"Please don't hurt us."

# 30

I don't resort to foul language as a rule, but that first session with the counselor yesterday was bloody ridiculous. I started crying in front of Dr. Temple at the end of her stupid empty-chair exercise, and then she actually said, with faux gentleness, that our session had to draw to a close and that she'd see me next week at the same time. She basically hustled me out onto the street, and I found myself standing on the pavement, shoppers bustling past me, tears streaming down my face. How could she do it? How could one human being see another so obviously in pain, a pain she had deliberately drawn out and worried away at, and then push her out into the street and leave her to cope with it alone?

It was 11 a.m. I wasn't supposed to be drinking, but I wiped away my tears, went into the nearest pub and ordered a large vodka. I silently raised a toast to absent friends and drank it down fast. I walked out before any of the daytime drinkers could begin an interaction with me. Then I went home and got into bed.

≈

Raymond and I continued to meet for lunch in our usual café while I was off work. He would text me to suggest a time and date (the only texts I had received on my new mobile telephone so far). It turned out that if you saw the same person with some degree of regularity, then the conversation was immediately pleasant and comfortable—you could pick up where you left off, as it were, rather than having to start afresh each time.

During the course of these chats, Raymond asked again about Mummy—why I hadn't told her I'd been unwell, why she never visited me, or I her, until finally I gave in and provided him with a potted biography. He already knew about the fire, of course, and that I'd been brought up in care afterward. That, I told him, was because it wasn't possible for me to live with Mummy afterward, not where she was. It was, I'd hoped, enough to keep him quiet, but no.

"Where is she, then? Hospital, nursing home?" he guessed. I shook my head.

"It's a bad place, for bad people," I said. He thought for a moment.

"Not prison?" He looked shocked. I held his gaze but said nothing. After another short pause he asked, not unreasonably, what crime she had committed.

"I can't remember," I said.

He stared at me, then snorted.

"Bullshit," he said. "Come on, Eleanor. You can tell me. It won't change anything between us, I promise. It's not like *you* did it, whatever it was."

I felt a hot flush streak right up the front of my body and then down my back, a sensation I can only liken to being given a sedative prior to a general anesthetic. My pulse was pounding.

"It's true," I said. "I honestly don't know. I think I must have been told at the time, but I can't remember. I was only ten. Everyone was really careful never to mention it around me . . ."

"Oh, come on," he said. "She must have done something really terrible to . . . I mean, what about at school? Kids can be little shits about stuff like that. What about when people hear your name? Although, come to think of it, I don't think I remember reading anything about a crime involving an Oliphant . . . ?"

"Yes, I suppose you would have remembered an Oliphant in the room," I said.

He didn't laugh. It wasn't a very good joke, on reflection. I cleared my throat.

"Oliphant isn't my real name," I said. I liked it, always had, and was extremely grateful to whoever had selected it for me. You didn't come across many Oliphants, that was for sure. Special.

He stared at me, like he was watching a film.

"They gave me a new identity afterward, moved me up here . . . it was meant to stop people recognizing me, protect me. Which is ironic."

"Why?" he said. I sighed.

"Being in care wasn't always much fun. I mean, it was completely fine, I had everything I needed, but it wasn't all picnics and pillow fights."

He raised his eyebrows, nodded. I stirred my coffee.

"The terminology's different now, I think," I said. "They call young people in care 'looked after.' But *every* child should be 'looked after' . . . it really ought to be the default."

I heard myself sounding angry and sad. No one likes hearing themselves sound like that. If someone said, Please could you describe yourself in two words, and you said, "Erm . . . let me see . . . Angry and Sad?" then that really wouldn't be good.

Raymond had reached out then and, very gently, he squeezed my shoulder. It was superficially ineffectual, but, in fact, felt surprisingly pleasant.

"Do you want me to find out what she did?" he said. "I bet I could, quite easily. The magic of the Interweb, hey?"

"No thank you," I said curtly. "I'm more than capable of finding out myself, should I ever wish to. You're not the only person who knows how to use a computer, you know," I said. His face went very pink. "And in any case," I went on, "as you so thoughtfully pointed out, it must have been something fairly horrendous. Don't forget, I still have to talk to her once a week—it's hard enough as it is. It will be completely impossible if I know that she's done . . . whatever it is that she's done."

Raymond nodded. To his credit, he looked slightly ashamed, and only a tiny bit disappointed.

He really isn't prurient, unlike most other people.

After this chat, he still asked questions, but they were normal questions that anyone would ask about their friend's mother (friend! I've got a friend!)—how she was, whether we'd spoken recently. I asked him the same questions back. It was normal. I didn't tell him most of what Mummy said during our chats, of course—it was too painful to repeat, embarrassing and humiliating. I was sure Raymond was already acutely aware of my many physical and character defects, and so there was no need to remind him of them by relating Mummy's bon mots.

Sometimes, he made me stop and think. We'd been talking about holidays, about how he planned to go traveling when he retired, so that he would have enough money to do it in style.

"Mummy's seen so much of the world, lived in so many different places," I said. I reeled a few off. Raymond, surprisingly, looked distinctly unimpressed.

"How old is your mum?" he said. I was taken aback. How old *was* she? I started to work it out.

"So . . . I'm thirty, and I think she must have had me when she was very young—nineteen, twenty? So she'll be . . . I'd guess she'd be in her early fifties now, something like that?"

Raymond nodded.

"Right," he said. "So . . . I'm wondering . . . I mean, I don't have kids, so what would I know—but I imagine it can't be easy, lodging in an opium den in Tangier if you've got a toddler with you? Or . . . what was the other thing? Working as a blackjack dealer in Macao?" He spoke very gently, as though he were afraid to upset me.

"I mean, if you added up all the things she said she'd done, wouldn't it cover a longer period than thirty years? Unless she did it all before you were born and she was still a teenager. And if she did . . . well, I'm wondering . . . where did she get the money from, to do all that traveling, and wasn't she a bit young to be going to places like that on her own at that age? What about your dad? Where did she meet him?"

I looked away. These were important questions that I couldn't answer. Questions I wasn't sure I wanted to answer. But really, why hadn't I ever thought about them before?

≈

This conversation with Raymond came back to me the next time I spoke to her.

"Hello, darling," she said. I thought I heard a hiss of static, or perhaps the malign buzz of strip lighting and another noise, something that sounded a bit like the clanging of bolts being drawn.

"Hello, Mummy," I whispered. I could hear chewing.

"Are you eating?" I said. She exhaled, and then there was an awful honking sound, like a cat trying to cough up a furball, followed by a moist splat.

"Chewing tobacco," she said dismissively. "Ghastly stuff—I'd advise against it, darling."

"Mummy, I'm hardly likely to try chewing tobacco, am I?"

"I suppose not," she said. "You never were very adventurous. Don't knock it till you've tried it, though. I indulged in some paan now and again, back when I lived in Lahore."

As I'd told Raymond, Mummy has lived in Mumbai, Tashkent, São Paulo and Taipei. She's trekked in the Sarawak jungle and climbed Mount Toubkal. She's had an audience with the Dalai Lama in Kathmandu and taken afternoon tea with a maharaja in Jaipur. And that's just for starters.

There was some more throat clearing—the chewing tobacco had clearly taken its toll. I took advantage of the opening.

"Mummy, I wanted to ask you something. How . . . how old were you when you had me?"

She laughed, unamused.

"I was thirteen . . . no, wait . . . I was forty-nine. Whatever. Why do you care? What's it to you, daughter mine?"

"I was just wondering . . ." I said.

She sighed. "I have actually told you all this before, Eleanor," she said briskly, "I do wish you would listen." There was a pause.

"I was twenty," she said calmly. "From an evolutionary point of view, that's actually the peak time for a woman to give birth, you know. Everything just springs back into place. Why, even now, I still have the pert, firm breasts of an early-career supermodel . . ."

"Mummy, please!" I said. She cackled.

"What's wrong, Eleanor? Am I embarrassing you? What a strange child you are! You always were. Hard to love, that's what you are. Very hard to love."

Her laughter trailed off into a long, painful-sounding cough.

"Christ," she said. "I'm starting to fall apart."

For the first time I could remember, I heard a note of sadness in her voice.

"Aren't you well, Mummy?" I asked.

She sighed.

"Oh, I'm fine, Eleanor," she said. "Talking to you always revitalizes me."

I looked at the wall, waiting for the onslaught. I could almost feel her gathering herself, ready to strike.

"All alone, aren't you? No one to talk to, no one to play with. And it's all your own fault. Strange, sad little Eleanor. Too bright for your own good, aren't you? You always were. And yet . . . in so many ways, you're incredibly, spectacularly stupid. You can't see what's right in front of your nose. Or should I say *who* . . ."

She coughed again. I did not dare to breathe, waiting for what would come next.

"Oh, I'm so, so *tired* of talking. It's your turn, Eleanor. If you had even a modicum of social savoir-faire, you'd know that conversation is supposed to be a to-and-fro, a game of verbal tennis. Don't you remember me teaching you that? So, come on, tell me—what have you been doing this week?"

I said nothing. I wasn't sure I'd be able to speak.

"I must say," she went on, "I was surprised when you told me you'd been promoted at work. You've always been more of a follower than a leader, haven't you, darling?"

Should I tell her that I'd been signed off sick? I had managed to avoid any talk of work recently, but she'd raised the topic now. Did she already know about my absence, and was this therefore a trap? I tried to think on my feet, but that's something I've never been good at. Too slow, Eleanor, too late . . .

"Mummy, I . . . I've been unwell. I'm off work at the moment. I'm on sick leave for a while." I heard a deep breath. Was she shocked? Concerned? The same breath rushed out of her, down the phone and into my ear, heavy and fast.

"That's better," she said, sighing happily. "Why on earth would you chew tobacco when you could smoke a lovely, delicious Sobranie?"

She took another deep drag on her cigarette and spoke again, sounding, if anything, even more bored than before.

"Look, I haven't got long," she said, "so let's keep it brief. What's so wrong with you that you're skiving off work? Is it serious? Life threatening? Terminal?"

"I've got clinical depression, Mummy," I said, all in a rush.

She snorted.

"Stuff and nonsense!" she said. "There's no such thing."

I thought back to what the GP and Raymond had said, and how kind and understanding Bob had been. His sister had depression for years, he'd told me. I'd had no idea.

"Mummy," I said, as defiantly as I dared, "I have clinical depression. I'm seeing a counselor and exploring what happened during my childhood, and—"

"NO!" she shouted, so loud and sudden that I took a step back. The next time she spoke, she was quiet—dangerously quiet.

"Now, you listen to me, Eleanor. Under no circumstances are you to discuss your childhood with anyone, especially not a so-called 'counselor.' Do you hear me? Don't you dare. I'm warning you, Eleanor. If you start down that path, do you know what will happen? Do you know what I'll do? I'll—"

≈

Dead air.

≈

As always, Mummy was scary. But the thing was, this time—for the first time ever—she'd actually sounded scared too.

# 31

A few weeks passed, and the sessions with Maria Temple had become a natural part of my routine. It was nice to be out, despite the wind, and I decided to walk instead of taking the bus, enjoying what remained of the sun. There were plenty of other people with the same idea. It felt good to be part of a throng, and I took gentle pleasure in mingling. I dropped twenty pence into the paper cup of a man sitting on the pavement with a very attractive dog. I bought a fudge doughnut from Greggs and ate it as I walked. I smiled at a spectacularly ugly baby who was shaking his fist at me from a garish pushchair. Noticing details, that was good. Tiny slivers of life—they all added up and helped you to feel that you too could be a fragment, a little piece of humanity who usefully filled a space, however minuscule. I was pondering this as I waited for the lights to change. Someone tapped me on the arm, and I jumped.

"Eleanor?" It was Laura, looking cartoonishly glamorous as usual. I hadn't seen her since Sammy's service.

"Oh hello," I said. "How are you? I'm sorry I didn't manage to speak to you at your father's funeral."

She laughed. "Don't worry about it, Eleanor—Ray explained that you were a bit tiddly that day," she said.

I felt my face flush and looked down at the pavement. I suppose I had drunk rather a lot of vodka that afternoon. She punched my arm gently.

"Don't be daft, that's what funerals are for, aren't they—a wee drink and a catch-up?" she said, smiling.

I shrugged, still averting my gaze.

"Your hair's looking good," she said brightly.

I nodded, glanced up into her kohl-rimmed eyes.

"Several people have remarked upon it, actually," I said, feeling a bit more confident, "which leads me to think that you must have done a very good job."

"Och, that's nice to hear," she said. "You can pop back into the salon anytime, you know—I'll always try to fit you in, Eleanor. You were lovely to my dad, so you were."

"*He* was lovely to *me*," I said. "You were very lucky to have had such a delightful father."

Her eyes started to brim, but she blinked the tears away, aided no doubt by the enormous artificial lashes she had glued along her upper lids. The lights at the pedestrian crossing started to flash.

"Raymond mentioned how fond of him you both were," she said quietly. She checked her watch. "Oh God, sorry, I'll need to run, Eleanor—the car's on the meter, and you know what those wardens are like if you go a minute over."

I had absolutely no idea what she was talking about, but I let it pass.

"I'm seeing Ray this weekend, actually," she said, touching my arm. She smiled, "He's actually quite nice, isn't he? He kind of slipped under my radar at first but then, once you get to know him . . ." She smiled again. "Anyway, I'll let him know you were asking after him on Saturday, Eleanor," she said.

"No need," I said, bristling slightly. "I've recently had luncheon with Raymond, as it happens. What unfortunate timing—I could have let him know that *you* were asking after him."

She stared at me. "I wasn't . . . I mean, I didn't know you two were close," she said.

"We lunch together weekly," I said.

"Ah, right—lunch," she said, looking happier, for some reason. "Well, like I said, got to run. Nice seeing you, Eleanor!"

I raised my hand and bade her farewell. It was incredible how she managed to run so nimbly in those heels. I feared for her ankles. Fortunately, they were rather on the chunky side.

≈

Maria Temple was wearing yellow tights today, teamed with purple ankle boots. Yellow tights did not, I noticed, flatter a sporty calf.

"I wonder if we might revisit the subject of your mother, Eleanor? Is that perhaps something we could—"

"No," I said. More silence.

"Fine, fine, no problem. Could you tell me a bit

about your father, then? You haven't really mentioned him so far."

"I don't have a father," I said. More of that awful silence. It was so annoying, but in the end, it actually worked, her refusal to speak. The quiet went on for eons, and in the end I simply couldn't bear it any longer.

"Mummy told me she was ... I assumed she was ... well, she didn't tell me directly when I was a child, but as an adult, I've come to understand that she was the victim of a ... sexual assault," I said, somewhat inelegantly. No response. "I don't know his name and I never met him," I said.

She was writing in her notebook, and looked up. "Did you ever wish you had a father, or a father figure in your life, Eleanor? Was it something that you missed?"

I stared at my hands. It was difficult, talking openly about these things, dragging them out for inspection when they'd been perfectly fine as they were, hidden away.

"You don't miss what you've never had," I said eventually. I'd read that somewhere and it sounded as though it ought to be true. "For as long as I can remember, there's only ever been me and ... her. No one else to play with, to talk to, no shared childhood memories. But I don't suppose that's particularly unusual. And it didn't do me any harm, after all."

I could feel the impact of these words in my stomach, acidic and bitter, swirling around inside.

She was writing in her notebook again and didn't look up.

"Did your mother ever talk about the assault? Did she know her assailant?"

"I stated quite clearly on the first day I came here that I didn't want to talk about her," I said.

She spoke gently. "Of course. Don't worry—we won't talk about her, Eleanor, not if you don't want to. I'm just asking in the context of your father, trying to find out more about him, your feelings about him, that's all."

I thought about it. "I don't really *have* any feelings about him, Maria."

"Did you ever consider trying to find him?" she said.

"A rapist? I shouldn't have thought so," I said.

"A daughter's relationship with her father can sometimes influence her subsequent relationships with men. Do you have any thoughts about that, Eleanor?"

I pondered. "Well," I said, "Mummy wasn't particularly keen on men. But then, she wasn't keen on anyone, really. She thought most people were unsuitable for us, regardless of their gender."

"What do you mean?" Maria said.

Here we were, talking about Mummy, after I'd expressly forbidden it. However, I found, much to my surprise, that I was actually starting to enjoy holding court like this, having Dr. Temple's undivided attention. Perhaps it was the lack of eye contact. It felt relaxing, almost as though I was talking to myself.

"The thing is," I said, "she only wanted us to socialize with people who were *nice*, people who were *proper*—that was something she talked about a lot. She always insisted that we spoke politely, behaved with decorum . . . she made us practice elocution, at least an hour a day. She had—let's just say she had quite *direct* methods of correcting us when we said the wrong thing, did the wrong thing. Which was pretty much all the time."

Maria nodded, indicated that I should go on.

"She said that we deserved the best of everything, and that, even in straitened circumstances, we should always conduct ourselves properly. It was almost as though she thought we were some kind of displaced royalty, you know . . . the family of a deposed tsar or an overthrown monarch or something. I tried so hard, but I never managed to look and behave the way she thought I should, to behave appropriately. That made her very unhappy, and very angry. Mind you, it wasn't just me. No one was ever good enough. She was always telling us we had to be on the lookout for someone who was good enough." I shook my head. "I suppose that's how I ended up here," I said. "Trying to find someone like that, and then getting confused and making a giant mess of everything."

I realized that my whole body was shaking like a wet dog on a cold morning. Maria looked up.

"Let's move on, for now," she said gently. "Do you want to tell me something about what happened after you and your mother parted company, about your experience of the care system? What was that like?"

I shrugged.

"Being fostered was . . . fine. Being in residential care was . . . fine. No one abused me, I had food and drink, clean clothes and a roof over my head. I went to school every day until I was seventeen and then I went to university. I can't really complain about any of it."

Maria spoke very gently.

"What about your other needs, Eleanor?"

"I'm not sure I'm quite following you, Maria," I said, puzzled.

"Humans have a range of needs that we need to have met, Eleanor, in order to be happy and healthy individuals. You've described how your basic physical needs—warmth, food, shelter—were taken care of. But what about your emotional needs?"

I was completely taken aback.

"But I don't *have* any emotional needs," I said.

Neither of us spoke for a while. Eventually, she cleared her throat.

"Everyone does, Eleanor. All of us—and especially young children—need to know that we're loved, valued, accepted and understood . . ."

I said nothing. This was news to me. I let it settle. It sounded plausible, but it was a concept I'd need to consider at more length in the privacy of my own home.

"Was there ever someone who fulfilled that role in your life, Eleanor? Someone who you felt understood

you? Someone who loved you, just as you were, uncon-
ditionally?"

My first response was to say no, of course. Mummy
most certainly did not fall into that category. Something—someone—was niggling at me, though, tugging at my sleeve. I tried to ignore her but she wouldn't
go away, that little voice, those little hands.

"I . . . Yes."

"No rush, Eleanor. Take your time. What do you
remember?"

I took a breath. Back in that house, on a good day.
Stripes of sunshine on the carpet, a board game set
out on the floor, a pair of dice, two brightly colored
counters. A day with more ladders than snakes.

"Pale brown eyes. Something about a dog. But
I've never had a pet . . ."

I felt myself becoming distressed, confused, a
churning in my stomach, a dull pain in my throat.
There was a memory there, somewhere deep, somewhere too painful to touch.

"OK," she said gently, passing me the much needed
box of man-sized tissues, "time's is almost up now."
She took out her diary. "Shall we agree to meet at the
same time next week and come back to this?"

I couldn't believe it. All that work, I was so close,
so close now, and she was throwing me out on the
street again? After everything I'd shared, all the things
I'd uncovered, was about to keep uncovering? I threw
the tissue on the floor.

"Go to hell," I said quietly.

## 32

Anger was good, she'd said, while I was putting my coat on. If I was finally getting in touch with my anger, then I was starting to do some important work, unpicking and addressing things that I'd buried too deep. I hadn't thought about it before, but I suppose I'd never really been angry before now. Irritated, bored, sad, yes, but not actually angry. I supposed she had a point; perhaps things had happened that I ought to feel angry about. It wasn't an emotion I enjoyed feeling, and it certainly wasn't fair to direct it toward Dr. Maria Temple, who was, after all, only doing her job. I'd apologized profusely straight after my outburst, and she was very understanding, even seemed quite pleased. Still, I wouldn't be making a habit of telling people to go to hell. Obscenity is the distinguishing hallmark of a sadly limited vocabulary.

On top of all this, I was trying to find a new routine, but it wasn't easy. For more than nine years, I'd got up, gone to work, come home. At the weekends, I had my vodka. None of that would work now. I decided to clean the flat from top to bottom. I saw how grubby it was, how tired. It looked like I felt—unloved, uncared for. I imagined inviting someone—Raymond,

I supposed—for lunch. I tried to see it through his eyes. There were things I could do to make it nicer, I realized, things that didn't cost much but which would make a big difference. Another houseplant, some brightly colored cushions. I thought about Laura's house, how elegant it was. She lived alone, had a job, her own business even. She certainly seemed to have a life, not just an existence. She seemed happy. It must be possible, then.

The bell made me jump, mid-clean. It wasn't a sound I heard often. I felt, as I usually did, slightly apprehensive as I unbolted the door and threw the locks, noted the increase in my heart rate, the gentle tremor in my hands. I peered around the chain. A youth in sports clothing stood on my doormat, his trainer-shod foot tapping. More than that; his whole body was vibrating with energy. His cap was on backward. Why? Instinctively, I took a step back.

"Oliphant?" he said.

Apprehensively, I nodded. He dipped down to the side of the door, out of sight, then reappeared with a huge basket filled with flowers, wrapped in cellophane and ribbons. He made to hand it over and I unlatched the chain and took it from him gingerly, fearing some sort of trick. He rummaged in his jacket pocket and pulled out a black electronic gadget.

"Sign here, please," he said, handing me a plastic pencil which had, horrifically, been lurking behind his ear. I produced my special autograph, which he did not even glance at.

"Cheers!" he said, already skittering off down the stairs. I had never seen so much nervous energy contained in one human body.

A tiny envelope, like a hamster's birthday card, was affixed to the cellophane. Inside, a business card—plain white—bore the following message:

> Get well soon, Eleanor—we are all thinking
> of you. Love and best wishes from Bob and
> everyone at By Design xxx

I took the basket into the kitchen and put it on the table. Thinking of me. The scent of a summer garden, sweet and heady, was released when I removed the cellophane. They'd been thinking. Of me! I sat down and stroked the petals of a red gerbera, and I smiled.

~

Flowers placed carefully on the coffee table, I continued my slow progress around the flat, and as I cleaned, I thought about what it meant to make a home. I didn't have much experience to draw on. I opened all of the windows, tuned the radio until I found some inoffensive music and scrubbed each room in turn. Some of the stains in the carpet wouldn't come out, but I managed to lift most of them. I filled four black bags with rubbish—old crosswords, dried-out pens, ugly knick-knacks that I'd collected over the years. I sorted out my bookshelf, making a pile to take (and in some cases, return) to the charity shop.

I'd recently finished reading a management tome

which seemed to be aimed at psychopaths with no common sense (quite a dangerous combination). I have always enjoyed reading, but I've never been sure how to select appropriate material. There are so many books in the world—how do you tell them all apart? How do you know which one will match your tastes and interests? That's why I just pick the first book I see. There's no point in trying to choose. The covers are of very little help, because they always say only good things, and I've found out to my cost that they're rarely accurate. "Exhilarating" "Dazzling" "Hilarious." No.

The only criterion I have is that the books must look clean, which means that I have to disregard a lot of potential reading material in the charity shop. I don't use the library for the same reason, although obviously, in principle and reality, libraries are life-enhancing palaces of wonder. It's not you, libraries, it's me, as the popular saying goes. The thought of books passing through so many unwashed hands—people reading them in the bath, letting their dogs sit on them, picking their nose and wiping the results on the pages. People eating cheesy crisps and then reading a few chapters without washing their hands first. I just can't. No, I look for books with one careful owner. The books in Tesco are nice and clean. I sometimes treat myself to a few tomes from there on payday.

$\approx$

At the end of the process, the flat was clean, and very nearly empty. I made a cup of tea and looked around the living room. It just needed pictures on the walls and a rug or two. Some new plants. Sorry, Polly. The flowers would have to do for now. I took a deep breath, picked up the pouf and squashed it into a bin liner. It was quite a fight to get it in. As I grappled with it, I thought about what I must look like, my arms wrapped around a giant frog, wrestling it to the ground. I snorted a bit, and then I laughed and laughed until my chest hurt. When I stood up and finally tied the handles, a jaunty pop music song was playing and I realized what I felt . . . happy. It was such a strange, unusual feeling—light, calm, as though I'd swallowed sunshine. Only this morning I'd been furious, and now I was calm and happy. I was gradually getting used to feeling the range of available human emotions, their intensity, the rapidity with which they could change. Until now, anytime that emotions, feelings, had threatened to unsettle me, I'd drink them down fast, drown them. That had allowed me to exist, but I was starting to understand that I needed, wanted, something more than that now.

I took the rubbish downstairs and when I came back into the flat, I noticed that it smelled lemony. It was a pleasure to enter. I didn't normally notice my surroundings, I realized. It was like my walk to Maria Temple's office this morning: when you took a moment to see what was around you, noticed all the little things, it made you feel . . . lighter.

Perhaps, if you had friends or a family, they might help you to notice things more often. They might even point them out to you. I turned off the radio and sat in silence on the sofa, drinking another cup of tea. All I could hear was the breeze whistling softly through the open window and two men laughing in the street below. It was a weekday afternoon. Normally, I'd be at work, watching the hands tick round until five, waiting for pizza and vodka time and then Friday night and the three long sleeps until Monday. With the exception of the shot I'd had in the pub, I hadn't drunk any vodka for some weeks now. I'd always thought that it helped me sleep, but in fact I'd been sleeping more deeply than ever before, untroubled by disturbing dreams.

An electronic noise startled me and I almost spilled my tea. Someone had sent me a text message. I ran into the hall for my phone. The little envelope flashed:

> U about early evening? Can I
> come over? Got a surprise 4
> u! Rx

A surprise! I replied immediately.

> Yes. Eleanor O.

No one had ever asked to come and visit me before. The social worker made an appointment, and the meter reader just turned up. I was conscious that Raymond's previous visits had not been very pleasant for him—or me—and decided to try to make amends.

I put on my jerkin and headed out to the corner shop. Mr. Dewan looked up from reading a newspaper at the sound of the electronic alert. It must drive him to distraction, bleeping all day like that. He smiled cautiously at me. I took a basket and got some milk, Earl Grey tea bags and a lemon to slice, in case Raymond preferred his tea that way. I spent a considerable amount of time in the aisles, somewhat overwhelmed by the choice. In the end, I plumped for Garibaldi biscuits, throwing in a packet of pink wafers too—apparently, it's nice to offer guests an option. I wondered if Raymond might prefer something savory, and so I got some cream crackers and a packet of cheese slices. All bases covered.

I stood in line with my basket, not eavesdropping but nonetheless forced to overhear the conversation of the couple in front of me as we waited our turn. Eventually, I felt compelled to intervene and provide assistance.

"It's 'tagine'," I said.

No reply. I sighed, and leaned forward again.

"Tagine," I repeated, speaking slowly and clearly and, I thought, in a passable French accent.

"Sorry?" the woman said, not sounding sorry at all. The man simply stared at me, in a manner best described as mildly hostile.

"Neither of you can remember the word for the—as you described it—'ceramic pot with the pointy lid' that 'Judith'—whoever she is—had put on her wedding list, leading you"—here, I indicated the woman with a gentle nod of my head—"to describe her as a 'pretentious cow'." I was quite enjoying the occasional use of the waggling finger gesture now that I'd got the hang of it.

Neither of them spoke, so I felt emboldened to continue.

"A tagine is a traditional cooking vessel of North African origin," I said helpfully, "generally made from fired clay and decorated with a brightly colored glaze. It's also the name of the stew that is cooked within it."

The man's mouth had fallen open slightly, and the woman's had slowly changed shape to form a very thin, very tight line. She turned back to him and they began to whisper together, looking round more than once to steal a quick glance at me.

Nothing more was said, although they glared at me as they walked out, having paid for their goods. Not a word of thanks. I gave them a little wave.

≈

Mr. Dewan smiled warmly at me when I finally reached the till.

"The levels of rudeness and the complete lack of awareness of the comme il faut among the general population never ceases to disappoint me, Mr. Dewan," I said, shaking my head.

"Miss Oliphant," he said, smiling in an understanding way. "How nice to see you again! You're looking very well."

I felt myself beaming in response.

"Thank you very much, Mr. Dewan," I said. "It's nice to see you too. Pleasant day today, is it not?"

He nodded, still smiling, and scanned my items. When he'd done that, his smile faltered slightly. "Will there be anything else today, Miss Oliphant?"

The bottles behind him glittered in the glare of the overhead lights, red and gold and clear.

"Yes!" I said. "I'd almost forgotten." I leaned over to the newspaper stand and picked up a *Telegraph*— I was itching to get back to the crossword again.

~

Back home, I lit the gas fire and laid out the teacups. I wished that they matched, but I was sure Raymond wouldn't mind. I sliced the lemon and arranged the biscuits as alternating spokes on a wheel on my nicest plate, the one with flowers on it. I decided to keep the savory items in reserve. No need to go crazy.

Being somewhat out of practice, I was only half-way through the crossword when the doorbell rang, a bit later than I'd been expecting. Due to hunger pangs I'd been forced to have a few biscuits, so a couple of the spokes on the wheel were missing now. Too bad.

Raymond was holding a cardboard box with handles in one hand, and a huge, bulging plastic bag in the other. He seemed very out of breath, placed both items gently on my hall carpet without being asked, and started to take off his jacket, still puffing and blowing like a beached porpoise. Smoking kills.

He passed me his jacket and I looked at it for a moment before realizing I was supposed to hang it up. I didn't have anywhere suitable, so I folded it into a square as best I could and then put it on the floor in the corner of the hall. He didn't look very pleased, although I had no idea why. It wasn't an expensive-looking jacket.

I showed him into the living room and offered him tea. He seemed quite excitable. "Later, maybe. I've got to tell you about the surprise first, Eleanor," he said.

I sat down.

"Go ahead," I said, bracing myself. My experience of surprises is limited and not particularly positive. He fetched the cardboard box from the hall and placed it on the floor.

"Now," he said, "you don't have to do this. My mum will be more than happy to oblige. I just thought . . . well . . ."

He opened the lid very gently, and I instinctively took a step back.

"*Come on, darling*," he said, in a soft, crooning voice that I'd never heard him use before. "*Don't be frightened . . .*"

He reached in and lifted out the fattest cat I'd ever seen. It was, in theory, jet black, the darkness extending even to its nose and whiskers, but its thick fur was covered in bald patches which looked all the paler by comparison. He held it close to his chest and continued to whisper endearments in its ear. The creature looked distinctly underwhelmed.

"What do you think?" he said.

I stared into its green eyes, and it stared back. I took a step forward and he offered her to me. There was a bit of awkwardness as he passed her over, trying to transfer her bulk from his arms into mine, and then, all at once, it was done. I held her like a baby, close against my chest, and felt, rather than heard, her deep, sonorous purring. Oh, the warm weight of her! I buried my face in what remained of her fur and felt her turn her head toward me as she gently sniffed my hairline.

Eventually, I looked up. Raymond was unpacking the other bag, which contained a disposable litter tray, a squishy cushion bed and a small box of kibble. The cat squirmed in my arms and landed on the carpet with a heavy thump. She strolled over to the litter tray, squatted down and urinated loudly, maintaining extremely assertive eye contact with me throughout. After the deluge, she lazily kicked over the traces with her back legs, scattering litter all over my freshly cleaned floor.

A woman who knew her own mind and scorned the conventions of polite society. We were going to get along just fine.

～

Raymond declined all of the biscuits on offer and also the tea. He requested beer or coffee, but I had neither. Taking care of guests was more challenging than I'd thought. Eventually, he settled for a glass of water, which he didn't even drink. Desi, one of his flatmates, had rescued the cat from the back court of his flats last night, he told me. Someone had put her in a metal dustbin and set it alight—Desi had heard the screams when he was returning home from work. I stood up and ran toward the bathroom, where I vomited up the pink wafers. Raymond knocked gently on the door, but I shouted at him to leave me alone. When I came back, both he and the cat were sitting separately on the sofa. I sat down in the chair opposite, and they both watched me carefully.

"Who would do such a thing, Raymond?" I said, when I could finally speak. Both he and the cat looked sad.

"Sick fucks," said Raymond, shaking his head. "Desi brought her in and we made sure she was OK. He's allergic, though, so we can't keep her. I was going to take her to the Cats Protection, or see if my mum wanted another one, but then . . . I dunno, I thought she might be a nice bit of company for you, Eleanor? Just say if not. It's a big deal, having a pet—a lot of responsibility . . ."

This was tricky. On the one hand, I could not deny that I was drawn to her. She had an undeniably rakish, alopecia-based charm and a devil-may-care attitude that would melt the hardest of hearts. I could tell that she was a cat that brooked no nonsense. She was, at the same time, a vulnerable creature, one which needed looking after. Therein lay the rub. Was I up to the task?

I thought back to the counseling sessions, how we'd talked about thinking things through rationally, recognizing unhelpful patterns of behavior and being brave enough to try doing things differently. Come on, Eleanor, I said to myself. Be brave. This is not the same as before, not even close to it. She's a cat, and you're a grown woman. You're more than capable of doing this.

"I will assume the mantle of care, Raymond," I said, firmly. "This creature will be looked after assiduously."

He smiled.

"I'm sure she will be. She looks at home here already, right enough," he said. The cat was now sprawled across the sofa cushions, for all intents and purposes asleep, although one ear twitched intermittently as she monitored the conversation.

"What are you going to call her?" he said.

I put my head on one side while I considered this. After a while, Raymond stood up.

"I'm going to nip downstairs for a fag. I'll leave the door on the latch," he said.

"Don't blow the smoke toward my windows!" I shouted after him.

When he came back ten minutes later, I told him that her name was Glen. He laughed.

"Glen? That's a boy's name, surely?"

I thought about all of those red labels, all those empty bottles. "She's named after an old friend," I said.

~

The next day I woke with a start to find Glen lying beside me, her head on the pillow and her body under the covers, just like a human. Her huge green eyes were staring intently at me, as though she had willed me awake. She followed me into the kitchen and I gave her some water, which she ignored, and some kibble, which she bolted down and promptly vomited back up onto the kitchen floor. I turned away to get some cleaning materials from under the sink, but when I looked around, she was eating her sick back up again.

"Good girl, Glen," I said. Low maintenance.

Raymond had only brought the bare minimum for her to spend the night, so, while she was snoozing on top of the duvet, I snuck out of the flat and took the bus to the retail park, where I knew that there was a big pet supplies store. I bought her a bigger, comfier bed, a proper litter tray with a covered roof for privacy, four different kinds of wet and dry food, and a sack of organic cat litter. I picked up a bottle of oil that was supposed to be good for her coat—a teaspoon was to be mixed in with her food every day. I didn't care if her coat grew back or not, because she was fine just as she was, but I felt that she might be more comfortable without the bare patches of skin. She didn't strike me as the type to enjoy playing with toys, but just in case, I bought a glittery ball and a huge fluffy mouse, the size of an old man's slipper, which was stuffed with catnip. When I took the trolley to the till, I realized that I was going to have to call a taxi to get it all home. I felt quite proud of myself.

The driver wouldn't help me carry it upstairs, so it took me a few trips, and I was sweating by the time I got everything indoors. The expedition had taken over two hours, from start to finish. Glen was still asleep on the duvet.

I spent the day pottering around the flat. Glen was good company: quiet, self-contained, mostly asleep. That evening, as I sat with a cup of tea and listened to a play on the radio, she jumped onto my lap and began kneading my thighs with her paws, claws partially unsheathed. It was slightly uncomfortable, but I could tell that she meant it kindly. After doing that for a minute or so, she settled herself carefully onto my lap and went to sleep. I needed to go to the bathroom about twenty minutes later, a necessity exacerbated by the fact that she was far from slender and was lounging with her full body weight directly atop my bladder. I tried to gently shift her to one side; she resisted. I tried again. On the third attempt, she got to her feet slowly, arched her back and then shuddered out a long, judgmental sigh, before dropping down onto the floor and waddling off toward her new bed. Once ensconced there, she glared at me as I left the room, maintaining the expression when I returned, and continued to glower at me throughout the evening. I wasn't worried. I'd dealt with far, far worse things than an irritated feline.

Raymond paid a visit again a few days later to see how Glen was settling in. I'd invited him and his mother, as he'd mentioned that she was keen and I imagined, as a cat obsessive, she'd enjoy meeting Glen. In any case, there were still plenty of biscuits left over from his previous visit, so it was not as though it was any trouble.

They arrived in a black cab, which Mrs. Gibbons was very pleased about.

"The driver was lovely, Eleanor, wasn't he, Raymond?" she said. Raymond nodded, and I thought I detected a hint, just a tiny one, of weariness, as though it wasn't the first time she'd gone over the topic during their short journey from the south to the west of the city. "Oh, he couldn't have been nicer, helped me in—and out!—of the taxi, held the door open while I got my walking frame . . ."

"That's right, Mum," he said, tucking her walking frame into the corner of the living room while she settled herself on the sofa. Glen, ever the iconoclast, had immediately gone to bed—my bed—as soon as they arrived, and there was nothing to see of her but a lightly snoring lump under the duvet. Mrs. Gibbons was disappointed, but I left her to peruse some photos on my phone while I went to make tea. Raymond joined me in the kitchen, leaning against the work top while he watched me pour. He placed a carrier bag next to me.

"It's nothing much," he said. I peered inside. There was a white cardboard box, from a bakery, tied with ribbon. There was also a tiny tin of "gourmet" cat food. "How lovely!" I said, delighted.

"I wasn't sure what you liked, didn't want to come empty-handed . . ." Raymond said, blushing. "I thought, well . . . you seem like the kind of person who likes nice things," he said, looking up at me. "You *deserve* to have nice things," he said firmly.

This was strange. I must confess I was somewhat lost for words for a moment or two. Did I deserve nice things?

"It's funny, you know, Raymond," I said. "Growing up with Mummy was very disorientating. Some—times she gave us nice things, other times . . . not. I mean, one week we'd be dipping quail eggs in celery salt and shucking oysters, the next we'd be starving. I mean, you know, literally, deprived of food and water," I said. His eyes widened.

"Everything was always extreme, so extreme, with her," I said, nodding to myself. "I used to long for *normal*. You know, three meals a day, ordinary stuff—tomato soup, mashed potatoes, cornflakes . . ."

I untied the ribbons and looked inside the box. The sponge cake inside was an artful confection, chocolate ganache scattered with bright raspberry jewels. It was an ordinary luxury, which Raymond had chosen, especially for me.

"Thank you," I said, feeling tears threaten to well up. There was really nothing else I needed to say.

"Thanks for inviting us, Eleanor," he said. "Mum loves to get out, but she doesn't often get the chance."

"You're welcome anytime, both of you are," I said, and I meant it.

I set the cake on a tray with the tea things but, before I could pick it up, Raymond did the honors. I followed behind. He had had his hair cut, I noticed.

"How are you feeling, Eleanor?" Mrs. Gibbons asked, once we were all settled. "Raymond mentioned that you'd been a bit under the weather recently?"

She wore an expression of mild, polite concern, nothing more, and I realized, flushed with gratitude, that he hadn't provided her with any details.

"I'm feeling much better, thank you," I said. "Raymond's been keeping an eye on me. I'm very lucky." He looked surprised. His mother did not.

"He's got a heart of gold, my boy," she said, nodding. Raymond's face looked like Glen's did the time she noticed that I'd seen her trying and failing to jump from the sofa to the windowsill. I laughed.

"We're embarrassing you!" I said.

"No, *you're* embarrassing you," he said, "rabbiting away about nothing like a proper pair of old biddies. Anyone want some more tea?" He reached forward for the teapot, and I saw he was smiling.

The Gibbonses were easy, pleasant company. We were all slightly surprised at how quickly time had passed when the prebooked taxi honked its horn in irritation an hour later, I think, and their departure was, by necessity, somewhat rushed.

"Your turn to come to me next time, Eleanor," she said, as they struggled out of the door with the walking frame, Raymond shrugging on his jacket at the same time. I nodded. She kissed me quickly on the cheek, the scarred one, and I didn't even flinch.

"Come again with Raymond one Sunday, have your tea, stay for a while," she whispered. I nodded again.

Raymond lumbered past me, then, before I could do anything about it, leaned in and kissed me on the cheek like his mother had done. "See you at work," he said, and he was off, manhandling both her and her wheels down the stairs in a very precarious fashion. I put my hand to my face. They were quite a kissy family, the Gibbonses—some families were like that.

I washed up the cups and plates, at which point Glen finally decided to make an appearance. "That wasn't very sociable, Glen," I said. She stared up at me and let out a short sound, not really a meow, more of a chirp, strangely. The import—namely, that she didn't give a fig—was abundantly clear. I spooned the special cat food that Raymond had brought into her bowl. This was met with considerable enthusiasm, although, regretfully, her table manners were sadly reminiscent of her benefactor's.

Raymond had left his tabloid newspaper behind on the chair in the living room—unfortunately, he often carried one rolled up in his back pocket. I leafed through it, just in case it had a halfway decent cross-word, and stopped at page nine, my eyes drawn to the headline.

*Glasgow Evening Times*

**Entertainment News**

**PILGRIM PIONEERS DISCOVER AMERICA:**
**Glasgow band tipped to be "bigger than Biffy"**

> Scottish band Pilgrim Pioneers are celebrating
> this week after reaching number five in the
> American Billboard Top 100.
>
> The Glasgow-based four-piece look set to
> crack the lucrative US market after years of gig-
> ging locally in pubs and clubs.
>
> Their single "Don't Miss You," written after
> the acrimonious departure of their previous front
> man, was picked up last month by an industry
> insider via YouTube. Since then, it's been broad-
> cast nightly across the USA as the sound track to
> a big budget advert for a telecoms company.
>
> The band is set to head Stateside next month
> on a coast-to-coast tour.

Reading this, I was taken straight back to another
place, another person; the person I was trying to be
and the changes I was trying and failing to make, to
myself and in my life. The singer wasn't ever the point,
really; Maria Temple had helped me see that.

In my eagerness to change, to connect with someone, I'd focused on the wrong thing, the wrong person.

On the charge of being a catastrophic disaster, a failed human being, I was starting to find myself, with Maria's help, not guilty.

The story didn't mention what Johnnie Lomond was doing now. It really didn't matter. I folded up the newspaper—I could line Glen's litter tray with it later.

@johnnieLrocks 7h
Massive congrats to the
guys—great news and really,
really well deserved. So
chuffed for them #usa
#bigtime
[no likes]

@johnnieLrocks 44m
Fuck. Fuck fuck fuckety fuck
fuck.
[later deleted]

# 33

Maria seemed in a good mood when I arrived at her office, and I was too. It was an effort to switch my brain to alert mode when she started talking about the past again.

"We haven't spoken much about the fire. I wonder . . . are you happy to talk a bit about it?"

I nodded, warily.

"Good. Now, can you try closing your eyes for me, please, Eleanor? Sometimes it's easier to access memories that way. Take a deep breath in, and then let it all out. Great. And another . . . good. Now, I want you to think back. You're at home, and it's the day before the fire. What do you remember? Anything? Take your time . . ."

I'd been feeling so light and free earlier, so centered in myself, that I hadn't had a chance to prepare myself properly for this. As I closed my eyes and exhaled to Maria's count, I had the worrying realization that, before I was even properly aware of it, my brain was off accessing memories in places I didn't want it to go, scurrying into rooms before I'd had a chance to block them off. My body felt heavy, in contrast to my mind, which floated, balloon-like, just beyond my reach. Now that it was happening, though, I accepted it with equanimity. There was a certain pleasure in ceding control.

"Mummy. She's angry. Mummy was sleeping but we've woken her up again. Mummy's had enough of us now." I feel tears on my cheeks as I relate this, but I don't feel particularly sad. It's as though I'm describing a film.

"That's great, Eleanor, you're doing really well," Maria said. "Can you tell me more about Mummy?"

My voice is tiny. "I don't want to," I say.

"You're doing great, Eleanor. Let's try to keep going. So, about Mummy . . . ?"

I said nothing for the longest time, allowing my mind to wander where it needed to go in that house, letting the memories out like trapped birds. Finally, I whispered. Two words.

"Where's Marianne?"

# 34

Sunday. I had to leave the house at twelve to meet Raymond for lunch. Glen was dozing in her new bed, and I used the camera function on my mobile telephone to take some more shots of her. In the final picture, she had one paw covering her eyes as if to block out the light. I knelt down on the floor beside her and buried my face in the biggest patch of fur. She wriggled slightly, then increased the volume of her purring. I kissed the softness on the top of her head.

"See you later, Glen," I said. "I won't be long." She appeared blissfully untroubled by my imminent departure.

When I was ready to leave, I opened the door as quietly as I could and tiptoed into the living room to check if she was still asleep. I found her on top of the giant catnip-stuffed mouse, both she and the rodent facing me, its glazed button eyes staring straight ahead. She had her front paws thrown over its mousy shoulders and was lazily kneading them while she humped it energetically from behind. I left them to it.

Ever since the session, all I could think about was Marianne. Marianne Marianne Marianne; I turned

the name over and over in my mind like a coin
between my fingers. Dr. Temple had asked me to prepare myself to talk about her again in our next session. I wasn't sure how I felt about that. Is knowing
always better than not knowing? Discuss.

Raymond, untroubled by philosophical questions,
was already there when I arrived at the Black Dog,
reading the *Sunday Mail* and sipping a pint.

"Sorry I'm late," I said.

His face was paler than usual, and when he stood
up to hug me, I could smell old as well as new beer,
in addition to the usual reek of cigarettes.

"How's it going?" he said, his voice sounding
scratchy.

"How are *you*?" I said. He didn't look well.

He groaned. "I nearly texted you to cancel, to be
honest," he said. "Had a bit of a late one last night."

"Did you and Laura go on a date?" I said.

He boggled at me. "How on earth did you know
that?" he asked, sounding incredulous.

I remembered something I'd seen Billy do in the
office, and tapped the side of my nose with my index
finger knowingly.

He laughed. "I think you might have a bit of witch
in you, Eleanor," he said.

I shrugged. I even had a black cat now to prove it.

"I bumped into Laura a while back, actually," I
explained. "She told me you were seeing each other."

He took a big gulp of his pint.

"Right. Yeah, she's been in touch a few times, asking if I wanted to meet up. We went to see a film last night, had a couple of drinks afterward."

"That sounds nice," I said. "Is she your girlfriend now, then?"

He signaled to the waiter to bring him another pint.

"Laura's a lovely girl," he said, "but I don't think I'm going to be seeing her again."

A staff member brought Raymond's beer and some menus, and I asked for a Dandelion and Burdock. Weirdly, considering it was a smart bar in the city center, they didn't have any, so I had to make do with a Dr Pepper.

"Why not?" I said. "Laura's very glamorous."

Raymond sighed. "It's a bit more complicated than that, Eleanor, isn't it?" he said. "I think she's probably a bit . . . high maintenance for me, if you know what I mean?"

"Not really, no," I said.

"She's not my type, to be honest." He took a noisy mouthful of beer. "I mean, looks are important, of course they are, but you've got to be able to have a laugh, enjoy each other's company too, you know? I'm not sure me and Laura have got that much in common."

I shrugged, not knowing how best to respond. It was hardly my area of expertise.

We were silent for a moment. He was looking terribly pale and uncomfortable. Classic hangover symptoms. Thankfully I never suffered from them, blessed as I am with an iron constitution.

I ordered an omelet made by the chef, Arnold Bennett, and Raymond went for the full cooked breakfast with extra fried bread.

"Had quite a lot of Jack Daniel's with Desi after I got home last night," he explained. "That should soak it up."

"Don't make a habit of the drinks, Raymond," I said sadly. "You don't want to end up like me, do you?"

Raymond reached for my arm, held it for a moment.

"You're doing just fine, Eleanor," he said.

The food came, and I tried not to look at Raymond as he ate. It was never a pretty sight. I wondered how Glen was doing. Would it be possible to bring her out somewhere like this, if she could sit in some sort of high chair at the table with us? I could see no reason against it but for the small-minded anti-feline contingent who might complain.

"Look, Raymond!" I said, thrusting my phone in his face. He glanced at the first four pictures.

"Ah, that's nice, Eleanor," he said. "She looks really settled at your place."

"Keep scrolling," I said. He flicked through a few more in a desultory fashion; I could tell he was losing interest. Pearls before swine.

We talked about inconsequential matters as we waited for our coffee. When it arrived, there was a lull in the conversation, and Raymond poured a sachet of sugar onto the table. He began to draw in the grains with his forefinger, humming tunelessly as he tended to do when he was feeling anxious. His cuticles were bitten and his nails didn't look too clean—he could be such an annoying man sometimes.

"Eleanor," he said, "look, I've got something to tell you, and you've got to promise not to be angry with me."

I sat back and waited for him to continue.

"I've been doing some research online about your mum, about what happened back then."

I stared at the grains of sugar. How could each one be so tiny, and yet so perfectly angular?

"Eleanor?" he said. "I'm not sure if what I found is right, but I googled arson, and the year it happened, and London, and there are some newspaper articles you might want to take a look at. We don't have to if you don't want to. I just wanted you to know, in case . . . well, in case you changed your mind about finding stuff out."

I went to the happy place in my mind for a moment, the pink and white fluffy place with bluebirds and gentle babbling streams and, now, a semi-bald cat purring noisily.

"Where did you say your mum is these days?" he asked, very gently.

"I don't know," I mumbled. "She's the one who contacts me. It's never the other way around." I tried to fathom his expression. I find it hard to work out people's expressions sometimes. The cryptic cross-word is much, much easier. If I had to guess what was showing on his face, I would have said: sadness, pity, fear. Nothing good. But the underlying feeling was one of kindness, gentleness. He was sad and afraid for me, but he wouldn't hurt me, and didn't have the slightest desire to do so. I took some comfort in that.

"Look, we won't talk about it anymore, OK? I just wanted to say that . . . if anything comes back to you . . . in counseling or whatever . . . I might be able to give you some answers, you know? But only if you want them," he added quickly.

I thought about this. I began to feel the vague inklings of irritation.

"Raymond," I said, "I really don't think it's appropriate for you to try to direct me toward this, not before I'm ready. I'm making perfectly good progress on my own, you know," I told him. Be patient, Marianne. I'm coming. I looked at his face, which was even paler now than when he first sat down. His mouth hung open very slightly and his eyes were glassy and tired. It wasn't an attractive look.

"You're not the only person who knows how to use a search engine, you know. It's my life, and when I'm good and ready, I'm more than capable"—I treated him to one of my more direct looks—"of finding out exactly what happened for myself."

He nodded, and started to speak. I held up my hand, palm facing forward, to stop him. It was a very rude gesture and I must confess to an illicit thrill of pleasure as I made it. I followed this up by taking a long, pointed draft of my Dr Pepper. Unfortunately, it was almost finished, and the straw made a very unpleasant slurping sound, but I think I managed to get my point across quite effectively nonetheless.

After I finished my drink, I caught the waiter's eye and indicated that I'd like him to bring the bill. Raymond had his head in his hands, not saying anything. I felt a rush of pain in my chest. I'd hurt his feelings—Raymond. I put my hand over my mouth and felt tears form. He looked up at me, then leaned over and took both my hands, quite assertively, in his. He puffed out some stale air from inside his hairy little beard.

"I'm so sorry." We both spoke the words at exactly the same time. We tried again, and the same thing happened. Suddenly, I laughed, and he did too. Short bursts, at first, and then for longer. It was proper, genuine laughter, the kind that makes your whole body shake. My mouth was wide open, my breath slightly wheezy, my eyes shut tight. I felt vulnerable, and yet very relaxed and comfortable. I imagined that vomiting or going to the lavatory in front of him would feel the same way.

"Look, it's totally my fault," he said, when we'd finally calmed down. "I'm so sorry if I upset you, Eleanor. I shouldn't even have brought it up, especially today when I'm hung over—my brain feels mashed," he said. "You're absolutely right. It's your business, and your decision. One hundred percent."

He was still holding on to my hands. It was extremely pleasant.

"It's fine, Raymond," I said, and I meant it. "I'm sorry if I overreacted. I know that you're a kind man who means well, and you were only trying to help." I ventured a small smile at the sight of his face, which was full of relief.

He let go of my hands very gently. I hadn't really noticed his eyes before. They were green, flecked with brown. Very unusual.

He smiled again, then put his palms up to his face and rubbed it, groaning quietly.

"Christ," he said. "I can't believe I've got to visit my mum now and see to the cats. I just want to crawl back to bed and sleep until Tuesday."

I tried not to smile, and paid the bill—he protested, but I took full advantage of his weakened state.

"Do you want to come with me?" he said. "She'd love to see you."

I didn't even consider it. "No thank you, not today, Raymond," I said. "Glen will have had a bowel movement by now, and I don't like to leave her feces in the tray for more than an hour or two, in case she needs to urinate again afterward."

Raymond stood up quickly. "Just nipping to the Gents," he said.

≈

I bought some cat food for Glen on the way home. The thing about Glen is that, despite her offhand manner, she loves me. I know she's only a cat. But it's still love; animals, people. It's unconditional, and it's both the easiest and the hardest thing in the world.

Sometimes, after counseling sessions, I desperately wanted to buy vodka, lots of it, take it home and drink it down, but in the end I never did. I couldn't, for lots of reasons, one of which was that if I wasn't fit to, then who would feed Glen? She isn't able to take care of herself. She needs me.

It isn't annoying, her need—it isn't a burden. It's a privilege. I'm responsible. I chose to put myself in a situation where I'm responsible. Wanting to look after her, a small, dependent, vulnerable creature, is innate, and I don't even have to think about it. It's like breathing.

For some people.

# 35

We had increased our counseling sessions to twice a week, which had sounded excessive when Maria first proposed it, but I was finding, to my surprise, that this was barely enough. I hoped I wasn't turning into one of those needy people, though, the kind who are always droning on about themselves and their problems. Boring.

I was slowly getting used to talking about my childhood, having spent the best part of thirty years studiously avoiding the subject. That said, every time the topic of Marianne came up, I sidestepped it. Before each session, I told myself that *this* would be the right time to talk about her, but then, when it came to it, I just couldn't do it. Today, Dr. Temple had asked about Marianne again of course and, when I'd shaken my head, she suggested that it might be helpful to think about my childhood as two discrete periods; *before* and *after* the fire, as a way of getting to the topic of Marianne. Yes, I said, it might be helpful. But very, very painful.

"So what's your happiest memory from *before* the fire?" she said. I thought hard. Several minutes went by.

"I remember moments here and there, fragments, but I can't think of a complete incident," I said. "No, wait. A picnic, at school. It must have been the end of term, or something like that—we all were outside, at any rate, in the sunshine." It wasn't much to go on, and certainly not a detailed recollection.

"What was it about that day that made you feel so happy, d'you think?" She spoke gently.

"I felt . . . safe," I said. "And I knew Marianne was safe too."

Yes, that was it. Marianne—*don't think too hard*—that's right, her nursery class was there that day too. We all got a packed lunch, cheese sandwiches and an apple. The sunlight, the picnic. Marianne and I had walked home together after school, as we always did, going as slowly as we could and telling each other about our day. The walk home wasn't long. It was never long enough. She was funny, a gifted mimic. It hurt to remember how much she'd made me laugh.

School had been a place of refuge. Teachers asked how you got your cuts and bruises, sent you to the nurse to have them dressed. The nit nurse combed your hair gently, so gently, said you could keep the elastics because you'd been such a good girl. School dinners. I could relax at school, knowing Marianne was at nursery, safe and warm. The little ones had their own special peg to hang their coats on. She loved it there.

It wasn't long after the picnic that Mummy found out Mrs. Rose had been asking about my bruises. We were homeschooled after that, all day every day—no more escaping from nine till four, Monday to Friday. Worse and worse, quicker and quicker, hotter and hotter, fire. I'd brought it on myself as usual, my own stupid fault, stupid Eleanor, and, worst of all, I'd dragged Marianne into it too. She'd done nothing wrong. She'd never done anything wrong.

≈

Dr. Temple pushed the tissues toward me and I wiped the tears from my cheeks.

"You mentioned Marianne a lot there," she said gently, "when you were talking about your day-to-day life."

I was ready to say it out loud. "She's my sister," I said.

We sat for a moment and I let the words crystallize. There she was: Marianne. My little sister. My missing piece, my absent friend. The tears were coursing down my cheeks now, and Maria let me sob until I was ready to speak.

"I don't want to talk about what happened to her," I said. "I'm not ready to do that!"

Maria Temple was very calm. "Don't worry, Eleanor. We'll take this one step at a time. Acknowledging that Marianne is your sister is a huge thing. We'll get to the rest, in time."

"I wish I could talk about it now," I said, furious with myself. "But I can't."

"Of course, Eleanor," she said, calmly. She paused. "Do you think that's because you *can't* remember what happened to Marianne? Or is it because you don't want to?" Her voice was very gentle.

"I don't want to," I said slowly, quietly. I rested my elbows on my knees and put my head in my hands.

"Be gentle with yourself, Eleanor," Maria said. "You're doing incredibly well."

I almost laughed. It certainly didn't feel like I was doing well.

Before and after the fire. Something fundamental had gone missing in the flames: Marianne.

"What do I do?" I said, desperate, suddenly, to move forward, to get better, to *live*. "How do I fix this? How do I fix *me*?"

Dr. Temple put down her pen and spoke firmly but gently.

"You're doing it already, Eleanor. You're braver and stronger than you give yourself credit for. Keep going."

When she smiled at me then, her whole face crinkled into warm lines. I dropped my head again, desperate to hide the emotion that flamed there. The lump in my throat. The pricking of more tears, the swell of warmth. I was safe here, I'd talk more about my sister soon, however hard it was going to be.

"See you next week, then?" I said. When I looked up, she was still smiling.

~

Later that day, Glen and I were watching a televisual game in which people with a fatally flawed understanding of statistics (specifically, of probability theory) selected numbered boxes, each containing a check, to be opened in turn, in the hope of unearthing a six-figure sum. They based their selections on wildly unhelpful factors such as their birth date or that of a person they cared about, their house number or, worst of all, "*a good feeling*" about a particular integer.

"Humans are idiots, Glen," I said, kissing the top of her head and then burying my face into her fur, which had grown back with such resplendence that she could now afford to shed it all over my clothes and furniture with gay abandon. She purred her assent.

The doorbell rang. Glen yawned extravagantly then jumped down from my lap. I wasn't expecting anyone. I stood before the door, thinking that I ought to get one of those spy holes installed, so that I would know who was there before I unlocked it. I found the trite theatricality of it rather dull. Who's behind the door? Boring. I don't like pantomimes or whodunnits—I like to have all the relevant information at my disposal at the earliest opportunity, so that I can start to formulate my response. I opened the door to find Keith, Sammy's son, standing on the doorstep and looking nervous. Mildly surprising. I invited him in.

~

By the time Keith was sitting on my sofa with a cup of tea, Glen had disappeared. She only really enjoyed her own company. She tolerated mine, but fundamentally she was a recluse at heart, like J. D. Salinger or the Unabomber.

"Thanks for the tea, Eleanor. I can't stay long, though," Keith said, after we'd finishing exchanging the usual pleasantries. "My wife's got Zumba tonight, and so I need to get back for the kids." I nodded, wondering who Zumba was. He reached into the backpack he'd brought with him, pushed a laptop to one side and took out a parcel, something wrapped in a carrier bag—a Tesco one, I noted with approval.

"We've been clearing out Dad's stuff," he said, looking directly at me and keeping his voice even, as though he was telling himself to be brave. "This isn't much, but we wondered if you might want it, as a keepsake? I remember Raymond saying how much you'd admired it, after that time you helped Dad . . ." The words snagged in his throat and he trailed off.

I unwrapped the parcel carefully. It was the beautiful red sweater, the one Sammy had been wearing on the day Raymond and I found him in the street. I could smell it, still faintly scented by its wearer with apples and whiskey and love, and I squeezed it tight, feeling the softness and the warmth against my palms, the gentle, exuberant Sammyness of it.

Keith had gone to the window and was staring out at the street, an action I completely understood.

When you're struggling hard to manage your own emotions, it becomes unbearable to have to witness other people's, to have to try and manage *theirs* too. He couldn't deal with my tears. I remember, I remember.

"Thank you," I said. He nodded, his back still turned. Everything was there, obvious to us both, but it all remained unsaid. Sometimes that was best.

After he'd gone, I put the sweater on. It was far too big, of course, but that made it even better, with more of it to go around me, anytime I needed it. Sammy's parting gift.

# 36

Getting to Dr. Temple's office involved a bus journey into town and then a short walk. My travel pass had expired, and it was symptomatic of my general feeling of *Weltschmerz*, of anomie, that I hadn't even bothered to renew it last week. Marianne. Everything else was just trivia. I dropped two pounds into the driver's slot, caring not one whit that it bore an ugly sticker saying *No Change Given*, and that I had therefore needlessly sacrificed twenty pence. Who gave a fig about twenty pence, when it came down to it?

All of the seats already had an occupant, which meant I was going to have to position myself next to a stranger. In a different mood, I enjoyed this game: one had ten seconds to scan the occupants and select the slimmest, sanest, cleanest-looking person to sit next to. Choose wrongly, and the fifteen-minute journey into town would be a much less pleasant experience—either squashed beside a sprawling fatty, or mouth-breathing to minimize the penetration of the reek emanating from an unwashed body. Such was the excitement of traveling on public transport.

I took no pleasure in the game today, however, and merely seated myself as close to the front as possible, taking no interest in the merits or demerits of my companion. As luck would have it, she was an elderly woman, slightly on the plump side but not inconveniently so, who smelled of hairspray and kept herself to herself. Good.

She got off at the next stop and then I had the seat to myself. More people got on, and I watched a handsome young man—tall, slim, with disproportionately large brown eyes—play the scanning game in order to select a seat. I looked forward to sitting next to him, being sure that he was neither mad nor malodorous.

However, he walked straight past me and sat on the other side of the bus, next to a short, rough-looking man in a sports jacket. I couldn't believe it! Two people got on at the next stop—one went upstairs, the other, once again, eschewed the spare seat next to me and walked toward the back of the bus, where, I noticed when I turned around to look, she seated herself next to a man with no socks on. His bare ankles looked distressingly white above his oxblood leather brogues, which he had teamed with green jogging bottoms. A madman.

I stared at the floor, my mind racing. Did I . . . did I look like the kind of person who ought to be avoided in a game of bus seat selection? I could only conclude, in the face of the evidence, that I did. But why?

I would have to reason my way to the answer. I wasn't overweight. I didn't smell—I showered daily, and I laundered my clothes regularly. That left madness, then. Was I mad? No. No, I wasn't. I was suffering from clinical depression, but that was an illness. It wasn't madness. Did I look mad, then? Act mad? I didn't think so. But then, how would I know? Was it my scar? My eczema? My jerkin? Was it a sign of madness even to think you might be mad? I rested my elbows on my knees and placed my head in my hands. Oh God oh God oh God.

"You all right, hen?" a voice said, and I felt a hand on my shoulder, causing me to startle and sit up again. It was the man with no socks, who was en route to the front of the bus.

"Yes, thank you," I said, not making eye contact. He sat down next to me while the bus approached the next stop.

"You sure?" he said kindly.

"Yes, thank you," I repeated. I risked a look at his face. He had very gentle eyes, the same delicate shade of green as newly emerged buds on trees.

"Just taking a wee moment, hen?" He patted me on the arm. "Everybody needs to take a wee moment to themselves now and again, eh?" He smiled, full of warmth, and stood up to leave. The bus was slowing down.

"Thanks!" I called after him. He didn't look round, but raised a hand in salutation, trousers riding up past his bare ankles as he left.

He wasn't mad. He just didn't have any socks on.

Eleanor, I said to myself, sometimes you're too quick to judge people. There are all kinds of reasons why they might not look like the kind of person you'd want to sit next to on a bus, but you can't sum someone up in a ten-second glance. That's simply not enough time. The way you try not to sit next to fat people, for example. There's nothing wrong with being over-weight, is there? They could be eating because they're sad, the same way you used to drink vodka. They could have had parents who never taught them how to cook or eat healthily. They could be disabled and unable to exercise, or else they could have an illness that contributes to weight gain despite their best efforts. You just don't know, Eleanor, I said to myself.

The voice in my own head—my own voice—was actually quite sensible, and rational, I'd begun to realize. It was Mummy's voice that had done all the judging, and encouraged me to do so too. I was getting to quite like my own voice, my own thoughts. I wanted more of them. They made me feel good, calm even. They made me feel like *me*.

## 37

Old routines, new routines. Perhaps even, sometimes, no routines? But twice a week, for as long as it
was going to take, I made the journey to town and
climbed the stairs to Dr. Temple's consulting room. I
no longer found it nasty—I was beginning to understand the efficacy of neutral, unattractive surroundings, tissues, chairs and an ugly framed print. There
was nothing else to look at, save oneself, nowhere to
retreat to. She was smarter than she first appeared,
Dr. Temple. That fact notwithstanding, her dream
catcher earrings today were, frankly, abominable.

I was about to take to the stage and say my piece.
I wasn't acting, though. I'm a terrible actor, not being,
by nature, a dissembler or a faker. It's safe to say that
Eleanor Oliphant's name will never appear in lights,
and nor would I want it to. I'm happiest in the background, being left to my own devices. I've spent far
too long taking direction from Mummy.

The subject of Marianne had caused me so much
distress, me trying furiously to build up my courage
and direct my memory into places it didn't want to
go. We'd agreed not to force it, to let her appear naturally, we hoped, as we talked about my childhood. I'd

accepted this. Last night, as Glen and I listened to the radio, the memory, the truth of it, had come to me, quite unbidden. It had been a perfectly ordinary evening, and there was no fanfare, no drama. Just the truth. Today was going to be the day I spoke it aloud, here in this room, to Maria. But there had to be some preamble. I couldn't just blurt it out. I'd let Maria help by leading me there.

There was also no escaping Mummy in the counseling room today. It was hard to believe that I was actually doing this, but there it was. The sky didn't fall in, Mummy wasn't summoned like a demon by the mere mention of her name. Dr. Temple and I were, quite shockingly, having a reasoned, calm conversation about her.

"Mummy's a bad person," I said. "Really bad. I know that, I've always known that. And I wondered . . . do you think I might be bad too? People inherit all sorts of things from their parents, don't they—varicose veins, heart disease. Can you inherit *badness*?"

Maria sat back, fiddled with her scarf.

"That's a very interesting question, Eleanor. The examples you gave are physical conditions. What you're talking about is something different, though— a personality, a set of behaviors. Do you think that behavioral traits can be inherited?"

"I don't know," I said. I thought about it. "I really, really hope not."

I paused for a minute. "People talk about nature

and nurture. I *know* I haven't inherited her nature. I mean, I'm a . . . difficult person sometimes, I suppose . . . But I'm not . . . I'm *not* like her. I don't know if I could live with myself if I thought I was like her."

Maria Temple raised her eyebrows.

"Those are very strong words, Eleanor. Why do you say that?"

"I couldn't bear it if I thought that I would ever actually *want* to cause someone pain. To take advantage of weaker, smaller people. To leave them to fend for themselves, to . . . to . . ."

I broke off. It had been very, very hard to say that. It hurt, a real, physical pain, as well as a more fundamental, existential ache. For goodness' sake— existential ache, Eleanor! I said to myself. Get a grip.

Maria spoke gently.

"But you're *not* your mother, are you, Eleanor? You're a completely separate person, an independent person, making your own choices."

She gave an encouraging smile.

"You're still a young woman—if you wanted to, you could have a family of your own one day, and be a totally different kind of mother. What do you think about that?"

That was an easy one.

"Oh, I'll never have children," I said, calm, matter-of-fact. She indicated that I should keep talking. "It's obvious, isn't it? I mean, what if I passed it on, the Mummy thing? Even if I don't have it, it could skip a generation, couldn't it? Or . . . or what if it's the act of giving birth that brings it out in a person? It could be lying dormant all this time, waiting . . ."

She looked very serious.

"Eleanor, I've worked with several clients over the years who've had similar worries to yours. It's normal to feel that way. Remember, though—we've just been discussing how different you are from your mother, the different choices you've made . . ."

"But Mummy's still in my life, even after all this time. That worries me. She's a bad influence, a very bad influence."

Maria looked up from the book where she was taking notes.

"You're still talking to her, then?" she said, her pen poised.

"Yes," I said. I clasped my hands and took a deep breath. "But I've been thinking that it needs to come to an end. I'm going to stop. It has to stop."

She looked as serious as I'd ever seen her.

"It's not my role to tell you what to do, Eleanor. I will say this, though—I think that's a very good idea. But, ultimately, it's your decision. It's always been your decision," she said, excessively calm and ever so slightly aloof. It was as though she was trying just a bit too hard to be neutral, I thought. I wondered why.

"The thing is, even after everything that she's done, after all of it, she's still my mummy. She's the only one I've got. And good girls love their mothers.

After the fire, I was always so lonely. Any mummy was better than no mummy . . ."

As I paused, in tears, I saw that Dr. Temple was completely sympathetic, that she understood what I was saying and was listening without judgment.

"Lately," I said, starting to feel a bit stronger, a bit braver, buoyed by her kind eyes and supportive silence, "lately, though, I've come to realize that she's . . . she's just *bad*. She's the bad one. I'm not bad and it's not my fault. I didn't make her bad, and I'm not bad for wanting nothing to do with her, for feeling sad and angry—no, furious—about what she did."

The next bit was hard, and I looked at my clasped hands as I spoke, scared to see any change in Dr. Temple's demeanor in response to the words coming out of my mouth.

"I *knew* that something about her was very, very wrong. I've always known, as long as I can remember. But I didn't tell anyone. And people died . . ."

I dared to look up, and felt my body slump with relief when I saw the expression on Maria's face, unchanged.

"Who died, Eleanor?" she said quietly. I took a deep breath.

"Marianne," I said. "Marianne died." I looked at my hands, then back at Maria. "Mummy set a fire. She wanted to kill us both, except, somehow, Marianne died and I didn't."

Maria nodded. She didn't look surprised. Had she already worked it out? She seemed to be waiting for me to say something else, but I didn't. We sat in silence for a moment.

"It's the guilt, though," I said, whispering. It was very hard to speak, physically hard, trying to force out sound. "I was her big sister; I should have been looking out for her. She was so small. I did try, I really did, but it just . . . it wasn't enough. I failed her, Maria; I'm still here and that's all wrong. It should be her who survived. I don't deserve to be happy, I don't deserve to have a nice life when Marianne . . ."

"Eleanor," she said gently, once I'd calmed myself, "feeling guilty about surviving when Marianne didn't is a perfectly normal reaction. Don't forget, you were only a child yourself when your mother committed her crime. It's very important that you understand that it's not your fault, that none of it was your fault."

I was sobbing again.

"You were the child and she was the adult. It was her responsibility to look after you and your sister. Instead, there was neglect and violence and emotional abuse, and there were terrible, terrible consequences for everyone involved. And none of that is your fault, Eleanor, absolutely none of it. I don't know if you need to forgive your mother, Eleanor," she said. "But I'm certain of one thing: you need to forgive yourself."

I nodded through the tears. It made sense. I wasn't sure that I quite believed it—yet—but it certainly made logical sense. And you can't ask for more than that.

Blowing my nose, unembarrassed by the trumpeting, which was as nothing compared to the horrors I'd already laid before Dr. Temple in this room, I made my decision. It was time to say a final good-bye to Mummy.

# 38

Raymond had insisted on meeting outside the counseling rooms that day to take me for coffee. I watched him amble toward me. His peculiar loping walk was almost endearing now—I wouldn't recognize him if he started to walk as normal men did. He had his hands in the pockets of his low-slung denim trousers, and was wearing a strange, oversized woolen hat that I hadn't seen before. It looked like the kind of hat that a German goblin might wear in an illustration from a nineteenth-century fairy tale, possibly one about a baker who was unkind to children and got his comeuppance via an elfin horde. I rather liked it.

"All right?" he said. "I nearly froze my bollocks off on the way over here." He blew into his cupped hands.

"It is rather inclement today," I agreed, "although it's wonderful to see the sun."

He smiled at me. "It is, Eleanor."

I thanked him for taking time off to come and meet me. It was kind of him, and I told him so.

"Away you go, Eleanor," he said, putting out his cigarette. "Any excuse for a half day. Anyway, it's nice to talk to someone about something that isn't software licenses and Windows 10."

"But you *love* talking about software, Raymond," I said, sniffing, and then I nudged him in the ribs, very gently, very bravely. He laughed, and nudged me back.

"Guilty as charged, Miss O," he said.

We went into a branch of a café chain—I'd seen lots of them around town. We queued, and I asked for a grande mochaccino with extra cream and hazelnut syrup. The young man asked my name.

"Why do you need to know my name?" I said, puzzled.

"We write it on your cup," he said, "so the drinks don't get mixed up."

Ridiculous.

"I haven't heard anyone else order an identical drink to mine, so far," I said firmly. "I'm sure I'm more than capable of identifying my chosen beverage when the time comes."

He stared at me, the pen still poised in his hand. "I have to write your name on the cup," he repeated, sounding firm but bored, as people in uniform are often wont to do.

"And *I* have to maintain a modicum of privacy by not sharing my given name with all and sundry in the middle of a cafeteria," I said, equally firmly.

Someone further back in the queue tutted, and I heard someone else mutter something that sounded like *for fuck's sake*. It appeared that we had reached something of an impasse.

"Fine, all right then," I said. "My name is Miss Eleanor Oliphant."

He boggled at me.

"I'll just put, eh, Ellie," he said, scribbling. Raymond was silent, but I could feel his large shoulders and misshapen body quivering with laughter. It was his turn next.

"Raoul," he said, and then spelled it out.

When we'd collected our drinks—with no problem whatsoever—we sat at a table in the window and watched people pass by. Raymond stirred three sachets of sugar into his Americano, and I resisted the urge to suggest that he make healthier choices.

"So," he said, after what I recognized was a comfortable silence. "How did it go today?"

I nodded. "It was OK, actually," I said. He looked closely at me.

"You look like you've been crying," he said.

"I have," I told him. "But it's fine. It's normal to cry when you're talking about your dead sister."

Raymond's face contorted with shock.

"She died in the house fire. Mummy started it on purpose. We weren't meant to survive, but somehow I did. My little sister didn't, though," I said. I sounded strangely calm as I said these words. I looked away when I'd finished, knowing that Raymond's face would be expressing emotions that I wasn't quite ready to relive yet while he processed this information. He started to speak, but struggled.

"I know," I said calmly, giving him a minute to compose himself. It was a lot for anyone to take in. It had taken me decades, after all. I told him a bit more about what had happened to Marianne, about what Mummy had done.

"Now that I've finally been able to talk about what she did to me and what she did to Marianne, I can't possibly continue to have Mummy in my life. I need to be free of her."

He nodded.

"Does that mean you're going to . . ."

"Yes," I said. "Next Wednesday, next time I speak to her, I'm going to tell her that we're done. It's time to cut contact, for good."

Raymond nodded, almost approvingly. I felt calm, sure of the way forward. It was a novel sensation.

"There's something else I need to do too. I need to find out everything that happened to me, to us, back then. I remember some of the details, but now I need to know all of it." I cleared my throat. "So, will you help me, Raymond, help me find out what happened, the fire?" I said, not looking at him, my words barely audible. "Please?"

Asking for help was anathema to me. I'd told Maria that. "And how's that been working out for you so far?" she'd said. I didn't appreciate her somewhat pointed tone, but she was quite right. That didn't, however, mean that it was easy.

"Of course, Eleanor," he said. "Anything. Whenever you're ready. Whatever you need." He took my hands in his and squeezed them gently.

"Thank you," I said, quiet, relieved. Grateful.

"I think it's amazing, what you're doing, Eleanor," he said, looking at me.

This is what I felt: the warm weight of his hands on me; the genuineness in his smile; the gentle heat of something opening, the way some flowers spread out in the morning at the sight of the sun. I knew what was happening. It was the unscarred piece of my heart. It was just big enough to let in a bit of affection. There was still a tiny bit of room left.

"Raymond," I said, "you can't know how much it means to me, to have a friend—a genuine, caring friend. You saved my life," I whispered, scared that tears might come, here in the café, and embarrass us both. Now that I'd started crying in public more often, it seemed that I would do it at the drop of a hat.

Raymond squeezed my hands tighter, and I fought, and won over, the urge to whip them away and put them behind my back.

"Eleanor, don't thank me. You'd do the same for me, you know you would."

I nodded. To my surprise, I realized that he was right.

"I remember the first time I met you," he said, shaking his head and smiling. "I thought you were a right nutter."

"I *am* a right nutter," I said, surprised that he'd think otherwise. All my life, people had been telling me that.

"No, you're not," he said, smiling. "Aye, sure, you're a bit bonkers—but in a good way. You make me laugh, Eleanor. You don't give a fuck about any of the stupid stuff—I don't know, being cool, office politics or any of the daft shite that people are supposed to care about. You just do your own thing, don't you?"

I was crying now—there was no avoiding it. "Raymond, you swine," I said. "You've made my smoky eyes dissolve." I was quite annoyed when I said it, but then I started to giggle, and he laughed too. He passed me one of the café's inferior paper napkins and I wiped off the dark remnants.

"You look better without it," he said.

Afterward, we walked toward the point where we'd part in search of our respective bus stops.

"See you soon, then?" he said.

"Oh, you'll be seeing me sooner than you think!" I said, smiling at him.

"What do you mean?" He looked puzzled, and mildly amused.

"It's a surprise!" I said, gesturing with my hands and shrugging extravagantly. I'd never seen a magician perform onstage, but that was the look I was trying for. Raymond burst out laughing.

"I'll look forward to it," he said, still smiling as he fumbled in his pockets for his cigarettes.

I took my leave of him in a somewhat distracted frame of mind, my thoughts returning to Marianne and to Mummy. I had work to do now. The past had been hiding from me—or I'd hidden from it—and yet there it was, still, lurking in darkness. It was time to let in a little light.

# 39

Back to work! A cockerel's dawn crowing had woken me from my slumbers. This glorious morning sound was powered by an AA battery and delivered through a tinny speaker, and was brought about by my setting my alarm clock the previous evening, rather than, as is the case in our avian friends, raised levels of testosterone and sunlight. It is fair to say that my bedroom is a testosterone and sunlight-free zone at present. But winter does pass, I told myself—remember that, Eleanor. Glen was slumped over my feet on top of the duvet, keeping them warm as she did her best to ignore the alarm.

Excited at the prospect of the day ahead, I dressed in a new white blouse, a new black skirt, black tights and the boots I'd got a while ago for a gig I should never have gone to. I looked smart, practical, *normal*. Yes, I was going back to work.

Years ago, one of the foster families I lived with had taken me, alongside their own children, on a "back-to-school shopping trip." All three of us were allowed to choose new shoes and a new schoolbag, and were kitted out with a brand-new uniform (even though my skirt and blazer from the previous year still fit perfectly well). Best of all, the trip culminated with a visit to WHSmith, where the riches of the stationery aisle were ours to plunder. Even the most recondite items (set squares, butterfly pins, treasury tags: what were these for?) were permitted, and this booty was then zipped into a large, handsome pencil case which was mine, mine, mine. I am not generally a wearer of perfume, preferring to smell of plain soap and my natural musk, but, were it possible to purchase a bottle in which the scent of new pencil shavings and the petroleum reek of a freshly rubbed eraser were combined, I would happily douse myself with it on a daily basis.

I ate breakfast (porridge and a plum, as usual) and left in good time to catch the bus. Glen was still asleep, having moved under the duvet to occupy the warm space as soon as I vacated it. I left her some fresh water and a big bowl of kibble but I doubted she'd even notice I'd gone until she heard my key in the lock again tonight. She was very easygoing that way (although not, it had to be said, in lots of other ways).

The walk to the bus stop was more interesting than I remembered, perhaps because I was seeing it with fresh eyes after such a long absence. There was an excessive amount of litter and no litter bins; these two facts were surely correlated. This part of the city was aggressively gray, but green life still struggled into being: moss on walls, weeds in guttering, the occasional forlorn tree. I have always lived in urban areas, but I feel the need for green as a visceral longing.

Just as I was about to reach the junction where I cross to catch the bus, I stopped dead, my eye drawn to a sly movement, a measured dash of brownish red. I breathed in, the morning air cold in my lungs. Under the orange glow of a streetlight, a fox was drinking a cup of coffee. He wasn't holding it in his paws—as has been clearly established, I'm not *insane*—but, rather, had dipped his head to the ground and was lapping from a Starbucks cup. The fox sensed me watching, looked up and stared assertively into my eyes. "What of it?" he seemed to be saying. "A morning cup of coffee, big deal!" He went back to his beverage. Perhaps he'd had a particularly late night out by the bins, was finding it hard to get going on this cold, dark morning. I laughed out loud and walked on.

~

While I'd been off, Bob had told me to pop into the office anytime, or phone for a chat whenever I wanted. Last week, a few days before my sick note was due to expire, I was still undecided as to whether to revisit the doctor and seek an extension, or else return to work on the following Monday, so I had called him, not wanting to go into the office for fear of encountering intrusive questions from my coworkers without having prepared some appropriate responses first.

"Eleanor!" Bob had said. "Great to hear from you! How are things?"

"Thank you for the flowers," I said. "I'm fine . . . that's to say, I'm much better, thank you, Bob. It's been difficult, but I've been making good progress."

"Brilliant," he said, "that's brilliant news! So, do you know when you're, eh, when you're likely to be back?" I heard an intake of breath as he worried about what he'd just said. "No rush, now . . . no rush whatsoever. I'm not pressuring you—take as long as you need. Not until you're absolutely ready."

"Don't you *want* me to come back, Bob?" I said, daring an attempt at humor.

He snorted. "Eleanor, the place has been falling apart without you! Jesus Christ, Billy hasn't the first clue how to raise an invoice, and as for Janey . . ."

"Bob, Bob, I was joking," I said. I smiled, and I must admit to feeling slightly gratified at how poorly my colleagues had coped in my absence.

"A joke, Eleanor! Well, that's a great sign—you must be on the mend, then," Bob said, sounding relieved, either because of the joke or because I was getting better—or both, I supposed.

"I'll be back on Monday, Bob," I said. "I'm ready." My voice was firm, confident.

"Great! And you're sure it's the right time? Och, that's grand, Eleanor," he said. "I'll look forward to seeing you on Monday, then." I could tell he was being genuine because of all the warmth that was coming down the phone. Your voice changes when you're smiling, it alters the sound somehow.

"Thank you very much for being so understanding about all of . . . about everything, Bob," I said, a lump forming in my throat. "Thank you for your support. I've been meaning to say . . . I'm sorry if I haven't always been a very . . . enthusiastic employee over the years . . ."

"Ach, away you go," he said, and I could almost picture him shaking his head. "The place wouldn't be the same without you, Eleanor, it really wouldn't. You're an institution."

I heard his mobile phone ringing. He tutted.

"I'm so sorry, but I've got to get this, Eleanor—it's a new client. Now, you take care of yourself, and we'll see you on Monday, right?"

"Right," I said.

I remember thinking, as I put the phone down, that I really, really hoped that Janey wouldn't bring in one of her homemade cakes to mark my return, as she often did when people had been off. Dry doesn't even come close to describing the arid desert texture of her coffee-and-walnut sponge cake.

~

When I arrived at work, the exterior of the office was as unenticing as ever, and I hesitated outside. I had been absent for almost two months, and heaven alone knew what sort of unsubstantiated rumors had abounded as to the reasons behind it. I had not given—had not been capable of giving—a thought during that time to my spreadsheets, to accounts receivable, purchase orders and VAT. Could I still do my job? I wasn't confident that I could remember anything. My password? Of course. Three words, *Ignis aurum probat.* "Fire tests gold." The rest of the phrase: ". . . and adversity tests the brave." How true. A strong password, strong indeed, exactly as required by the computer system. Thank you, Seneca.

Ah, but I felt the beginnings of a fluttery panic in my chest. I couldn't do it. Could I? I wasn't ready to face it. I would go home and telephone Bob, let him know that I would be taking another week's leave. He'd understand.

There was a shuffling sound behind me on the path, and I quickly wiped away the tears that had formed while I was staring at the squat building before me. With no warning, I was pulled 180 degrees around and crushed into an embrace. There was a lot of wool (hat, scarf, gloves) and scratchy bristles, and a smell of apples, soap and Marlboro Reds.

"Eleanor!" Raymond said. "So that's what you meant when you said you'd see me soon."

I let myself be held, moved closer into the embrace, in fact, because, I was forced to admit, at that particular time and in those particular circumstances, and feeling the way I did, the sensation of being held by him was nothing short of miraculous. I said nothing, and, very slowly, my arms crept up, tentative as winter sunlight, so that they were placed around his waist, the better to bury myself into the embrace. My face rested against his chest. He said nothing either, intuiting, perhaps, that what I needed most at that moment was that which he was already providing and precisely nothing more.

We stood this way for some moments, and then I stepped back and rearranged my hair, wiped my eyes. I looked at my watch. "You're ten minutes late for work, Raymond," I said.

He laughed. "So are you!" He stepped forward again, peered closely at me. I stared back at him, rather like the fox had done earlier.

He nodded. "Come on," he said, holding out his arm, "we're both late now. Let's go in. I don't know about you, but I could really do with a cup of tea, eh?"

I linked my arm through his and he walked me inside, all the way to the door of the accounts office. I disengaged from him there as quickly as I could, anxious that someone might see us together like this. He bent down and put his face close to mine, speaking in rather a paternal manner (at least, I assume that's what it was—fathers are hardly my area of expertise, after all).

"Now then," he said, "here's what's going to happen. You're going to walk in there, hang up your coat, put the kettle on and get started. No one's going to make a fuss, and there won't be any drama—it'll be like you've never been away."

He nodded once, as if to reinforce his point.

"But what if—"

He spoke over me. "Honestly, Eleanor—trust me. It's going to be absolutely fine. You've been unwell, you took some time off to get better and now here you are, back in the fray. You're great at your job, and they'll be over the moon to have you back. End of," he said, earnest, sincere. Kind.

I did actually feel better after he said this—quite a bit better.

"Thank you, Raymond," I said quietly.

He punched me on the arm—gently, not a real punch—and smiled.

"We're so late!" he said, eyes wide in faux horror. "Meet you for lunch at one?"

I nodded.

"Go on then, get in there, give 'em hell!" he said, smiling, and then he was off, lumbering upstairs like a circus elephant learning a new trick. I cleared my throat, smoothed down my skirt and opened the door.

~

First things first: before I went to my desk and faced everyone, I had to have the dreaded back-to-work interview. I'd never had one before, but I'd heard the others muttering about them in the past. Apparently, HR forced you to have a meeting with your boss if you'd been off for more than a couple of days, ostensibly to make sure you were fully recovered and fit for work, and to see if any adjustments needed to be made to ensure you stayed well. In reality, however, the popular view tended toward this process having been designed to intimidate, to discourage absence and to check whether you'd been—what was the word?—ah yes, *skiving*. Those people didn't have Bob as a boss, however. Only the section managers reported to Bob. I was one of them now, the Praetorian Guard, the elect. Bob was an odd kind of emperor, though.

He stood up and kissed me on the cheek, and while he hugged me, his little potbelly pressed against me and made me want to laugh. He patted my back a few times. The whole thing was excruciatingly embarrassing, but really, really nice.

He made me a cup of tea and fussed around with biscuits, making sure I was comfortable.

"Now then, this interview. It's nothing to worry about, Eleanor, a formality—HR gives me a hard time if I don't do these things, you know what it's like." He made a face. "We just need to ticky boxy" (what?) "and sign the form, and then I'll let you get back to it."

He was slurping from a mug of coffee and had spilled some down his shirtfront. Bob wore thin shirts, a vest visible beneath, which added to the overall impression of an overgrown schoolboy. We went through a list of insultingly banal prescribed questions from a form. It was, to the visible relief of us both, a painless if somewhat tedious process.

"Right then," he said, "that's done, thank Christ. Is there anything else you wanted to talk about? It's a bit soon to get into specifics, I know," he said. "We can meet again tomorrow when you've had a chance to get up to speed with everything, if you like?"

"The Christmas lunch," I said, "is it all arranged now?"

He screwed up his little round face, and swore in a most uncherubic fashion.

"I totally forgot about that!" he said. "There were so many other things to sort out, and it just kind of, I don't know, slipped off my radar. Shit . . ."

"Fear not, Bob," I said. "I shall address it post-haste." I paused. "I mean, after I've caught up with all the accounts, of course."

Bob looked worried. "Are you sure? I really don't want to put any extra pressure on you, Eleanor—you're just back, and I'm sure you'll have more than enough on your plate . . ."

"No problemo, Bob," I said confidently, giving him a double thumbs-up sign, thereby trying out a favorite phrase and gesture of Raymond's for the first time. Bob's eyebrows shot up. I hoped I had used them correctly, and in the appropriate context. I'm very good with words as a rule, but this sort of thing does, I must confess, trip me up sometimes.

"Well, if you're one hundred percent sure . . ." he said, not, it must be noted, sounding particularly sure himself.

"Absolutely, Bob." I nodded. "Everything will be confirmed and arrangements put in place by the end of the week. You can count on it."

"Ah, well, that'd be brilliant," he said, scribbling on the form, which he then passed to me. "I just need you to fill in that section at the bottom, and that's us done," he said. I signed with a flourish. I don't have much opportunity to use my signature in day-to-day life, which is rather a pity, as I have a very interesting "John Hancock," as our cousins across the pond would have it. I don't mean to boast. It's just that almost everyone who's seen it has remarked on how unusual, how special it is. Personally, I don't see what all the fuss is about. Anyone could write an "O" as a snail-shell spiral if they wished to, after all, and using a mixture of upper- and lowercase letters is simply good sense—it ensures that the signature is difficult to forge. Personal security, data security: so important.

~

When I finally sat down at my desk, the first thing I noticed was the flowers. They'd been obscured by the monitor as I'd approached, but now I saw the vase (well, it was actually a pint glass; the office never had enough vases, cake knives or champagne flutes, despite employees celebrating life events on what seemed to be a weekly basis). It was filled with blooms, sea holly and agapanthus and iris, and it was glorious.

An envelope was propped against the arrangement, and I slowly opened the seal. There was a card inside, a stunning photograph of a red squirrel eating a hazelnut on the front. Inside, someone (Bernadette,

I suspected, from the childlike scrawl) had written WELCOME BACK ELEANOR! and a multitude of signatures, accompanied by Best Wishes or Love, were scattered across both sides. I was somewhat taken aback. Love! Best wishes! I wasn't at all sure what to think.

Still mulling this over, I switched on my computer. There were so many unanswered e-mails that I went straight to today's, thinking that I'd simply delete all the others. The senders would get in touch again if they were important, surely. The most recent one, sent only ten minutes ago, was from Raymond. The subject heading read: READ ME!!!

> Thought I'd better put that as u probs have about ten billion unread messages in your inbox right now LOL. I meant to say the other afternoon, I've got two tickets to a concert, it's classical music, I dunno if you like that sort of thing but I kind of thought you might? It's two weeks on Saturday if you're free— maybe go for something to eat afterward?
>
> See you @ lunch
> Rx

Before I had a chance to reply, I realized that my colleagues had assembled in a circle around my desk without my noticing. I looked up at them. Their expressions ranged from bored to benevolent. Janey looked mildly concerned.

"We know you don't like a fuss, Eleanor," she said, having clearly been nominated as spokeswoman. "We just wanted to say that we're glad you're feeling better, and, y'know, welcome back!" There were nods, murmured assent. As speeches went, it was hardly Churchillian, but it was yet another very kind and thoughtful gesture.

I wasn't one for public oratory, but I sensed that they would not be satisfied without a few words.

"Thank you very much indeed for the flowers and the card and the good wishes," I said, eventually, eyes on my desk while I spoke. There was a bit of a silence that no one, and certainly not me, quite knew how to fill. I looked up at them.

"Well," I said, "I don't suppose those overdue invoices are going to process themselves, are they?"

"She's back!" Billy said, and there was laughter, including my own. Yes. Eleanor Oliphant was back.

# 40

Wednesday night. High time.

"Hello, Mummy," I said. I heard my own voice—it sounded flat, emotionless.

"How did you know?" Sharp. Irritated.

"It's *always* you, Mummy," I said.

"Cheeky! Don't be insolent, Eleanor. It doesn't suit you. Mummy doesn't like naughty girls who talk back, you know that."

Old ground, this—a reprimand I'd heard so many times before.

"I don't really care what you like anymore, Mummy," I said.

I heard her snort; short, derisive.

"Oh dear. Someone's in a strop. What is it—time of the month? *Hormones*, darling? Or something else . . . let me see. Has someone been filling your head with nonsense? Telling lies about me? How many times have I warned you about that? Mummy isn't—"

I interrupted. "Mummy, I'm going to say good-bye to you tonight."

She laughed. "Good-bye? But that's so . . . final, darling. There's no need for that, come along now. What would you do without our little chats? What

about your special project—don't you think you ought
to keep Mummy updated on your progress, at least?"

"The project wasn't the answer, Mummy. It was
wrong of you, very wrong of you, to tell me that it
was," I said, not sad, not happy, just stating facts.

She laughed. "It was *your* idea, as I recall, darling. I merely . . . cheered you on from the sidelines.
That's what a supportive Mummy would do, isn't it?"

I thought about this. Supportive. Supportive
meant . . . what did it mean? It meant caring about
my welfare, it meant wanting the best for me. It meant
laundering my soiled sheets and making sure I got
home safely and buying me a ridiculous balloon when
I was feeling sad. I had no desire to recount a list of
her failings, her wrongdoings, to describe the horrors
of the life we'd led back then or to go over the things
she'd done and not done to Marianne, to me. There
was no point now.

"You set fire to the house while Marianne and I
were asleep inside. She died in there. I wouldn't
exactly call that supportive," I said, trying my best to
keep my voice calm, not entirely succeeding.

"Someone *has* been telling you lies—I knew it!"
she said, triumph in her voice. She spoke brightly, full
of enthusiasm. "Look, what I did, darling—anyone
would have done the same thing in my situation. It's
like I told you: if something needs to change, change
it! Of course, there will be inconveniences along the
way . . . you simply have to deal with them, and not
worry too much about the consequences."

She sounded happy, glad to be dispensing advice. She was, I realized, talking about killing us, Marianne and me, her *inconveniences*. In a strange way, it helped.

I took a breath, although I didn't really need to.

"Good-bye, Mummy," I said. The last word. My voice was firm, measured, certain. I wasn't sad. I was sure. And, underneath it all, like an embryo forming— tiny, so tiny, barely a cluster of cells, the heartbeat as small as the head of a pin, there I was. Eleanor Oliphant.

And, just like that, Mummy was gone.

# Better Days

# 41

Although I felt completely fine and, indeed, ready to get back into the thick of it all, HR had insisted on a "phased return," whereby I only worked during the mornings for the next few weeks. More fool them—if they wished to pay me a full-time salary for part-time hours, it was their lookout. At lunchtime on Friday, the end of my brief working day and my first week back, I met Raymond for the second time that week.

Since then, we'd been communicating solely by electronic means. I had spent the previous evening searching online. It was so easy to find things. Too easy, perhaps. I'd printed two newspaper articles without reading beyond the headlines, then sealed them in an envelope. I knew Raymond would have found them already himself, but it was important to me that *I* did the searching. It was *my* history and no one else's. No one else alive, at any rate.

As requested, he'd joined me in the café, so that I wasn't alone when I read them for the first time. I'd tried to cope alone for far too long, and it hadn't done me any good at all. Sometimes you simply needed someone kind to sit with you while you dealt with things.

"I feel like a spy or something," said Raymond, looking at the sealed envelope that lay between us.

"You're completely unsuited to a career in espionage," I told him. He raised his eyebrows.

"Your face is too honest," I said, and he smiled.

"Ready then?" he said, serious now.

I nodded.

The envelope was a buff manila self-sealing A4, which I had purloined from the office stationery cupboard. The paper had come from there too. I felt slightly guilty about it, especially since Bob, I knew now, had to factor this sort of thing into his running costs. I opened my mouth to tell Raymond about the stationery budget, but he nodded toward the envelope encouragingly, and I realized that I could delay matters no further. I eased it open, then held it toward him to show him that there were two pages of A4 inside. Raymond shuffled even closer, so that we were touching, sides together, congruent. There was warmth and strength there and, gratefully, I drew on it. I started to read.

*The Sun*, August 5, 1997, p. 2

### "Pretty but deadly" kiddie killer
### "fooled us all," neighbors say

"Killer Mum" Sharon Smyth (pictured), 29, had been living in a quiet Maida Vale street for the last two years, neighbors said, before deliberately starting the fire that ended in tragedy.

"She was such a pretty young woman—she had us all fooled," said a neighbor, who did not wish to be named. "Her little ones were always properly turned out, and they spoke so nice—everybody said what lovely manners they had," he told our reporter.

"As time went on, you could tell something wasn't right, though. The kiddies always seemed terrified of her. Sometimes they had bruises, and people heard a lot of crying in that house. She'd go out a lot. We just assumed there was a babysitter, but looking back on it . . .

"One time, I was talking to the older girl—she was only nine or ten, I'd say—and the mum shot her such a look, she started to shake like a little dog. I dread to think what went on in there behind closed doors."

Police confirmed yesterday that the fatal blaze at the property had been started deliberately.

A child (10), who cannot be named for legal reasons, remains in hospital in critical condition.

I looked at Raymond. He looked at me. Neither of us said anything for a while.

"You know how it ends, right?" Raymond said, gentle, quiet, looking me in the eye.

I pulled out the second article.

***London Evening Standard,***
September 28, 1997, p. 9

**Maida Vale murder latest:
two dead, plucky orphan recovers**

Police confirmed today that the bodies recovered
from the scene of last month's Maida Vale house
fire belonged to Sharon Smyth (29) and her youngest daughter Marianne (4). Her eldest child, Eleanor
(10), was released today from hospital after making
what doctors described as a "miraculous" recovery
from third-degree burns and smoke inhalation.

The spokesman confirmed that 29-year-old
Smyth started the fire deliberately, and died at
the scene as a result of smoke inhalation as she
fled the property. Tests on both children revealed
that a sedative had been administered, and provided evidence that they had been physically
restrained.

Our reporter understands that Eleanor Smyth
initially managed to free herself and escape the
blaze. Neighbors then reported seeing the badly
injured ten-year-old re-entering the house before
the emergency services arrived. Firefighters allegedly found her attempting to open a locked wardrobe in an upstairs bedroom. The body of her
four-year-old sister was recovered inside.

Police have been unable to trace any living relatives of the child, who is being cared for by Social Services.

That's all I found too," Raymond said, as I pushed the printouts toward him.

I looked out of the window. People were shopping, talking on mobiles, pushing prams. The world just went on, regardless of what happened. That's how it works.

Neither of us spoke for a while.

"Are you OK?" he said.

I nodded.

"I'm going to keep seeing the counselor. It helps."

He looked at me carefully. "How do you feel?" he said.

"Not you as well." I sighed, and then I smiled so that he would know that I was joking. "I'm fine. I mean, yes, obviously, I've got a lot of things to work through, very serious things. Dr. Temple and I are going to keep talking about all of it—Marianne's death, how Mummy died too and why I pretended for all those years that she was still there, still talking to me . . . it's going to take time and it's not going to be easy," I said. I felt very calm. "Essentially, though, in all the ways that matter . . . I'm fine now.

Fine," I repeated, stressing the word because, at last, it was true.

A woman jogged past, running after a Chihuahua, shouting its name in an increasingly anxious tone.

"Marianne loved dogs," I said. "Every time we saw one, she'd point and laugh, then try to hug it."

Raymond cleared his throat. More coffees came, and we drank slowly.

"Will you be OK?" Raymond said. He looked angry with himself. "Sorry. Stupid question. I just wish I'd known sooner," he said. "I wish I could have helped more." He glared at the wall, looking as though he was trying not to cry. "No one should have to go through what you've been through," he said finally, furious. "You lost your little sister, even though you tried your best to save her, and you were only a child yourself. That you could come through that, all of it, and then spend all those years trying to deal with it on your own, it's—"

I interrupted him. "When you read about 'monsters'," I said, "household names . . . you forget they had families. They don't just spring from nowhere. You never think about the people that are left behind to deal with the aftermath of it all."

He nodded slowly.

"I've requested access to my files from Social Services now. I've had cause to review my opinion of the Freedom of Information Act, Raymond, and let me tell you, it's actually a splendid piece of legislation.

When it arrives, I'm going to sit down and read it cover to cover—the Bumper Book of Eleanor. I need to know everything—all the little details. That's going to help me. Or depress me. Or both."

I smiled, to show him I wasn't worried, and to make sure that he wasn't worried either.

"It's more than that though, isn't it?" he said. "All those lost years, wasted years. Terrible things happened to you. You needed help back then and you didn't get it. You've got a right to it now, Eleanor—" He shook his head, unable to find the words.

"In the end, what matters is this: I survived." I gave him a very small smile. "I survived, Raymond!" I said, knowing that I was both lucky and unlucky, and grateful for it.

~

When it was time to leave, I noticed and appreciated Raymond's effort to move the conversation toward something else, something normal.

"What have you got planned for the rest of the week, then?" he said.

I counted things off on my fingers. "I've got to take Glen to the vet for her vaccinations," I said, "and I've got a Christmas night out at the safari park to organize. Their website says that they're closed for winter, but I'm sure I'll be able to persuade them."

We went outside and stood by the doorway for a moment, enjoying the sunshine. He rubbed his face, then looked over my shoulder toward the trees. He cleared his throat again. One of the many perils of being a smoker.

"Eleanor, did you get my e-mail about that concert? I was just wondering whether—"

"Yes," I said, smiling. He nodded, looked closely at me and then slowly smiled back. The moment hung in time like a drop of honey from a spoon, heavy, golden. We stood aside to let a woman in a wheelchair and her friend go inside. Raymond's lunch break was almost up. I had the rest of the day to spend however I wanted.

"Bye then, Raymond," I said. He pulled me in for a hug and held me for a moment, tucking a strand of hair behind my ear. I felt the warm bulk of him, soft but strong. When we broke apart, I kissed his cheek, his bristles all soft and ticklish.

"See you soon, Eleanor Oliphant," he said.

I picked up my shopper, fastened my jerkin and turned toward home.

# Acknowledgments

Thank you to my friends and to my family, and also to the following people and organizations:

Janice Galloway, for always being wise and inspiring.

My amazing agent Madeleine Milburn, and her colleagues at the agency, for their enthusiasm, expertise, advice and support.

My editors, Martha Ashby in the UK and Pamela Dorman in the US, who took meticulous care of the book and brought insight, wisdom and good humor to the editorial process. My thanks also to their talented colleagues at HarperCollins and Penguin Random House, respectively, who were involved in designing, producing and raising awareness of the book. I am very fortunate to be in such good hands.

The Scottish Book Trust selected me to receive the Next Chapter Award, which, among other things, allowed me to spend time writing and editing at Moniack Mhor Creative Writing Centre. I'm very grateful to both organizations.

My writers' group, for constructive feedback, helpful discussion and good company.

George and Annie, for their generous hospitality and unstinting encouragement.

Finally, thanks to George Craig, Vicki Jarrett, Kirsty Mitchell and Philip Murnin. I'm very grateful for their supportive friendship, editorial insight and good humored encouragement while I was writing (and not writing) this book.

**A READERS GUIDE TO**

# ELEANOR OLIPHANT
# IS COMPLETELY FINE

Gail Honeyman

# An Introduction to
## *Eleanor Oliphant Is Completely Fine*

*"My life, I realized, had gone wrong. Very, very wrong. I wasn't supposed to live like this. No one was supposed to live like this. The problem was that I simply didn't know how to make it right." (p. 278–279)*

Twenty-nine-year-old accounting clerk Eleanor Oliphant tends to stick to her routine: work all week, buy a supermarket pizza and two bottles of vodka on Friday, and spend the weekend alone in a drunken stupor waiting for Monday to arrive. Eccentric, awkward, and judgmental, Eleanor might sound like the very definition of an antiheroine, yet in debut author Gail Honeyman's hands, she is refreshingly honest and utterly relatable. With a sharp, albeit unintentional sense of humor and a deeply flawed self-image that makes her all the more sympathetic, Eleanor Oliphant has become one of the most lovable characters in recent fiction—and her creator, Gail Honeyman, has become one of the most celebrated new authors on the international literary scene.

As the novel begins, Eleanor is an opinionated young woman who makes sweeping and often laugh-out-loud pronouncements on everything from duffle coats to bikini waxes. But what first appears to be the narrative of a prudish and harmless loner soon gives way to reveal darker undercurrents, from Eleanor's childhood in foster homes to an adulthood punctuated by abusive phone calls from her absent mother. In fact, entire years seem to be missing from Eleanor's past, and ominous memories rise up which she can't explain to anyone, most of all to herself.

Two events, however, begin to coax Eleanor out of her shell. First, she develops an unexpected crush on a local musician, Johnnie, and, despite never having met him, she embarks on an imaginary love affair—convinced they have a future together. Second, Eleanor and her colleague Raymond rescue an injured elderly man, Sammy, and this act of kindness sets off a ripple effect in which she both builds a relationship with Sammy and his family and forges a friendship with Raymond. Eleanor may be tone-deaf to social convention, but with Raymond's bemused guidance, she begins to imagine leading the kind of normal life that she never thought possible before.

But just when Eleanor begins to feel truly happy, she discovers the crushing truth about her beloved singer, and her broken fantasy sends her into a spiral of depression and self-harm. Thankfully, Raymond's friendship saves Eleanor from herself, in ways large and small, and at his urging, she agrees to see a counselor. As she begins to heal, her past is revealed to her in its entirety—and a stunning twist casts the events of the novel in a brand new light.

# QUESTIONS FOR DISCUSSION

1. Knowing the truth about Eleanor's family, look back through the book to revisit her exchanges with her mother. Did you see what was ahead? How did Honeyman lay the groundwork for the final plot twist?

2. What are the different ways that the novel's title could be interpreted? What do you think happens to Eleanor after the book ends?

3. Eleanor says, "These days, loneliness is the new cancer—a shameful, embarrassing thing, brought upon yourself in some obscure way. A fearful, incurable thing, so horrifying that you dare not mention it; other people don't want to hear the word spoken aloud for fear that they might too be afflicted" (p. 273). Do you agree?

4. What does Raymond find appealing about Eleanor? And why does Eleanor feel comfortable opening up to Raymond?

5. Eleanor is one of the most unusual protagonists in recent fiction, and some of her opinions and actions are very funny. What were your favorite moments in the novel?

6. "Did men ever look in the mirror, I wondered, and find themselves wanting in deeply fundamental ways? When they opened a newspaper or watched a film, were they presented with nothing but exceptionally handsome young men, and did this make them feel intimidated, inferior, because they were not as young, not as handsome?" (p. 89). Eleanor's question is rhetorical and slightly tongue-in-cheek, but worth answering. What are your thoughts? If men don't have this experience, why not? If they do, why is it not more openly discussed?

7. Eleanor is frightened that she may become like her mother. Is this a reasonable fear? What is the balance of nature and nurture?

8. Is it possible to emerge from a traumatic childhood unscathed?

9. Eleanor says, "If someone asks you how you are, you are meant to say FINE. You are not meant to say that you cried yourself to sleep last night because you hadn't spoken to another person for two consecutive days. FINE is what you say" (p. 273). Why is this the case?

# A CONVERSATION WITH GAIL HONEYMAN

*Where did the idea for Eleanor Oliphant come from?*

*Eleanor Oliphant Is Completely Fine* started with two related ideas. The first was loneliness, an issue that's now thankfully starting to receive more attention as we begin to understand more about its often devastating consequences. I remembered reading an article in which a young woman, living in a big city, said that unless she went out of her way to make arrangements in advance, she'd often find herself not speaking to another human being from the time she left work on Friday night until her return to the office on Monday morning, and not by choice.

I started to wonder how such a situation could come about. When loneliness is discussed, it's often in the context of the elderly, but I began to think about how it might manifest in younger people, and whether the issues might be slightly different for them. Was it harder to talk about, or even to identify, because their loneliness didn't result from, say, the death of a spouse after decades of marriage, or from becoming housebound due to age-related illness? Did social media have an impact and, if so, was it positive or negative? Was it worse or better to find yourself lonely in a big city rather than in a small town or a village? In the end, it wasn't difficult to imagine how a young woman with no family nearby could find herself in the situation described in the article; moving to a new city, she might rent a one-bedroom apartment, take a job at a small firm where she had nothing in common with her colleagues . . . narratively, the possibilities began to intrigue me.

The other strand that helped inform the book was the idea of social awkwardness. Only a few fortunate people are blessed with the ability to make effortless, charming small talk with strangers, and the rest of us just try to muddle along as best we can. However, most people have, at some point, found themselves struggling to maintain a more than usually stilted exchange with someone whose conversation and demeanour just seem a bit . . . awkward. It struck me that I'd never given much thought as to whether there might be a reason for this, something that helped to explain that person's awkwardness. Might there perhaps be something in their background or childhood experiences, some life event that had helped to shape them in this particular way?

I realized that I wanted to tell a story about someone like this, or, rather, someone who'd ended up like this, living a small life. A lonely person, a slightly awkward person, and someone in whom loneliness and social awkwardness had become entwined and self-perpetuating. I wanted to tell the story of how this had happened to her, and of what happened to her next, and this became the story of Eleanor Oliphant.

*Many of Eleanor's coworkers know nothing about her. Some of this can be contributed to her reluctance to interact with others, but it largely has to do with her unusual appearance and odd personality. Why do you think we are so hesitant to accept the "other"?*

That's a good question, and a very difficult one. In Eleanor's specific case, I think that her colleagues, faced with what appears to be extreme and perhaps rather misplaced self-confidence, coupled with an inability to fit in socially and a complete lack of interest in attempting to do so, find her to be quite challenging, and possibly even a slightly threatening character. Of course, the reader can see the difference between who Eleanor really is and how she might appear to others, but unfortunately most of the people she encounters don't have access to the full picture—her thoughts and feelings and experiences—which could help them understand why she seems to behave in particular, and sometimes quite irritating, ways.

*In the beginning of the story, Eleanor falls in love with a local musician, Johnnie. She believes he is her soulmate, even though they haven't actually met. Her relationship with him is completely one-sided, and exists solely online. Romantic idealism isn't a new concept, but do you think that social media gives it a new platform?*

When I was writing about Eleanor and Johnnie, I began thinking about what he might reveal about himself online, either knowingly or, perhaps more interestingly, unknowingly—the tiny background details in photographs, for example. From following Johnnie's various and frequent social media posts, Eleanor very quickly forms a completely false sense of intimacy with him—a person she's never met—because she's able to see where he goes and who he spends time with, and in a matter of days, she comes to know a tremendous amount about his life. This provides a lot of narrative possibilities in a compressed time period, which is very useful for a writer.

*Eleanor is so literal but so funny. Though there's plenty of darkness in her story, she never fails to make us laugh. How did you come up with Eleanor's inimitable voice?*

I'm absolutely delighted to hear that she's making people laugh! Darker aspects of the story aside, the character of Eleanor Oliphant was so much fun to write, partly because she has no filters and very little self-awareness, and so she often ends up saying things out loud that most of us wouldn't ever dream of saying. Eleanor is also largely unaware of social conventions, or, when she is aware of them, pays them no heed. Because of all these factors, she looks at other people and at the world—even the most mundane, routine situations and encounters—from a very particular point of view. She's not much influenced by preconceived ideas or social pressures to conform, and trying to create a character who spoke with that particular voice and had that particular view of the world was such an enjoyable challenge.

*Eleanor Oliphant Is Completely Fine is your first novel, yet it was already on the shortlist for the Lucy Cavendish Prize in the UK. How long did it take you to write this novel, and how did you feel when you found out it would be published?*

It took me around two years to write it—I had a full-time job, so I was writing before or after work, or on weekends when I could. I was completely thrilled when I found out it was going to be published—even now, I'm still pinching myself.

*What is it about the other characters—Raymond, Sam—that finally get Eleanor to open up her life to others?*

I think it's partly a question of timing—when we first meet Eleanor, she has reached a point where something has to give, and these characters come along at exactly the right time in her life. I think it's also that they're very nonjudgmental; they take Eleanor as they find her, with all her quirks and idiosyncrasies. They're happy to let her be herself, and, at the same time, are gently trying to help her be the best, happiest version of herself, without ever thinking or implying that what she is at the moment is anything other than completely fine. That's an important aspect of helping to build her trust, I think. The other thing, perhaps the most important thing, is that they are kind, and their kindness works its own particular magic.

*If there's one piece of advice you would give to Eleanor, what would it be?*

I suppose if I had to suggest anything to Eleanor, it would be that she should keep trying to open up. It's great that she's self-sufficient and confident in her abilities, but other people have so much to offer, and she's been missing out on this. The other thing is that while it's wonderful to receive help when you need it, it's also a lovely feeling to be able to give it, knowing that you've been useful or made a difference in someone's life, however small. If Eleanor opened up more and, in so doing, let people in, she'd also be giving them the gift of helping her—it's a positive, virtuous circle.

*What are you working on now?*

I don't want to say too much about it at this early stage, but it's a novel that moves between the 1940s and the present day, with a male protagonist and a female protagonist who are related to each other, and it's set in both London and Scotland. I've loved spending time with Eleanor in her world, but I'm really enjoying writing something very different and exploring different voices right now.